Onansburg, IOWA

a novel

Onansburg,
IOWA

PEGGY LAMMERS

GREENLEAF
BOOK GROUP PRESS

Published by Greenleaf Book Group Press
Austin, Texas
www.gbgpress.com

Distributed by Greenleaf Book Group

For ordering information or special discounts for bulk purchases, please contact Greenleaf Book Group at PO Box 91869, Austin, TX 78709, 512.891.6100.

Design and composition by Greenleaf Book Group
Cover design by Greenleaf Book Group
Cover Images: ©iStockphoto.com/yanjf

Publisher's Cataloging-in-Publication data is available.

Print ISBN: 978-1-62634-723-6

eBook ISBN: 978-1-62634-724-3

Part of the Tree Neutral® program, which offsets the number of trees consumed in the production and printing of this book by taking proactive steps, such as planting trees in direct proportion to the number of trees used: www.treeneutral.com

TreeNeutral

Printed in the United States of America on acid-free paper

20 21 22 23 24 25   10 9 8 7 6 5 4 3 2 1

First Edition

Onansburg, Iowa is dedicated to my children,
Lisabeth Lammers and Jon Lammers,
who are now older than I was
when I wrote the first pages.

Prologue

*C*loris clutched him to her chest, and he wrapped his legs around her waist as he had when he was a toddler. He peered cautiously over his sister's shoulder as she rushed him from the receding tunnel of the dimly lit hallway. The thick cord dangling from the bare bulb dated the austere passageway, as did the linoleum runner bordered by wide oak floorboards. No pictures or photographs graced the faded wallpaper. His eyes widened at the sight of his father treading purposefully toward them, and he hid his eyes on Cloris's shoulder. With relief, he heard the footsteps stop and his mother's whimper. Raising his head, he saw his father grasping his wife's arm, jerking her to her feet, then shoving her along the hallway toward the room they shared.

When Cloris threw the door of his bedroom open, it made a resounding clunk when it bounced against the teat of the rubber doorstop, but it couldn't shut out the sound of his father's rage nor his mother's sobbing. Cloris thrust him under the thin sheet and then the quilt, pieced from salvaged woolen garments gleaned from church rummage sales and the family's own retired clothing. The random pieces became a patchwork of the legacy of happy days and sad days crudely sewn into new utility. Its meager length and width was folded in quarters for warmth.

Sonny burrowed under the quilt, then covered his head with his sparsely stuffed pillow, shutting out the other noises: hurried footsteps, doors closing, his mother's whimpering, Cloris's shouted defiance of their father. But he couldn't shut out the horror he encountered when awakened in the night.

Cloris's admonition was imprinted forever into his consciousness, the only memory that survived the night. "Be the best little boy you can be, Sonny. Be the best boy."

One

Sweat concentrated at Sonny's lower back, forming a damp delta below his waist. He hoped it would not soak through his clothing. His misery in the relentless heat and humidity would be forever baked into his memory of the day. As he waited patiently for the pallbearers to perform their final duties, a tear slid around his nose and into the furrow above his upper lip. Sonny shifted his weight to his other foot and removed his once-pristine white handkerchief from the right rear pocket of his new gray suit trousers. He mopped his face, refolded the linen square carefully, and tucked it back into the pocket from which it came. He sighed at the irony of his funeral attire; it had been Polly insisting he buy a new lighter-weight suit, not three weeks ago.

Remembering, he had briefly protested. "Dammit, Polly. I never wear a suit this time of year! Khaki pants or shorts—we don't go anywhere that I wear a suit, much less a new one."

She nodded her agreement with him as always, so it was not quite so much a surprise that he'd found himself at the cash register of Jameson's Men's Store, paying for a summer-weight suit.

And it wasn't a surprise, but still he marveled at Polly's foresight when he dressed himself in the suit on the morning of her funeral service. From the walk-in closet in their bedroom, he'd selected the new suit coat, matching trousers, white button-down collared shirt, black wing-tip shoes, and dark blue repp stripe tie, all from his designated space within the sunny closet that was, during daylight hours, illuminated by the window, the upper half bejeweled with stained glass squares of cobalt, ruby, and amber, dividing the space equally. *Thank you, darling,* he'd breathed to himself. *I don't have to think about what to wear.* Shutting the louvered closet door behind him, pausing to hear the latch click in place, he crossed the bedroom to the dresser, where he retrieved a clean handkerchief from the top drawer.

On one hand, since Polly's death he had been like an automaton, coordinating funeral home arrangements, church arrangements, floral arrangements, cemetery arrangements, transportation arrangements. There'd been no mindful thinking of anything beyond the task at hand. With the family, friends, and neighbors surrounding him, food had appeared in his kitchen as if by magic; the grass had been miraculously mowed and trimmed; the porch was swept, and the cushions on the porch swing were fluffed and straightened.

At the end of the memorial service at their church, Little Flock Chapel, Steve Fetters, Onansburg's sole funeral director, and his assistants had pushed the chrome trolley transporting Polly's casket from the sanctuary of the church. Sonny had followed behind, reflexively clasping the outstretched hands of sympathetic well-wishers as he traveled along the center aisle, the family cortege behind him.

The same doors that led in and out of the chapel were opened to allow the passage of the casket. His breath caught in his throat, and his eyes widened when he saw that the Cadillac hearse had been backed up to the opening and was waiting to swallow Polly, casket and all, for her final ride to the cemetery. The cemetery, the long-ago spot where young couples had driven to park, to turn out the car lights to exchange kisses, swallow tongues, and fumble caresses.

The generation that Sonny and Polly inhabited as teens some thirty years ago had witnessed the birth of rock 'n' roll, the new frontier of dance, and the invention of sex. It was an era marked by the Castro takeover of Cuba, the first moonwalk, and the Cold War, coupled with the angst of the civil rights movement. They had been filled with newly awakened hormone highs of puberty, driven by Elvis, Buddy Holly, the Big Bopper, Richie Valens. The highs plummeted when the latter three died in an airplane crash in a muddy Iowa farm field. But later, hope resumed when the Beach Boys extolled the freedom of life on the Southern California beaches. Then tales of Haight-Ashbury and the musical debauchery of Woodstock in a New York farm field trickled back to the Midwest. The Beatles swarmed the USA during the British invasion, and Rod Stewart dropped his pool cue to return to school. The Pepsi generation rallied.

It was a heady time in history, and they'd neatly discounted the Depression and WWII sacrifices of their parents. Automobiles sporting loud mufflers and modified by lowered bumpers carried teenagers traveling the tidy streets where, intersecting with one another, each street formed unseen hash marks at each corner with the other, squaring up the courthouse lawn. Onansburg, Iowa, county seat of Choctaw County, was organized around a town square, in the middle of which was the courthouse. This was the place in the county to pay taxes and register marriages, births, deaths, or liens in whatever order they occurred in citizens' lives.

No one knew the origin of the town's name for sure, but Choctaw County was clearly named for the Native American heritage of the grassy prairie. It was likely that the namesake tribe had never come close to Onansburg, but local lore said a contingent of residents claimed land in an area of what came to be known as Choctaw Ridge. The settlers, German immigrants, first landed in Oklahoma, where the Choctaw Nation was settled following exile by the US government from Mississippi, the Choctaw Nation's first resettlement. Then, immigrant families, finding the Oklahoma terrain unsuitable for their farming practices, chose the Iowa countryside, founded the outpost of Onansburg, and proclaimed it as the county seat of the newly named Choctaw County.

Sonny and Polly Dawson had lived and always belonged in Onansburg. Their lives began there; Polly's life ended there.

In 1960, the year Sonny graduated from Choctaw County High School, the elderly federal-style courthouse presided over the town square like a nodding senior citizen in her last years of stately existence. The clock on the bell tower hadn't marked time for years; like major human organs that had to be replumbed or retooled with heart bypasses, transplanted kidneys, new hips and knees, the courthouse needed extensive updating with central heating, air conditioning, and plumbing. The faded architectural grand dame would, in 1964, suffer the indignity of being torn limb from limb, revealing her secrets hidden so many years under her brick skirts and white petticoat of rotten wooden timbers.

During the sixties when they were dating, Sonny and Polly had laughed at the antics of local teens and their hot rods tricked out with exotic paint jobs, lowered bumpers, and fuzzy dice hanging from the rearview mirror. When one of the fuming, farting modified street machines would zip past them, it was Sonny who'd yelled sarcastically, "Go, Cat. Go!" Sonny had shared the phrase in the remarks and memories he'd collected to give to Pastor Fred for Polly's funeral service; Polly had, without fail, to the day she died, giggled at his dated exclamation.

Now, Sonny stood apart from the others, just outside the doors where the yawning maw of the waiting hearse swallowed Polly's rich, polished casket. He clasped his hands to quiet their shaking, and his perspective narrowed as the double doors of the funeral coach closed with solid finality. He stood numbed with darkness closing off the periphery of his vision. It was as though he was the lone survivor watching his ship sink into black waters; then darkness closed around him.

Suddenly, Pastor Fred was at his side, his hand on Sonny's arm, steadying him. "Go, Cat. Go!" he whispered.

Sonny's vision cleared, and he dropped his hunched shoulders. Fred's attention eased his tension for the moment. The hearse departed with practiced finality. With a relieved half-smile to Pastor Fred, he watched until the coach took its lead position and pulled up at the junction of the concrete path from Little Flock Chapel and Lone Tree Road to allow the procession to form for the short drive to the cemetery.

Upon arriving at the church for the service, Sonny had parked his own Oldsmobile behind the limousine that was for the transport of the pallbearers and Pastor Fred. Cloris and Skip, his older sister and her husband, brought Dolores, the middle child of the three siblings, with them and parked their car at Sonny's home, arriving promptly at twelve noon, as he'd directed. Along with the Shaw family, Polly's people had gathered at Sonny's invitation for a quick lunch. The group departed for the short ride to the church en masse promptly at one p.m. for the one-thirty service.

Motioning to Cloris and Dolores, who followed him from the church, Sonny directed the seating for the ride to the cemetery, this time giving Dolores the honor of riding next to him, although Cloris had claimed the privilege on the ride to the church. When he'd opened the front door and guided Dolores's entry into the front seat, she covered her pleased smile with her hand. She fastened her seat belt without Sonny reminding her to do so, then smoothed her good black dress where the belt scrunched it into creases. Sonny closed the door for her, then wordlessly climbed into the driver's seat and quickly fastened his own seat belt.

Cloris and Skip took the unassigned places in the back seat, with Skip directly behind Sonny. A backward glance from Sonny reminded them to fasten their own seat belts. Cloris, her bottle-blonde hair piled high in 1960s cocktail waitress style, was wearing a white pique dress with big black polka dots, her black patent slings, and had a bag to match. Her smoke-coarsened skin and purple-veined nose bespoke her addictions. Now, the sister's physical appearances denied any familial traits. Cloris's abuse of alcohol caused her eyes to be perennially bloodshot with puffy bags of flesh that dripped onto her cheekbones, while Dolores's eyes, despite her weight, appeared sunken and hopeless with dark circles beneath them.

Skip, uncomfortable in his light beige suit, was accustomed to the clothes of the working man, a tee shirt with the name of his employer emblazoned on both front and back, then tucked into Levi's or Dickies work pants. He had loosened the fingered, frayed knot of his polyester necktie and unbuttoned the top button of the shirt beneath the released knot.

Cloris and Skip had been relieved when Sonny asked them to ride in his car to the funeral and to the cemetery. Sonny had guessed they would prefer to ride with him so they wouldn't have to drive alone in their old car. They had been, over the recent few days when they'd been thrown together with Polly's family, uneasy and awkward with the Shaws' reputation and affluence. Yet Sonny felt his family had acquitted themselves well.

While the Dawson family waited for the procession to form, the congregation of mourners streamed from the same exit doors, then took to their own automobiles. The pallbearers—Polly's brothers, Walter, Darrell, and Tom, and their respective sons—rode in the Fetters' limousine just behind the hearse. Then, according to funeral decorum, Sonny was next followed by Polly's family—the three brothers' wives together in one car, her sister Dorothy and Dorothy's husband in another, plus assorted Shaw nieces and nephews in a station wagon. He glanced into the rearview mirror before he followed the limousine from the church parking lot, and recognized three of the automobiles behind him as belonging to the Shaw family. Their cars were pristine in appearance, noticeably different from their customary coating of dust stirred by the graveled country roads that led to their homes.

Beyond pallbearers, hearse, and immediate family, there was no established pecking order for the stately drive to the cemetery. Before departure, the Fetters Funeral Home attendants had stopped briefly at each car, instructing the driver to turn on the headlights, the mark of their entitlement as part of the funeral cortege. Each driver fell in line, politely deferring to parking lot directional arrows. Claude Bray, the night marshal pressed into duty for funerals and other state occasions, stopped traffic long enough for the line of cemetery-bound cars to follow the hearse without interrupting the procession, from the parking lot onto Lone Tree Road. A twenty-five-mile-per-hour top speed allowed the caravan to form up and stay together.

Traffic at the intersection of Main Street and the exit road from Highway 35 was stopped by a Choctaw County deputy sheriff to allow the line of cars to proceed unimpeded by stop signs or cross traffic. Main Street was the direct route to Onansburg's only cemetery.

Cloris, ever the back-seat driver, leaned forward over Dolores's shoulder. "Sonny, don't follow the limo too close. You don't know who's driving, and he might stop sudden! Sonny, do you have your lights on like he said?"

Sonny stirred, then turned his head to catch Cloris's eye and replied, "Cloris, do you want to drive? We're going fifteen miles an hour right now. How much trouble can I get into?" Sonny regretted the edge in his voice and spoke quickly to soften his words. "Thanks. I know you're trying to help."

Be the best boy you can be, Sonny. Be the best little boy.

The words had occurred at other times, unbidden as an unexpected descant above conscious thought. As before, Sonny pushed them away.

The occupants of the car were silent but for desultory remarks during the remainder of the ride.

From Dolores, the subject was weather. "I don't like the looks of that sky."

From Skip, a man of few words: "The *Choctaw County Republican* should be out by later today."

Cloris studied her newly groomed nails.

Sonny drove close behind the slow-moving hearse and pallbearer's limousine following tree-lined city streets to the town cemetery on the south edge of Onansburg. As soon as he turned into the narrow cemetery lane, he could see from a distance of perhaps one hundred yards from the front gate of the cemetery the tent erected over the gravesite.

Sonny had chosen the plot, hereafter known as the Dawson Plot, during an on-site visit accompanied by Steve Fetters and the city clerk of Onansburg, who maintained cemetery records. It was with surprise when he realized the plot would be legally conveyed to his ownership by a warranty deed from the Town of Onansburg. He'd never thought of there being legal title to a piece of land only used as a necessity, and after the burial of loved ones no one would argue possession. Cemetery plots didn't fit his definition of prime real estate.

He had examined the available spaces carefully and chose one close to but not contiguous to the space already occupied by Polly's parents. A decorative granite bench under a nearby tree offered its stony solace to visitors.

He followed the hearse and the limousine when they edged to the left side of the lane, the side closest to the gravesite, and parked slightly off the gravel on the grass. Slowing his car to a crawl for the last few yards, he then parked behind the limousine as directed by Steve Fetters. Steve, studying the front of Sonny's car, stood directly behind the limo with arms and hands outstretched toward Sonny's car, waggling his fingers toward himself until he signaled a stop with hands turned outward in a push-back motion. He moved quickly to open the door for Dolores, then took her hand as she exited her place of honor in the front seat. Sonny, Cloris, and Skip pre-empted Steve's assistance. The siblings were directed up the slight incline to the front row of navy blue draped folding chairs under the tent, where they were joined by Polly's sister, Dorothy, and by Polly's three sisters-in-law filling in the three rows in turn as the front row of chairs were filled. Sonny solicitously stood until they were seated. Skip and Dorothy's husband took places behind the chairs.

Others from the congregation crowded under the tent but left room for the pallbearers to fill in behind the family with those left outside jostling gently for position to see and hear the grave-side service. The casket was disgorged from the hearse into the waiting arms of the pallbearers.

Sonny watched intently. With stony countenances, the three Shaw brothers, along with their respective sons, joined in carrying Polly to her grave, led by Pastor Fred. The Shaw family took care of their own.

Fat, pregnant raindrops began to plop onto the grass and on top of the green tent covering overhead. The raindrops fell faster for a few moments, beating their blunt tattoo on the tent. The rain stirred the parched late-summer grass, releasing a cloud of dust to cake the shoes of those standing outside the tent. There was a rustling of rain-coats, plastic rain bonnets, and the pop of inflating umbrellas. Under the tent, a wrinkled green cloth masquerading as grass protected the nearest's and dearest's footwear. The mourners stood in silence until after a few moments, as though to placate the bereaved, the beat softened as the rain shower moved on past the cemetery.

The casket was placed on the bier that dominated the funeral tent. Sonny and his sisters had chosen Polly's casket. Smooth, ebony wood with antiqued-silver fittings. The interior was of pale shell pink. The luxuriously lined boxes displayed at the funeral home reminded Sonny of the heart-shaped boxes lined up on the drugstore shelves for lovers and the dutiful to choose for Valentine's Day. Every year Polly, a frequent visitor to the seasonal display, had exclaimed over his choice of the frilly boxed chocolates and assured Sonny he had chosen her favorite. "How do you always know which one?" she'd ask, pulling him close.

Sonny's breath caught. He exhaled slowly and deeply when he imagined soft pillows cushioning her head and satin lining trimmed with ruched ribbon enfolding her as the casket was placed to enter the waiting grave.

No more Valentine's Day candy, no more sunlit smiles of pretended surprise.

His eyes fell away from the casket when he noted the pall-bearers had completed their ritual duty. With lowered eyes and somber expressions, the men of the Shaw family stepped away from the bier and joined the mourners, each standing just behind the row of folding chairs on which Sonny, his sisters, Polly's sister, Dorothy, and the three Shaw wives were seated. Their sons took their places just behind their fathers. Sonny turned and nodded to them collectively.

Sonny's eyes flitted to the crowd at graveside. His forehead creased into a frown when he noticed some unexpected faces just outside the tent. He hadn't expected Larry and Julia Hayes to attend the graveside service, but they were clustered with his other employees, Ruby Shelton and Thelma Jane Hyatt, along with Ruby's husband, Harold. When Pastor Fred directed his gaze at Sonny, eyebrows raised in question, Sonny turned and nodded his attention to him as he read from his Order of Service.

"Here we are gathered in memory of Polly Shaw Dawson to perform our final duty: to place her remains in their final resting place. Let us join in prayer and meditation in a time of silence."

Following the interval of silence, the short pastoral prayer was concluded by the attending congregation, uttering respective "Amens" following that of Pastor Fred. He resumed speaking.

"We continue to the reading of the passages of scripture, the words of comfort from Ecclesiastes 3. 'To every thing there is a season: a time to be born, and a time to die, a time to plant, a time to reap . . . '"

Tears again welled up and spilled from Sonny's eyes upon hearing the familiar verses. Dolores placed a tissue in his hand while Cloris, seated to his left, rustled around in her handbag for one as well. One of Polly's brothers sniffed audibly from the rows behind Sonny.

Pastor Fred, his voice steady and strong as he began his remarks, spoke briefly to urge family and friends to remember Polly's life with its best examples of her grace, strength, generosity, and wisdom; to feel her loss deeply; and last, to let grief and pain transcend to warm memories.

"Her grace, one who knew she was a recipient of God's grace, not taking it for granted but living knowing she was one of His. She was strong, resolute in her faith. Polly gave and shared her gifts of service and wisdom, generously. Last, Polly was filled with love and loyalty for Sonny, her family, and community." His voice, with its soft, southern inflection, broke when he listed the attributes of Polly's character.

Pastor Fred concluded the graveside service with the finality of the phrase "What has come from the earth, returns to the earth." Then, raising his right hand with his palm open, he bowed his head, cradling his Bible and Order of Service in his left, and asked that all recite the Mizpah, the benediction requested by Sonny.

"May the Lord watch between me and thee, while we are absent, one from the other."

Pastor Fred then dismissed the congregants with the final blessing. "In the name of the Father, the Son, and the Holy Spirit. Amen." The mark of the cross from the hand extended to heaven encompassed the casket and the mourners, and authorized the conclusion of the service and leave-taking from the grave.

The crowd stirred when Sonny stood up. He took Dolores's arm to indicate she should stand beside him. Cloris, Skip, and the three sisters-in-law, Molly, Carla, and Jenny, surrounded him with quiet embraces until Pastor Fred approached from his place at the head of Polly's casket. Drying their eyes, the sisters-in-law unobtrusively slipped closer to their husbands.

Cloris gestured toward the casket. "Sonny," she asked, "do you want one of the lilies from the bouquet?" The floral spray from Sonny, dozens of white Casa Blanca lilies surrounded by lush greenery, covered the casket. He had known that white flowers were Polly's favorite.

"No, I don't, but if you and Dolores do . . ." He nodded his permission. As Cloris stepped toward the casket, Sonny indicated with a beckoning of his arm that his sisters-in-law were welcome to the blossoms as well.

"God be with you, Sonny." Pastor Fred, his flushed face radiating sympathy and heat, pressed his palm into Sonny's right hand, then flexed his other fist against Sonny's arm in a manner that left Sonny no choice but to turn to those waiting dumbly to offer cuds of comfort—round bovine expressions of sympathy and curiosity, lower lips scooping out ruminates of wisdom.

Sonny snorted softly to himself with a slight, tight smile that threatened to break his face. Brother Billy Bob Clergy. The compactly built pastor had been born and raised in Alabama. His first twenty years of pastoral experience had been in the Deep South, before he petitioned the church's governing body to transfer him to northern climes.

Years before, upon first encountering the Rev. Fred and his deep-seated southern accent, during visiting hours at the hospital wearing a badge that proclaimed its bearer "CLERGY," he and Polly had dubbed him Brother Billy Bob Clergy.

Pastor Fred had been in daily attendance to Sonny since his loss of Polly. Following their initial encounter with the newly arrived minister at the hospital, Polly and Sonny had come to know Pastor Fred and respected him as a friend. Much of the Dawsons' social life revolved around church activities; Polly helped serve in the kitchen for weddings, funerals, and anniversary parties. Sonny served on the church council and attended the Methodist Men's monthly meetings and special dinners.

After several minutes of greetings, somber conversation, and hugs of comfort, gentle custodial hands herded Sonny from the grave; but, turning back for a last look, he longed to stay. Then his inner voice directed him.

Don't look back, Sonny. Come back when you can be alone. It went so fast. Do it all again. The memory snapshot isn't enough. Everyone leaves while the city workers do their work filling in the grave, smoothing it over, covering it with sod. I'd feel better if I could have stayed to help. Even if I had to do it by myself. I need to be alone with Polly.

Sonny climbed into the driver's seat of the Oldsmobile. The script had been written. He had only to follow it. Quickly, he started the car. The fan from the air conditioning first blew out hot air. He reached over and turned it up to HIGH, then gradually, it began to cool the interior. He pressed his forehead against the driver's side window, studied the scene and the company of friends in small groups of two or three, hesitantly moving slowly away from the grave. A few glanced or nodded in his direction.

Cloris and Skip escorted Dolores back to Sonny's car. This time, Skip assisted Dolores to her front-seat place in the car. He and Cloris reassumed their same back-seat places by default. Seat belts were fastened without direction. Sonny carefully pulled out from behind the emptied hearse and the car inched its way down the graveled cemetery road, once more in the lead of the cars that had parked behind him. The rush from the air conditioning finally began to overtake the heat in the Oldsmobile's leather-lined interior cabin.

Sonny glanced in the rearview mirror at the rear-seat occupants and caught a glimpse of Skip's raised eyebrows. Leaning back slightly and turning over his right shoulder to comment over the shrapnel pellets of gravel doing a rat-a-tat drumming on the car's underside, Sonny responded to Skip's nonverbal question.

"Yeah, we'll go on back to the church, Skip. Everyone's invited back to the church."

Sonny glanced through the car window to the unhappy sky with its roiling, tumbling clouds, then slumped back against the warm leather seat and allowed the air conditioning to blow away the perspiration from his forehead. He realized, too late, he could have taken his suit jacket off before he got out of the car for the brief service, and then the other men and the pallbearers could have followed his lead in the sweltering heat.

He tried not to listen to Dolores's sotto voce conversation with Cloris and Skip, yet felt annoyed at being left out. They were talking about how many people had come out for the funeral. Polly's cousins—so many from around town. Sonny interrupted.

"Yes, yes! It was great that so many came. Yeah, probably half the town was there. Yeah, it was nice to see old friends. Several of Polly's cousins and old friends of ours drove in just for the service."

Then he frowned, remembering a face he'd glimpsed in the crowd outside the tent. He hadn't been able to place the person at first, but it came to him now.

I haven't seen Drennan McCormack in years. He looks so much older. Sure as hell didn't expect him to show his face.

Sonny's gaze slid out of focus as he puzzled through the disbelief of the past few days yet again.

Once more, Sonny remembered Polly, the way she looked when she went out the door just five days before. Their home was so filled with Polly, so it was impossible to know if it was a manifestation of her psychic energy reluctantly left behind or if it was the physical imprint of her recent being that made Sonny see her everywhere he turned. Coming around the corner from the dining room into the kitchen, there she was at the stove. Walking the sidewalk from the garage to the back door, she was waiting to give him a welcome-home hug. His memory caught the faint scent of her lavender fragrance when he'd nestled his face along hers and tucked her in his embrace.

The wrinkled sleeves of her jacket left hanging in the closet indicated a willingness to bend at the elbows; muddy garden gloves stiffened in the shape of her busy hands; her glove-soft slippers beside the bed were ready to take her direction. Spats, the black-and-white tomcat, waited impassively to share Polly's chair, not knowing she wouldn't be back for him.

Sonny suddenly became aware of his older sister's voice and spoke grudgingly in reply. "Yes, Cloris, I'm watching the road."

Taking a more direct route to the church than the funeral procession had traveled, Sonny drove along one side of the square of lawn surrounding the courthouse and with a start noted the preparations for Old Settlers. The mowing had been finished and the city workers were pruning bushes and trimming around light poles and trash cans.

Sonny shook his head in disbelief; the physical arrangements for the celebration had been his responsibility for fifteen years on the second Saturday in August. He'd compiled folders and notebooks clearly marked with the year of the celebration in bold letters. Each year, necessity dictated that he tweak the diagrams and maps for placement of the refreshment stands, the Cattlemen's group selling burgers and barbecued beef; the pork people selling pork chops on a stick, bratwurst and sausage sandwiches. There were hastily constructed stands and booths for civic fundraisers; support for the Choctaw Independent Theatre, donations to the pet rescue fund and the wildlife conservation fund at the Waterworks Park. Other tables staffed by their creators featured handmade crafts, crocheted and knitted creations, Barbie doll wardrobes.

In addition, he had been in charge of assigning the front display windows of participating stores to the civic groups and Onansburg High School class reunions. Every year, windows were decorated with the composite of high school graduation photos from the class celebrating its twenty-fifth, thirty-fifth, even fiftieth reunion at the current Old Settlers. And classmates who had passed away, some from accidents or illnesses even during their high school years, were remembered with the placement of gold stars above their individual photos. Other windows were filled with remembrances of Onansburg history, but all windows were unified by the theme chosen for the current year as determined by the Old Settlers committee. This year, "Old Settlers Salutes the Family" was announced in July for the 1994 theme.

Most years, the positioning of the benches in front of the bandstand where the program and entertainment were presented were essentially the same. He had mapped out dimensions and positions of the benches years earlier when he first took on the responsibility of the physical arrangements, but each year, he reviewed the diagram to accommodate any changes. Driving by now, he saw with relief the city works department trucks loaded with concrete blocks and stacks of planks, each twelve feet long. The blocks would be positioned so the planks were evenly and substantially supported. A few park benches would be claimed by early arrivals, but the remainder of the crowd would occupy the benches or bring their own lawn chairs.

Now he was chagrined. How could he have forgotten to check on the arrangements for which he was responsible? Then, his mind reeling, he recalled the afternoon of the last Old Settlers committee meeting. He'd come home from the meeting in time to answer the front door to Pastor Fred and the delegation of Polly's friends. They'd come to tell him that Polly was dead.

I'll play catch-up, but not today. This is my work for today.

He drove by Franklin Hardware, the business he and Polly

owned for the last twenty years. Polly and the business had filled his heart and soul, but today it was closed in observance of Polly's passing and funeral, as it had been since the previous Saturday following her death on Friday.

Sonny slid the car into the empty parking spot in front of the church. He was ready to get out of the car and shed the tension his sisters were giving off. Plus, his tolerance for Skip was running short. Skip had been accompanying Cloris, helping as needed in the last few days with errands or serving coffee or soft drinks to those who called and gathered at Sonny's home. On guard against Skip's obsequious attitude in the presence of Polly's family and friends, Sonny's patience had been tested and tried. Skip had stopped just short of fawning over Sonny's guests with unaccustomed hospitality. In the past, whenever Sonny grew impatient or churlish with Skip, Polly gently reproved him, saying, "Now, Sonny . . . " It was usually all she needed to say to bring him up short.

Skip spoke up. "Looks like we're the first ones here. Shall we go on inside, get some iced tea, some coffee before everyone else gets here?"

Well, hell yes, we're the first ones here. We left the cemetery first.

"I'll go on inside," Sonny said now, bursting from the driver's side door. "The ladies from the church didn't go to the cemetery; they'll be here. Just tell everyone to come on in when they get here."

Sonny was glad to have a reason to absent himself from Skip, and even Cloris and Dolores. More than anything he wanted to be alone, with the freedom to weep and wail or rage and curse. The wish had been his constant thought since Polly died, but even when he'd had small moments to himself, he couldn't tap into the surge of emotions he knew he needed to release. On the night of the day she'd died and the ones after, when he was finally alone, all he could do was fall into their bed, dry-eyed with shock.

Sonny made his way through the side door of the white frame church and headed down the stairs to the basement; the cement steps shone slightly damp from the humidity. The dimly lit passageway, with its sudden coolness, was welcoming after the sticky August heat outside.

Descending into the Sunday school smell he associated with old church basements, Sonny was reminded of the dank odor of old pop machines of his childhood, the kind that had iced, cold water to cool the innocent favorites, grape, strawberry, orange soda. Sonny wasn't ever allowed to choose cola, only fruit flavor on semi-rare occasions. When a bottle of soda pop was allowed, it was shared out to the three Dawson siblings equally in glasses, no ice. The family Kelvinator wouldn't have stored ice even had there been some.

His mouth suddenly felt dusty and old. His face was gritty, the salt from his tears and sweat mixed with the dust from the cemetery. He felt even more keenly the ache of his loss, but then Sonny termed his thoughts as maudlin. He was annoyed with himself.

He negotiated the sharp turn at the bottom of the steps but bumped his shoulder on the sharp corner and swore under his breath. Rubbing his shoulder, he passed the ladies' room, then gave the door of the men's room a shove with an outstretched arm and pushed through the door. He heard Cloris and Dolores, the heels of their dress shoes tapping down the concrete stairs behind him.

The door banged shut behind him, and Sonny entered the first stall, then locked himself in. Without unzipping or lowering his trousers, he seated himself gratefully on the commode, leaning sideways against the ubiquitous institutional roll of tissue jutting out from the sides of the metal stall. A minute to catch his breath, to be alone before facing the congregation of good people now arriving, slamming car doors, noisily stomping cemetery dust and mud from their shoes, taking up life again. The last part of the ritual was coming up.

Get up, Sonny. Get going.

"Sonny? Sonny? Are you OK in there?"

"I'll be right out, Cloris."

Sonny hauled himself to his feet, flushed the toilet to legitimize his tenure in the men's room, and then slid the recalcitrant metal lock open. He brushed white dusty lint left by the tissue from the right sleeve of his suit coat with his hand. Crossing in front of the row of three stalls and the urinal, he allowed himself a look at the wavy image in the mirror above the lavatory. The webbed distortion in the surface of the glass added a surreal dimension to a face Sonny hardly recognized.

He heard Cloris just outside the restroom door. "Sonny's inside. He'll be out in a minute." He didn't know to whom she spoke.

Sonny twisted the handle of the water faucet, cupped cold water from the sputtering tap in his hands, and splashed it on his face. He dried his face and hands with brown paper towels from the dispenser beside the sink. He remembered Polly in front of a mirror. She had been a flurry of activity, fluffing her hair with her fingers, patting her nose and cheeks with a tissue or powder puff. He wouldn't think of her now in the candy-box casket.

Responding to Cloris's plaintive inquiry through the men's room door, Sonny left the caricature of himself behind in the looking glass.

God knows, let's not upset the sisters anymore. They're all over me as it is with their concern! I needed to wash up, so what's the hurry? It's all but over now.

He chided himself for his petulance, crumpled the paper towel in his hands, and fired it into the empty metal waste can. He hastened to the door and jerked it open.

When he stepped out of the men's room both sisters were waiting for him, their bulk nearly filling the narrow corridor leading from the side door down the stairs, past the restrooms and on to the fellowship hall. Sonny, still annoyed at having been called away from the privacy of the men's room, led the way to the fellowship hall. Dolores followed just behind Sonny, bleating about having taken the pictures of Polly in her casket.

"She looked so natural, just like she's sleeping. I took a whole roll of film . . . " Dolores, noting his inattention to her, abandoned her attempt to evoke a response as they approached the hall.

He could hear the conversation coming from the fellowship hall, the congregation arriving, coming down the wide stairway from the main entrance to finish the work of death and funerals, the proper responses, the offerings of flowers and food, conventional offers of "if there's anything I can do."

He turned to Dolores. "Dolores, honey, thanks. I'll appreciate the pictures. It was good of you to take them. Just don't show them to anyone. I'll want to see them first."

Sonny knew he wouldn't want to see the pictures, and he sure as hell didn't want anyone else to see them either. God, he hated the idea of Polly being photographed in her casket, so vulnerable, so exposed, so dead. Better to picture her toasting him with her glass of wine; standing knee-deep in her colorful flower garden playfully threatening him with her garden shears, urging him to help her; bringing his first cup of coffee to the breakfast table. Sonny didn't want Dolores to know he was distressed about the photography session.

Everyone tried too hard to do something to ease his pain. The gift of time that it would take to bring any comfort was not theirs to give. To let them make their noises, to parry their kind offers of help, were both part of the ritual of death and loss.

Sonny took Dolores's hand in his as he led the way, with Cloris following on down the narrow corridor toward the fellowship hall. Sonny noted that while there was the low hum of voices, there was no punctuation of laughter. At first, the crowd didn't notice his entrance, and as they, one by one, saw him and his sisters in the doorway, conversation fell away.

He wondered how it would be if there were no prescriptions or proscriptions for handling a loved one's death. What if, rather than prescribed behavior surrounding experiences of liminality, people were forbidden to react with emotion, whether grief or joy? In the case of reacting to the death of a loved one, would people hurt more or hurt less if they were not sanctioned to mourn?

Sonny paused, still within the dimly lit corridor. The bright gathering place before him made him sense he was joining a play already in progress. Concerned faces and tentative smiles welcomed Sonny and his sisters as they joined the crowd.

He noted Jean, Karen, and Norma, Polly's card-club friends, standing in a small cluster near the coffee urn. Lars Swenson and Terry Mathews, standing close by their wives, turned toward him as he entered. Jean, divorced and single, continued to be welcomed as part of the group of close friends.

Sonny gave them all a quick wave with his open right hand to his forehead in a quasi-salute. They'd been among the family and friends in regular attendance at his home, checking in with him every day by phone, sweeping sidewalks, watering Polly's outdoor plants, and it was Norma and Karen who'd come, along with Pastor Fred, to tell him that Polly had passed away suddenly. It had been the four women's every-other-week Friday card game, bridge on the days they didn't play poker.

Ladies from Polly's Martha Circle were busy serving cookies, pieces of cake festooned with frosting, small sandwiches filled with egg salad, ham salad, cream cheese with cucumber. There was fruit punch and coffee. The room was crowded, warm with body heat and sentiment. It was yet another tribute to Polly that so many people had taken the time to come to her service and reception.

Skip was slouched in a chair at the corner of the exit door, looking ready to make a getaway at the first opportune moment. While he knew many of those who were in the room, it was only by sight and perhaps by name.

From the neighbors two blocks over: "Sonny, we've been so concerned." "Thank you, Margaret. It was good of you and Verle to be here with us."

From Polly's former high school English teacher, now in her

eighties: "Sonny, this is so hard on everyone. At my age, it should have been me, not Polly." Sonny had heard that phrase from several octogenarians over the past few days. "Yes, Miss Cook, this is hard work for everyone."

From the president of the Chapel's Women's League: "Sonny, everyone will miss her so." "Yes, Marcella, we all will."

Sonny accepted the platitudes and made the obligatory responses knowing they were part of the ritual. These good folks would resume their lives; go to their jobs, clean their homes, pay bills, buy groceries. Their attendance on this day would conclude the work of Polly's death for them. Others would call, bring an occasional plate of cookies. Still others would earnestly say they'd remember Sonny in their thoughts and prayers, and in return, Sonny wondered if they really would. One by one or in small clusters, friends sought him out to announce their departure and bid him goodbye. Some reminded him, "Let us know if you need anything, just give us a call."

Calmer now, consciously donning a pleasant expression, Sonny skirted around still-occupied chairs and tables where friends were finishing their cake, dusting cookie crumbs from chins, bosoms, and mustaches. He went toward the kitchen where, through the open serving window, he could see the ladies from Polly's circle clearing up, hand-washing the glass snack plates and cups. With a flash of memory, he saw her working, moving among the women.

A number of those in attendance were members of Little Flock Chapel, but along with friends and family, the crowd at the funeral had grown to more than two hundred. The Shaw family, in its entirety, was still present at the reception. Its prominence in Onansburg, both in agricultural business and community affairs, had added even more to the numbers for Polly's service. Darrell had served on the school board, while Walter was a member of the board of directors of the locally owned bank, Second National Bank of Onansburg.

The Shaw family was close-knit, bound in business by the shared ownership of the family farm and by ascription of shared values passed down by the generations preceding them. Three sons and two daughters, including Polly, had been born to Mahlon and Tillie Shaw in the square white farmhouse five miles southeast of Onansburg. Dorothy followed the twins, Darrell and Walter, into the world two years later, with Polly nearly three years younger than she. Tom, the brother Sonny felt closest to, followed Polly in the birth order after another three years. Polly and Dorothy were fine-boned with Dorothy fashionably thin, while Polly had always been softer in appearance.

Now at the end of the funeral observances, in contrast to the hushed voices of the visitation at the Fetters Funeral Home and the funeral, there was a relieved energy in the voices. Stress, fostered by empathy and vicarious grief of those in attendance, was dissipating. There was even occasional quiet laughter. While groups genially moved aside to allow him passage, Sonny was but midway across the big room toward the kitchen when he heard yet another voice seeking his attention. He stopped and turned toward the summons.

"Sonny? I don't know whether you remember me."

Though phrased as an inquiry, there was no question in the voice; its owner knew the answer. A tall man, massively built, regarded Sonny steadily from several feet away. He'd been standing with the Shaw family. His appearance commanded attention, yet Sonny had missed seeing him among the others at the reception.

Drennan. And here he is . . . with the Shaws.

Like a gunfighter who has been called out, every sense came to attention. His scalp prickled, the skin along his spine crawled as though the teeth of a giant zipper were closing from its base to the top.

Now, tension snaked through the room. Many present, and certainly Polly's family, knew Drennan as the long-ago romance in Polly's life. The conversation among those close to where he was standing faltered and died. He heard Cloris's little gasp, felt Dolores's hand tighten on his arm. He turned toward the voice. His response was slow, measured.

"Hello." He paused. "Yes, I remember you," he responded assuredly.

Now aware of the interest stirring the crowd, Drennan relied on convention to carry the conversation. "Yes, I thought you would." He nodded his head affirmatively. "My brother Mike called me. He knew I'd want to know about Polly. He told me it was her heart?" he said, ending with a question in his voice.

Sonny took a deep breath and made obligatory answers. "Yes, her heart. And sudden, but that's what Burt, Dr. Cook, said it was."

McCormack moved closer to Sonny. Polite but intentional conversation resumed among the members of the little groups of two and three standing close by. With attention seemingly fixed on one another, they chewed iced chocolate cake and cookies with pink frosting, pointedly allowing the two men a semblance of privacy. The men and women of the Shaw family turned away from the two. Curious glances, while feigning interest in contents of coffee cups and iced tea glasses, peered over bifocal frames and surreptitiously watched the two men, now face-to-face. Cloris retreated to the corner where Skip was slouched on a folding chair. Dolores alone remained, glancing openly and curiously from one to the other.

Drennan tilted his head toward Sonny, lowering his voice. "I want to visit with you. Just to talk about old times. But not here. Before I leave town." His demand was in the guise of a request, but there was no question that he expected agreement from Sonny.

Though balding now, in contrast to Sonny's full head of silvery-blonde hair, Drennan McCormack was still an impressive figure and a handsome man. His demeanor was that of a man accustomed to authority, of governing attention. The energy of his presence was one from which it was hard to look away. His dark, close-set eyes were fixed on Sonny and faithful Dolores, still attached to his arm.

Sonny frowned, and his voice was firm in reply.

"I can't think there's anything we need to talk about, Drennan. What do you want to say that you can't just say here?" Turning and speaking softly to Dolores, Sonny said, "Sweetheart, would you get some coffee for me?" Dolores smiled and slipped away from his side.

"Just to talk," Drennan repeated. "Just to talk. We've sure never been friends, but we never got to know each other. It was Polly I knew . . . " He paused, then finished lamely, "as a friend. I'll call first, then plan to come by your house sometime later."

He turned on his heel, responded to a few faint greetings with a nod to each, and moved purposefully through the crowd to the steps leading to the front door. Sonny, turning away from Drennan's leave-taking, stood alone for a few moments. Dolores reappeared at Sonny's side with a cup of coffee. "Do you want your coffee? Don't you want it black? They were out of cream, so I brought it without milk. Was that the man that was sweet on Polly years ago? I knew I'd seen him before. What is he doing here?"

Relieving Dolores of the coffee, he drank a few sips, giving himself a few minutes to collect his thoughts. He took a deep breath, transferred the cup to his left hand, put his right arm around her shoulders, and steered her toward his original destination, Pastor Fred and the ladies in the kitchen.

"Don't worry about it. He was just someone who used to live here."

"But, Sonny, I know . . . "

"It's just someone Polly and I knew a long time ago. Forget it. I think we can leave now. We'll tell Cloris and Skip . . . I'll drop you all off. Let's give Reverend Fred and the ladies in the kitchen our thanks for all they've done." He set his cup on a nearby table with a smile at its occupants.

When he caught Cloris's eye she rejoined her brother and sister, and together, they went to interrupt the work in the kitchen. The women, all busy with washing, drying, and putting dishes and silverware away, paused, turning toward Sonny. Their choir of conversation stopped, as if on cue from a director.

"Thank you, ladies. Thank you, one and all." His voice broke but he continued. "Your being here has meant a lot to me and my family, and Polly would have been so happy to know you were together here on her behalf. Again, my sincere thanks."

Most of the women stood with bowed heads, hands clasped over their aprons at their midsections. They had been Polly's friends. Those standing close reached out to touch Sonny's shoulder as he passed by them.

He shepherded Cloris and Dolores ahead of himself, through the kitchen door and then out through the main entrance to the fellowship hall toward the same stairs McCormack had taken. Skip fell in behind Sonny from his corner outpost. Dolores huffed and puffed as Sonny took her arm to assist her up the stairs.

"You must be so tired, Sonny," said Cloris. "Why don't Skip and I just catch a ride home with Sally and Chase." She gestured toward their neighbors, a few cars away. Sonny accepted her excuse, knowing the ride would inevitably lead them to the Cozy Tap, Cloris's and Skip's home away from home. He resigned himself to the thought when he realized it had been a long day for them too. He nodded a little and embraced Cloris for a moment longer than usual.

Sonny and Dolores drove to her house in silence. When they arrived, he followed her wearily up the five steps into the trim bungalow and went through the motions of exorcising gypsies, tramps, and thieves from under the beds and inside closets. It had come to be a mechanical task. He declined her invitation to come back later for dinner. "I'll fix you tuna melt sandwiches . . . You really like those, I know," she said, nodding her head importantly.

"Not tonight. Thanks, but I'm really tired."

Back again in the quiet of his car, driving toward the home he'd shared with Polly, Sonny thought to himself, *This is it*. Over the past few days, he'd heard this time described as being the hardest, the time when you finally go home alone, knowing this new reality is the way it will be forever.

Be the best boy, Sonny. Be the best little boy. You can do it. I know you can do it.

Two

---

*S*onny parked the car in the drive, walked to the front of the house, and climbed the eight cement steps up to the front porch of the stucco Victorian home where he and Polly had lived for nearly twenty-five years. Following the earlier rain, the heat and humidity of the August afternoon were oppressive. Under a clearing sky, the nearby fields of corn, the individual stalks visible from the porch, stood nearly motionless, with only an occasional wave of hot air stirring the plumed tassels of the green army of plants, all standing at attention in regimental rows.

Sonny removed the mail from the mailbox, then slammed the lid shut. Picking a spent blossom from a Polly-pink geranium, Sonny caught himself thinking *Polly will want to water the plants on the porch tonight*. It had been a ghost of a thought. His conscious mind reneged on it before the thought was fully formed.

Mail in hand, mostly big white or colored envelopes denoting sympathy cards, Sonny knelt to pick up the weekly newspaper, the *Choctaw County Republican*, delivered sometime during the afternoon. He pushed on through the unlocked heavy front door into the quiet, artificial comfort. As in many small towns, locking the doors, if at all, was only done at night.

Once inside, Spats rushed to greet him, questioning Sonny in his garrulous tomcat voice. Tossing the mail onto the hall table, then gathering the cat into his arms, Sonny held him close for a few moments, nuzzling the soft dark fur. In turn, Spats first pushed his nose then the side of his face along Sonny's face. It was often in the past that Sonny would catch the fragrance of Polly—her skin, her hair, even the aroma of cooking spices—on Spats and know that she had recently held him close.

Pushing himself away from Sonny with the namesake white feet, Spats jumped down and led the way into the living room, looking back, inviting Sonny to follow. Retrieving the mail and the paper, Sonny followed, looking forward to the calming effect that the well-ordered home always had on him. Uneasy despite having wishes for nothing more than to be alone, Sonny felt no relief or release from the respite afforded by the end of his official duties as the bereaved. He tried to relax, to take pleasure where he'd always found it, in their home. He'd always thought of it as reflecting their love for one another.

God, we loved this house. She was so damn proud of it from the day we moved in.

Peeling wallpaper, scarred woodwork, hole in the ceiling, she loved it all. Sonny thought back to the hours that he spent on ladders, on his knees with paint and wallpaper brushes becoming accustomed extensions of his own arms.

Total renovation had been only the first phase of the love affair with their home. First the house, then the yard, then the garden, with Sonny doing the hard, physical labor, while Polly planted beds and corridors of beautiful flowers that were defined by graceful, curved delineations of blooming plants and shrubs. The birdbath in the center of one of the circular beds had been an anniversary gift from Sonny to Polly. The figure of an organ grinder's monkey stood in a shell-shaped bowl. With a fez to match his military-style jacket, the monkey held an umbrella from which water spouted up and over into the graceful bowl. Polly had been delighted when the surprise was unveiled.

Then it was "Oh, Sonny, think about a screened porch!" "What about a brick walk to the garden?" "We should have a gazebo!" Sonny knew he'd created a proverbial monster of "Honey-do this and Honey-do that."

Handsome antiques added yet another dimension to the work of their home. The Victorian walnut dining table, when extended for company, could seat twelve guests comfortably. A pier mirror with diamond dust ground into the glass reflected their appearance from its seemingly made-to-order spot at the foot of the stairs; an ornate sideboard featured a silver tea service, an antique Wedgwood cake plate, fresh flowers in season, or an antique oil painting of flowers surrounded by a gilt frame. They earned their satisfaction in the home with their hard work, even though the restoration was never quite done in Polly's eyes.

Suddenly, Sonny sensed that he was not alone in the house. The creak of a telltale floorboard sounded the warning that meant someone was in the library. Tom Shaw, Polly's brother, stepped into the living room from the adjoining room.

"I didn't know anyone was here," Sonny said.

"Sorry. Didn't mean to startle you. Jenny dropped me off; I let myself in. She went to do some errands before we go on home."

Sonny noted he seemed uncharacteristically tense. Tom was the brother Polly had always favored. He and his wife, Jenny, were easily her best friends in the family of five siblings. They were frequent visitors; their children made Aunt Polly's home a depot for their arrivals and departures from high school activities. Sometimes, Polly and even Sonny filled in for Jenny as the driver for their children on one of their innumerable trips between town and their parents' farm home.

Since Friday of the week before Old Settlers, when Sonny made his hushed telephone calls advising her brothers of Polly's death, he had been surrounded by family and friends. Polly's three brothers, Walter, Darrell, and Tom, rushed to Sonny's home upon receiving the news. Walter, the oldest of the triumvirate brothers, arrived first. Even as he was bounding up the front steps, two at a time, Darrell and Tom pulled up in another of the farm's powerful Chevy trucks, dark green in color with the words "Shaw Family Farms" stenciled on the door. All the vehicles owned by the farm business were green and displayed the same logo.

None of the three men, in their shock and disbelief, had stopped to change from their work clothes. Levi's, plaid shirt, chambray shirt, Iowa State Fair tee shirt. The warmth of their bodies emanated the residual heat of the ninety-degree outside temperature, and their clothing with its strong, outdoor aroma of sun-warmed hay and grain recalled the work of their day.

"What's going on? Where is she? What's happened to her? Was there an accident?"

Walter demanded answers to which Sonny could barely respond. With elbows tight to his sides and upturned palms, Sonny could barely make himself heard. Haltingly, he choked out the words.

"I don't know, I don't know for sure yet. Polly went to play bridge with her club at Jean Thomas's. I was at the store, went to the Old Settlers committee meeting, then picked up the dry cleaning, dropped off a baby gift at Thorensen's . . . "

Walter cut him off short. "I don't care what you did, what about Polly? What happened?"

"Listen, I don't know anything more than Polly was at Jean's. She collapsed, and she was gone. Just like that. I ran to the hospital, Burt was there, and he said it was her heart or a stroke. There was no warning . . . " He covered his mouth with both hands to hide his grimace. He broke down, sobbing.

The three brothers turned away.

Hurried footsteps on the porch announced the wives of the three men; Carla, Molly, and Jenny Shaw knocked on the front door, then pushed it open. Carla, always in charge, like a herd mare to the Shaw family women, demanded the same answers

Sonny had already offered. "What's happened to Polly? Where is she? Can we see her?"

The telephone shrilled a demand for attention. Their sister, Dorothy, having been alerted by Carla before she left her home to meet Molly and Jenny at the sale barn corner, the common meeting place for the family, was calling from her California home in shocked surprise. Annoyed by the intrusion of the telephone, Sonny grabbed the phone and answered the phone call tersely.

"Yes, yes. It's true." He quickly passed the receiver to Carla. "It's Dorothy."

"No, no. We don't know anything for sure yet. Sonny just came back from the hospital." She paused for Dorothy's questions. "No, no. No arrangements yet. This just happened. We just got here to Polly's . . . " Her voice dropped at the familial claim to the home. An expression of sudden dismay passed across her face—it was no longer Polly's home.

Darrell and Walter, twins so alike in appearance and manner, they were, even at age fifty-five, nearly indistinguishable. Handsome men with salt and pepper gray hair, snapping blue eyes, florid coloration, and work-hardened bodies. Both were the same five feet eleven inches tall and weighed within three pounds of one another.

Dorothy, having long since moved to California, was a rare visitor to Onansburg. She came for Polly's funeral, accompanied by her husband Ted Hughes, a Los Angeles attorney. They had been strained, silent, seemingly removed from the family's grief. They'd preferred to stay at the Onansburg Inn rather than one of her brothers' homes.

Tom, the youngest at forty-five, was ten years younger than his brothers, and accordingly, Darrell and Walter fostered parental attitudes toward Tom from the time he was born. He was similar to his twin brothers in stature, but having assimilated a keen interest in health, diet, and exercise during his college years, he appeared even younger.

After their father's passing, their mother, as the sole owner of the farm according to the simple will, left the farming enterprise to her five children when she passed away, some seven years later. If there were questions of ownership based upon old customs, they were resolved with the incorporation of the family farm business. The corporation's holdings extended to nearly two thousand acres, with the five Shaw siblings owning an equal number of shares of the corporation.

Sonny recalled his answer to Polly at the time the family business was legally organized. "No, darling. If you need help to understand all of this, get an appointment with Kent Field. He'll explain everything to you, and I'll take care of his bill. I can handle my own business, but I don't have any experience with corporations, shares of stock, or how everything works in corporate business. Kent's the one to help you with that."

Sonny considered the matter closed between Polly and himself. For each year, dividends were paid once the predetermined benchmark of profit was met. Some years netted each shareholder more but for some years less, and it was an unwritten understanding that spouses weren't to participate in discussion of farm business with anyone other than their respective spouse. Sonny found it easy to comply with that prohibition; he had no wish to butt heads with Polly's brothers over business decisions for a business about which he knew nothing.

Now, looking at Tom Shaw's features, Sonny recognized the legacy of the cleft in the chin and wide-eyed guileless expression as Shaw family traits. "Did you just come here from the church? All of you, your family, were still there when I left. That was around three-thirty or so. A lot of your neighbors were there with you, and I didn't think about you coming on over here, figured you'd be going on home to chores. It was after four by the time I dropped Dolores off at her house, came on home."

It was a tacit understanding among farmers and their families that chores, morning and evening, had to be accommodated as part of their rural existence and business. Animals to be fed and accounted for, equipment to be shut down and maintained.

Sonny kept up a one-sided conversation, giving himself time to puzzle through the unexpected visit. He picked up the *Choctaw County Republican*, shook it open. Old Settlers was the front-page topic, the activities lineup, pictures of the musical groups slated to entertain. Sonny was glad that he had never been asked to book the entertainment as he thought that was clearly out of the limits of his understanding or experience.

"Have you seen the paper yet?" he asked, knowing that Tom wouldn't have had an opportunity to read the weekly publication. He hoped to draw Tom out, to learn why he had dropped by. His reticent attitude suggested to Sonny that he wasn't there on a social call.

Tom moved to the window, restless yet tight-lipped. He unbuttoned his cuffs, rolled up the sleeves of his white dress shirt. He didn't meet Sonny's eyes as he moved away from the window but then appeared to study the collection of family photographs on the fireplace mantel, all of which he'd seen numerous times.

"We didn't get to talk very much today; lots of people there. You want a drink?" Sonny gestured toward the small alcove between the dining room and the kitchen, originally a compact butler's pantry, now converted to a full bar with modern accoutrements. "I have pop, oh, Scotch or bourbon? Some wine? It's close enough to five o'clock."

Sonny had longed for privacy, even as he had been surrounded by family, friends, and neighbors as soon as Reverend Fred and Polly's friends delivered the shocking news of Polly's passing to him five days earlier. He'd hoped the whirlwind of activity would calm and he would be left to manage his new existence, but now, with Tom's presence, he found himself impatiently trying to draw him out.

To Sonny's distress, Tom's voice broke as he rushed into the message he was charged with bringing. "I said we have no business talking about this with you right now; you know the twins, though. Darrell and Walter want this settled. They want to know. They . . . "

"What? What do they want to know?"

"Dammit! It's the land, the goddamn land. Wouldn't you know. Darrell and Walter insisted I come in to talk to you about the land." Tom fumbled for words. "You know, Polly's shares of the farms."

Sonny felt a wave of relief wash over him; he had expected this conversation would come sooner or later. He hadn't expected Tom to be the one to initiate the questions.

"I told them it wasn't right. It isn't decent to come in here talking about Polly's will, asking questions and such on the day she's buried. I told them, 'Sonny'll probably throw me out, I come in talking about this today.'"

Now approaching a gentle forty-five years of age, sandy haired, lean, and sunburned with the forever-young look that sometimes graces blonde men, Tom had gone off at the family's behest to Iowa State University to major in agribusiness and finance. Darrell and Walter knew management of the farm operation and cash management, but they were far-sighted. They realized the business would need a partner with more knowledge of accounting, finance, and trends and influences on the domestic and international commodities markets.

Upon graduation, Tom didn't turn out to be the messiah of business for which the family had hoped. Instead, imbued with the strong work ethic of the Shaw family, Tom turned to the love of big machines, behemoths that lurked in cavernous aluminum lairs through months of every year to emerge mechanical, growling, snarling predators at harvest time, feasting on field after field. He loved the power, the sheer energy of the equipment consuming row after row of crops, corn, grain, soybeans, belching exhaust fumes and spewing the waste on the ground behind as they passed. When he tended the needs of the mechanical beasts—John Deere, Massey Ferguson, a well-preserved Oliver 88—Tom felt a kinship with past generations of Shaw men who once tended the needs of the great Percherons—Iowa Chief, Sadie Satin, Boomer, Crowder. Their nameplates still hung above empty stalls in the cavernous barn.

Sonny removed his suit coat and hung it over the back of a dining room chair that had been pulled away from its regular place at the dining room table. He frowned at it being out of place then remembered it had been pulled into the living room by one of Polly's nephews. There'd been a group of younger cousins, Tom's kids included, who sat together for the buffet lunch prior to the funeral service.

Sinking into one of the pair of damask-covered Victorian chairs, the gentlemen's chair and the ladies' chair, as always, he chose the gentlemen's chair. The other had been Polly's chair. He leaned against the back and cocked his foot up on the opposite knee in a relaxed position. He looked at his leg approvingly; there was no gap between his trousers and his black stockings. Sonny gestured for Tom to seat himself opposite.

Sonny sighed, searched for the right words, then chose them carefully; Tom was the last member of Polly's family he would offend. He resigned himself to the discussion.

"Well, okay. Let's discuss this going forward. I guess we need to talk about Polly's property, as it concerns your family." He pushed himself back in the chair, then leaned forward, resting his elbows on his knees. He tried to make direct eye contact, but Tom looked away and gestured his acquiescence. "Now, I haven't looked at Polly's will; I've never seen it. She wanted me to read it when she signed it, but I told her that it was all up to her. All I have is a general understanding of what she intended to do. The will itself is in the safe at Kent Field's office; I'll contact him. He drew up both our wills. The three of us talked about Polly and me having mirror wills—that's what Kent called them—the exception being the shares of the farm."

He spoke firmly. "What I think she did is this: her share of the family land holdings, her shares in Shaw Farms, Incorporated, is to go back to all of you in equal parts, however the mechanics of the transfer of shares works legally. That didn't ever have anything to do with me, but what we acquired together, what we bought for each other, with each other, our bank accounts, all of that, she planned to leave to me."

Tom shifted uncomfortably in his chair. He stood up, extended both hands, locking the fingers of one hand to the other hand's fingers, then pushed one against the other. Straightening his back with an audible crack of his spine, he looked over his shoulder toward the front door as if looking for an escape.

Puzzled and uncomfortable with Tom standing over him, Sonny stood up to face him.

"Sit down. Please, I'm not finished. You know we're not wealthy. We're set okay, but it's not big dollars. We've planned pretty well, set aside enough for some investments, mutual funds. We own the store building, plus the building next door that we lease to the bank. We're planning to buy the Crawford lot next to us here so we can put a retaining wall behind our garage. And we're going to . . . " Sonny realized he was rambling about a future that was no longer going to happen. He glanced down and brushed at the creases of his trousers.

He redirected his gaze on Tom. "Tell the others I'll start right away, getting stuff together, seeing to Polly's will. I'm sure she named me as executor of her estate. I've always known how Walter and Darrell feel about me. We've never had any trouble, anything like that. I don't want any now. Who knows about Dorothy? Living so far away, all she cares about is getting her checks."

Tom continued to stand and spoke firmly, in turn locking eyes with Sonny. "No one wants any problems. But you know how we are about the land. The land that the corporation holds, it's always been understood that the shares in the corporation will stay in the family. That means ownership stays in the bloodlines of the family." Tom set his mouth in a hard line, broken only by the gentle curves of his upper lip. He fixed his eyes on Sonny as though daring him to challenge him.

Sonny felt the old feeling, his old enemies, dread and anxiety, creep over him. He dropped his eyes. Suddenly stiff and mechanical, he tried to fix his face in a pleasant expression, tried not to betray his dismay over the adversarial direction of the conversation from Tom. Finally, raising his eyes to meet Tom's, Sonny could only nod in agreement. The family closes ranks.

Yeah, I know how you all are about the land.

"Like I said, Tom. There shouldn't be any problems. The land has been, always will be, a family deal, and Polly knows, knew that." Sonny, growing impatient, was terse.

Tom pushed the conversation harder. "The rest of the family thinks that the dividends from this fiscal year that ended June 30 shouldn't be paid out. We held a shareholders meeting yesterday, since Dorothy was already in town, and that is what we decided. This coming year isn't looking as good as last, and we're thinking we should hold on to the cash. And in some years, you and Polly . . . Polly, that is, came into a pretty fair amount of cash." Tom plunged on. "I don't know what Polly was thinking when she made out her will. No one planned for this. But the biggest problem is that we're all thinking that Polly left her shares of Shaw Family Farms to you! Walter, Darrell, and I went to see Kent Field this morning. His dad always did our legal work, but Kent said he couldn't discuss our questions about Polly's shares with us. We all thought the deal was between all of us Shaws, and no one other than a Shaw would ever inherit shares of stock. We wanted to discuss what we needed to do to bring the shares back into the corporation; did we need a meeting of the shareholders, how would the value of the shares be determined, would there be inheritance taxes to pay? We tried to ask the questions, and Kent just said that he represented you and Polly's estate, and he couldn't discuss Polly's will or shares with us. So, we pretty much figured out that Polly must have left her shares to you."

Sonny's mind was reeling. He jumped to his feet.

"Now you look here. I told you I haven't seen her will. But I do know this: I'm going to do whatever her will says I must do. To give in and do whatever you all say to do would be denying everything we had together. I loved your sister with every ounce of my being, and you all know that she loved me in the same way. She cared about all of us, and whatever she worked out with Kent, I'm sure she had her reasons!"

Holding his open hands in front of his chest, his long, slender fingers were curled like talons. He shook both hands at Tom with each word. He raised his voice to yet a higher pitch. "I only wish to God that we could have had children, so this never had to come up! What if we had adopted children, Tom? Would the family issue a rule about adopted children not inheriting family land? There's more to family than just bloodlines, Tom, and you guys never get that! Bloodlines be damned! You all *knew* we'd never have our own children!"

Tom stared at Sonny, incredulous. Shaking his head in amazement, Tom turned on his heel and with long strides headed for the door. Abruptly, he turned back to Sonny.

"I didn't mean for you to take offense. I understand it's too soon for you to have gotten to settling Polly's estate affairs. But Polly made some pretty good money, a pretty fair chunk of change from the farm. It doesn't seem fair that it went into your pocket, not to mention the future earnings if she left her shares to you."

"Fair doesn't have a damned thing to do with it! You know what the issue is here! We're not talking land *or* money! This is about Darrell and Walter never being able to accept Polly loving me or she and I being together. Never mind anything else. Drennan McCormack is the one you guys wanted for Polly. That's the real issue. Go on, just leave! Get out of here!"

Tom fixed Sonny with a baleful stare and said in a low flat voice, "I've never seen you act like this. If you were anyone else, I'd say you just stepped on your own dick and then walked all over it!" Tom jerked the front door open inward, slamming it against the doorstop, then stalked through it. He stormed across the porch and down the steps, cutting across the lawn to his car.

Sonny rushed to slam the door shut behind Tom, using both hands and all his strength. The door and its frame shook from the onslaught. Watching Tom through the beveled glass in the heavy door, Sonny noted that Jenny, wisely, had opted to wait in the car when she'd returned from her opportune errands.

Pacing back into the living room, he saw the sun was starting to fade, leaving long shadows where there'd been bright hot light. Hands on his hips, Sonny went to the window to watch the car pull away. His anger continued unabated, his breathing hard and fast.

"My God, what are they *thinking?* How could he have agreed to come in to stake a claim for the family? Where are those chicken-shit older brothers? Why did they send their little brother? *Tom!* Acting like *I'm* trying to take their land!"

Sonny shrieked and raged, roaring back and forth across the living room and the adjoining parlor. He stalked through the dining room, through the kitchen to the back door, then back to the living room. He replayed the spoken and unspoken insults of the conversation in his mind, and the inference that he'd been greedy. From the corner of his eye, he saw the dark shadow of the cat, slinking to a hiding place under the sofa.

And they think I'm going to inherit her shares? Polly! What the hell is going on? What is their rush about all of this?

But there was no answering voice of reason to mollify or modify what had been said. Sonny was never hasty in formulating answers to questions or to conflicts. He had always avoided allowing himself anger, equating anger with loss of control. He always listened for cues from his inner voice. The voice served him well most times. But now it was silent.

He fell to a crouch, then to one knee, panting, sobbing, exhausted. Then, as if suddenly demented, he charged across the living room to the stairs to the second story, through Polly's little office at the top of the stairs, and into their bedroom. His face, his body felt as if it were glowing, burning white-hot. He wrenched at his necktie till it loosened; he tore the buttons of his shirt open. Seizing the door of their dual closet, tearing it open, he attacked Polly's side of the orderly room. He jerked garments from their padded hangers, her sporty fur jacket, her beaded party dress, skirts, jackets. Scooping the shelf clear of the boxes of shoes and handbags, he gathered up as many garments as he could carry, tripping and stumbling over them.

Rushing to the open stairwell, Sonny heaved the whole lot down the stairs. He gave the shoe that first landed on the top step a kick so vicious the heel left a mark where it struck the doorframe at the bottom.

Back and forth to the closet, Sonny pushed on. "Take it all. Hell, just take it all! You want her things? You think you're entitled to her things? Here they are! Come and get them. Take it all! Oh, hell yes. Bring a truck!"

When the contents of Polly's closet were finally exhausted, Sonny's fury turned suddenly to despair. He stood at the top of the stairs, staring at Polly's clothes littering the steps. All her lovely things. The memory of her in them still fresh in his mind.

A wave of nausea hit him. Then another. His burning fever turned to cold sweat. He reeled into the bathroom, gagging and retching. Standing over the toilet, he was sick. Again and again, he vomited, until there was only black bile. Finally, a fulminating diarrhea purged him.

The cold discomfort from the white tile floor finally awakened him. Sonny didn't know how long he had lain there, but little by little, he returned to full consciousness; his trousers and underwear were around his knees. He finally opened his eyes without lifting his head and watched a ubiquitous pubic hair stuck to the base of the toilet stir each time he exhaled. Sonny lay motionless for a few minutes longer, breathing deeply and evenly.

Must have slept. Can't move yet, not yet. Just stay here. Soon. I'll get up soon.

Raising his eyes to the leaded panes of the octagon window set high on the wall above the commode, he judged from the fading light of the pewter sky that it had been more than an hour since Tom left. Sonny knew his rage had been subdued by the violent physical reaction of his body. He was quiet. In control again.

After another ten minutes or so, stiff from lying on the floor, Sonny moved to get up. Grasping the edge of the vanity, an antique sideboard that had been modified to accommodate modern plumbing fittings, he pulled himself first to a sitting position, then scrambled to his feet. Reaching to untie his dress shoes, he looked away from the spattered surface of the smooth-toed Oxfords. He stepped out of his trousers and soiled boxer shorts, and leaned on the vanity. Supporting himself on the marble surface with both hands, he peered at himself in the mirror.

I look so old, tired, washed out. Dark circles under my eyes. Hollows under my cheekbones.

Shaking his head sadly, he dropped his eyes from his countenance, then looking into the glass once more, he thought he saw Polly standing behind him, her eyes sad. But it had been only an ethereal glimpse; he longed to feel her arms around him, comforting him, even if just for that instant.

The debacle of the closet shamed him. The rage, or was it a tantrum? Violence appalled him. But he had been violent when he plundered the closet. Now, Polly's clothes, shoes, handbags, belts were strung in a progression from the closet and down the stairs. Polly had a lot of clothes, pretty clothes.

He regretted his behavior, his loss of control, his inability to reach down in the center from which he operated to maintain his equilibrium. As a child, he had hated the accusing finger pointed at

him by another child in mock severity. When that child shamed him
by stroking a forefinger in his direction with the other forefinger,
Sonny had hung his head. Now he had come too far from that child
to regress to those same feelings.

It is done. Just pick up the mess. Get on with it.

He walked slowly from the bathroom into the bedroom. Then he
turned back to gather his trousers and shorts from the bathroom floor.
Heading into the closet once more, he wrinkled his nose at the rank,
feral smell of the garments. He dumped the trousers into the hamper
for the dry cleaners and tossed the shorts into the wastebasket. With
a second thought, he finished by wrapping them in the plastic liner
of the basket. Sonny avoided looking at the empty side of the closet
while he stripped himself of the rest of his wilted clothing, his tee shirt
and the white shirt now minus two of its buttons. Sonny stripped off
his socks, added them to the discarded shirt and tee shirt, and left the
pile on the floor of the closet. Then, looking back at the mess, he guiltily retrieved them. Dumping them in the laundry basket, he headed
for the bathroom once more.

In the while-tiled cavern, the needle-sharp spray from the
shower attachment injected anesthetic relief for his weariness.
Toweling himself dry, his use of fresh towels reminded him of the
need to check the laundry baskets to see what needed to be laundered, a new responsibility. Polly had always taken care of the
laundry and the needs of the household. To him, the washer and
dryer were no more than mysterious twins occupying the same corner of the laundry room.

Promising himself to look at the question of what to do with the
laundry, Sonny was relieved to find clean underwear in his dresser
drawer even though he hadn't noticed an absence earlier. Dressed in
slacks and shirt, Top-Siders but no socks, he stood in the doorway
to Polly's closet, empty now with its empty hangers scattered on the
floor, and faced the chore of doing something with her belongings.
He couldn't stand to see her dresses guarding the closet like silent

sentinels. The best plan, he decided, was to just go ahead and pack everything up, and give it away later.

Methodically, Sonny gathered and folded the garments he collected from the floor and staircase, collating everything into categories. Blouses here. Skirts there. Slacks and jeans. Good suits and dresses on the bed. He retrieved Polly's luggage from the shelves of the guest room closet and filled each bag as carefully as if she would be unpacking it to wear later. She had chosen everything carefully and coordinated garments and accessories with meticulous care. In turn he placed jackets, slacks, blouses, shirts in coordinated groups, as he remembered her wearing them. He wished he could send the bags to her.

From the corner of his eye, he saw the cat stealthily creeping across the floor toward the suitcases. "Come here, you rascal." Spats had always considered open suitcases an invitation to climb in to make a nest for himself. Sonny and the cat regarded one another for a moment. Then Spats jumped onto the bed, stepped into a suitcase, and made himself comfortable on top of Polly's fur jacket. He curled up with his feet tucked under his body and regarded Sonny with cool feline detachment. "She'll miss you, little guy. But she couldn't take you with her. I need you. Come here."

Retrieving Spats from the suitcase thoughtfully with both hands, Sonny cradled the furry friend like a baby. He stroked the side of the pointed face, scratching behind the little felt ears. He rubbed the white-vested chest and tummy with the grain of the fur until Spats purred with contentment. The khaki-green eyes narrowed and squinted, then blinked open again.

"Let me finish here, Spats."

He carefully placed Spats on the bed, supporting him until the cat deigned to stand on his own four feet, then started toward the dresser. But he turned, retrieved Spats, and returned him to his chosen spot on Polly's fur jacket. Spats arched his back in a stretch, then settled back onto the jacket, tucked his feet beneath himself once again. Sonny then emptied Polly's dresser drawers, her lingerie, sweaters, and scarves into the last big case, shut and locked the bags, twirling the combination locks.

Seven sixty-seven. The month and year we met, July of 1967. Polly was twenty-three and I was twenty-six.

Sonny thought back to 1967, a quick memory of Japanese paper lanterns, soft music, pastel dresses on a soft summer night. They had danced to the song, the ten-year-old "Moonglow/Theme from *Picnic*"; he let the song and its melody go quickly. The memory was too sweet, too dear for now when his feelings were so raw.

Polly's clothes. What to do with them? Dolores is too heavy, Cloris too big, too tall. I can't bear to see them on someone else. No surprise—I don't want to see someone else wearing her things. I'll keep her jewelry for now anyway. She didn't have so much; her pearls, her rings, her diamond stud earrings. Dorothy has their mother's things; nothing here for the Shaws to claim!

He'd been surprised when Steve Fetters had handed him, in a sealed envelope, the rings and jewelry Polly had been wearing when she died; he thought she would be buried with the rings he'd given her. He'd wanted that. But Steve had returned them, saying, "Things aren't like they used to be, Sonny, even here in Onansburg. This way you know for sure where the rings are. Funeral directors won't assume the liability for jewelry nowadays."

Thinking of Steve reminded Sonny of the chores still to be done. Thank-you letters to write, casserole dishes and plates to be returned, a gravestone to be purchased, and the other, the will.

I'll get to it all. Lots to do. Lots to do.

"Come on, Spats. Here, kitty, kitty." At the head of the stairway he stopped, doubled back to find Spats curled up on Polly's side of the bed. Then, with feline disdain, Spats announced his intention to nap by closing his eyes. "Just stay there then. Just don't plan to prowl around all night just because you've already slept . . . "

Sonny went on talking to himself as much as to Spats. He flipped some lights on as he descended the steep stairway and was still talking when he emerged from the stairway into the living room to find Dolores seated on one of the damask chairs, studying the view from the window over the sofa.

"Dolores? How did you get here? You didn't walk, did you?" Sonny had rightly guessed from her appearance that she had, indeed, walked. Dolores was not physically fit, and her cheeks were still flushed from exertion.

"I thought you might need me, Sonny. I tried to phone. Where were you? I was worried that you might, that you could . . . hurt yourself or . . . " She searched for words. "Have an accident."

Sweet Jesus. How long will it be before everyone else's need to care for me, to assuage their own grief would be abandoned? This is so tough. And I'm so tired. It's sure as hell not like hearsay about someone else going through it. Maybe Dolores is right to worry. I've never had a complete loss of control like that.

The service to those recently bereaved from others carried its own reward capital. The well-meant kindnesses in turn were rewarded by becoming privy to the stuff from which local myths, even legends, are born. Sonny had overheard conversations at the café, at their country club, in his own store. For the few days surrounding the passing of a local, for example, when his customer Lois Fenimore died after a long illness, the family circle of the bereaved grew incrementally with the enmeshed interest of those who were relatives, friends, or just acquaintances. All claimed special privilege of private information. It was said of her husband: "He was a real trouper through all of this. We all know what he went through. She was sick for so long. He is devastated, just devastated."

Dolores's reappearance didn't surprise Sonny. She was an enigmatic woman. The middle Dawson child had been attractive enough, a pretty little girl, but then she became a frankly plain older woman. Now, at age fifty-seven, she could be anywhere between fifty and eighty, and no one would know or care.

In trying to explain Dolores to Polly, Sonny had been puzzled. He had taken for granted that she was different from Cloris, different from himself and from Cloris's penchant for creating turmoil with her behavior in their childhood home and in school. Dolores was affectionate to him and obedient to their parents, even docile. He finally characterized her to Polly as one who never got off the bench to play in the game of life.

Sonny retrieved the mail from the table in the foyer and gathered the *Choctaw County Republican* from where it had ended up on the floor sometime during Tom's visit. Sonny consulted the outside envelope of each piece of mail briefly.

"Have you seen this week's paper yet?" Without waiting for her response, he continued. "Polly's obituary must be in it. Have you read it yet?"

Dolores didn't respond but continued to gaze through the window where the descending sun filtering through gauzy clouds fabricated an opalescent sky. Cicadas droned their reminder of the intransigence of nature. She seemed distracted, her lower lip caught between her teeth.

Sonny, suddenly sarcastic, waved the folded newspaper and gestured dramatically toward the window. "Ladies and Gentlemen. For your viewing pleasure. One of nature's most beautiful sights . . . " Sonny's voice trailed off in disgust at his lame remark, and he tossed the paper onto the sofa next to Dolores.

"Come on now. I'll take you home." Sonny went to his sister, grasped her plump arm gently, giving it a little upward tug. "Dolores?"

Dolores turned away from Sonny, pulled her arm from Sonny's grasp, her downcast eyes studying her sensible good shoes that she had worn for the funeral. Sonny followed her gaze to her feet. Dolores's small-world self-focus had always included explaining details to Sonny and sometimes to Polly ad nauseum. For example, she categorized her choice of footwear in terms of how, what, when, and where she chose to wear them.

Margaret, White Elk, size 8M. Her good summer shoes worn only between Memorial Day and Labor Day. The rest of the year, for good, she wore Margaret, Black Calf, size 8M. Her choice of footwear was restricted to a style that would accommodate her bunions and could be purchased at Bonita's Bootery on the Square. She bought one pair of black Margarets every year, and one pair of White Elk Margarets every other year. For everyday, she wore flat rubber-soled canvas shoes, black for winter, white for summer, the lack of support of which contributed to back trouble, but allowed expansion for bunions.

She had further explained that Dan Jenkins, the proprietor of Bonita's, encouraged Dolores to "break loose, have a little fun, choose something else for once, like this nice Coquette, ebony, size 8M."

Dolores told Sonny that she was pretty well sold on Margarets, and despite Dan's suggestion, she had no interest in wearing Coquettes on her Margaret feet. Plus, she wasn't sure that Dan wasn't poking a little fun at her. She'd tittered, "He's such a tease." Ever since his wife died, Bonita Jenkins had been memorialized on the town square by the sign that proclaimed the establishment "Bonita's Bootery."

But Dolores hadn't ever been sure about Dan. "After all," she told Sonny and Polly, "he wears the same shoes, day after day." And sometimes recounting her visits to the store, she said, "I smelled liquor on his breath." She'd reiterated her stance; there wasn't a thing wrong with her Margarets.

Suddenly resolute, she stood, pushing herself from the chair with one hand. With some effort, she retrieved the paper Sonny had thrown and refolded it. "Sonny, I've been thinking. Maybe I should come look after you for a while. You know you aren't good with the house. You couldn't cook if your life depended on it. Polly took care of you and everything else around here. She spoiled you plenty, and I could . . . " She saw Sonny's frown, and her voice trailed off, even as she began to warm to her subject.

"Not now, honey. I can't think about that right now. I know you want to help. You've been a big help since Polly died, but I just can't think about it right now."

Dolores looked away, her downcast eyes evidencing her disappointment. Sonny knew he had to be definite, unwavering in making his position clear to her, but then he weakened to using a bribe. Knowing Dolores had an inordinate fondness for Peanut Buster Bars from the Dairy Queen, he continued.

"Now come on, don't look that way. Not tonight. This day has been too tough already. Just stay awhile this evening. I'll take you home later. We can stop at the Dairy Queen. Honey, can you help me sort out the cards that were on the flowers from the cards that were with the memorial contributions, then later I'll write nice notes to everyone. That's what Polly would want. Steve Fetters said he'd bring thank-you cards and envelopes by the house. I have to open the store again tomorrow, but you could help me tomorrow night too."

Sonny's voice took on a desperate note; it had been a hard day. He was exhausted. His eyes felt as though huge thumbs were pushing them deeper and deeper into their sockets. And he didn't want to deal with any more problems.

Just let me finish out this day. And let me sleep tonight.

"All right then. We won't talk about it anymore tonight. But this won't be the end of it. You're going to need someone in the house. And to take care of Polly's plants and the flowers outside. I could do all the cooking along with the cleaning. You could let Charlene go. You'll want company, Sonny. This is a big old house for you to just rattle around in."

An hour later, a careful organization of the tasks gave Sonny some small feeling of accomplishment. The rich walnut surface of the dining room table was covered with neatly sorted piles of cards from those who'd sent plants and flowers, checks and envelopes with cash to be passed on to the church memorial fund, sympathy cards, and plates and casserole dishes—each marked with its owner's name on masking tape—ready to be returned.

Permanent rooms had not been assigned to the several blooming plants, delivered since Polly died. They stood awkwardly out of place in the foyer, on the floor of the dining room, in the library, like new kids on their first day of school waiting to be assigned a seat. Sonny examined the penile protrusion on the bloom of the anthurium plant, commonly called the little boy plant. He smiled to himself. *A curious choice!*

The house seemed strangely empty after the constant attendance of family and friends over the past few days, but it was time to take Dolores home. Sonny shook his head. It wasn't like Dolores to be so assertive. Not like her at all. It was obvious that she felt she had a lot at stake.

As they exited the rear door of the house, Sonny reached back to turn on the light above the kitchen table. He preferred a lighted sentry rather than enter a dark room, any dark room.

Dolores picked her way carefully along the brick walk from the back door to the driveway and allowed Sonny to open the passenger door for her. Settling herself tenuously on the upholstered leather seat, she deposited her handbag on the floor of the front seat and fastened her seat belt before Sonny could remind her to do so. Sonny backed down the short drive onto the street, but Dolores sighed regretfully as Sonny shifted into DRIVE.

"Wait," she said seriously, as if just reconsidering their earlier conversation. "Sonny, now Sonny, it's not too late. I guess I can stay tonight if you really want me to. I tucked my gown in my bag. I can just as well stay as not. I probably just should. I might as well just come on back with you after the DQ."

Sonny smiled at her cunning reversal. "That's all right. I know you like your own bed. After such a hard day, you better just try to get a good night's sleep. I'll just have to get along without you."

They drove the rest of the way to the Dairy Queen on Jackson

Street in silence. The few blocks were interrupted by only one stop sign at the corner of Jackson and Main. There were no illuminated stoplights in Onansburg, but a flashing yellow orb blinked its warnings to motorists before and after school hours during the school year.

"Is it that peanut and chocolate thing you like? I'll get it and bring it out to you. We'll just sit here in the parking lot and eat." Sonny knew if Dolores went inside, she would vacillate between several choices and then default to the peanut buster bar; far better to ask her to make her selection in the car. Inside, Sonny exchanged pleasantries with the high school kids working the counter and the soft-serve ice cream machine. After paying the tab and poking a one-dollar bill into the tip box, Sonny carried the treats back to the car, the peanut buster parfait for Dolores, a vanilla and chocolate twist cone for himself. He felt a pang of nostalgia when he remembered that Polly's favorite Dairy Queen treat had been a vanilla cone dipped in chocolate.

Exchanging but a few comments—"Yours good? Yes, is yours? They do a good business here. Yes, it's a little gold mine"—Sonny started the car, backed out onto Jackson Street, and they were homebound for Dolores's cottage.

The new digital clock above the front door of the bank reminded them it was 9:10 p.m. As they coasted past the side of the deserted town square, the neon advertising in the window of the Cozy Tap beckoned its welcome. Dolores caught sight of Cloris and Skip just as they pushed the glass door of the Cozy shut behind them. Moving shadows behind the glass spoke to the sociability of the remaining crowd.

Dolores fumbled for the button to lower the electric window and began waving at Cloris and Skip even before they spotted Sonny's car. "Stop. Stop. There's Cloris. And Skip."

Dismayed at acquiescing yet again to his family's intrusion into his time, Sonny pulled in parallel to the curb across the yellow painted lines designating angled parking slots in front of the Cozy and waited while Cloris teetered around to his side of the car on her too-high sling-back heels. Skip followed then propped himself against the front fender of Sonny's car to distance them from himself and the smoke from his cigarette.

Cloris exhibited the vestigial remains of an attractive woman. When yet a teenager she exhibited a voluptuousness that turned men's heads, made them envy the boy who was currently the object of her considerable affection. The first time she married, she said she married for love, and she left town on the back of Nate Cullen's Indian motorcycle. The next time, she said, it was for fun. And no one knew how to categorize all those who came in between. Sonny didn't know how many times she had been married before she met Skip Easley. He couldn't have said for certain that they were even married.

Skip came to Onansburg in the early 1980s with a construction crew to work on the addition to the high school, a new gymnasium and locker rooms. He was well muscled and tanned with dark brown collar-length hair that was hidden beneath the hard hat during the day and curled up at the edges of the baseball hat he wore most other times. He and Cloris met, and he didn't bother to move on to the next job. The Cozy Tap and the bar at the American Legion Hall hosted their romance.

Appearing pleasantly numbed from the evening's consumption, Cloris leaned through Sonny's window. He pushed himself back against the leather seat, trying to avoid her well-ginned breath. She leaned closer. Surreptitiously reaching for the electric control lever, he moved the seat back and back even farther with Cloris leaning in to examine his face, his eyes. He smiled broadly then snickered at the thought of the sight of her polka-dotted rear end protruding from his car window. In trying to disguise his amusement, his snicker turned into a whinny of laughter.

"Sonny! Goddammit Sonny! You been drinking? Skip, goddammit Skip, Sonny's drunk. Oh shit, now what should we do?

Poor Sonny, poor Sonny, poor baby. He's always been my little boy; my best little boy."

Cloris started to cry the broken blubbery sobs of a drunk. Skip moved to comfort her in his staggering embrace, clutching her, stroking, patting her big behind with his work-hardened paws. Looking through the open window at the couple, Sonny thought, with their unsteady grappling, they looked like dancing bears in costume.

Dolores leaned forward, her eyes wide and mouth open in astonishment as she watched Cloris and Skip. Sonny leaned over, face down on the front seat next to Dolores, shaking with laughter. Taking her cue from Cloris's and Skip's maudlin snuffling and what she took to be Sonny's distress, Dolores started to cry noisily, stroking Sonny's head and back, making soothing sounds between her sobs. "I'll take care of you, Sonny. It'll be all right, it's all right now."

Sonny tried to regain his composure to avoid the tears that were precariously close behind the laughter, when the headlights of another car bounced off the tableau. Suddenly, the scene was under the scrutiny of a spotlight, and Claude Bray, the night marshal, screeched to a stop. Bilious green in color, his ten-year-old Dodge was nicknamed the Vomit Comet by Onansburg teenagers who fled in mock fear when it appeared.

"You folks there! Break it up! You'd better just break it up now and get on home! Skip! Skip Easley? That you again?"

Heaving himself from the patrol car, the spotlight still trained on the little group, Claude cocked his head to look closer. "Well! Sonny! I'm sorry. Didn't know that it was you. Sure didn't expect to see you up here tonight."

Cloris, above her too-high heels, withdrew from the window, jammed both hands on her hips, and attempted to fix Claude in a cold, hard stare. "Now, see here, Claude Bray! Don't you go pickin' on Sonny. He was just passing by and offered us a ride home." The effect of her bravado was lessened by the noticeable slur in her words.

Keeping a wary eye on Cloris and Skip, Claude strode up to Sonny's car window to look closer at Dolores's distress and Sonny's discomfiture. The interior of the car had become heated. Sweat beaded Sonny's forehead. A lock of his hair had fallen out of place, hanging over his ear; his eyes were red and watering. Dolores was snuffling loudly.

Sonny turned to look past Claude to Cloris's face, full on, at the same time she turned away from Claude to Sonny. Catching her eye, Sonny saw shame and embarrassment cross her expression. She dropped her eyes and turned her head away. It was a momentary flash of cognizance, of recognition of the tawdry scene even from her dimmed, alcohol-induced awareness.

"Say, you need help, Sonny?" Claude asked, casting a glance at Cloris and Skip. "Need a ride home or anything?"

Sonny struggled for composure so that he could respond to Claude, but his thoughts turned to dismay when he thought of this story hitting the South Side Café first thing in the morning. Claude would, no doubt, hold forth to the early crowd at the café. He could imagine the night marshal's exposé of the Dawson family debacle.

"Yup. Just drunk as lords. The whole damn family. Yeh, even that Dolores. She the one that's not quite right? Yeh, her too. Right in front of the Cozy. The way they was raised, nice and respectable. Religious too. Would you think it of them? The parents, they were good, God-fearing people. They went to that off-beat church, but they went to church, doesn't matter which one.

"Sure a shame, about the Missus, uh, Polly, you know. Dropped like a stone they said. And she was only fifty. Well, guess you can understand Sonny getting his snoot wet, feeling so bad and all. Told them all they better just get on home, sleep it off.

"Didn't ever have much use for that no-good Skip Easley, but Cloris, now, she's quite a woman, lot of problems with her drinking and all the men she ran with, but she's a good woman. Truth is, there's a time she could have turned my head. Before I met the wife, of course. Dolores, now, there's a sad story; since she got out of the state hospital over at Clarinda, hadn't been for Sonny, she'd have had a hard time of it. Cloris, though, she could have been something, really something."

Puny Sorenson, the early cook at the South Side, would lean over the counter to Cy Luftkin, one of the café regulars, to dispense the wisdom for which he considered himself famous, at least in Onansburg.

"Old Claude always did have a hard-on for Cloris; she might just have been a little too much woman for old Claude. Don't think he could have handled her. Might have been fun to try in her day though, before she had so many miles on her. Now she looks like she's been rode hard and put away wet."

The story would be told and retold, magnified each time.

"I guess they were all drunk, wanted to fight old Claude Bray; he was just doing his job, you know."

"That poor sister, you know the one, Dolores, she cooks at the school, they even had her with them."

"They say Sonny was just a mess, just drunk out of his mind. Well, he'll just have to get hold of himself. Person like that's got responsibilities. Business to run and all. He's on the church council too, isn't he?"

Seeing Sonny's discomfort, Claude interceded in the family drama. "Sonny, you all need help getting on home? You want me to take the Easleys to their place? Looks like they might have a little trouble getting home on their own. Sure be glad to help."

One of the nice things about a small town and one of the sad things about a small town is that most people have known each other for years, maybe a lifetime. And preformed social judgments govern many of the interactions between residents of a small community. Claude knew Sonny's family, went to school with Cloris.

Sonny collected himself, then taking hold of the door handle, opened the door slightly. Claude stepped back, and Sonny opened the door farther, got out of the car; putting his left hand on Claude's upper right arm, as if to restrain him, but at the same time reaching to shake Claude's hand.

"Thanks, Claude. Thanks a lot. This has been a tough day and now this tonight." Sonny shrugged, and Claude nodded his head sadly. Sonny continued, "I'll just get this little group on home—can't thank you enough."

Twenty minutes later, Sonny had escorted Dolores into her home, snapped on the lights, and checked the house yet again for strangers. After a wordless trip to the edge of town, Sonny deposited Skip and Cloris in the driveway of the little bungalow near the train tracks. When Sonny turned into the drive, the headlights swept the darkened windows that stared blankly back at them. The rented house was devoid of personality or charm. Neither bushes nor flowers nodded a welcome; no vigilant nightlight waited patiently for them to return.

Sonny waited in the drive, watching to be sure that Cloris and Skip had successfully negotiated the intercourse between the front door lock and its mate, the key. The light blinking on under the peaked ceiling of the diminutive foyer signaled the Easleys were home. Sonny knew the home to be immaculate, but its starkly furnished, sterile interior offered no more clues about its occupants than did the mowed and clipped exterior. It could have been anybody's house or nobody's house.

Sonny shook his head, exhausted. He stroked his chin between the thumb and forefinger of his right hand. He could feel the fatigue tugging him downward into a pool of weightless weariness, yet his mind raced on. A collage of images of the day pooled into messy sequence without order or importance to be stored in his memory, the faulty bank of recollections.

Three

He would reopen the hardware store tomorrow. It had been closed since Polly died. It couldn't, shouldn't be closed another day. He knew Onansburg depended upon the store being open.

He thought back to the day after, without Polly, and the stricken faces of Ruby and Thelma Jane when he went to the store, to tell them to lock up until after the funeral. They had been waiting for him when he arrived at the parking lot of four spaces at the back of the store. It wasn't seven-thirty yet, but he had guessed correctly that they would be there getting ready to unlock the front doors promptly at eight.

He knew they would have known that Polly was dead within a very short time after he knew she was gone. The word-of-mouth telegraph in Onansburg would have been spreading the sad news within minutes of the summons to Burt Cook and Steve Fetters and within minutes of Sonny's frantic trip to the hospital.

Ruby Shelton and Thelma Jane Hyatt had worked at the store for ten years and seven years, respectively. It seemed likely that Ruby would work at the Franklin Hardware store until she was dead or disabled; it was her retirement job. At age sixty-three, she had raised her two children, taken care of their home, gardened and canned, and sewed and knitted, along with a little work in her church circle. After Harold Shelton, two years older than Ruby, retired from the dairy, things just weren't so good around home anymore; he was there all day, making suggestions about this and about that, generally making a nuisance of himself until Ruby decided she just couldn't live with Harold anymore if he was going to be around and underfoot all the time. She knew nearly everyone in town. Honest and reliable, quick to learn, she was the ideal employee. In no time, she was devoted to Sonny and Polly.

Generously proportioned with wide hips and pendulous breasts, Ruby hustled around the store on legs that, in contrast, were girlish and shapely. She dispensed requested and unrequested advice on any one of a number of topics, mostly cooking, cleaning, the use of gadgets and home appliances sold at the store. She not only sold a baby high chair, she suggested what should be fed to its miniature occupants. "Yup. Then when they're ready for some table food, a few mashed potatoes, little bit of gravy, some bread and jelly. That'll make them grow. Look at my kids, they turned out pretty good, didn't they?"

She not only sold a Foley food mill, she demanded a high standard for its care and maintenance. "Now, see this little nut on the bottom here, see where it connects to the crank? That's the key, the key to the whole thing. You lose that, you're out of business. Might as well throw the whole thing away. You just take care of that, just wash it separate, set it up on the sink to dry, this'll last you your whole life. Never need to buy another. Now Harold, he knocked mine off the sink one time, like to scared me to death until I found it. I told him, just don't you go messing around with things you don't know nothing about. Oh, I suppose I could have gotten another nut from the Foley food mill folks, but that would have been foolish, a waste of money. I would have been embarrassed to tell them I'd gone and done such a foolish thing. Now you just take good care of this, you hear, now?"

It was her manner of speech, her reference to Harold-he-did-this or Harold-he-did-that, that prompted Sonny and Polly to refer to Ruby, privately, as Ruby-she. Mrs. Harold-he Shelton and her children Billy-he and Janet-she, long since grown, married and with their own families to whom Ruby also dispensed wisdom and advice.

Thelma Jane was as quiet, as retiring, as Ruby was loquacious. A painfully thin maiden lady, Thelma Jane had been companion and nurse to her elderly mother until her mother's death six years ago, in 1988. The two had lived in genteel poverty in the big house that Thelma Jane's father, Judge Hyatt, built in 1948. Thelma Jane watched her friends go off to college, then watched them marry from under one or another of the versions of the little veiled hats of the perennial bridesmaid. She never caught the bridal bouquet, nor the fevered hope it symbolized.

All the while, Thelma Jane was her father's, the judge's, good little girl, who stayed home to help him care for his wife. After the judge's death in 1955, the two women continued to live in the brick house even while it fell into shabby disrepair. There was no way the judge could have anticipated the rise in the cost of living; he thought he had provided amply for his women.

Thelma Jane spent her most productive years caring for her dipsomaniac mother. First shielded from the public by the judge's wealth and influence, then by the isolation enforced by her debilitation, Mrs. Hyatt finally set Thelma Jane free by dying. But it was years too late for Thelma Jane to recover any of her youth. She had faded from the bright, lively girl she had been to a wispy, stringy little old maid. With her graying hair, faded from its once glorious sable, tied into a low knot on her neck, she wore the clothes and shoes that said "old."

When Sonny hired Thelma Jane to work at the store, Polly had voiced her approval, remembering Thelma Jane when she, Polly, had been a teen.

"It's not as though she's not attractive, Sonny. She was pretty when she was younger. It was just that disappointment and all that hard work, living in that old house and taking care of her mother, wasted her. She was popular, I guess everyone called her 'T. J.' then. Her old friends, the ones that are still around, say she used to be lots of fun. You know, I guess she and Cliff Simmons were really serious about one another in high school. But then Cliff and all the rest went off to Iowa State; that's where he met Rosalee, and they grew apart. Thelma Jane just fell behind. Don't you wonder, Sonny . . . " Here, Polly lowered her voice conspiratorially, "if they ever made love, if Thelma Jane's ever been loved, had sex. Can you even picture her with a man? Even an escort? Pretty hard to imagine now, isn't it?"

"Polly sweetheart, it's not just hard to think about, it's really scary to think about, the way she is now. She and Cliff Simmons, eh? Well, quit worrying about her. We're not running a dating service here. You just worry about you and me." With that, he spun her around so they were face-to-face and then kissed her soundly. Then, he ran his hand up under her loose shirt and fingered her breasts through the fabric of her lacy bra. "Oh, oh! Your nipples are already perked up—have you been standing in front of the freezer again?" He nuzzled her neck and continued his attention to her nipples, making circular motions with the flats of his hands against the thin fabric of her blouse and bra. "You want to go upstairs and mess around a little?"

"Sonny," she replied with mock ferocity, pushing herself away from him. "We were talking about Thelma Jane and Cliff."

"Yes, and now I'm horny!"

"Thinking about Thelma Jane? Please, Sonny—don't even joke about it."

Thinking back to that conversation, Sonny ached for Polly. The laughing, teasing, sharing. The closeness, the intimacy of mind and body.

And my sex life is over! I knew every inch of her body—and she knew mine. No one would ever want me like she did.

Polly had admired his body but teased him about his flat derriere. "Sonny, I don't know what you sit on; you have no rear end. And you're so slender, almost thin."

Sonny's eyes filled again, and he reached for the individual packet of tissues that Polly left for him in the storage compartment of the car. Pulling up to the front of the Franklin Hardware store, Sonny sighed deeply, wiped his eyes. He hadn't meant to stop at the store, but it was as though the car turned by rote into one of the newly repainted diagonal parking slots that ornamented the town square like yellow rays from a paint-can sun. Sonny acknowledged that in Polly's absence, their store was the other mate to his life. It was Polly first, and then the store, and he needed to feel its comforting presence envelop him, to feel the aura of satisfaction and pride that it evoked in him.

The store. He and Polly had always said "the store," a formal title. The store had been established by one John Franklin in 1922. After old Mr. Franklin retired, the Franklin family retained ownership and Franklin's son-in-law ran it until Sonny bought it in 1975 from the remnants of the Franklin family.

Sonny had worked at Franklin Hardware store after school and during summer vacation from the time he was fifteen. In addition to his general duties around the store—sweeping, dusting, occasionally being allowed to wait on customers—it had immediately fallen to Sonny, being the youngest employee and the most physically able, to tend the furnace at the store during the winter and to bathe the Franklins' dog, Topsy, during warm weather.

And he had hated that damned dog. Years later, he even hated that dog's memory. Topsy was a dog given to excesses. In the days before the town of Onansburg passed a city ordinance not to allow dogs to roam free, Topsy was allowed to roam at will, satisfying his libido. It was not unusual for Mr. Franklin to receive a stuttering phone call from the owner of a female dog in season.

"Mr. Franklin, uh, John. This is, I mean, well, uh, Margaret

Grimes. It's," she cleared her throat, "it's Topsy, your dog, you know. Perhaps you should come for him. It, ah, it seems he's passed out on our lawn. Mr. Franklin, I, ah-hh, I'm, m-m-m, sure I don't know. Perhaps, he's, ah, he's overextended himself. I think you should come and get him. Soon. Very soon, please."

And the phone call was sometimes not phrased in such delicate terms. "John, this here's Ott Davis. Yer dog is over at the Grimes' place. Stuck to the Grimes' bitch. Mrs. Grimes's all upset, tried to run ol' Topsy off with a broom. You might want to bring a bucket of cold water along. They're stuck tight all right."

John Franklin, in his dotage during Topsy's salad days, took a pleasure in Topsy's escapades that was frighteningly akin to envy. Anthropomorphic vicariousness. It was rumored that John, in his day, was quick to prove his sexual prowess to his comely assistant manager, Nelle Myer. Those days now long past, John Franklin's pleasure in Topsy's conquests heightened the memory of his pleasure in his own long-ago libido. The memory didn't extend to the responsibility of retrieving the dog from his misadventures.

When the calls came complaining of Topsy's exploits, Sonny would be dispatched to extract Topsy from the depths of doggy depravity. And in the summertime, when the rendering truck hauling decomposing animal carcasses passed through town, Topsy would often lay in wait at the stop sign at the corner of the cemetery road and Highway 17, hoping for a quick roll in the malodorous liquid dripping from the truck bed. Sonny, again, would be called to rescue Topsy from disgrace.

The doggy bathtub on legs at the farthest reach of the store basement saved only Sonny's back, not his clothes and certainly not his pride. Sonny hated the fuzzy Airedale with reason and malice. At bath time, Topsy, associating Sonny with the good times, exhibited his most affectionate canine grin and displayed his glistening pink doggy erection that John Franklin admiringly called the Red Rocket for Sonny to admire.

It seemed good business to Sonny not to change the name of the store after he purchased it. Not that it would have done much good if he had done so. Most in Onansburg would have continued to call it Franklin's for at least ten or fifteen years, the South Side Café being an example. It had been the First National Café for at least that long after the café followed the First National Bank's occupancy of the space. It would have taken time for Sonny himself to call it something other than Franklin's. Name changes came slowly in Onansburg, even years after a marriage had taken place. "Oh yeah, she was one of the Schoenhutt girls"—the girl having been married to Clayton Stout for thirty years.

The exterior of the store probably didn't look so different than it did when it was built. The red brick front formed a handsome support to the decorative stone cornice that the building wore like a dowager matron's dignified hat. The buildings along the north side of the town square all featured variations of the same ornamentation carved into the stone featured in the turreted courthouse. Rebuilt in 1915 after fire destroyed the original north side businesses, the north side thought well of itself as the best real estate in Onansburg.

The front of the awning was scalloped, bordered with a narrow ribbon of white, with white block letters spelling out FRANKLIN HARDWARE. He'd wanted to add STORE to the title, but Polly had pointed out that adding it would, by necessity, diminish the rest of the letters in size. He'd been pleased that he'd deferred to her judgment, as the store name could be read from any place on the town square.

Sonny loved the store. It was part of his history, part of how he had made his way in town, part of how he belonged and contributed to the people of Onansburg. The store was filled with memories of Polly. The way she moved between aisles and shelves, the sound of her voice as she asked after customers and friends, the feel of her hands on his shoulders or head when she entered the office to check on him.

Key ring in hand, Sonny approached the front door of the store. Tonight, he found himself at the front of the building, as he felt too weary to go to his usual parking spot at the back door. It seemed too remote, too far away, too much work to drive to the rear of the building. He had been drawn to the store tonight just as he and Polly had stopped there on their way home from an event or an evening ride. "I just want to check on something." Sometimes Polly had come inside with him. Other times, she waited in the car.

The keys to the front door were on the same key ring, a vinyl badge spelling out "Franklin Hardware," as were the car keys. Two streetlights, one just in front of the store and the other across the street on the courthouse lawn, were conveniently placed so that they strategically cast their rays on the store, the display windows, and the front door. Security lights mounted high above the merchandise displays provided enough light by which to navigate the interior even in darkness.

He fit the key into the deadlock on the door, heard the resounding thunk of the hefty bolt clearing the lock. As he gave the door, swollen with heat and humidity, an extra shove, he caught a fading glimpse of a face, pallid in the weak light from the street lamp, and eyes round with surprise looking back at him through the door's plate glass window.

Dammit! Not Larry. Not tonight. I should have thought of him being here before I stopped.

The heavy door first caught, then sprung open with a vibrating shudder. The chime of the old-fashioned shopkeeper's doorbells sounded its three-note melody discordantly, as if alarmed by the forceful entry, instead of sounding its customary melodious tones. He made a mental note to use spray silicone lubricant where the uneasy union of door and frame created friction.

He had resisted replacing the heavy wooden door with a

contemporary aluminum-framed plate glass door. The old door with its beveled glass, if not original to the 1915 building, which was rebuilt after the fire, was an early replacement for the original. Glowing with the patina from years of careful attention, still with its original polished brass hardware, Sonny thought it denoted the quality, the respectability that he wanted associated with his business.

When Kent Field was remodeling his law office on the south side of the town square, directly across from Franklin Hardware, he had asked Sonny if he would be interested in selling the door to him. Kent was restoring the building where his father and grandfather began their practice and he wanted a door in keeping with the original quasi-federal style he was trying to recapture. It was balm to old wounds to be in the position of denying Kent Field, the man who grew up with everything Sonny had wished for himself.

Pushing the door closed with some of the same force he used to open it, Sonny manually snapped the solid bolt shut again. The lights from the street lamps framed his own shadow on the checker-board pattern tile floor. A looming, distorted, dusky harlequin. Without reaching for the light switch, Sonny looked around, seeking the owner of the face he had seen in the window. He walked behind the checkout counter with its centerpiece, the cash register, relying on the streetlights and store security lights.

"Larry? Larry, where are you? I saw you through the window. I know you're here. Where are you? Come on now. I'm too tired to play games."

"Here I am, Sonny. I'm back here."

The gondolas supporting the merchandise shelves ran the length of the store, and it was from between two of the eight-foot sections that the slight figure emerged. When Larry passed from the shadows through one of the beams of light that stabbed into the store's interior from the mercury vapor streetlights, Sonny caught the reflection of wetness, hastily scrubbed from the wounded cheeks. With eyes still bright from tears, Larry advanced toward Sonny hesitantly. His lips were pressed tightly together, forming deep pockets at the corners of his mouth to keep his chin from trembling. His arms hung at his sides, bent slightly at the elbows, palms opened and extended.

Sonny didn't want to understand his own ambivalence toward the boy, but he felt there to be even more to his rancor. Larry Hayes never asked for anything, for favors, for attention, but resentment and anger welled up in Sonny whenever he was around the kid. A reminder of a shameful episode in the not-so-distant past.

Sonny regarded the forlorn figure steadily for a few moments. A slight figure. Larry Hayes was sixteen, but no taller, and even smaller than most thirteen-year-old boys who had not yet begun to lock themselves in bathrooms to examine downy hairs for signs of impending coarseness. His blonde hair was neatly combed; round blue eyes stared in perpetual astonishment or perhaps a perpetual apprehension about to give way to fright. A severe case of acne was his only concession to puberty; he wore the blooming rosary of pustules embedded deep into his sallow cheeks as his stigmata. His appearance otherwise was that of an elderly child.

Larry's penchant for absolute order was a rigid, inflexible requirement to which he held himself. He was an excellent student with his schoolwork and exams always near perfection. His was the name that was ubiquitous on the honor roll, but now also with things people only dared whisper about.

Larry's job was the counterpart of Sonny's job when Sonny had first started at Franklin Hardware, but minus a Topsy. Sonny was not surprised to find Larry at the store even so late at night. He knew the boy frequently stayed on after he finished sweeping out, restocking, and checking in new inventory after Sonny was gone for the day. He was an ideal employee. His work at the store, like his schoolwork, was nearly flawless, so near that it would have been a gross injustice to point out the few fine details that escaped Larry's attention. As the business had been closed since Polly's death, Sonny surmised that Larry waited once his work was finished for his mother to get off work.

On Monday through Friday nights throughout the school year, Larry stayed on to do homework in the employee lounge, as Ruby and Thelma Jane laughingly called the room at the back of the store that hosted the refrigerator and microwave oven. The work tables that were used for sorting, inventory, and pricing would have had a comfortable jumble of coffee cups, paper napkins, and artificial sweetener, but he knew that Larry would have compulsively arranged it all in a neat row on the cabinet next to the sink. During the summer, Larry appeared for work before the six o'clock closing time, but came directly from school during the school year.

Larry was more comfortable, secure in the well-lit room than in his own home. By staying late, he could escort his mother home from her work at the bulk milk plant just off the square. It was originally because of his late-night trek home with his mother that Larry came to work at the store. And it was because Polly had called to Sonny's attention what he and others had failed to see, or refused to acknowledge. It was one of the few times that Polly and Sonny had ever been in conflict.

One weekday evening during the previous winter, they had just come home from having a quick dinner at the Burger'n'Brew, a quasi-roadhouse just off the interstate close to the Town Pump, the convenience store. Sonny had wanted to fill the car with fuel; the gauge was at the half-full mark. As they came up the steps from the sidewalk from the garage and into the kitchen, he made the offhand remark that he might look for someone to fill in at the store, to clean up and restock shelves at night. Polly had immediately suggested Larry Hayes. Sonny's response was immediate and definite. He slapped his leather gloves down on the kitchen table.

"No. I'm not going to have that kid around at my business. It's not good to have him around. People don't like being reminded about what happened to him."

Polly turned on him, her eyes flashing, her voice raised. "Sonny Dawson! Shame on you! Larry and his mom have fallen on hard times."

Sonny raised his voice in kind. "Yes, and that mother of his. Where was she when all that was happening to him?"

Polly pushed back, but her voice was sad and plaintive. "After that mess with that Wildfang guy, I think Julia is really down and out. She hadn't been working before all that happened to Larry."

"Oh yeah! And that son of a bitch that abused him! What was she thinking? Didn't she notice anything going on?"

Polly looked away, recusing herself for a moment, and then continued thoughtfully. "I think all the insurance money that came with the accident that killed her first husband, Larry's dad, must be gone. Wildfang probably got into her pocketbook as well as . . . " Then seeing Sonny's face, she stopped as he advanced toward her.

Sonny came back at Polly with vehemence. His voice was low and menacing, his eyes narrowed. "Now you look here! Don't you ever suggest that I, we, need to make up to someone for a bad experience of their own making. She, she, she . . . " he stuttered, unable to articulate a stronger disparaging epithet for Julia Hayes Wildfang.

Polly spun around from where she stood by the coat closet in the hall between the kitchen and the library. Still wearing her winter coat, she stood toe to toe with him, fixing him in her glare.

"And just let me tell you a few things, Sonny Dawson. You don't know everything, y'know! Whatever, however, it happened to them, it wasn't their fault. Julia came dragging back to Onansburg with Larry; they rented a little one-bedroom house. And then she got that job as night clerk at the milk plant, where Larry's dad worked. She's thin as a rail. Looks like a little old stray cat. And Larry—not even the school bullies bother him now. He's that pathetic!"

Sonny made a motion with his hand as though to dismiss Polly along with the subject of Larry and his mother. He turned back toward the kitchen. Incensed, her eyes flashing and hoarse with emotion, Polly stormed after him.

"But, Mr. Big Shot! Mr. Above It All! Did you notice that they only have one coat between them? Have you seen them? Sonny, they trade off wearing that big old military-style coat—like army surplus stuff. Did you notice that? Did you?"

Larry and his mother indeed shared a coat. In the wintertime, in the bitter cold, they had only one warm coat between the two of them. Larry and his mother had worked out a relay system for the coat. Julia walked Larry to school with Larry wearing the coat. Julia had use of the coat throughout the day, but Larry took possession after school until eleven o'clock when Julia clocked out at the milk plant.

No, Sonny hadn't noticed that they were sharing a coat. He averted his eyes when he saw them on the street. He delegated Ruby or Thelma Jane to wait on either of them when they came into the store. It was as though they were manifestations instead of humans; he tried not to let them impact his conscious thought.

Sonny had been aghast at the argument between Polly and himself and at the reason for it. In retrospect, he was never sure to whom he was making amends when he hired Larry. Was it for Polly, who had never taken up for someone with such passion, not even for his attitude toward his sisters? Or was it a make-good for his cavalier attitude toward Julia and Larry?

Larry reported five days a week after school, working until six o'clock. Then he waited for his mother until she was finished at work, so they could walk home together. Saturdays, he worked the day at the store so that Ruby and Thelma Jane could take a day off. Sonny, too, worked at the store on Saturdays.

"Larry?" Sonny pushed himself past his aversion to Larry, past his regret that he had stopped in at the store. If his conscious mind had been alert, he would have known that Larry would be at the store until a few minutes before eleven o'clock. Sonny's lack of attention was a rare lapse.

Sonny was always alert, thinking, aroused. He expended great amounts of psychic energy. He usually knew what others would say before they could articulate their thoughts; he frequently finished aloud a sentence yet barely formed in the mind of a companion. Polly scolded him for this in her gentle way. Don't try to control everyone, everything, every conversation, even the flow of thoughts.

Larry stood tense and waiting. It was because of Polly that he had a job at the store, a refuge. And Larry knew that Sonny had limited tolerance for him. It was Polly who gave Larry and Julia courtesies and attention that had been withdrawn from them after the debacle of Julia's alliance with Kenny Wildfang, the marriage so heartily supported and then so shamefully ended.

The unfortunate experience hung over Onansburg as though the community had a proactive part in what happened. When Julia Hayes met Kenny Wildfang at the Ranch, the townspeople wisely shook their heads affirmatively, nodding sagely in their collective wisdom, agreeing it was a good match. Now, more than two years later, everyone wanted to forget their earlier opinion on their own mistaken judgment.

Kenny Wildfang was an over-the-road trucker, hiring out, contracting to wholesalers requiring a semi-trailer truck to deliver their goods to the Southwest. He owned a mega-monster truck. By day, it was an impressive piece of machinery, so polished that a panorama of the countryside played on the black aluminum skin of the trailer in a constantly changing mural. Red-scripted letters embellished with metallic gold on the side of the tractor spelled out "Wildfang Transport." Highly polished chrome frosted every available space, and small red electric bulbs, runner lights, outlined the trailer.

But at night, it was larger than life with an existence independent of its driver. Looking back, in retrospect, it was ominous and menacing, its winking red lights foretelling the presence of evil. An individual hearing the deep, throaty growl of its engine recognized its approach like distant thunder that is heard before one is ever aware of an impending storm.

Kenny Wildfang was from Hamilton, nine miles south of Onansburg. He and his rig had become familiar over the years, as he had to pass through Onansburg to get to Interstate 35. Even now, with him gone, the sound of any big truck, first the rumble of the truck gearing down to the twenty-five-mile-per-hour speed limit through town, then gathering speed for the big hill on the way out to the interstate, caused listeners' eyes to snap to attention, to lock briefly with others' in a moment of mutual alarm.

Sonny and Polly heard about the magic couple on Monday after the Saturday night they met at the Ranch, a quasi-nightclub founded in a rural barn. Twenty bucks gained locals admittance that allowed the loosely gathered congregation a prodigious amount of beer, country music, and dancing. The Onansburg grapevine worked overtime, winding its way through the community on that Sunday, in time for Ruby to announce to Sonny on Monday that indeed, Julia Hayes had met herself a "ma-yn."

"Oh, you know him, Sonny, that trucker from over in Hamilton. He comes through here all the time, the one with the big fancy rig. He stopped in here to pick himself up one of those big flashlights once. Remember?"

Sonny remembered the man. Good-looking guy, maybe forty, forty-two. Not too tall, five-eleven or so, with a compact build. Dark hair but gone silver in odd contrast with his unlined, baby-fine skin.

Single women from around Choctaw County tracked the comings and goings of the master of the flashy rig, and his polite, disinterested flick to the brim of his hat in response to their friendly waves only fueled their interest. Lonely women patrolling the airwaves all along Interstate 80 listened eagerly for his soft, seductive voice when he responded on his CB radio. Waitresses in his favorite restaurants looked forward to his regular stops. His manner was always cordial, but always distant, removed as though he was saving himself for someone, somewhere.

The legend of his broken heart persisted even after three years. He returned from one of his trips west to find his wife and children gone. Their home was abandoned intact, but their $10,000 savings account accompanied Sarah Wildfang and her sons on their search for a new life. Divorce papers were served and finalized without Kenny ever knowing of their whereabouts. He kept mostly to himself, occasionally joining the weekenders at the Ranch or the crowd at the Hamilton Tap. He worked hard, it was generally acknowledged, probably driving too many hours with too little time between trips.

"Oh, he probably could've tried harder to find them, but what's the use," was the common sentiment. "A woman like that, just takin' off with a man's hard-earned money. Who'd want her back anyway. Damned ungrateful kids! You'd think they'd want to get hold of their own dad. The mother probably poisoned their minds. Those boys—seemed like odd ones—never looked you in the eye."

"A boy should be with a man, not just his mother all the time. Larry needs a little toughening up. Bob Hayes would have wanted Larry to have a dad. Take him hunting, fishing, and stuff like that."

When Julia met Kenny Wildfang, Larry was very much part of the picture. A man missed having a son. And indeed, it was in everyone's best interest when single attractive people met and married. Better to have that temptation out of the way.

Julia and Kenny were married the next spring, the year Larry was thirteen, and moved to Hamilton, seven miles away, to the house that Kenny had occupied with his first family. All of Julia's friends, even casual friends like Sonny and Polly, who knew Julia at church when she was married to her first husband, went to the party at the Ranch in celebration of the wedding. Blessed by Julia's minister, Fred James, applauded by Larry, cheered by the revelers at the

Ranch, the couple began their life of wedded bliss. And just short of a year later, Julia's world fell in around her.

From nearly the first moment Julia and Kenny and Larry were pronounced man and wife and son, Kenny's behavior changed. In retrospect, it seemed that he dropped his publicly proclaimed love and affection for Julia and Larry along with the pants to his wedding suit. Later, stripped of her defenses, having survived the assaults on her self-esteem, she knew the marriage had been under assault from the first day.

To Julia, he was sullen, secretive, withdrawn. He was no longer attracted to her sexually. The alteration left her bewildered, but it was Larry who paid the highest price. And when she understood, without question, what had happened, she was quick to act.

Looking back, she would wish that she had taken a more temperate approach. Less public knowledge, less public outcry might have been better for Larry. Even for herself. Dr. Cook, the sheriff, and the county attorney advised that discretion about the assault on Larry might serve both the boy and his mother better than the full hue and cry of public retribution.

It was a wicked crime that Ken Wildfang (the diminutive, Kenny, was dropped by all when they learned of the assault) committed against his stepson. While discretion would have kept knowledge of the crime from spreading like an infectious disease, the interest and privacy of the victim was forfeited in the contest between retribution and discretion.

"I hope he gets to be some bad man's girlfriend in prison!"

"They need to lock him up and throw away the key."

"Let's make damn good and sure there's not any more like him out there."

And Julia found herself in a no-man's-land of suspicion between her own guilt and the public's clamor for accountability that demanded, "Where was she when all of this went on?"

That night, with Larry heavily sedated, Dr. Cook insisted that

Julia go home to prepare to accompany Larry to Des Moines for surgery. Jim Saunders, the coach at the school, was dispatched to drive her to her home in Hamilton. In silence, he saw her to her door.

Once Julia was alone in the house, postponing the time when it would be necessary to reflect on what had happened, she drifted through the house, adjusting the curtains, cleaning the contents from the refrigerator, arranging and rearranging the throw pillows on the sofa. She prepared the house for her absence but closed the door to Larry's bedroom when she first entered, unable to face the quiet reproach of the still darkness.

Later, she forced herself on the pristine silence of the room. Bracing herself against the opening of the doorway, surveying the careful order of the room, the smooth unblemished surface of the crimson bedspread, the shoebox files of baseball cards, the baseball autographed by Mickey Mantle that had belonged to Larry's dad, she looked at the accusing emptiness of the room as though she were only an impersonal observer. She could no longer envision Larry there in safety.

With a fresh swell of anger rising in her, engulfing her, carrying her in its wake, Julia strode purposefully to her own bedroom. The same one she had, until this night, shared with Ken Wildfang. Flipping on the overhead light, she crossed the room to her dresser in three strides. With a broad sweep of her forearm, she cleared the top of the walnut cabinet, then coldly surveyed the wreckage of broken picture frames, her jewelry box and its spilled contents, an abandoned coffee cup broken in two with the dregs of the morning brew splattered against the wall.

Glimpsing the few coffee grounds stuck to the wall, Julia's mind flashed back irrationally, remembered her nearly blind grandmother spraying bug killer on coffee grounds spilled in her sink, screeching in alarm, "Ants! Look! Ants everywhere!"

Quietly then, almost reverently, Julia opened the top drawer and removed the silver concha earrings so carefully protected in their black velvet case. They had been a gift from Wildfang from one of his trips to New Mexico. Fixing her eyes on the stricken face framed in the mirror above the dresser, but finally meeting her own stare in the mirror, Julia stabbed the posts of the earrings through her ears, relishing the pain. She would wear them as a constant reminder of her mistaken judgment, as penance for marrying a man who preferred her son to her.

She tossed her glorious mane of hair in the flirtatious gesture of a woman who feels beautiful, if only for a moment. The polished silver pendants dropping from the turquoise stones flashed and danced, turning, dipping, and swaying. Leaning into the mirror, she pinched her cheeks for color, moistened her lips, and shot a brilliant smile at herself in the mirror, her fingers framing her beautiful face. Holding the pose, she hummed a rhythm to a tune with no melody, shuffled her feet in a parody of the Texas two-step until, like a music box dancer, she slowed and stopped.

Slowly dropping her arms until her hands hung motionless at her sides, her shoulders dropped, and she stepped back from the mirror to regard her own image. The smile faded, the warmth of the brown eyes dulled and teared. Her face crumpled in anguish. She turned her back on the reflection. When, early the next morning, Julia left the home, she took her own suitcase along with one for Larry.

<hr />

If Sonny had been less preoccupied by Polly's death, he would have remembered that Larry would be at the store until a few minutes before eleven o'clock. Larry stood tense and waiting.

Sonny reached for the wall and fumbled for the light switch, locating it so that the fluorescent lights overhead would wink into action, fixing the store and its well-ordered inventory under the steady gaze of their benevolent artificial beams. Larry quickly wiped his face with the back of an arm, blinking as he squinted down at his shoes. He stood, unbidden, uncertain before Sonny. Sonny felt a surge of unreasonable jealousy and anger. As though he could control who mourned for Polly! He had been jealous of Polly's friendship with Larry, her careful attention to Julia Wildfang, now Hayes again. He resented that he and Polly had quarreled about Larry. Sonny ignored Larry's tears.

While he recognized nothing would have changed materially during the three days the store was closed, Sonny pretended to busy himself, checking the cash register, examining the accounts receivable ledger. "So, Larry. You just finishing up?" he asked without looking up. "It's late. You can get on home. I just came in to pick up the cash register tape and the bank deposit from Friday's business. Ruby counted the cash and checks. I'll make the deposit at the night drop on the way home. Looks like everything is in pretty good shape for tonight. You go ahead. Get your things. I'll lock up."

Giving Sonny an affirmative nod, Larry padded toward the back room almost noiselessly, only the sibilant hiss of one Levi-clad leg swishing against the other marking his passage. Sonny noted that Larry wiped his eyes with his outstretched fingers and smeared the dampness against his pant leg. He watched Larry disappear into the back room and swatted the air in frustration as though he could rid himself of Larry's sorrowful image as he would an errant gnat on a kamikaze night flight.

Sonny fell into the category of those of Onansburg who, while they had mixed feelings about Julia and the questions surrounding her involvement with her ex-husband, and sympathy for Larry, wanted to remain distant, emotionally uninvolved with the details of the Wildfang case. Sonny didn't want to know, didn't want to discuss what had happened to Larry with anyone, not even Polly.

Some had tried to intellectualize what had happened, tried to institutionalize the recognition of the crime from a remote, detached vantage point in terms of deviance, pederasty, sexual abuse, sodomy, pedophilia. Many were left with only an ideogrammic understanding of the abuse; a void existed between their pictured understanding of what had happened and the name, the terms used to describe not the physical act, but a word that described the perversion and revulsion that accompanied it.

Others had grieved torturously for the violation of a thirteen-year-old boy, turning the incident over and over in their own minds, nursing the graphic implications like a festering wound. They recoiled from the notion that their own imaginations could inflict this outrageous act on their conscience for consideration. They vehemently denied its occupation of their mind's space from the fear that they could be titillated by their recognition of Larry's rape.

Even others, for lack of the desire or ability to pursue any analysis or understanding of the incident in any form, gossiped and speculated about it sotto voce, from behind hands cupped to their mouths in imagined privacy. With the simple, intentional cruelty of children.

The morning after Larry had been transferred to St. Luke's Hospital in Des Moines for surgery, Sonny appeared for his customary coffee break at the South Side Café. Every workday morning, except Saturday when Franklin's was too busy with weekend fix-er-uppers and would-be handymen for Sonny to leave the store, he made the pilgrimage to the café. There was coffee to be drunk at the Franklin Hardware store, to be sure, for employees and customers alike in Styrofoam cups imprinted with the yellow and orange logo of the store's national franchiser. But Sonny thought it was good business to make an obligatory appearance at the café.

With a smile and a nod for the waitress, Mary Lou Acheson, Sonny approached a seat at the freshly wiped Formica counter. He carefully placed his hand-carried copy of the *Des Moines Register*, so as to avoid the dampness of the soon-to-be-dry faux marble. Watching for a moment until the wetness left by the recent application of a damp towel gradually receded, Sonny mounted the round stool, leaned forward, resting on his elbows, expectantly waiting for Mary Lou to bring his coffee and make a pro forma query: "What'll it be, Sonny? The whole wheat toast or a doughnut this morning?"

As Mary Lou started forward to take his order, Puny Sorenson, the early cook at the South Side, abandoned his post behind the serving window and came powering up to the front line of the counter, obviously intent on having a word with Sonny.

Puny dispensed breakfasts and lunches six days a week at the South Side Café, his seemingly disembodied arms presenting plate after plate at the window. He was like a robot in the domain of the kitchen, tirelessly coordinating the cooking of eggs, sausages, pancakes, and toast, then hamburgers, fries, chicken and noodles, and pot roast, collating them without error onto plates for delivery. No parsley bouquets adorned the plain-cooked fare; Puny displayed clerical aptitude versus creative flourish.

Puny ruled the kitchen from five-thirty a.m. until one-thirty p.m., when the lunch business was officially over. Only Phil Larson, proprietor of the South Side, could enter Puny's workspace on official business only, for which he was subjected to a baleful glare.

Puny occupied the small but efficient stainless-steel kitchen fully and would often crouch, with his hand shading his eyes against the glare of the overhead lighting, to squint through the serving window. It was easy to imagine Puny as a WWII tank commander. He peered through the window, measuring the opposition, assessing the targets, mentally computing coordinates of roast beef, gravy, and mashed potatoes to chicken and biscuits, coleslaw. He barked out his commands to his crew in a steady voice that brooked no disobedience: "Hurry it up now. Pick it up! Pick it up! Come and get it!"

Waving Mary Lou aside, Puny, his arms rhythmically treading air as he abandoned his post, stalked up to Sonny, an agenda clearly in mind. Eyes slid surreptitiously to watch the unaccustomed sight of Puny leaving his kitchen.

Puny always wore the traditional cook's white uniform to work; he affected the white paper campaign-style hat of a butcher versus the traditional chef's hat. Even with no head covering, Puny's hair wouldn't have been a threat to the cuisine; a short butch haircut delineated his hatchet-shaped head. A local wag had once suggested that Puny wear a hairnet, after which he was banned from the South Side by Puny's refusal to serve him. With the seam of his white trousers splitting the halves evenly, Puny's massive rear end appeared like a great, bifurcated full moon. It was in balance with the firmly rounded paunch in front. Observing Puny from the waist down, only the direction of his shoes would tip an onlooker off as to which direction he was facing.

With his hypertensive color in full flush, a light sweat broke on Puny's brow. He swung his bulk onto the vacant stool next to Sonny, leaned close, and spoke in guarded tones. "Did you hear about the mess over at the school yesterday? Over at the junior high? You didn't? Oh, Jesus. It's just a *hell* of a thing." Puny plundered on with his narrative, assaulting Sonny with the story, in the only terms he knew. They were graphically horrific. Rushing toward the conclusion of the tale, Puny took no notice of Sonny's lack of response. "I guess they took the kid on to Des Moines. Going to have an operation. Heard they was going to give him a rubber butthole. Ain't it something? Ain't it just the shits? That asshole, Wildfang! I'd like to get my hands on him, just for a few minutes. Tearing up a kid like that! That dirty motherfucker!"

From the beginning of Puny's diatribe, Sonny sat speechless, motionless. His vision grew dark around the peripheries, and then he stared at Puny's moving lips, as if they were at the end of a receding tunnel in a dimly lit hallway. Then he straightened, pushed himself back from the counter with outstretched hands. He couldn't draw a breath. He tried to speak, but no air flowed past his vocal cords. He could not shut out the sudden image of Kenny Wildfang treading purposefully and threateningly down a long hallway toward Larry

Hayes. Sonny felt very cold. A prickly sensation crept from the base of his scalp, down the back of his neck, down his spine.

Everything, everyone appeared to be in slow motion as he elaborately, with exaggerated slow motion, pushed himself to his feet. He turned, walked between tables and staring eyes, putting one foot carefully in front of the other, opened the door, and exited wordlessly into the brightness of the day outside.

Puny watched the departure in puzzled silence. Cy Luftkin, one of the regulars at the South Side, turned to Puny, regarding him steadily. "Puny, you dumb shit! Why in hell would you go and tell Sonny all that about the kid? And about his getting a rubber butthole? Don't you got no sense at all?"

Perplexed, confused by Cy's vituperative attack, Puny shook his head, cupped his hand over his meaty lips. Pulling at his mouth, wiping the moisture from his upper lip, he headed back to the unguarded kitchen.

Small communities tend to remember. Even while memories fade or are replaced by newer events by local residents, those who move away are left with the image they carry with them, part and parcel, the baggage from their lives there. A constantly changing reel-to-reel tape is playing for the resident community while the transplanted sojourner carries a still photo, a picture that is flashed into memory on a generally unbidden cue. History would carry a slide of Larry, to be clicked up on personal screens of individual memory, the stigmatized victim of his stepfather's perversion. The kid with the mythical rubber butthole.

Feigning interest in the contents of the cash register, Sonny watched from under lowered lids when Larry returned to the front of the store, schoolbooks under his arm.

"Ahem." Sonny seemed not to hear. "Ahem. Uh?"

"Larry?"

"Uh, I went to Polly's funeral today. Went with Ruby and Harold and Thelma Jane. So we'll, I'll, miss her, Sonny. I'll miss her a lot."

"Go on, Larry. Go on home."

Sonny turned away. He heard the back door open, then close as Larry made an otherwise noiseless exit. When he knew he was alone, he buried his face in his hands.

Polly, oh Polly. You wouldn't have liked that. I'll go home now. Polly. Let's go home.

Sonny picked up the rectangular canvas deposit bag containing receipts from the day Polly died. A light breeze stirred the humidity as he emerged from the store to go to his car. It was the kind of Iowa night when the old-timers say you can hear the corn growing. The redolent air was heavy with the fragrances of blossoming plants and flowers even while the same full ripening reminded of the passing of the seasons.

Sonny drove through the drive-up window at the Second National Bank, deposited the bag in the night drop drawer, then drove slowly home.

Four

Sonny awoke the next morning to a grinding, throbbing orgasm. Emerging reluctantly from the delicious euphoria, he had never been so happy. Polly was with him again, wearing a new blue dress. Her face and her hair looked different. Somehow both were rearranged. In the dream, he knew that Polly was changed, but they were together in a beautiful, sunlit room where they had never been before. He was so happy to be with Polly again. Smiling, smiling until his face ached from the force of the smile. He longed for her. She had seemed so close. He reached for her but could never quite touch her. Disjointed, fragmented visions of Polly. And of himself with Polly. To hold her once more.

Sonny's eyes snapped open. In breathless panic, he pushed himself to his knees amid the tangled bedclothes; his heart pounded. He was flushed and aroused. Then, sick with disappointment, he sank back down, his face against Polly's pillow. He pressed his face deeper into her pillow, as he had on the other nights since she was gone. Her lavender essence lingered. Rolling over onto his back, he slowly pulled his feet closer to his body, hugged his legs. Looking between his knees to the foot of the antique bedstead, he saw that Spats had been witness to his ecstasy and then his anguish when the dream disappeared. Spats gazed at him, a dispassionate, implacable witness.

With fingers outstretched, he pressed his fingertips against his cheekbones, sliding them back to his temples. He pressed tightly to quell the tears he felt beginning to form. Dragging his hands along the sides of his face, he finally joined them in clasped union, one gripping the other tightly as if in fervent prayer. Then he dropped them loosely to his sides, his palms flat against smooth cotton sheets. Taking a deep breath, he exhaled forcefully through his mouth.

Pushing himself over the side of the high walnut bed, he stood for a moment, his hand gripping the bedpost with its massive cannon-ball finial. He was shaken by the dream, by its intensity. By his own despair. He was frightened for his aloneness.

From time to time in the past few days, Sonny had wondered if his pain would have been less acute if the circumstances had been different. If she had not died so suddenly, so unexpectedly. Could he handle it differently? Better? Sonny thought a lot about his performance as it might be compared to others.

A glance at the brass carriage clock on Polly's nightstand, and Sonny realized that his dream had wakened him far earlier than his usual six a.m. The artificial atmosphere of the bedroom with the hum of the air conditioner and the drapes drawn tight against the early sun and heat gave few clues about the outside world.

Sonny started for the bathroom, then returned for the clock. It would work as well on his side of the bed, he reasoned, as he carefully placed it so it could more easily be seen from his side, the one closest to the door. But then, Sonny returned the clock to Polly's side.

Soon, showered and dressed in khaki slacks and a blue Oxford button-down shirt, Sonny descended the stairs eagerly and hurried to the kitchen. Breakfast was his favorite meal, but no clatter of breakfast things or hot coffee welcomed him to the day. The empty kitchen mocked him; only the impersonal hum of the refrigerator greeted him.

No paper. Where the hell is the Des Moines paper?

With chagrin, Sonny realized that the paper hadn't ever traveled from the porch to the breakfast table on its own, since Polly always brought it to the kitchen to share with their meal. He had taken it for granted. He had taken her many small courtesies for granted.

Take a deep breath. You're not the first to go through this. Yeah, but this is the first for me. God, think of people who are widowed more than once. Sure as hell would take a lot of getting used to more than once.

Sonny's internal dialogue carried him along through the house while he opened the same drapes and blinds pulled protectively closed by Dolores the night before. When he opened the front door to retrieve the paper, the warm, moist air carrying the late summer plague, ragweed, tickled his sinuses, making him sneeze explosively.

He picked up the newspaper and started back into the house, but the faint, repetitive thud of running feet caused him to turn. The porches on the sides of the house ran parallel to two streets, 5th Avenue and Wall Street, and converged at a ninety-degree angle, the point of which was sliced off by the width of the concrete steps rising from the brick sidewalk. The steps climbed up to the porches at what would have been the apex of the angle formed by the porches. At the time their home was built, in the late 1890s, the airy porch was the only relief from the heat of the Iowa summers. But the porch swing was now used only in milder weather. And the chintz-cushioned white wicker armchairs were mostly decorative.

A solitary jogger came into view on Fifth Avenue. His gray tee shirt was soaked with perspiration; a v-shaped wetness on his back extended from his shirt to his running shorts. Pretending to examine the newspaper headlines, Sonny glanced at the man without seeming to notice him. He had seen him running before, but he was unremarkable except for a curiously simian appearance. An uneven gait on disproportionately short, bandy legs, broad sloping shoulders extending to long muscular arms with one hairy arm hung seemingly longer than the other. The fingers of that hand curled loosely as though its owner might suddenly yield to temptation and fall forward to balance on the ever-ready appendage.

Noting Sonny standing on the porch, the man, someone Sonny had once worked with on the parade committee, raised his arm in wordless greeting.

With a mental lurch, Sonny realized that the weekend of the festival was upon him, and he had obligations, responsibilities to the Old Settlers committee. And then at the thought of Old Settlers, Sonny's mind flipped back to Polly's funeral, the people who had come—church friends, people around town, the Shaws, Drennan McCormack.

Drennan McCormack! Did he come for Polly's services or did his visit just happen to coincide with Old Settlers?

Sonny thought back; he couldn't remember Drennan returning for the celebration previously. If Drennan had been in town for some previous Old Settlers, wouldn't it have been in the paper? Sonny thought about his festering angst over Drennan. Was it comparison with the importance of a professional man of achievement or comparison with the young man Drennan had once been?

The newspaper, the *Choctaw County Republican*, which had arrived yesterday, printed the Onansburg's business, civic, and social news in columns titled, appropriately enough, LOCAL NEWS. And each surrounding community, be it ever so small, was given space in the paper for its local news, with items of social intercourse compiled by the local correspondent.

The space given in the paper was a concession, a living memorial to small aggregates of civic-minded folks whose effort was never quite enough to warrant an incorporated town. The little clumps of homes and farm outbuildings could, at most, be called villages; once a school, perhaps a small depot and a general store served the hopeful that lived there. Now, there were mostly just memories of those appurtenances for the neighborhoods that remained. Their mailing addresses would likely be Onansburg or Hamilton instead of New York or Bethlehem, the former being incorporated survivors of early settlements.

From time to time, the paper would carry news of Drennan

McCormack having visited his brother and family; Sonny always took note of Drennan's visits. But he couldn't remember Drennan having been in town for Old Settlers.

The *Choctaw County Republican* carried reprints of news of events from years past in columns headed FIVE YEARS AGO, TEN YEARS AGO, TWENTY-FIVE YEARS AGO, FIFTY YEARS AGO. But, just two years ago, it was reported that "Dr. Drennan McCormack, Professor of Sociology at the University of Minnesota, visited the Michael McCormack family in Onansburg en route to San Francisco where he was to present a paper to The American Sociological Society."

TEN YEARS AGO.

"Dr. Drennan McCormack of Minneapolis, Minnesota, was a weekend guest of his brother and sister-in-law, Mr. and Mrs. Michael McCormack. Dr. McCormack is on sabbatical leave for the current academic year from the University of Minnesota and will be leaving the country to teach and conduct research in China having been awarded a Fulbright Scholarship."

TWENTY YEARS AGO.

"Dr. Drennan McCormack, formerly associated with Duke University in Durham, North Carolina, has accepted a position at the University of Minnesota as an associate professor of sociology. It will be remembered that Dr. McCormack, the son of Emmett and Genene McCormack, graduated from Onansburg High School. His brother, Michael, and his family reside in Onansburg."

And once in the SOCIETY NEWS, Sonny had seen Polly linger on a particular article.

"Mr. and Mrs. Harold E. Withrow III of Raleigh, North Carolina, announce the engagement of their daughter, Susan Elizabeth, to Drennan James McCormack of Durham, North Carolina. Dr. McCormack, formerly of Onansburg, is a teaching fellow at Duke University and was awarded the degree Doctor of Philosophy in Sociology in June of last year."

The distinguished professor drifted in and out of town once a year, sometimes again for holidays. Polite interest in his work disguised the lack of understanding about his profession. Drennan was heard to say once, by way of explanation, "A sociologist is someone who spends $40,000 to discover a whorehouse that everyone else knew was there."

No one in Onansburg questioned that Drennan did not, in fact, marry Miss Susan Elizabeth or anyone else. But the cancellation of the engagement always caused Sonny a certain amount of discomfort; Drennan and Polly had been in love before he and Polly knew each other. With Drennan a year older than he and Polly two years younger, Sonny had been out of high school before he ever noticed either of them.

But Polly and Drennan had been high school sweethearts. Years later, at the time of Drennan's engagement announcement, the unusually insensitive neighbor Wanda Wainwright, knowing Drennan and Polly had dated, had asked Polly, at a neighborhood potluck dinner, if they had once been serious. Polly, with a self-conscious little laugh, had responded glibly. "Of course, we were serious! All high school romances are serious!" But at the time, Sonny had known the quick answer was not so easily given; it had cost Polly to toss off her relationship with Drennan so lightly, even if it was just to diffuse Wanda's nosy interest. She had loved Drennan; he was the first man to know her, and she had promised herself to him.

But then she met Sonny. That was nearly thirty years ago.

Once, just a few years ago, he and Polly had been in Des Moines. Following a day of shopping and a movie, they were having dinner at an Italian restaurant they favored on the west side. A young man came in, following the hostess to a table. Polly, in gleeful surprise, had exclaimed, "Look! It's Drennan!"

Impatient and annoyed, Sonny had turned to her and said tersely, "That's not Drennan. That man is not twenty-five years old. Drennan is older than *you* are now." In truth, the man did look very much like Drennan had looked at age twenty-five or so. But Polly was non-plussed, flustered. She dropped her eyes and looked aside to pick up her spoon, which she then dropped onto her napkin from where it continued its journey to the floor. She was shaken and embarrassed to the point that Sonny took pity on her.

"It's all right. I've done the same thing. Gotten caught in a time warp," he said, picking up the spoon for her. "Young people come into the store that look so much like their parents did when they were young, and I confuse them."

Thinking of Polly and Old Settlers, Sonny's rumination was cut short when he recalled his impending responsibility to the arrangements on the town square. He hurried back into the house with the paper and headed through the living room and dining room on his way to the kitchen to get his car keys and pocket paraphernalia, a tin of breath mints, and his money clip. Sonny stopped short in dismay.

What the hell! Just look at this room! What's going on here?

In addition to the coat of his suit, still covering the chair upon which he had parked it last night, yesterday's *Choctaw County Republican* had fallen open from the chair where it had been tossed, the stacks of correspondence and cards still covered the dining room table, silver and china waited to be restored to the built-in oak sideboard, some of the drapes were still drawn. And the odor!

"Spats, dammit, I smell cat poop! Dammit, Spats! What did you do?"

With the aura of the cat's wrongdoing in the air, Sonny's nose quickly led him to one of the new plants that had been delivered since Polly died, and there it was. Spats had defecated in the soil surrounding the tall ficus tree that had been parked in the sunny window next to the sofa, and then in trying to cover it, had kicked loose dirt all over the French blue carpet. Sonny knew he would have to remove the offending pile, vacuum the carpet, plus replace the soil that had been kicked out from around the plant.

Sonny felt himself swell with indignation, but even while the adrenaline charged his arteries, he felt the conflict of rage against the surge of self-pity and tears that welled up simultaneously. He knew he was about to break again.

No, no. Catch hold. Come on. Ease up. Ease up.

His heart pounded. He caught sight of himself in the heavy gilt mirror hanging over the Victorian credenza and could see his face was mottled with white splotches over the angry blush. He bent at the waist, pressed his tightly clenched fists together against his thighs, pressing, pressing hard as if he could push the tension from his body. His eyes were wide and staring, but tears didn't come. He slowly raised his head.

The door. The basement door. As he fought for reason to return, he caught sight of the door to the basement just inside the kitchen. It was firmly closed, which explained the neat pile Spats made in the nearest receptacle resembling his litter box.

Sonny looked around for Spats but wasn't surprised not to catch sight of him. Spats was a cat of great presence and dignity with impeccable manners. Defecating, even by necessity, in a plant would not have been to his liking, and Sonny knew Spats blamed him for the door having been closed. Spats would know that had Polly been here he would have not been so humiliated. He punished Sonny with his absence.

When the odorous onus was removed, Sonny checked the library to be sure there were no other surprises left by Spats; he didn't know how long the door to the basement had been closed. Entering the powder room from the hall connecting the library with the kitchen, Sonny carefully washed his hands in the sink, making a froth of lather with the soap and using the hottest water he could stand.

He dried his hands quickly, then realized he needed to put out fresh hand towels. The crowd of family gathered yesterday before the funeral had taken its toll on the lavatory and its supplies. He mopped up the sink with a used towel but abandoned the thought of doing more than a quick wipe-up.

Later, maybe later. It's already seven-fifteen. There's too much to take care of right now.

He recognized then that the kitchen too needed attention. It was bewildering to him that he hadn't noticed this earlier. Stacks of paper plates, cups, napkins, one abandoned cookie with a bite taken from it and the ensuing crumbs, along with mysterious foil-wrapped packages from visitors the day before, cluttered the counters. He noticed he'd also left his keys on the kitchen counter rather than hanging them on the rack next to the outside door as usual.

Dropping the morning paper on the table, he fed the cat and took a look around. He decided to leave everything for later, since Old Settlers needed his attention more. Sonny picked up his keys, located his briefcase in the hallway, and let the door slam behind him as he headed down the brick walk to the garage.

As he hurried to his car, Sonny ticked off in his mind the list to be accomplished before lunch. Then, his heart plummeted, descended to the now familiar gut-wrench. There would be no thoughtfully engineered luncheon respite from a busy day. He was on his own. He and Polly generally expected to have lunch together each day, either at home with soup, a sandwich, and fruit, or even leftovers. On occasion, Polly brought a hot casserole, full to the brim with noodles or rice, sausage or chicken in a savory sauce, to the store for Sonny, Ruby, and Thelma Jane. When she treated them to lunch, she always made a smaller casserole for Larry to take home for dinner.

In the car, Sonny headed for the town square to the store, trying to think it was to be just another day's work for all of them. Back to normal, which meant Sonny would arrive first, cranking out the old-fashioned awning, maneuvering the seasonal display racks to the outside, hosing off the sidewalk if necessary, then checking the contents of the vending machine that dispensed live fishing worms.

He worked at Franklin Hardware full-time after high school until the opportunity came to buy the business. By the time he was twenty-three, he was the manager of the business for the Franklin family. When John Franklin passed away and after a time of inconvenient absentee ownership, he became the natural selection to whom the Franklin family proffered the purchase. With down payment conveniently supplied to him as an heir to his mother's estate and the balance of the purchase price tendered by a business loan by then-Second National Bank, successor to the failure of First National Bank, Sonny purchased Franklin Hardware. The bank was eager to keep a venerable business in place on the town square and Sonny had already proven his ability to run the business profitably.

Sonny liked his solitary morning routine. Greeting other merchants, catering to the emergency needs of a customer knocking on the door brandishing a broken faucet before the store officially opened, mixing paint orders for his commercial customers, all served to organize the corners of his mind. Sonny's customers knew that if Sonny was at the store, they were welcome.

Despite being later than he wished to be arriving that morning, Sonny turned from the asphalt trajectory to the store toward the cemetery, as if drawn by an invisible cord. Upon reaching the cemetery, he slowly circled Polly's gravesite by driving through the cemetery's center lane, then alongside it on the waterworks road. Sonny didn't stop. The drooping heads of the blossoms of the floral offerings mounded over the grave were already turning brown from the heat of the morning sun.

Ashes to ashes, dust to dust. We return to the soil.

Unreasonably, he wanted the flowers removed. He was repulsed. He drove away.

The wide avenue that led from the cemetery, Drake Avenue, was interrupted where it intersected with the courthouse square but resumed on the opposite side to continue its oak-lined progress to connect to Highway 30. In turn, Highway 30 connected to Interstate 80 by way of a short segment appropriately named Southwest Connector.

The homes along Drake Avenue were among the loveliest

examples of Victorian architecture that Onansburg offered: brick and stucco and frame all embellished with ornate wooden gingerbread trim. Many of the homes displayed the same motif carved into the gingerbread, the delicately scalloped wildwood flower denoting the same builder. A family of homes bespeaking common features, as distinctive as the bright blonde hair and dimpled cheeks of the eight children of Onansburg's largest family, the Rustows.

Trying hard now to refocus, to distract himself from his thoughts, Sonny looked blandly at the homes as he went slowly past. He and Polly spent many evenings gliding and riding, admiring flowers and shrubs, a new fence, fresh paint. When Sonny approached the corner of Drake and Tenth, he shot a quick glance down the cross street that had been his street. His eyes were drawn to the unpretentious, square house where he had lived as a child.

That was the closest, the closest my old man could ever get to Drake Avenue.

He knew it had been his father's greatest ambition to live in one of the large homes on Drake Avenue. His father had wanted a house that took itself seriously, that others took seriously. He worked hard to achieve his goal, to be respected, to raise his family to take their place in the society of Onansburg.

Remembering, Sonny shook his head and smiled again, outwardly this time, derisively. With a short, impatient chop at the steering wheel, Sonny snorted in derision. The dumb bastard never understood that Onansburg polite society didn't take applications.

In retrospect, his father's goals seemed so simple, yet they had cost so much; Sonny generally avoided thinking about the hard-bitten, driven man. To all appearances, his mother never softened in her resolute faith in his father, and he tempered his memory of his mother, even after she became feeble and slow-witted, knowing that she was compelled by the same demons, greed, lust, duplicity, that gnawed at his father.

He turned down Tenth Street and pulled up in front of his

former home, gazing across the oncoming traffic lane, currently devoid of traffic. The big square house looked happy now in contrast to its chilled, impersonal austerity of earlier days. The house was a bright white in clean contrast to the new green-shingled roof, and mounds of profusely blooming impatiens bordered the driveway next to the house. A tangle of bicycles rested where they had tumbled into the shrubs against the front porch, enclosed since 1970 against the crystal cold of Iowa winters. Now, white fluffy curtains framed the porch windows. In contrast, when Sonny's family lived there, there had been no flowers; the house had been neat and well painted, but cold, dark, and forbidding, as if it were hollow of life therein.

He remembered a brief period of a relationship with his father as a very little boy. Had he been three or four years old? When they lived in the little rented house on Cedar Street. Daddy's little buddy, but he didn't recall but a brief snapshot of that time. He thought of the intervening years between the time the Dawson family lived on Tenth Street until his father died and the years after when the wreckage of his sisters' lives became reality. Cloris left town, and Dolores was but a shell of a teenager.

Shifting uncomfortably on the leather seat now, Sonny pushed the meditation of his father back into a recess in his memory from which it could be necessarily summoned but could not unnecessarily clamor for attention. Relief from memories of him was a gift Sonny gave to himself.

Sonny had been told his father's father had been a pilgrim, a traveler, a wanderer. Sonny didn't remember his grandfather at all; he died long before Sonny was born. It was as well.

Five

_____

*C*harles Dawson Sr., to his family's everlasting shame, died, so to speak, in the saddle. Profligate, adulterous, philandering, he died in the bed of his occasional lady friend, Georgia Someone. If Georgia had been younger, she could have been called a party girl. She probably had a last name, but in the transition between marriages, it had been forgotten. She would be remembered as "Oh you know, that Georgia, ah Georgia—oh, you know who I mean."

She was always available, friendly, and above all, easy. She was not unattractive, tiny but with a well-rounded figure that had long since begun its liaison with gravity. Otherwise, she might not have been caught with a man with the reputation of a ladies' man and lecher, like Charles Dawson Sr., in her bed. And caught she was, screaming until the tenants of the apartment next door called the Choctaw County Sheriff's office to come and free her from the cooling corpulence of her late companion.

The Choctaw County Cocksman was no more. The Choctaw County Bull was dead. Morbid jokes accompanied his demise. Everyone had liked "old C. D." He was genial, charming. But indeed, C. D. died a legend in his own time. It was reported that he could, upon request, display thirteen silver dollars along the length of ol' Spike, as it came to be known among the locals. No one would attest to having witnessed a demonstration of this feat, but many swore to the validity of the statement.

His impact on his family was a different matter. C. D.'s son, Sonny's father, was barely twenty when his father died. By then, self-conscious and humorless, filled with the need to avenge his shame at C. D.'s dissolute and immoral behavior, Charles Dawson Jr. cursed his father's memory.

C. D. brought his family to Choctaw County by train in 1925. They arrived at the station on the eastbound Rock Island Rocket, to occupy yet another in the succession of small rented homes, each progressively poorer than its predecessor. The Dawson family never so much as alluded to their previous epochs, as though there were no links between from where they'd come and their new surroundings.

When C. D. and his wife, Rose, accompanied by their sixteen-year-old son, Charles Jr., disembarked from the Rock Island Rocket, it was as though a favorite son had returned, bringing his gifts to bestow on the community. Charles Dawson Sr. cut an impressive figure, and Rose complemented his self-assurance with her own confident composure, betraying none of the sense of itinerant failure that added its weight to their baggage. Their air of success was not reflected in their worldly possessions, consisting of a bag apiece and a trunk of household goods. Rose, with her neat shirtwaist and fashionable summer hat, and C. D., in his well-tailored dark suit and straw boater, were a handsome couple. A closer inspection might have betrayed the shiny fabric, worn cuffs, and frayed edges of their fashionable finery.

C. D. approached the stationmaster at the Onansburg depot with a broad smile and an outstretched hand. "How do you do? How do you do? The name's Charles Dawson Sr. Just call me C. D. This's the wife, Rose, and this is my son, Charles Jr. Step right up, Charles. Shake this man's hand. You're . . .? Nielsen? Oh, Niel. Niel. Nielsen? Good name! Good name!" He turned to his wife. "Rose, Rose here will be needing to make the acquaintance of the ladies here in Onansburg. The church ladies, of course. Rose will call on Mrs. Nielsen. You have a family? The boy here was sixteen in March. Maybe there's someone his age to show him around? Just as soon as we can get settled a bit. Yup, going to take on the old Butler place."

Mr. Nielsen pulled back from the handshake in surprise and shot a hard look at C. D. With raised eyebrows, he immediately countered C. D.'s self-confident bluster with a quick retort. "The Butler place. Guess there's not much left of that old wreck. No one's lived there for years. House is a ramshackle mess and the barn too. You're not going to live out there right away, are you?"

"Yup, yup. I'd have to agree. We might not want to stay there. I understand it's pretty rundown right now, and Rose and the boy, they need a good, clean place. We might have to look at a place to rent in town. There'll be a lot of work to do on the place. Now, my good man, Mr. Nielsen . . ." C. D. was careful not to presume by using a first name too readily, without being bidden. "Is there a conveyance we can engage? Ah, the dray. Perhaps the drayman can deliver our bags, the trunk. Yes, the trunk. We'll need a buggy for Rose and the boy. Is there a livery? Rose, my dear Rose, will you just wait until I can engage a horse and buggy and come for you? You and the boy?" Then, pausing, leaning closer as if to listen to Rose's soft voice, he continued. "Oh no, my dear, I couldn't let you. No, no." C. D. was definite in his refusal, but then he recanted. "Well, I suppose. I suppose. I guess since the dray is already here, we could just as well rather than wait in this heat. Yes, the heat."

John Tubbs, the drayman, already there to meet the train for cargo to be delivered, hesitated, looking doubtfully at C. D. Then, looking to Rose, he agreed to transport the human cargo. "Well, I reckon since you're needing to get to your place along with the trunk and your suitcases, I'd as leave take you."

So, without ceremony, C. D. loaded up his family with he, himself, on the wagon's front seat with the drayman, talking, gesticulating,

waving his arms expansively. Rose seated herself on the flat lid of
the faded trunk. At first, she crossed her ankles primly, but after the
swaying wagon ride began, she planted her feet wide apart to balance herself against the motion. At the back of the wagon, Charles
pulled his ungainly long legs up into the wagon and tried to make
himself comfortable leaning against the side of the cargo wagon.
Then, he swiveled his body ninety degrees, dropped his legs over the
end gate of the wagon, and braced himself against the jolting ride.
He hoped no one upon seeing him would remember him riding on
the unfashionable conveyance.

Staring dispiritedly down the red shale of Drake Avenue as it
passed between his black boots, Charles also wished the brim of
his only hat, a serviceable black felted wool, would hide his face
from anyone who might later recognize him as C. D.'s son. The
leather sweatband of his hat felt greasy against his sweat-damp-
ened brow in the June heat. He quickly removed the hat, mopped
his forehead with his outstretched hand, and jammed the hat back
on his head. The hat did little to shade his face, which was already
flaming with heat.

He listened to his mother's cheerful chatter without responding,
but he was offended, insulted, by her bright comments to C. D. even
while he was so miserable. Another sudden, furtive journey, running again from God only knew what scandal, the news of which
would eventually catch up to them. Rose always managed to survive
C. D.'s malfeasance. She was like a cat, always landing on her feet;
indeed, she displayed a cat's wily confidence.

He resented his parents' air of success and self-assurance, knowing the deception always came to light. He ridiculed them in his
mind for the insouciant attitude he had come to associate with those
of wealth and power or the very foolish.

The drayman's cart and its human load trundled along behind
the patient draft horses, while Charles Jr. appraised the substan-
tial homes and manicured lawns of Onansburg's more prosperous

citizens from beneath the brim of the much-loathed hat. Other boys, young men his own age, sported a summer straw, appropriate for the weather. A summer hat and a winter hat. A summer suit and a winter suit. Not the cut-down, cast-off clothing of a feckless father.

He wished for good clothing, quality boots; a home with shady trees and wide porches; in the summertime, light airy rooms and tall pitchers of lemonade cooled by ice chipped from the big block of dwindling ice in the oak icebox; and in the wintertime, chrome-plated, pot-bellied stoves glowing red-hot in the parlor, warming fingers and toes. Charles wished for stability, constancy in his life; for tenure in a community that would place him in the mainstream instead of the fringe. He had always been "the new boy." And yet, until a later point when he surmised for what reason it became time to move on, he never knew for sure. Each move meant traveling lighter, leaving more behind them. This time, it meant leaving Omaha with only what they could carry themselves.

Lost in his rumination, Charles suddenly realized the wagon had come to a stop. The adults' lively conversation had ceased; even C. D. had fallen silent. They were at the top of a dirt lane that wound and curved its way down a long, gradual hill, past a barn, leaning on its fieldstone foundation toward its companion, the house. Weathered to a silvery gray, the dwellings stood derelict, overgrown with weeds, and abandoned. From a second-story window of the house, the remnants of a torn curtain flapped, forlorn in the hot wind. Pigeons poked in and out through the broken windowpane. Sagging and decrepit fences corralled farm implements, rusting and useless. The windmill rattled noisily above its rusted steel tower. Long since disengaged from the pump in the well, it was still turning endlessly, like a gambler's wheel but with no winners.

"This's it! This's the Butler place! Your new home!" The drayman took a perverse pride in announcing the disappointing news to the Dawson family. Charles was dismayed by the assumption that the three of them were indeed a family that could consider this wreckage as a home. He wanted nothing quite so much as to have C. D. renounce the Butler property on the spot, to say there was a mistake that they were there. Tubbs shook the reins over the backs of the team to move them on.

The sun bore down on them. The rhythmic crunching of the horses' heavy hooves at a trot, accompanied by the percussive jingle of the harness, seemed deafening as the wagon ground down the hard-packed lane, rutted from years of heavy loads. Charles felt rivulets of sweat breaking out under his shirt, running down to the small of his back. Glancing at Rose, he could see that glistening beads of moisture had formed on the bridge of her nose; he could smell her scent of moist talcum powder and the mysterious other, the mysterious woman smell that tantalized yet offended him because it was his mother's.

C. D. was unusually silent, studying the shabby buildings, each in turn. Charles looked questioningly to him, surprised by his unusual reaction. Then came Rose to his rescue. This had long been their game. No one else, particularly Charles, ever seemed to learn the rules to the clever repartee that served them so well.

Standing up in the wagon, her hands on her hips, Rose looked around, shaking her head. "Well, C. D.!" she laughed. "You've done it this time. Now this place is a real challenge." The drayman, Tubbs, looked at her curiously. She continued, "Well, when did you tell the carpenters to be here? Why aren't they here, working? The house is a sight! And the privy'll have to be rebuilt before we can spend a night here. But C. D., just look. This place will shine again. It's a diamond in the rough. The orchard is overgrown but look at the summer apples setting on. There'll be asparagus and strawberries in the spring. Bet there's a raspberry patch back there too." Mr. Tubbs looked quizzically from one to the other.

C. D., grabbing the lifeline to his ego that Rose had thrown him, responded quickly. "Rose, Rose, this place will be better than ever when we get it into shape. You're right. This place has all we need.

And Mr. Nielsen at the station will let us know when the livestock arrives." Aside to John Tubbs, he said, "Blooded stock, you know. Thoroughbreds and blooded stock. Coming out later so we could get the fences repaired and painted before they arrive." Then, gazing with proud eyes on the property, he called out to his family, "Yup, yup. Didn't I tell you? This'll be a great little place for horses and cattle." Turning to the drayman again, he continued, "You see, we kept the pick of the crop from the ranch, only the best. Only the best for the Dawson bloodline. A breeding farm will be sure to bring a lot of business into this place. The boy here. A natural with the stock." At that statement, Charles could hardly conceal his incredulousness. He barely knew one end of a farm animal from another. "Yup. Doing this for him. Get a good working place going for him, then Rose, Rose and I'll move on in a few years. Start up another operation. Yup, this's the way we do it! Always on the move. Making something out of nothing. Now, we'll just get the bags down here now. No, no, we won't be staying here for a few days. One of your local carpenters, a builder, a Mr.—Mr.—what's the name?"

Tubbs looked away from the play in action, puzzled, but obligingly muttered, "Sutton? Ted Sutton? Or Max Lytle? Or . . ."

Again, C. D. grabbed the verbal lifeline thrown to him, this time unwittingly by John Tubbs. "Yes. That's it. I'm sure Mr. Lytle will be out here this afternoon. We'll be here, working right along until he comes, then we'll just ride back to the hotel with him. Rose has our plans and blueprints in that bag over there. Yup, yup. We'll be busy, alright."

Tubbs clucked to the team and drove the wagon up close to a sagging wire fence that separated the overgrown drive from the front yard with its patches of grass, unmown and untended, blowing in the wind. There was a curious combination of grass where there should have been none, and none where there should have been some. With a low "whoa" to the team, Tubbs drew to a halt, eased down from the wagon seat, tied the lines fast to the brake on the wagon, then wrapped the lead lines around the sturdy hitching post. The team threw their heads, blew their heavy breath through their nostrils, stomped their hooves, rattled the harness in a barnyard chorus. They were at rest.

C. D. jumped lightly down from the right side of the wagon and reached back for his coat, long since draped over the wagon seat next to him. He stood surveying the property while Charles helped his mother down from the back of the wagon. Charles retrieved the three bags from the wagon, one at a time, while Tubbs stepped back up to the wagon seat and slid around it to the trunk. He shoved it to the back of the wagon, then hopped down, steadying himself with one hand on the side of the wagon to where Charles was waiting. Together, he and Charles eased the trunk to the ground. Without bothering to open the twisted wire gate, they stepped over the fence where it had collapsed to the ground and each, with two hands on the leather handles, heaved the trunk up onto the porch.

C. D. strode purposefully back and forth, master of all he surveyed. "Just leave it there. Just right there'll be fine." C. D. followed the procession up to the porch, reaching into his coat for his wallet. Elaborately extracting several bills, he looked at Mr. Tubbs questioningly. "Now, what do I owe you?" In response to Tubb's request for one dollar, C. D. shook his head. "Now, now, Mr. Tubbs. You were good enough to drive the missus and the boy and myself out here as well. Take this with our thanks." C. D. transferred another bill from the roll in his left hand to join the dollar bill in his right hand and solemnly handed them over. Rose and Charles tried to look away from the transaction. "Charles Dawson Sr. always pays his way. Fair enough? It's been a business doing pleasure with you. Yes, sir. That's what I always like to say. It's been a business doing pleasure."

Tubbs unhitched the lines from the hitching post, one of the few items in good repair, backed then turned the team, and with a light flick of the reins and a wave, headed back to town. The family watched as Tubbs and the team wound their way back up the long lane, but Charles stood apart from the two of them, refusing to look at either of his parents, unwilling to take part in the family tableau. C. D. stood beside Rose, his arm around her waist, and waved until he could no longer put off facing his family. Rose's face became forlorn as the wagon wound up the lane. Rose stepped away from C. D.'s clutch, and Charles noted tears starting to spill down her cheeks. She faced C. D., shaking her head slowly in dismay.

As the dray turned the corner from the lane onto Lone Tree Road, Charles furiously ripped the heavy hat from his head. He flung it to the hard ground and fled. Rose and C. D. stared after him, their mouths agape. Leaping a low fence, barely breaking stride, he kept running. Through the orchard, past the berry bushes; his shirt caught, then tore on a low-hanging branch. His heavy boots banged against his ankles as he ran.

Finally, breathless and overheated, he slowed to a trot, then to a walk. Winded, he bent at the waist, hands gripping his knees, trying to catch his breath. His chest was heaving. He tried to push on, running a few steps, but stopping again, he conceded the race. He had run the race before and would run again against himself and the omnipresent self-conscious rage and shame that were his self-inflicted curse. He might have kept on going, right on back to town and the next train east, leaving his parents to their own misfortune. No one could blame him, he reasoned. There would be nothing here for him.

Now, looking back in the direction from which he had taken flight, Charles stood in indecision. He could keep on going, strike out on his own in final defiance, or he could turn back to the ram-shackle farmstead in tacit acceptance of C. D.'s terms. He fantasized about how badly C. D. and Rose would feel if he was gone. He reveled in his fantasy of C. D. in abject humiliation, begging him to return, begging his forgiveness for the sins he had inflicted on him.

He conjured up scenes of Rose hovering over his poor body,

broken and bleeding from some nameless accident, the fault of which was entirely C. D.'s. Wailing in anguish, she would revile C. D., castigate him for his failures, for his perfidious behavior, for the treachery that led to this fateful tragedy where her adored son lay near death. Rose would nurse him back to health, first tending to his injuries, touching him, washing his wounds, bathing him, caressing him intimately as she cared for him. They would live together, without C. D., in the mythical rose-covered cottage in a mythical town that C. D. had for years held out to Rose as bait, as appeasement for his transgressions, not in a ramshackle house on a derelict farm, more than a mile from the nearest neighbors.

Panting softly still, Charles stood erect once more and took a deep breath, exhaling it in a long sigh. Hands on his hips, mouth pulled into a thin line, he stopped and took stock of his surroundings from the back of his imagined horse.

Loosely piled humps of hay dotted the field. Charles squinted his eyes to narrow slits against the sun. The hay-buffalo appeared hazy and indistinct, peacefully grazing in the meadow. Stealthy now, Charles dismounted, pulled the Winchester from its scabbard on the saddle, inserted shells in the chamber, and took careful aim at each shaggy mound. He fired round after round, slowly, carefully at first, mouthing the crack of the repeating rifle, "Kscshoo! Kscshoo!" He reloaded and fired until the barrel of the rifle was so hot he could no longer hold it. Charles imagined blood spouting, gushing from the surprised animals. In his peripheral vision, he spotted one old hay-bull, protecting his cows from the slaughter, charging him. Charles swung around and waited until he was a mere ten feet away; then, calmly, he dropped him with a well-placed shot between the eyes. Blood from the dying beast splattered him, his fringed buckskin shirt and trousers, the gleaming mahogany boots.

Aroused to an erection, he quickly relieved himself. The imagined sight and smell of the warm blood pouring forth in mighty gouts filled his senses. With a theatrical bow, arms sweeping the ground, he received the homage of an unlikely but adoring crowd miraculously assembled to watch him destroy the peaceful animals. Then he stood with both arms upraised, the Winchester held high, waves of applause and adulation ringing in his ears. He heard his name shouted over and over.

Startled from his reverie, he looked back to see Rose looking for him, following the same lane that he had taken to the field. The cadence of her march told him his flight had had the desired effect. In the full charge of the mother of any species protecting her young, she was coming to implore him, cajole him into returning to the farm where she would, once again, strive to make things right for him, to make up for C. D.'s deficiencies. He watched her for a few minutes—her worry evident as her eyes sought him—before she saw him silhouetted against the haystacks and hurried across the field toward him. It was a big field; the abandoned hay from a previous year represented many man-hours of work wasted, since it was now molding and decomposing. It should have been long since gathered by strong men steadily forking the loose fodder up onto a hay wagon, matching the pace of the slow-moving team of horses.

Rose had removed her hat. Her loose knot of hair was sliding to one side of her head without the hat and its stiletto hatpin to anchor it. The stylish hat, black straw with red silk roses, was cleverly constructed in the latest fashion from bits and pieces of others' cast-off finery. The ribbon had been left in the Presidential Suite at the Hotel Lincoln where Rose had last been employed in Omaha; the roses were salvaged from an elegant ball gown, which she had redesigned when she worked for a dressmaker in Kansas City. The crown of the hat had been smashed and Rose had salvaged it from the trash at the milliner's shop that adjoined the dressmaker's. No one missed it when Rose left from work that night.

Tall for a woman, graceful and lithe as a ballet dancer, Rose's beauty could have carried her far had her ambition and will so dictated. Even given the quick, canny mind that served Rose so well, her vision was limited to acting on the choices she'd already made. Her minutely defined features under the canopy of abundant honey-blonde hair had set her apart even as a child, and from the earliest age, her violet-blue eyes seemed to consume the senses of those who happened to meet her all-encompassing gaze. Her countenance could change on a moment's whim from that of hilarious jocularity to a wanton licentiousness to inscrutable disdain. Her appearance had always served her well, and a commitment to acting as a secondary career to her marriage to C. D. was a necessity for her survival.

Her voice, with its low throaty timbre, caused strangers to turn their attention to her. Her diction was clipped and precise with a distinct, but undefined ethnic overtone in her pronunciation of words with "o" that made observers look to see if her pretty mouth was pursed in a momentary pout. She spoke softly, always, but there was no one who would say that it was difficult to hear her words. Once ensnared by the magnetic attractiveness of her appearance and her frankly sexual quality, men and women alike paid her homage with their rapt attention.

Her cheeks flushed from the heat, the fair, translucent skin on Rose's nose was already burned from its unaccustomed exposure to the relentless sun. The combination of the long grass, again of a length to be mowed for hay, her ankle-length skirt, and high spooled heels made walking over the uneven ground hard work. At her approach, Charles willed his eyes to tear; he began to snuffle.

When she reached him, breathless, she tried to gather his six-foot frame into her arms, as she had since he was a child. Now her words tumbled over each other. "Oh, Honey-Boy, don't be hard on Papa. He's doing the best he can for us; we'll be just fine, you'll see, just fine." Charles allowed himself to be pulled closer. "He feels so bad that you're hurting so. He thinks you don't respect him. He couldn't help losing his job in Omaha. Wasn't his fault he sold more than that old Mr. Willbury's son. That wasn't any reason to go and fire your papa. Just because he sold more furniture than the boss's son." Neither Rose nor Charles could have known that C. D.'s most recent termination was as it had been for others; Mrs. Willbury had responded most favorably to C. D.'s considerable charm.

Charles blubbered in self-pity. Pushing himself away from her ministrations, he sniffed and fumbled for his handkerchief to give himself time to respond. Graciously allowing himself to be comforted, and with Rose's encouraging promise that C. D. was gone and had walked to the nearest farm to make the acquaintance of their new neighbors, he shuffled along, managing an occasional sob to ensure her continued interest. As they left, Charles couldn't resist looking back at the now-dead humps of hay, the remains of his triumph.

"Come on, Honey-Boy! Just you wait and see! I'm going to start right away fixing up your room! I'll get to work right away on it."

Charles and Rose took their time walking back to the house with Rose imploring Charles, encouraging him, consoling him, all the while stifling her own impatience to begin her work of organizing yet another home for her menfolk. She absently brushed tendrils of luxurious hair back up on her neck from where they had escaped confinement. Her mind, while not well educated, was quick and alert and was now occupied with a systematic evaluation of their current status.

Rose took the role of wife seriously. She was no martyr, yet she was self-sacrificing. She was no Stoic, yet she accepted C. D.'s cavalier treatment impassively. Like a puppy chasing its tail, she was caught up in his cycle of repeated failure, and like an unquestioning little canine, she would fall down in exhaustion and confusion, only to repeat the exercise as soon as she regained her strength, never intervening, only remediating their downward cycle.

Approaching the abject farmhouse squatting in its little valley, Rose and Charles were already both exhausted and chagrined from the day. The afternoon sun had peaked, and Charles recognized there would be no welcoming evening meal or peaceful rest on clean linen for any one of the three of them. "What will we do? This is no place for us," he said, near wailing. "When will he ever think about you and me?" Rose studied her son in a moment's reflection and, without reply, took his right hand and wrapped his arm in her own.

The languid heat of the afternoon fell heavy on the somnolent farmstead; only the raucous jeer of an occasional crow broke the sleepy rhythm of the peeping songbirds. Still trudging along wearily, now arm in arm, Rose and Charles were astonished by the seemingly theatrical appearance of an unusual bird, strutting from beneath his watchful hideout of chokeberry bushes. He gauged the attention of his audience with his distinctive hesitation-step gait across the road. With an instinctive, calculated distance separating them, the amazing bird stopped as if in surprise and fixed them in the stare of one bright beady eye. They regarded him in astonishment without speaking, but both knew what this magnificent specimen of the bird kingdom must be. A chicken of sorts. A gamecock, a fighting cock. The iridescent green plumed tail feathers quivered with tension, and the proud head turned then inclined disdainfully toward them and regarded them from the other eye. Unlike its plump, barnyard cousins, born for the stew pot, this bird was bred an aristocrat.

Charles was thrilled. Even city boys knew about cockfighting, the age-old sport featuring clandestine matches between valiant little roosters, surrounded by bloodthirsty fans. Equipped with razor-sharp knives fitted to their own prominent spurs, the game birds fenced and parried and flew at one another, slashing with practiced precision until one was disabled, disemboweled, or dead. It was merciful when both roosters died, when neither lived to fight another day.

The possibility of catching the bird fostered nebulous thoughts, ill-formed images of himself as the owner of the fighting cock, training the bird for the fighting arena, seeking clandestine meets for illicit gaming. Charles's mind raced with the possibility of owning a gamecock. An instant new image of himself began to form as a man free from parental direction, a man among other men—successful, dashing, gutty, undauntable.

Rose stopped, clutched Charles's arm as he started forward to claim the rooster. "I aim to catch that rooster and make him mine. Mama, that's a real fighting bird!"

"Let's get Papa to help us catch him."

"No. I'll have to catch him if I want him for myself." The rooster crossed the road with his distinctive hesitation-step gait and disappeared into the bushes.

Charles hung his head dejectedly but studied her reaction from beneath lowered lashes. Ignoring the firmly latched but useless front gate, Charles pushed the sagging fence down to the ground, forcing its remaining tensile resistance with his foot so that Rose could step across. He handed her up across the splintered front step onto the porch, noticing as he did so that the trunk containing all their household goods had been dragged into the house. Following the path the trunk had taken through the front door, Charles noted it had already been opened. His lip curled with the surly recognition that he had not in fact been her first concern after his precipitous flight. He was, however, too fearful of her impatience or possible rejection to take issue.

Rose had opened the windows on the first floor of the house, allowing the hot wind to drive the musty air of accumulated neglect away. "Charles," she smiled engagingly, "help Mama now. There's enough kindling and firewood out there to get the old cook stove going. We'll fill the reservoir on the stove to have plenty of hot water for scrubbing. Just get this place cleaned up a bit, make up some beds. We'll camp out here for a few nights. It won't be so bad. You'll see." Rose handed Charles the bucket and met his eyes with the startlingly direct gaze that rarely failed to have its effect. She dimpled prettily as he accepted the bucket and started for the door.

Hours later, with the floors swept clean of the accumulated dirt and debris from prior tenants and then scrubbed relentlessly with a stout scrub brush, feather ticks, smooth but worn cotton sheets, and much laundered, embroidered pillowcases appeared from the recesses of the trunk to comfort the travelers on their first night in their reclaimed home. Many abandoned houses were treated cruelly by the elements and by nature's creatures, but this house was more the nature of a hollow tree trunk standing bleached and empty, stretching naked limbs skyward in silent supplication among its verdant neighbors. Preserved and dried by first the rains and then the winds to a silvery husk.

C. D. had reappeared sometime during the afternoon bearing gifts of hens' eggs, fresh baked bread, and newly churned butter from the family on the next farm east. C. D. recounted his noble sacrifice in refusing the family's invitation to join them at their midday meal. With longing in his eyes, he described the crusty fried chicken, fluffy mashed potatoes, thick, creamy gravy, and fresh butter beans. Glorious descriptions of cottage cheese, pickles, preserves, and apple pie from new summer apples tantalized Charles while he sopped up the liquid yolk of the eggs that Rose quickly fried up in the cast-iron skillet to accompany the bread that she sliced in generous slabs, spread with yellow butter. They ate their first meal in their new home standing at the scarred table that had been shoved against the wall, kitty corner from the cast-iron stove that dominated the kitchen.

C. D. officiously helped clear the few dishes, bailed scalding-hot water from the reservoir on the side of the stove to fill the enameled blue dishpan, but begged off helping with the dishes to visit the erstwhile privy. Rose and Charles washed and dried the dishes, then Charles was dispatched to hang the feed-sack dish towel on the sagging clothesline outside.

Rose stood in the center of the wood-planked kitchen floor and took stock of what had been left by those going on to better things. There was no doubt that the scarred pine kitchen cabinet and rustic table with its gimpy leg had seen better days, but she had had better and had had worse. She wasted no time longing for creature comforts, and her own sense of style provided the aesthetic quality to her life with her ability to make a home comfortable and attractive with little. She'd moved their household possessions from place to place, from one makeshift home to the next, in the old immigrant trunk. The massive wooden vessel was festooned with faded decorative rosemaling, her only tie to her Norwegian-born parents, long since dead. She carried her home, if not on her back like a turtle, with her.

Returning from his lengthy inspection of the privy, C. D. stole quietly into the kitchen, startling Rose when he approached her softly, grasping her slender shoulders as she straightened from yet another foray into the depths of the trunk. Gently, he turned her to face him. A sheen of perspiration shone on her forehead. Dark shadows of fatigue underlined her eyes, adding depth to their violet-blue hue. Wrapping his arms about her, he pulled her close, grasping her backside with both hands to pull her hips against his. Moving against her, rubbing their loins together, he found her lips, his tongue hungrily exploring, seeking hers, reminding her of the incipient pleasure it could bring. He teased the protruding prominence of her upper lip, nibbling it carefully with his even white teeth, flicking it with his tongue. His mustache bristled against her mouth, yet stimulated her as her body betrayed her fatigue and, as always, responded to C. D.'s skilled ministrations. It would have been hard to say whether C. D.'s libido had a cause-and-effect relation with his physical endowment or whether there was a social component, a learned response from his own recognition of his surfeit dowry.

"No, the boy. He'll . . ." she protested. But he wasn't detracted.

Pressing his right hand lightly against her mouth while holding her close with his left arm, his hand slid to the buttons on the front of her shirtwaist and expertly unfastened each tiny pearl knob from the fabric loop that encircled it. Her rounded breasts, surprisingly large on a woman so slender, were visible through the fabric of her undergarments. He wasn't detracted. His voice husky, he said,

"We're alone. I sent him down to the first farm west to see if he could buy a couple of setting hens. It's just you and me here."

C. D.'s desire was fueled partly by the promise that Rose's body held for him and partly by the admiring glances he had received earlier from the neighbor's sloe-eyed daughter. Even as he and Rose engaged in foreplay, he thought back to the girl's comely figure, her pert upturned breasts, and the promise of shapely legs under her thin summer dress. He had caught the girl, more than once, examining him from beneath her sooty black lashes. *God,* he had thought at the time. *What a baggage she is!* But she was young. Too young and the schoolteacher to boot.

C. D. turned his full attention back to Rose. His lips traveled to her ear, down her neck to the swell of her breasts, stopping before he found the rosebud nipple with his hungry mouth. Rose moaned softly and pressed his head to her breast, leaning back against his strong arm, so he could reach her easily. He pushed the straps of her thin cotton shift down and covered her breasts with soft kisses, brushing them with his mustache. With the two of them leaning back against the edge of the table, their hands exploring each other's bodies, he alternately tongued, then gently sucked her nipples and the soft flesh around the swollen aureoles. C. D. scooped his hand up under the gingham skirt into which she had changed for housework and groped for the split-seam opening of her drawers. He slipped a probing finger through the opening and located the soft velvet cleft that was hidden deep in the thick mat of hair. Sensing their mutual readiness, C. D. quickly withdrew his hand from under Rose's skirt to unbutton his trousers, which he allowed to slide to his knees, freeing himself. Then, he lifted her to the edge of the poor old table. Raising her skirt higher, he stood in the V made by her legs, which she rested at his waist in a practiced motion. Her eyes widened in anticipation, then she leaned languorously back on her elbows, offering herself fully, her eyes heavy and half-closed. Knowing Rose was ready to receive him, C. D. thrust into her.

Suddenly, with their motion, the table shifted on its game leg, and Rose and C. D. were jolted momentarily from their pleasure. Neatly stepping out of his trousers, C. D. lifted Rose down to the floor from the table and stripped her of her modest cotton drawers. Sweeping her up into his powerful arms, he kissed her deeply and carried her to their bedroom, just off the kitchen, only that afternoon designated as such from the wreckage of the first floor of the old house. Its location had purposely been chosen by default, as the farthest from the bedroom assigned to Charles.

As C. D. maneuvered his precious burden into the airy bright room, past the abandoned oak dresser with its cracked and splintered mirror, Rose traced the tiny buds of C. D.'s nipples with her fingernail through his shirt, but his magnificent erection needed no reminder of its urgency. Depositing her on the soft feather tick, C. D. threw her skirt up and mounted her quickly, with Rose's deft hands guiding him, encouraging him. She took him gladly, and they began their practiced rhythm. They didn't hear Charles's soft step on the porch, nor did they hear him enter through the door to the "L" of the kitchen that adjoined the bedroom.

Despite the fact that he'd been dispatched on the errand by his father, Charles was pleased with his purchase of two fine red hens for a quarter apiece. He had hastened back from the neighbors to show his prize to his mother, to receive her praise for a job well done. Cradling a bright-eyed hen under each arm, Charles slipped into the kitchen. He noted quickly the tangle of his mother's drawers mingled with his father's trousers on the floor. He paused instinctively, just short of the opening to the bedroom, without making his presence known. At the angle it was placed between the doorway and the bed, the old dresser, had its mirror not been cracked, would have too graphically revealed Rose and C. D. in the full throes of their lovemaking, but the broken mirror offered only multiple fragments of the scene of their thrusting, heaving motion and their partial nudity.

Charles felt his face flame. His stomach and throat seized and retched. He backed quickly and stealthily from the vision and slid out the door without a sound. Fiercely tossing each puzzled hen into the scrubby grassy area outside, Charles stormed to the opposite corner of the house to the long sweet grass that surrounded the fruit trees in the orchard. The pungent aroma of fallen apples, damaged and spoiling on the ground, stung his nostrils as he crept under the canopy of branches, hanging low with their burden of fruit.

After a while, Charles felt rather than heard a sound behind him and turned to see C. D. standing at the end of the porch looking toward him. C. D. spotted Charles in the shadows of the adjacent orchard even though Charles thought he had hidden himself well back under the thickest of branches. C. D. wore a half-smile of arrogance and satisfaction. His shirt was opened, revealing his well-muscled, hirsute chest. He smoked a cigarette down to the butt, then flipped it over his shoulder onto a barren patch of the would-be lawn. Giving Charles a casual nod, he returned to the house.

Six

*A*nd the days of summer passed, but not so quickly as Charles would have them. Time on the farm passed slowly; there were few opportunities for social interaction with other young people. Charles longed for relief to his boredom.

Due to Rose's effort, the house, over the summer, became livable. The clean look of newly whitewashed walls and spare rough furniture with its simple lines lent it the minimalist temporary look of a summer home. Graceful bouquets of wildflowers, strategically placed, and the rich patina of the single ornate silver candelabra, Rose's only inheritance apart from the trunk and a rocking chair from her family long since dead, lent their charm to the family's rooms. Her improvised decorating was born of need, a chic austerity perhaps harkening back to some faint inherited memory of an ethnic flavor. Her Norwegian grandparents would have been comfortable in Rose's home. Their massive flat-topped painted trunk had been pressed into service as a primitive sideboard in the dining room. Her touches marked the home as hers, as did the ruffle from her second-best petticoat that became a pristine white curtain for the bedroom that she and C. D. shared. A banquet cloth, once discarded from the Hotel Lincoln, was darned and re-embroidered over worn spots and holes by Rose and served as a counterpane over the bleached sheets covering the feather tick. The yardage from her wool plaid skirt, draped and swagged just so, caught back with lengths of scarlet ribbon, graced the windows of their small sitting room.

Charles stubbornly resisted her attention to his bedchamber, preferring the stern severity of a monk's cell. The room formerly designated as the parlor served as an anteroom to the bedroom. The parlor with its sole occupant, a derelict piano, served to hold his few pieces of clothing. Rose fashioned curtains over the west window to shut out the heat of the afternoon sun, but otherwise abandoned her attempts to bring comfort to the room. The plastered walls had long ago been ripped out, exposing the clapboard siding of the old house. His wooden bedstead, abandoned by a previous tenant, was made of Osage orange tree limbs that had begun their sapling life as hedgerow fences. No pictures graced his faded gray walls.

Another dimension, hard work, was added to Charles's life during those long summer months. He began to hire out to neighboring farmers who frequently needed a hand for some portion of their summer work. Planting, putting up hay, then threshing, separation of the wheat from the chaff, and later picking field corn. It was his work, in addition to Rose's, again as a dressmaker, that put food on their family's table and bought their few necessities. He became, in fact and in practice, the manager of the family fortunes.

When he didn't have work at others' behest, Charles turned to the actual business of clearing the forgotten junk and overgrown weeds from their own family farmstead, repairing and painting the fences, tending the milk cow that placidly awaited the arrival of the mythical blooded stock from the likewise mythical ranch. The cow, a well-tended escapee from some neighboring farm, wandered down the lane one day and was promptly sequestered in the orchard. She was nondiscriminatory about who received her milk or otherwise cared for her.

Charles longed for diversion from the rigor of his self-imposed collection of precepts, yet like a piece of southern Iowa clay, his emerging perspective became less malleable as it was baked by the hot summer sun. His attitude coagulated and hardened like a scab on a wound. He put his childhood, his youth behind him and assumed the air of the possessor of divinely imparted wisdom, of maturity, never understanding its relative and arbitrary nature.

His self-consciousness translated into a quiet seriousness, an attitude of solicitous interest toward others that masked his condescension. In the egoism of youth, he imagined himself to be the only person to learn what he considered to be great truths of human nature. It was his self-inflicted indictment, a charge against his mental and emotional development, that he would not subject his rigid beliefs to the critical scrutiny of continued growth.

"No, ma'am. I don't need nothing from the library. Nothing there to do but look at books. I need to keep busy. No, Mama. High school isn't for me. We need the money I bring in—those high school boys don't know up from down. They need to get out in the real world like me. Algebra, geometry, football, baseball. None of that is going to help me in my work or put food on our table." He was proud that he could be a self-made man, more productive than his father and respected by members of the community.

Charles's physical features combined the best from each parent. Startling deep-set blue eyes contrasting with thick unruly hair of the same deep sable color as C. D.'s set off the burnished mahogany tan burned on by the summer sun. He affected no awareness of his appearance despite the attention it created for him. He was reserved and polite to the men for whom he worked, and to their satisfaction, affected a disinterested attitude in their daughters.

As was the custom, he took his noon meal, dinner, with the families for whom he labored. He displayed his best manners. He washed up at the basin of warm water offered on a bench outside the kitchen door, made sure to wash with lots of soap so that he didn't leave a grimy residue on the huck toweling. He wetted the common comb with water from the washbasin, combed his hair straight back, and entered the house by invitation through the kitchen door to take the place assigned him at the table. He bowed his head for grace, passed the dishes in the direction indicated by the rest of the family, spoke when spoken to, and otherwise kept his mouth shut and his eyes on his plate. His appearance was by far his most interesting characteristic.

The farmer's daughters were always happier to help their mothers in the kitchen when Charles Dawson was "the hand," and his presence at the table did not displease their mothers either. Daughters wore their best workaday dresses, perhaps spruced up with a new ribbon, and the women put on their best display of culinary skill, serving gargantuan meals from the maw of the cast-iron cook stove. "Charles, now help yourself to plenty. There's pot roast and gravy, mashed potatoes and coleslaw, and fresh-picked green beans. More biscuits coming right out of the oven in a minute. There's applesauce and tomatoes. Lucy there, pass Charles the butter 'n the jam for the biscuits. There's pie and cake both for dessert! Do you want coffee or milk with your meal?" The hospitality also called self-righteous attention to a woman's work, and to produce a fine meal was important. It was hard for a man whose wife didn't set a good table to hire help.

It was important to Charles that he secure a reputation as a good worker to counter the embarrassing image of his father. Charles assumed that all knew of C. D.'s reputation for shiftlessness and self-importance, while in truth the few that knew didn't really care. But Charles's egoism and obsessive fear that he and his parents were the subject of interest whenever a cluster of people met teetered on the edge of paranoia, and sometimes it descended.

C. D. delivered Rose, when she had work, in a secondhand, run-down buggy drawn by the spirited horse that C. D. bought for himself to ride. An automobile was a luxury far beyond their means. Charles had polished the buggy and the tack, but it was still obvious from the worn upholstery and loose wheels that the buggy had seen better days. That, coupled with the folly of a high-spirited horse that was not trained to being driven as opposed to ridden, made their trips into town an adventure worthy of notice. The saddle horse took exception to being pressed into duty with the buggy. Its limited experience with dragging a buggy with passengers made him first rear and plunge in the traces and then skitter ahead a few yards before stopping so suddenly the buggy threatened to overturn. Even C. D., the only family member who barely qualified to drive the recalcitrant beast, was hard put to maintain his aplomb as the conveyance stuttered and stopped only to lurch forward again; the passengers were, of necessity, constantly on their guard.

Charles preferred to walk the few miles to town or to be dropped off at the outskirts rather than brave the scrutiny and smiles that their arrival generated. He watched his parents' arrival from a safe distance as though they were only interesting strangers. He parted their company when they stopped just off the square at Philips Feed and Grain to buy a sack of oats even though he suspected that the high-spirited, five-gaited animal would not be bribed into submission to the yoke of the common carriage horse. He laughed to himself at the thought of C. D. trying to make a deal with the horse from hell. El Diablo, C. D. called him.

When the buggy clattered up to the rail in front of the Lockard Dry Goods Store in a cloud of dust, Rose was pink with embarrassment at the confusion of their arrival and C. D. equally flushed with exertion. They joined their neighbors for the traditional Saturday night in town, enhanced on this particular Saturday by the celebration called Old Settlers.

Charles was curious about it, having heard of Old Settlers from neighbors. The once-a-year festival had been hosted by the Town of Onansburg on the second Saturday of August every year since 1883 and featured not only a carnival but also contests and games for children during the morning and dances, cakewalks, musical performances, and programs featuring history and culture to adults during the afternoon and evening. Only a Chautauqua event he had once attended in a nameless Nebraska town had ever afforded him this kind of opportunity for entertainment. Even as he approached the center of town, when he could just barely catch the bright, hot scent of fresh popcorn, Charles could sense the carnival energy of the town square. Wagons loaded with families and buggies with couples hurried past him. Occasionally, someone for whom he had worked recognized him and saluted him with a wave and a smile, but Charles's taciturn disposition discouraged familiarity, so there were no friendly invitations to ride along or to join the family groups.

With no clear mission in mind, Charles shuffled along, self-consciously alone, his hands in his pockets, looking at store windows that were decorated in themes denoting the heritage and history of Onansburg. The store windows caught his solitary reflection in a cold, quiet void between the heat and light of commercial activity inside the store and the hurdy-gurdy bustle of the street; he regarded his appearance soberly, ever seeking his own approval. Others crowded around to peer into the windows, but he scrutinized only himself. Charles didn't know who he was, just who he was not, and his reflection gave him no clues.

Attracted by activity in the courtyard, Charles listened with interest to the last piece of the stirring performance by the fife and drum corps, the shrill pipe of the fifes over the drummed cadence. Charles couldn't help tapping his foot to the beat of the bass drum and the rattle of the snare drums. He smiled with pleasure at the performance. The quasi-military troop had been formed during the Spanish-American War to cheer the troops on to battle and then to welcome them home short months later. Older men, past the age of serving in the US Army when the troop was begun in 1898, they continued to practice and perform, an unofficial musical home guard.

"Hi, Mr. Byrd. Hi, Mr. Byrd. Over here, hi." One old gentleman interrupted his piping to wave to his grandchildren and to those youngsters who were current students from his Sunday school classes. Mr. Byrd had survived thirty years of teaching the fifth-grade boys' class.

Charles's disappointment that their performance ended was short-lived when he saw that the Onansburg town band next took the bandstand relinquished by the fifes and drums. After the months on the remote farm, the excitement from the festival of Old Settlers infected him. He watched with interest as the conductor stood at the podium and was impressed with the code of conduct followed by the musicians.

The band launched its performance with a John Philip Sousa march, "Semper Fidelis," after which Charles removed his hands from his pockets and applauded enthusiastically, forgetting his customary reserve. But looking around self-consciously, he scanned the faces in the crowd gathered for the performance; grandmothers and great-grandmothers had been accorded the privilege of seats on the board benches suspended between cement blocks. They sat nodding in time to the music, and some of the grandmas held babies or minded toddlers while their parents were busy. A few young people, seemingly well known to one another, teased back and forth between the segregated groups of boys and girls. Segregation between races was not a question in Onansburg; a long-standing town rule dictated that no person of color could spend the night in that small town. But the elderly Negro woman who had lived for years with old Doctor Ryan's widow was seemingly exempt from the statute, as evidenced by her presence on this night and by her acceptance by the community of Onansburg.

Charles's gaze swept over the groups but returned to focus on a particular girl. She stood almost by herself, not quite a part of any of the groups of young women, and he realized that her direct stare had commanded his attention. She lifted her arm and fluttered her fingers at him. Charles pressed his lips together, rubbed the back of his neck self-consciously, and examined the grass between his boots. And when he looked up, she was still staring, smiling directly at him.

He turned his head slowly and looked over his shoulder to see if there was someone else in line to receive the wave. The band began its last number, "Stars and Stripes Forever."

Confused, Charles turned away and walked toward the stores on the west side of the square. As he moved among the clusters and crowds of people, he looked back at the girl through the tunnel of darkness between the oasis of the bandstand in the center of the courtyard and the brightly lit storefronts. She was still watching him boldly. He knew both her name and that she lived on the next place east of theirs. She was older than he was. Nineteen to be exact, and the schoolteacher at Highlands Country School. He did not know, however, that she had caught his father's eye as well; that C. D. made regular forays to the Richards' farm ostensibly on business but always combined with the hope of seeing Miss Lydia.

Her mother's lineage occasionally produced a throwback to some early ancestor with olive skin and almond-shaped eyes so dark they were nearly black. With the addition of hooped earrings, Lydia could have been a gypsy, but her modest pastel summer dress with its ruffles and ribbons suited her poorly and spoiled the otherwise titillating but mysterious suggestion of the exotic. Instead, she looked awkward and raw-boned; her eyes were glittering black jet beads set above cheekbones so high that her face seemed disproportionately arranged under the tousled mop of dark curls that defied any order. Her features were large, bordering on coarse, but Lydia possessed an air of guileless sensuality that both confused and alarmed her parents. She refused convention, preferring the rough-and-tumble games and strenuous fieldwork of boys to the indoor activities of sewing and embroidery and kitchen work. Her frank admiration of men and boys and their ways had, in a sense, ensured her innocence.

When Lydia played catcher on the team with the guys and squatted behind home plate, wearing bloomers and a middy blouse, her mother despaired of her daughter's athletic prowess; there was no offset of pride in homemaking skills. If Lydia played in the field, she could sling the naughty chatter like the best of the boys. Young men of her own age, having known her since childhood, had not awakened to her charms that were too obvious to strangers like Charles and the nefarious C. D. Her male friends of her own age saw her as a companion, a rival to be bested in games and contests. And Lydia did not know that she could not best all men, unlike her local compatriots at their games.

Lydia was the teacher of Highlands Country School by both default and attrition. She had attended classes there in the one-room school, shared by children in grades one through eight, until the eighth grade and then went on to graduate from Onansburg High School. Many of her friends did not attend classes beyond the eighth grade, and some didn't attend beyond the sixth grade. Molly Simpson's mother died in childbirth, and she was needed at home to take care of little brothers and sisters. Jenny Shoop, with her crossed eyes and thick glasses, had no aptitude for school and so was excused from higher education after sixth grade. Elda Thomas's parent saw no need for a girl to know more than she had learned as an eighth grader.

As they completed eighth grade, some boys went to work on family farms, and some went on to high school. One bright young man, particularly ill suited for life on the farm after finishing high school, went away to Iowa State Teachers College in Cedar Falls for two years, but came back to teach at Onansburg High School. The position of teacher for grades one through eight at Highland Country School had fallen to Lydia Richards. The position would be hers until she married.

Charles had not so much as spoken a word with Lydia; she was older. He had no attraction to her even when he worked for her father and ate at the same table. He was always too painfully aware of himself to notice more than the business at hand, but now he examined his memory for what he knew of her. He remembered her seated across the table from him, and as a disembodied voice from behind the screen door of the kitchen informing him that "Mama's just dishing up; come on in to the table." And he remembered her downcast eyes when he made his obligatory "Much obliged, ma'am," to her mother for the meal.

That she was worthy of his notice was not in question, but rather what her interest was in him. He pondered the question over the next few days. His mind kept flashing to her image smiling and laughing at him as he walked away from the lights of the bandstand. He transformed the scene in his memory to picture her wearing a dark red, near crimson-colored dress with the brassy gleam of the band instruments surrounding her. And she smiled wickedly at him, beckoning him closer. Then, shaking his head as if to clear it, he would see her again as she was, a girl, not quite woman, in her ill-suited homemade dress.

August was hot and dry. The sparse grass turned down and crunched underfoot. Only an occasional thunderstorm wetted the hard-packed soil but it was enough to ensure the crops did not wither and die in the fields. Charles went to town on Saturday night a few more times through August, but the magic of Old Settlers was gone. Sometimes, he saw Lydia from a distance; she smiled and waved, but there was no hint of an unspoken message that had so confused him before. He had come to know a few more of the young people from the farms nearby through working either with them or for their fathers, but no one from town. Even as he nodded to young men waiting on customers in their fathers' stores, he felt uncertain and awkward in their presence. It was as though he had forgotten he had been a town boy himself, having lived in small cities all his life until Onansburg; he identified with C. D.'s and Rose's defeats as banishment to a lower status and could only work for the day when he could take his place in town with a good job. Charles was a natural to hard work on the farm, but he knew it would bring him none of the attention or recognition he deserved. None of the good, solid values of farm life inspired him.

The fighting rooster that Charles and Rose had come to call "Cock of the Walk" did interest Charles, however. The wily bird made frequent appearances but gave no hint of interest in his human neighbors or of becoming a domestic bird. While he performed the ceremonial duty of crowing at daybreak, his only other concession to the occupants of the farm was to examine the domestic chicken feed with some amount of interest. Charles intended to capitalize on that interest and to let the bird's taste for commercially prepared food betray him. Charles wanted to own the fighting cock, and the fowl's defiance of his intention irked him.

Now that he had come to know a few neighbors, he elicited the information that indeed the rented farm had once been a site for illegal cock fighting. A tenant on the old Butler place, one Les Randall, had sponsored a short series of fights in the derelict barn. A partially dismantled arena in the barn bore rusty, blood-stained evidence of its purpose. Charles's plan was to catch Cock of the Walk, train him to fight, and reinstitute the illegal sport right there in their own barn. Lack of any real knowledge of the clandestine sport didn't dampen his ambition; the first goal was to catch the bird.

Through the month of August and into September, Charles attempted, at least once each day, to snare Cock of the Walk. Box traps with a full measure of food failed, as did flinging a musty fishing net that Charles had found abandoned in the barn. By late August, discouraged by his futile attempts, Charles crafted a plan that finally succeeded in trapping Cock of the Walk in the corner of one of the empty pens in the barn.

For a week, Charles logged Cock's customary haunts and habits in his mind. A free agent in contrast to the domestic hens, nights found Cock outside and roaming about the farm in contrast to the recently purchased flock of setting hens, who were closed in the decrepit chicken house at dusk. Mornings found him companionably scratching at feed scattered in the newly enclosed chicken pen, all the while keeping watch against varmints or other intruders. Afternoons were spent on sentry duty in the guard-tower opening of the haymow. Cock had chosen the location of the showdown. Charles chose September 15 as the day of reckoning.

Charles entered the barn through the main door beneath the door of the haymow overhead. Seemingly disinterested in Cock's whereabouts, he cleared the soft piles of long since decayed dung from the main arena as though engaged in routine chores. Ever curious, Cock fluttered down from the haymow to perch on a sagging gate meant to confine cattle or horses and watched as Charles raked the waste toward the main door of the barn.

The worn but intact wooden door was mounted on a track, sliding open and closed on steel wheels attached to the top of the door. While corroded, resistant, and disused, Charles had cleaned and lubricated the hardware earlier during the week. It was noisily functional. Charles both tugged and pushed the door shut, sliding it, screeching, along its predetermined path. He closed and locked the smaller access door in and out of the barn with sliding bolt locks that he found in a pile of discarded scrap metal hinges, hasps, and pins. And Charles thought with his plans complete, he had as good as won.

Cock jumped to the ground to get a better look at Charles as he struggled with the barn door. Now, as the combatants took the measure of one another for the final battle, Cock eyed Charles warily, sensing the inevitability of the showdown. In the arena, now again the site of a cockfight, Charles stalked Cock back and forth in ever-smaller quarter circles, rushing closer to cut off any attempt he made to dart to safety. After several feints and parries, with nowhere to fly within the confines of the pen made by two solid walls and with Charles cutting off any possible escape route, Cock stood motionless except for the nervous dart of the amber eyes. A rivulet of sweat traced its way down Charles's face from his temple, and he slowly sank into a low crouch; the popping crack of his knee joints, the sudden noise in the hot and musty old barn, startled both opponents, breaking their concentration momentarily.

Charles straightened and tried to make eye contact with the nervous bird. They resumed their contest, Charles creeping closer and closer to a now motionless Cock. Slowly, slowly, Charles brought his arms up to a position ready to pounce, grab Cock, and fall on top of him. His plan was to use his own weight to render the bird powerless to use his spurs. But the canny bird was a veteran of opponents with more formidable instinct and experience than Charles. Sensing the moment Charles was ready to spring, Cock seized the initiative. He struck first, flying at Charles in a fury of shrieking and feathers, beating his wings against Charles's face and upper body to distract attention from the fighting bird's real weapons, the sharp, horned spurs.

With a scream of surprise and pain, Charles fell back onto the floor, and Cock escaped, leaving Charles, his trunk and arms and thighs slashed and bleeding, on the dusty floor of the arena. The pain gave way to rage, then to pain again. Gasping in shock, hardly daring to examine himself, Charles looked down, noting the rents in his clothing even as the white-hot pain of his wounds began to register. Blotches of bright blood began to appear on his cotton trousers, on the front of the striped work shirt. Quickly, he dropped his trousers, ripped open the buttons of his shirt. His stomach lurched and rolled sickeningly as he inspected his injuries. The striated gashes opened wide and deep below his breastbone, extended to his thighs. Only Charles's crouched position had saved his genitals.

Charitable in victory, having disarmed and beaten his enemy, Cock of the Walk vanished for several days while Charles, laid up by the several deep cuts in addition to the many scratches and scrapes inflicted in the battle, recuperated. When Charles stumbled into the yard dripping with blood, Rose had taken over, mustered C. D. to hitch the horse, and loaded Charles into the buggy. As a seamstress, she recognized the need for finer work than she could manage, and Rose negotiated the transaction, offering her services as a dress-maker to Doctor Ryan's wife. Stitches for stitches, as it were.

For the next few days, Charles reveled in the attention Rose lavished on him. She bathed and dressed his wounds daily per the doctor's instructions and generally gave him nearly all her attention with especially tasty dishes to tempt his appetite, reading aloud to him from a copy of *Riders of the Purple Sage*, Zane Grey's novel that she found discarded in the drawer of one of the abandoned dressers. The deep slashes on his chest and legs made him feverish and stiff. His injuries seemed out of proportion to his opponent, as did the effort spent planning his next strategy, a shortsighted revenge. He reveled in the plan he made even while he gave up his vision of him-self as the master of a magnificent fighting bird.

Lying on his uneven featherbed, his eyes hot and bright with fever and his forehead burning, Charles was confused; sometimes it was Rose moving softly into the bedroom, wringing out towels from the basin of cool water from the deep cistern. At others, it was Lydia. But this Lydia was the Lydia of his dreams in her gypsy earrings and satin dress. She smiled and flirted. "Charles, my Charles." She touched him lightly, caressing his face with her fingers, smoothing his eyelids shut so that he could sleep and dream of her. The brilliant color of her crimson dress reflected through the translucent skin of his eyelids, and her fingers danced their way downward over his body, carefully avoiding his wounds. Her hands found him under the cotton sheet, encouraging, promising. He felt the surge of his blood. But then, stir-ring to consciousness and willing himself to peer through the dark curtain of lashes from behind still-lowered eyelids, he knew he was alone in the room. The makeshift curtains moved silently at the open window, and he thought for a moment that she had just disappeared through their folds. He croaked her name, but it was Rose, not Lydia, who came to do his bidding. Dismayed, he looked down at the wet stickiness spreading through the sheet that covered him. A quixotic image flashed across the screen of his imagination, and he unwillingly revisited his foolish fantasies of his mother, not understanding their significance. He was grateful that Rose feigned interest in the view from the window.

A golden September passed into a bronzed October, and Charles recovered from his injuries. After the sickness of the acute fever passed, no one would have been aware of his wounds. He resumed his jobs even while still pale and drawn from the pain of the injuries. But now, during the hot days of the so-called Indian summer when he worked in the fields, he always wore his shirt to cover the jagged lines of angry pink scars that raked the smooth tan skin of his chest. Only his parents would have marked the change in an already taciturn nature, that he was more withdrawn and sullen with misdirected anger and resentment. Rose and C. D. had not asked more than indifferent questions about the injuries, having been aware of Charles's crusade if not his intentions toward Cock. But Charles seethed over what he saw as his humiliation by a smaller, less cunning adversary.

C. D. procured the shotgun that Charles requested and for which he paid secondhand, even against Rose's protest that she didn't like guns in her home. But C. D. overruled her on the basis of "teaching the boy to hunt." With fall would come pheasant and quail hunting; it would be nice to supplement their plain fare with the game birds. C. D. won the gun in a poker game financed with Charles's cash earnings. (It was testimony to the limited vision of father and son that they did not see the potential for a business venture, given C. D.'s skill at poker and Charles's money.) Charles willingly spent additional dollars from his carefully hoarded savings to buy enough shells for target practice, and C. D. encouraged Charles. Availing himself of both Charles's gun and his ammunition, C. D. practiced too, the gentlemanly sport of the gentleman farmer. C. D. liked the idea of hunting and shooting, patterning himself after the hero of a book he read once. If this wasn't Scotland, this was Iowa, but C. D. could rationalize his lifestyle so long as others could support him.

With single-minded purpose, Charles practiced until he had fair assurance that he could hit a target. On that day, he turned to the matter at hand, setting out to visit all of Cock's regular roosts until he found him. He came upon him at the first place he looked, as if by appointment, perching on a burned-out tree stump in the small pasture that was part of the barnyard. Cock stood on the fence, next to his companion, Pansy, the cow. Charles had laid his plan carefully. Along with target practice, Charles planned a final encounter.

The bright red comb cresting his proud head shone near orange in the bright sun. His feathers lay smooth, sleek and glistening, red and orange, amber and green. Cock turned to face his adversary expectantly, perhaps looking forward to another round of the battle. Charles gave him no quarter.

Rose, summoned by the sound of gunfire so close to the house, called out to Charles from the porch. "What did you shoot, Charles? Did you see a varmint?" Hurrying closer to inspect the kill, Rose met Charles on the path as he stalked back toward the house. Her eyebrows arched high in question, Rose caught at his arm, exclaiming, "Honey-Boy? What is it? A fox? A weasel?" His lips were pulled flat against his teeth in a tight smile, and he made no reply. Charles shrugged past the puzzled Rose. Climbing up to the second board of the fence and with her hand shading her eyes, she looked to see the kill. The bright spatters of blood over the grass and dirt directed her gaze to the small body lying motionless, dead, in the dust. The half-closed eyes were glazed. Already, the iridescent plumage seemed dull.

The puzzled Rose met the calm gaze of the sandy brown milk cow, the silent witness. The gentle animal had become a pet to Rose, an anthropomorphic friend. "Oh, Pansy!" she breathed weakly, grateful for the animal's calm presence, yet unsure of the source of her own misgivings. Her blood pounded in her head, throbbing in the glare of the sun, and her mind, though it churned questions, found no answers. She climbed carefully down from the fence. She first thought to walk back toward the house, to where Charles had disappeared with the gun. Then, instead, she opened the gate and slowly entered the barnyard pen. Carefully fastening the latch behind her, Rose waited until Pansy ambled closer. Taking a deep breath, she gradually loosened her clenched fists, scarcely noticing the pain where her fingernails had dug neat half-moons into the fleshy pads at the base of her thumbs. She passed her hand carefully between the curved horns and absently scratched Pansy's head. The cow's tail and ears twitched flies unceasingly, and she stomped her neat hooves. Some of the same flies began to buzz over Cock of the Walk, and their feasting on the sticky blood prompted Rose to act.

Grimly, she fetched the deeply rounded grain shovel from the barn and scooped up the small body from the dirt. With one hand on the handle, the other supporting the bowl of the shovel at the neck, she carried the burden to the open field. The weight of the shovel far exceeded that of Cock. Under a line of trees that bordered a fencerow, Rose clumsily dug a shallow grave with the heavy tool and laid the ruined body in it.

Charles turned seventeen in March while they were on the Butler place. Childhood had been, for Charles, a category tied to age only and which had never been defined as special or exempt from certain requirements, but it was devoid of certain privileges. Charles completed school upon graduation from eighth grade, and the remainder of his preparation for adult life came by experience. If he was a man at seventeen, he was a man limited by his own definitions and yet defined by his own limitations.

When John Richards asked Charles if he would be interested in hiring on as his permanent hand, a move that might have put him in an opportune position from which to pursue one of Richards's four daughters, especially Lydia, Charles solemnly told Richards he would consider it and let him know. After two months of deliberation, it shouldn't have been a surprise that Richards hired the Becker boy. John Richards had offered opportunity, and Charles, his coyness masquerading in the posture of careful thinking that he didn't want to seem too eager to leap at the opportunity, watched it come and go. When Charles protested that he meant to take the job, Richards's expression turned severe, and his response was derisive.

A tall man, and gaunt, Richards tugged his wide-brimmed straw hat down farther to better shade his eyes and looked down at Charles from the advantage of his superior height. "Son, I made you a good offer at decent money. You never told me you were so much as interested." He turned and stalked away.

———————

By default, Charles and Rose both recognized a new reality. For Charles, it was a welcome escape from the old Butler farm, as it was still known. For Rose, it was time to start over as she had so many times before, but this time without the overriding presence of C. D. This time, it was without the liability or responsibility to save C.D. from his own foibles.

———————

After C. D.'s ill-timed demise some years of folly later, Rose managed her grief and collected herself, landing on her feet as always, and even the shameful circumstances of C. D.'s death in the arms of another woman did not shake her resolute faith in herself. She set up a small shop in town from which she did tailoring and dressmaking, marked only by a discrete sign in the window: FINE SEWING.

At first, she lived in the two small rooms at the back of the shop, but later she bought the small home in which Sonny remembered her. She was frequently sought after to help out when families from the large homes on Drake Avenue were entertaining, having parties, weddings, baptisms, christenings. Rose's style and deft touch with food, flowers, and table settings made her service an enviable asset. "Mrs. Dawson will be coming to me to help out" became a mark of distinction among polite society of Onansburg. And, once her reputation was established, Rose could afford to be selective about where she chose to help out.

When, as children, Cloris, Dolores, and Sonny went to visit Grandma Rose, they coaxed her to tell them stories of when she and the grandpa they never knew camped out at the old Butler place. With elaborate parties of bread and butter sandwiches and cambric tea made of warm water, milk, sugar, and just a hint of real tea, Rose regaled them with jolly stories with no hint of the strange events so formative in their father Charles's life. That she took artistic license and colored in the details much differently was her privilege, she reasoned.

She spun endless yarns of the family's life on the farm. The children's favorites were the invented stories of the complex social lives of the wonderfully educated dogs and kittens that lived at the farm. Perhaps for Rose, the mythical animals she told the children about filled a void of longing or of loneliness. The animals always came with a name and a distinct personality designed by Rose; there was Petrice, Stan, Crooked Tail Ed, Mama Kitty, and collectively, they were known as the little Tit-Tats. But fiction can be kinder than truth. No dogs or cats were ever allowed to stay on the farm.

At the farm, Rose always tried to understand when Charles announced to her that one of the animals could not stay; they were a nuisance, he said. We can't afford to feed them, was the reason. And while Rose regretted their loss, she did not argue with Charles. And she didn't want to trust her intuition. Even then, she feared what she didn't understand about her son. She knew enough about rural life to know that the cats kept pests like rats and mice at bay and earned their keep on a farm. She did so regret that the companionable, short-legged toy terrier that had come as a stray was useless as a farm dog. Years later, Rose would have flashes of memory of the little spotted dog she called Tootsie looking wistfully back to her as Charles led her away on a length of frayed rope. She hoped that Charles disposed of her kindly and hated herself for her doubts. Even then she feared what she didn't understand about her son. Without the meager protection C. D. had afforded her, she deferred to Charles when confrontation or unpleasantness presented itself.

Grandma Rose's house was a warm memory for Sonny, a sense of being whole and complete when he was there. It became a sanctuary for Charles's children despite his disapproval of what he called his mother's frivolous nature. Rose frequently had one child or another to sleep over in the little room under the eaves. As little girls, Cloris and Dolores frequently vied over the privilege of spending a night away from home. At bedtime, Rose produced a small assortment of quiet toys she had miraculously saved from her own childhood. Long after Cloris was too old to be intrigued by the treasures, she pretended it was only to play with Dolores that she deigned to play tea party or with dollies.

A miniature teapot with no lid and one chipped cup. A tiny kaleidoscope, its brown leather cover camouflaging the jewels hidden inside. The tin-head Minerva doll with her painted complexion pockmarked with chips and dents, but complete with a wonderfully hand-sewn wardrobe to grace her blocky, sawdust-filled body. Rose frequently remarked to her clients that having the little ones around made her think of her happiest days, when Charles was a babe, when she and C. D. were young.

Rose's candor allowed the circumstances of C. D.'s shiftless life and ignominious death to fade quietly into Onansburg's long-term memory. If Rose had taken a stance of outraged virtue over the faithless husband, there might have been the opposite effect, but the forked tongues of the village harpies could take no pleasure in wagging about Rose. Her gentle composure and acceptance disarmed their vitriolic gossip and allowed a measure of sympathy to be doled out for her.

She paid a call to Georgia Someone after C. D.'s death, and it was said she spoke gently to Georgia, expressing her regret for the discomfiting circumstances and for her distress. As is the way, no one assumed the personal knowledge of the call; rather it was the collective "they" who told the tale. "They say" was the most frequent and best source of reliable information for the kind of news that was never published in the *Choctaw County Republican.*

Rose remained a beautiful woman; her body retained its youthful suppleness. And her beautiful hands on which she lavished time and attention were her livelihood. Their strength, likewise her character, belied her otherwise fragile appearance. Long after Rose's death, when he sometimes couldn't picture her face, Sonny could remember her hands, how they looked and how they felt, the smooth skin on the backs of her hands in contrast to the fine-webbed network of tiny creases etched under her eyes and over her upper lip.

As a child, when her attention was taken by others in his presence, he amused himself examining her hands, turning them over, back and forth, studying their contours and planes. Her arm became a road for an imaginary horse that Sonny never tired of riding. His fingers trotted up and down the arm, perhaps going as far as her neck before descending, skipping and slipping down the imaginary cliff of her shoulder, down the steep road.

Seven

---

*L*eaving his recollections of his childhood behind and turning reluctantly back toward the store, Sonny drove across the black asphalt ribbon of Highway 30. He felt a distinct longing to turn onto the rolling corridor of the old Lincoln Highway, to drive and drive, rolling along until he could go no further, clear to California, right into the ocean, maybe to China. Take 30 right on into China! Coasting along without thought, without purpose, never thinking, no turning back. Right on into oblivion.

Sonny sometimes wondered if they should have tried to take a trip abroad; he suddenly regretted never taking Polly to London, Paris, Portugal, or Spain, the faraway places they had seen only by viewing their friends' snapshots and slides. He always thought foreign travel presented too many challenges, too many obstacles for them.

I'll never know now. Could she have gone without me? On a tour with her friends.

Even while he thought of her traveling to foreign destinations, he was perversely comforted knowing she would never have gone without him. His mind immediately glimpsed a distant fantasy of her in pink, always in pink, at the Coliseum, the Louvre.

Did my own issues about such a journey cheat her? She knew I was cautious about travel, but I would have done anything for

Polly! Now I look back at all the things she hadn't done or seen. Because of me? And babies! What a wonderful mother she would have been.

Sighing deeply, Sonny decided not to torture himself further, at least not now. Intuitively, he knew such thoughts, like picking a scab, were counterproductive to the healing process, that they wouldn't help him get through this day.

A day at a time! Just a damn day at a time!

Just as he turned onto the town square, he saw the little covey of Carlson children, the older brother looking after his two younger sisters and his younger brother. He waved to the children, dispiritedly lifting only the fingers of his right hand from its one o'clock position on the wheel. They hurriedly danced their way across the hot pavement already sticky and soft from the morning sun, gingerly lifting one bare foot after the other, elbows lifted high in quick-step rhythm like dancing puppets across a stage.

A surprising swirl of dry leaves clattered noisily around them, incongruous in the summer heat. The leader called out a hello to Sonny with a broad grin. Sonny slowed to a stop and smiled back at the children, forcing himself to roll the electric window down and exchange greetings. Sonny's mind fired scenes, one after the other, of summer childhood into his memory; he could smell and feel and taste them.

The last few days of summer for the children. Like ex-patriots from their own history, they could never go back to the summers of their childhood, the blessed golden time, self-defined and marked forever in memory. A protected time and place inhabited too briefly and to which they could never return. Lazy, long days of freedom under the scalding sun. The refuge of a secret, mossy spot never before discovered by the world. Summer apples warmed by the sun and eaten unwashed, the juice spilling onto chins and the small hands holding them.

The delicious twilight of droning cicadas; the supplication of calling voices of the quasi-prisoners of children's games; give me a wave, give me a wave! The night songs of birds while daylight was yet again reluctantly tucked into the western horizon by the descending darkness. The yellow porch light against which mindless moths danced their lives away heedless of the rest of the world, driven by their fatal addiction to the fool's gold. Stuffy hot bedrooms, the cells of muggy heat to which sweaty somnolents were sentenced, giggling and complaining until the sandman came and carried them sweetly away.

Grudgingly, Sonny allowed himself glimpses of family memories that were not shrouded in prohibitions or remonstrance. A few evenings spent at the Onansburg municipal swimming pool, he and Dolores proudly showing their parents what they had learned in swimming lessons. Both Cloris and Dolores had taken lessons in years past, but Sonny hadn't taken lessons until he was five years old. He remembered five as the magic number. At five, he could go to school, and the summer after, he was allowed to take swimming lessons. When Sonny was age five, Cloris was already fifteen and well past taking lessons but not past parading around the pool in her modest swimsuit, garnering appreciation from boys and men alike. They couldn't know of the bruises, scabs, and scratches that covered her backside beneath the swimsuit.

Suddenly, Sonny suddenly couldn't wait for summer to be over, to be gone and to take his pain with it. He ached aloud. Time passes too slowly for the grieving, and he had been promised that time would heal; the morning had already gone on too long. *The days are a hundred years long without her.*

Unable to postpone the store any longer, Sonny directed the car to the square; as he pulled into the parking lot directly behind the store, he caught a glimpse of Thelma Jane peering out through the lone window at the back side of the store, her hand shadowing her eyes against the glare of the sun. With a self-conscious wave, she turned away from the window, probably to alert Ruby that he had finally arrived.

Sonny glanced at his watch, the Rolex that he had coveted so long before Polly had given it to him in 1987 on the twentieth anniversary of the day they met. July 15th of 1967. Sonny's memory flipped back to Polly, the way she looked when they first met. She had been Drennan's girl then. And Drennan. Drennan had always been a good-looking man. Tall, near six feet, four inches in lofty contrast to Polly's petite frame. And, for that matter, in contrast to Sonny's angular stature. Drennan was dark in contrast to Polly's fair coloring and soft gentle features, the Shaw dimple prominent on her chin.

Why the hell should I think about Drennan now. God! He's been in and out of town so many times over the years . . . why let it bother me now? He and Polly were lovers! So what! And Polly chose me! Goddammit, she chose me!

Sonny lifted his leather case from the back seat and started for the store, then shifted it to his left hand so that he could punch in the combination to the lock on the back door. He glanced back to check that he had cracked the car window for air to circulate. Briefly, he checked the sky and confirmed to himself that no rain was in sight; it would be a scorcher. Pausing just inside the door to accustom himself to the gloom was a ruse; he knew the inside of the store like the back of his hand. Someone had forgotten to switch on the back-room lights. His omnipresent aversion to darkness kicked in; he was ever wary of shadows, boxes, and shelving units. The full head of the mop standing erect in the scrub bucket gave him a momentary start.

No matter, he thought. The front of the store was always brightly lit during the hours the store was open, but the front room and back rooms were lit only by security lights at night, which turned off automatically at seven a.m.

He took a deep breath and went on through the narrow corridors of inventory stored on sturdy steel and plank shelving, then emerged onto the showroom floor to find Thelma Jane and Ruby very busy. Thelma Jane was unpacking and restocking the shelves with the new lunch boxes, complete with thermoses. Ruby was dusting merchandise on display in the plumbing supply section. Plumbing supplies, elbows and joints, bore a rudimentary resemblance to the surgical supply cabinet in an orthopedic operating room. She dusted a different section of the store daily with the turkey feather duster, which, for the rest of the day, would ride her backside, ready for instant use, tucked into the strings of her apron. It looked almost as glorious on Ruby as it had on its original owner, the feathers bobbing up and down and back and forth with the action of her large buttocks.

Sonny rested his briefcase against the wall and then stood at the back of the showroom until both women, having heard him enter the heavy outside door, turned inquisitively to him. "Sonny?" Both women spoke at the same time.

"Just take a few minutes, will you? This's a different day for us, for all of us. Let's have a cup of coffee and . . ." Sonny's voice cracked and broke. He forgot temporarily the remarks he'd planned to share. He'd been sympathetic to their grief and had planned to put them at ease.

He began again with false heartiness. "Ruby, do we have some fresh coffee? I could sure use a cup!"

He realized that he hadn't drunk his morning coffee requirement yet, hadn't eaten any breakfast.

The three of them trooped single file to the room that was more kitchen than lounge. Ruby busied herself with the coffee, pouring for the three of them, while Thelma Jane carefully arranged three cinnamon rolls on a tray from under a foil-covered baking pan. Sonny looked hopefully at the unexpected treats. She offered them to Sonny for him to have first choice, along with a white napkin. She kept her eyes shyly cast aside. Thelma Jane exhibited the same affectation as Princess Diana, always looking aside, never directly at the subject of her attention, from beneath lowered lashes.

When all were served and chewing dutifully, Sonny leaned against the counter and regarded the two women thoughtfully. Ruby broke the silence at the same time Sonny started to speak. A few awkward gestures later, Sonny spoke. He reminded them that it would be back to serving the customers who had no doubt missed the conveniences and merchandise provided by the store. "Business. Business as usual. Let's just try to carry on today."

Sonny had hoped that the two would be ready to go to work, with no further commiseration or sympathy. But even as he spoke, tears welled up in Thelma Jane's eyes, and Ruby's face reflected her sadness.

"Well," Sonny began again, relying on his planned remarks, "it's going to be different for all of us, that's for sure. But, let's try to keep on. We probably won't be too busy with customers this morning; folks won't be sure we're open yet, so let's just keep busy. We've plenty to do."

Having outlined his talking points in his mind earlier, Sonny paused briefly, remembering Larry's sadness of the night before, but then rushed on. "Oh, and we won't be needing Larry anymore. I'm going to have plenty of time to do some of the things that he did and there's no need for . . . " Sonny broke off when he met the eyes of the two women. Ruby's mouth fell open, and a frown creased Thelma Jane's forehead, reinforcing the already permanent lines.

"Like I said," he continued resolutely, "we won't be needing Larry. I'll let him know when he comes in tonight to sweep up. He can go ahead and clean up the rest of the week through Saturday and then I'll pay him two weeks' severance."

Ruby crumpled up the last of her cinnamon roll with her napkin and neatly deposited it under the swinging lid of the plastic trashcan. She left the room noiselessly on her crepe-soled sensible Oxfords. Thelma Jane left her roll on its napkin at the edge of the counter and, turning her back to Sonny, began to wash the coffee cups in the sink.

Dammit. Why did I even mention Larry to the two of them? My business is no business of theirs. But then he recognized he was being defensive and surly.

"Sonny," she said, her voice muffled under the sound of the running water, "Larry was already here this morning. He brought the cinnamon rolls; Julia made them for us. And he left a note for you. Ruby put it with your mail, but Larry said you would know what it is about."

"I'll be in the office, Thelma Jane. Doing some paperwork and making some phone calls. I need to catch up."

Sonny retrieved his briefcase and left the room, sparing himself the sight of the tears on Thelma Jane's fluttering lashes. He opened the door to his unlocked office and, noting the wire basket heaped with mail, nudged it through the door with his foot. Light from the store's overhead lights darted into the room.

Sonny propped the door open behind him with his briefcase and paused a moment to shrug off his tension, then reached back to the right to flip the wall switch. Sonny abhorred walking into dark rooms where they were filled with incomprehensible shadows, noises with an overlay of threats.

The ceiling fixture blinked the room into life. A small twelve-foot-square room, it had been carved out from the stockroom but afforded privacy for telephone calls and files. Polly had insisted on it having the few amenities that it boasted: good lamps augmenting the overhead fixture, a comfortable leather desk chair, carpet on the floor in contrast to the tiled floor of the rest of the building. His handsome mahogany desk occupied the center of the room, facing the door. The room's only serious flaw was that the doorway to the concrete steps to the basement opened from the office, a problem they had been unable to avoid when redesigning the layout of the store in 1988.

Still leaning against the door, his gaze took in the dust that had settled on the surface of the desk, on the computer table. As Sonny had regarded his office as his personal retreat from the common areas of the store, Polly had always cleaned his office. While the door was always unlocked, he knew none of the three employees would enter if he were not there. He winced at the sight of the drooping head of a Polly-pink rose in its Waterford bud vase just beneath the desk lamp. Could it have just been earlier on the day she died that Polly brought it to him? It seemed a lifetime ago. He tried to ignore its faded presence.

Crouching beneath the desk, Sonny plugged in the electrical cords to the computer and printer. Fearful of errant electrical storms, he was always careful to unplug both when he left at night. He switched on the desk lamp and lifted the basket of mail to the console behind his desk. Ruby made it her job to gather the mail from beneath the mail slot on the front door where Stinky Little dropped it when he made the early morning delivery, the so-called business route. With the proliferation of direct mail marketing, the polished brass mail slot in the old door was woefully inadequate; Stinky forced the delivery through in relays, catalogs and magazines first, then circulars and advertising, then first-class mail. Sonny sighed when he recognized the task of sorting and attending to it.

Despite a nonverbal warning to himself, Sonny's gaze traveled to the framed photographs, a collection of which was grouped on the console on the wall behind the desk. And to the eight-by-ten of Polly and himself, a copy of the one taken for the church directory. The pictorial directory was a newer innovation to Little Flock Church, judged both a convenient resource to some and an affront to those who saw no need for pictures and addresses of folks they'd always known. The Outreach and Membership Committee had fostered the directory, and even if it had no other good use, it gave families a likeness of loved ones who might not have otherwise bothered to have a formal photograph taken. A service indeed to have captured a likeness of one who passed away even before the proofs were received. With a few steps, he crossed the room and studied the portrait of Polly and himself.

Sonny thought back to the silly photographer that had posed them, arranging their limbs and appendages in an uncomfortable pose, his thumb tucked under the hand that rested on Polly's shoulder just so. A seedy man in appearance with brown shoes, the leather of which was so scuffed and the heels so rundown they more resembled velvet house slippers than street shoes, he seemed unsuitable for many lines of work, including that of snapping pictures of strangers in a church basement. Despite his foolish jokes and the cheery "Jesus loves you" that had challenged them both to a pleasant expression, they smiled confidently, happily, into the lens of the camera. Just last January! Who would have guessed that Polly would be gone in a few short months? If only he had known that Polly's tender heart had put her in jeopardy! Irrationally, he thought if only he had known, he could have prevented her death, he could have controlled her fate.

"And the sparrow shall fall from her nest," a phrase from an anthem the church choir had sung, repeated itself over and over in his mind. He thought of residents whom they knew at the Friendly Manor Nursing Home, some imprisoned in worn, frail bodies and others robust in body but with failing minds. They called on Susan Henderson, bedridden after a fall that broke her hip. She would never walk again, and told anyone who would listen that she prayed daily for death to take her. Later, on their way to the car, Polly had turned to him, her eyes brimming with compassionate tears.

"Sonny, do you know why poor Susan can't die? I think it's because she has work to do, her work for every day is to die. Because she has a mission, a plan for every day when she awakens . . ." Her voice trailed off. Then she completed her thought.

"It's because her goal and her work are at, oh, you know, are at . . ."

"Cross-purposes." Sonny finished her thought for her.

"Yes. That's it. She can't die because she has a goal, a purpose in life. But how can that be? To say she has something to live for? Yet that something is her wish to die. Oh, Sonny, I don't understand."

"Neither do I, sweetheart, neither do I."

Now, he was ashamed of himself for not including himself in his inventory of likely candidates for the arbitrary nature of fate. He

recognized that his nominations for an immediate place in the hereafter hadn't included himself.

He looked to the framed photo of himself and his sisters on
the console. The black-and-white snapshot had been taken with a
Kodak box camera, a concession by a neighbor trying to finish up
a roll of film, then passed along to the Dawson family. It was, perhaps, the only photo that had survived their childhood. Sonny didn't
remember other photos having been taken; there were no photos of
their parents. It was in later years that Sonny had had it reprinted
and enlarged; the resulting grainy streaking left their features indistinct in the indifferent lighting.

Fifteen, ten, and five years old they had been. The oldest, Cloris's
large expressive eyes stared back deep and sunken in their sockets as
she stood at attention for the photographer. She was physically attractive. Her shapely legs were camouflaged by the dowdy, long skirt and
white anklets descending into sensible brown Oxfords. The precocious
sexuality for which she was already known even at that young age
was masked; her hollow-eyed likeness was reminiscent of the haunting photos of the child that Sonny remembered from having read *The
Diary of Anne Frank*. There was an innocence portrayed in the picture that was not part of her character as he knew her, her mercurial
temper, her anger, her defiance toward their parents. The prayers, the
laying on of hands by his parents over their wayward daughter, their
exhortation for her to repent of her sinful ways was forever logged into
his memory. Now, the memory was too painful to touch.

But Dolores! The middle child, she had always been the most
attractive of the three Dawson children. There she was, a tousled
blonde with the merry blue eyes of a plump little Heubach doll,
one hand jauntily cocked on her hip, in such remarkable contrast
to the sister he knew now. Despite her modest, smock-like dress and
naturally curly corkscrew curls—everyone thought she looked like
Shirley Temple—she was a tease, a temptress. Her joy in life had
been sinful to his parents.

And now with so many problems . . .

His thoughts trailed off. He gave the third child in the photo, himself, thoughtful consideration. He usually took the image for granted, but now he regarded it soberly for a moment.

Could I go back if I wanted? Would I start over if I could— would it be different? The same choices?

He thought about how he'd been his father's little pal for a short time, perhaps only a few months. Until he wasn't.

What happened to us?

In mute answer to his own questions, he turned his attention back to the likeness of Polly and himself. He clutched the framed photo to his chest, then carefully replaced it at the center of the console. The other frames in the small collection held snapshots of Spats and the feline that had preceded Spats, Tuxy, also a black-and-white tuxedo cat.

Scolding himself for wasting time, he reached to his immediate right for the conveniently placed telephone and punched in the number for Kent Field's office. It was time to get Kent moving on the administration of Polly's estate. Since he'd been confronted by Tom Shaw on the disposition of Polly's holdings in the Shaw Farms Corporation, he wanted resolution of their questions and, for that matter, of his own. Particularly, he wanted to inform the Shaw family that he had things underway.

Instinctively, while the number connected and rang, he turned to regard the small safe discreetly crouching in the corner behind the door to the basement, which, when the door was opened, swung to hide the squatty steel box with its Cyclops eye fixed on him. Both a copy of his own individual last will and testament resided there as well as Polly's, along with both of their instructions as dictated by their living wills and healthcare directives. As he'd told Tom Shaw in the conversation that had turned heated on the day of Polly's funeral, he'd never read Polly's will. Now he resisted the compulsive urge to reread his own will.

"Jessie? Hello. This is Sonny Dawson. Kent in yet?" He listened to the response and replied evenly, "Okay, then. Have him give me a call. I'm here at the store. Thanks, Jessie."

Sonny spoke with an easiness that rang hollow to his ears, as though his voice came from someone else and merely echoed through a cavern somewhere inside of him. He replaced the phone in its cradle and shuffled through the stack of mail. He discarded a few pieces of advertising, but then his gaze fell on a plain white business envelope with only his handwritten first name on its exterior. The letter must have been dropped through the mail slot on the door and gathered with the rest of the mail by the faithful Ruby. He turned the envelope over while he fumbled for his letter opener from its narrow tray on the inside of the center desk drawer. The drawer was neat, orderly, and he retrieved the letter opener without even glancing into the drawer to locate it.

He slit the top of the envelope and removed the folded note it contained. The five-by-seven piece of paper was headed with the printed inscription: "From the Desk of Drennan McCormack."

The note read: "Sonny, tried to reach you last night. Thought I might catch you here early this morning. Please give me a call at 555-253-4416. I'm staying at my brother Mike's. I plan to leave Saturday afternoon or Sunday morning, but it's important that we talk. Please call." It was signed "Drennan."

Sonny pushed the desk chair back, balled the paper up, and with an expletive, shot the crumpled note into the trash basket that shared the knee space of the large walnut desk.

Will this man ever leave us alone! What the hell, he's well-educated, successful, hell, he's even written books! What could he possibly want now? To bury an old hatchet because Polly chose me over him?

As his mind coursed along, Sonny knew that there was a touch of irrationality to his thoughts, that Drennan had never bothered them, had not assaulted Polly with entreaties to further his own cause.

Sonny didn't forget that Drennan had come home from Vietnam, forced to confront in person what he had already learned from Polly's letter: that she had chosen someone else.

And the someone else was me.

He was suddenly gleeful, but then the match-strike flare of temper ignited a smoldering anger that Sonny rarely let surface.

But what can he want now! Well, if he thinks I'm going to talk about Polly to him, he's got another think coming. And I'm sure as hell not going to let him tell me about him and Polly; she told me everything I needed to know about the two of them. If it had been anyone other than me that Polly chose, Drennan wouldn't have dared make such a request.

Cooling his anger quickly, he admitted to a curious interest in Drennan. Sonny mused over the fact that through the years, Drennan had returned to Onansburg. His parents were both long gone; his brother, Mike, was absorbed with raising his own family. Was it Polly that brought Drennan back over the years? Or was it just his need to return to Onansburg where he had spent those brief, but good-bad, bittersweet formative years of adolescence? Was it to recapture some of the flavor of the shared culture, to answer some of the questions left from those years, to try to resolve relationships, to reaffirm triumphs?

Sonny remembered one of his class reunions when perhaps twenty or twenty-five of the class members present from the graduating class of sixty-two members stood up in turn to tell of their marriages, family, or jobs. One man, once a disliked nerd, but now successful and wealthy, summed up his experience with no mention of his personal life by saying, "If you didn't like me in high school, you probably didn't like me at our ten-year reunion, you probably didn't like me at our twenty-year reunion, and at our twenty-five year reunion, you probably don't like me more than you ever did. The difference is, now I don't give a damn."

Sonny supposed that as long as Drennan himself was alive,

someone in Onansburg could associate him with the names on his family's tombstones at the cemetery. Or is a hometown just a place where your memories are buried along with your kinfolk?

With full intention of returning to the work that had piled up on his desk, he paused yet once more when his attention fell on the framed snapshot of his grandma Rose. Taken the year before she died, her beauty was evident even in her old age. And while his mind drifted once again unwillingly to his parents, Charles and Priscilla, he pushed them from his conscious mind. Sonny only allowed himself to face off against his enemies, his memories of his childhood, when he was feeling strong and resistant to their effects.

Sonny focused on Polly's face in the photo, then on Rose's, then on Polly's, until the two became one through the haze of his thoughts. He sighed and passed his hand over his eyes, sweeping moisture away, concentrating on the likenesses of the two women. He focused on the faces that had become his talismans of courage and hope until he felt the surge of spirit from deep within summon control over his memories. A defense mechanism disengaged itself from his conscious, took over, and saved him once more.

He knew of Polly all there was, physically and spiritually. And he had always recognized how like Rose she had been; knew that the mystery of his attraction to her was somehow tied to Rose. Even though he could not exactly define or name the feature, the characteristic, the quality, it was in their grace he had identified their alikeness.

Then he turned his attention back to the mail piled up on his desk. He noted a folded piece of paper with only his name on the outside and presumed it contained the note from Larry. He pushed it under an advertising circular.

I'll get to it when I get to it. Sonny recognized that shoving the note aside was another symptom of his distaste for Larry. He prided himself on prompt responses to letters, requests, and questions, but now he'd denied both Drennan's and Larry's bids for his attention.

Eight

ose knelt on the hard wooden floor of the bedroom
she shared with C. D. She prayed with fragments of
supplication punctuated by phrases from scripture
from the Bible from her long-ago memory.

"Dear God, please give me strength. Please help me. I don't know
what to do for my son. I'm frightened for him."

Yea, though I walk through the valley of the shadow . . .

"Something has happened to him, Lord, something has happened
to my Charles. He's just so miserable, I could die for him. And his
thinking, it's his thinking that's all messed up. This is my only son,
the only one I'll ever have."

For God so loved the world he gave his only begotten son.

"Now take my son, Lord, take him under your wing. Please
show him the way."

Thy will be done, on earth as it is in heaven.

Rose heard the flat slap of the kitchen door closing. She closed
her prayer hurriedly. "Thank you for your blessings. In Jesus's
name, Amen."

Rose had come to attribute her survival to prayer. She prayed
on her knees while she scrubbed, on her knees at her bedside with
clasped hands and bowed head; she prayed for her loved ones while

she sewed, for their physical and spiritual well-being. She weighed
the odds of being granted spiritual gifts against material gifts, so she
hedged her supplications to the Lord in terms of gifts more likely
to be granted, those of guidance, solace, peace, salvation. She had
long ago been taught that God would provide for her needs and that
prosperity and comfort were secondary.

"Mama? Where are you?"

The fragrance and chill of the snappy November evening preceded Charles into the room. The pristine air redolent with the
smoky overtones of fall emanating from Charles's outdoor clothing was like balm to her spirit. Of all the seasons, fall was her most
favorite. The spirit of the harvest was a reminder of humanity's
interdependence that was too easily forgotten by God's children
in the plenty of spring and summer. Rose hoped that the stress
of their move to Onansburg a few months ago would be soothed
by days shortened to an early dusk, and the descending darkness
relentlessly signaled the changing season, by the gathering of their
little family for evening meals of comfort food, chicken and dumplings, beef stew, apple dumplings, by the physical proximity of
winter evenings when they gathered in one room, the dining room,
to read or play dominoes.

Rose quickly rose from her prayers and met Charles as he hurried into the dining room. He deposited two square white envelopes
on the dining room table and hastily pulled off his jacket and his
denim work hat, tossing them toward an empty chair where they
failed to land.

"Mama, look. Miss Lydia gave me these. They're invitations to
the exhibit. I worked at the Richards place today. When Miss Lydia
came home from school, she gave these to me. I already opened
mine." To Rose's puzzled expression, he nodded importantly. He
spoke to her as though she was slow-witted, unable to comprehend
what he was about to impart.

"Mama, the exhibit. At Highlands School, on Friday night. They, well, the school board and Miss Lydia, of course, invite all the parents and other folks to see the students' work and there's a social; you know, pie and cake. And Miss Lydia invited us. One invitation is for you and Papa and the other is for me."

Rose was having trouble following Charles's explanation. She shook her head in amazement. This Charles was different from the man who had been sullen, morose, seemingly despairing. Most days, he did his assigned chores around the farmstead, worked as bidden during harvest for neighbors, and otherwise, ate little and slept long.

He bent his head quickly, studying the invitation but not so quickly that Rose did not see the embarrassed flush creeping from his jaw up under his high cheekbones. Rose was pleased. The invitation surely heralded some acknowledgment of their presence in the rural community. Yes, she was pleased. She clapped her hands together excitedly and sat down to study the invitation with its elegant Spencerian script addressed to Mr. and Mrs. Charles Dawson Sr.

"Well, Charles. That's just lovely. You'll be going, won't you? Is it this coming Friday night? My, this is Tuesday already! I'll bet they're just all excited over at the school."

But suddenly the former Charles reappeared; frowning, querulous, and demanding. "Mama, you and Papa are invited to the exhibit too. You have to go! Miss Lydia invited you. It would be an insult not to go."

Without waiting for her reply, he hurried from the dining room, through the parlor and into his own bedroom, which was really an extension of the parlor. Rose heard him jerk back the curtain that she had fashioned at his insistence between the parlor and his sleeping place. When they moved into the old house, Rose and Charles had pushed a ruined useless piano from the bedroom, which had given testimony to its former use as a music room. The old upright with its lacquered finish checked by age was now the sole occupant of the parlor. The parlor and the bedrooms would be closed off when winter set in to preserve the heat for the kitchen and the dining room, where the nickel-plated pot-bellied stove would hold court. The beds were piled with extra quilts and warmed before bedtime with a copper bed warmer filled with embers from the generosity of the stove.

Charles rushed back to the dining room, wagging a shirt on a wooden hanger at Rose. "Mama, can you wash and iron this shirt for Friday night for me to wear? Can you?"

Rose, half-risen from her chair, fell back down onto the padded seat. "That shirt's been fresh washed and ironed. I wouldn't have put it away dirty."

"Oh, Mama. Look at it! I can't wear this! I don't have anything decent to wear to a social."

Surprise caused Rose's face to go blank, her mouth pursed in question. "That shirt's perfectly fine, and besides, you don't have another." Then she reconsidered. "Well, maybe you could wear Papa's striped one and he could . . . "

Charles rushed over her words of suggestion with his own decision. "I'm going to buy myself a new suit. And a new shirt. I'm going to ask Mr. Richards tomorrow to leave early, tell him I've got business in town to attend to. This is important."

Charles had continued to work for John Richards, Miss Lydia's father, even after the permanent job of hand had gone by default to the Becker boy, under the caveat that he would only be needed until Christmas. Richards made a concession to keep Charles on through the holidays whether out of empathy or recognition that the Becker boy was not near the hand that Charles had become. He needed good help to put his farm to bed for the winter ahead. An uneasy truce carried the unspoken misunderstanding. Charles hadn't understood that his delay in responding to the job offer was a breach in a working relationship. "I made you a good offer, son," Richards had said. Charles didn't share his termination with his parents.

Now, Rose retrieved the invitation, and using the tiny silver letter opener she received for her high school graduation gift from her parents, she quickly sliced open the invitation addressed to Mr. and Mrs. Charles Dawson Sr. It was nicely lettered in Lydia's best Spencerian hand. Nice, very nice indeed, she commented to herself.

Rose looked from Charles's invitation to the one, comparing the two. She quickly noted that Lydia had included a note urging him to attend at the bottom of Charles's invitation, which had been addressed to Mr. Charles Dawson Jr. Charles snatched it from her view but not before she noted that Lydia had done her homework regarding their proper names.

Rose knew without asking that C. D. would try to beg off going to the exhibit, and she rehearsed her reasons that they should both attend as a couple. Shortly, she heard Charles leave the house from the door closest to the privy, and she rehearsed her reasons so that she could gain his assent before he had a chance to dash Charles's plans.

"It's the first time that we've had an invitation to anything since we moved here. C. D., Charles is counting on us, and I think Charles might be sweet on Lydia. And after all, she seems such a lively girl. I think they might be a good match."

Her well-rehearsed pleas were not in vain. When she heard C. D.'s footsteps approaching from the barn where he had stabled the horse, Rose slipped out the kitchen door and met him on the porch before he had a chance to make his presence known. Greeting him with her customary kiss, she brushed her upper lip against his mustache. His breath was a mixture of sweet tobacco and the other fragrance that told her he had been drinking spirits. Burying her face against his shoulder, she leaned against the house, pulling him close to her, and breathlessly, she told him of the important invitations. Rose was surprised when C. D. easily acquiesced even as his hands kneaded her breasts through her shirtwaist.

"Of course, we'll go Friday night if it means that much to Charles. Of course. She's one of the Richards girls, yes, the Richards girls." C. D., of course, remembered the Richards girls, in particular Lydia, who he had come to know was the teacher at Highlands School. She was of interest to him from the first time he saw her at his neighborly visit to their home upon his family's arrival on the Butler place.

It was with almost unguarded pleasure and anticipation that Charles waited for Friday night to come. The new suit was purchased, and Charles bore it proudly home wrapped in heavy brown paper. Rose made some small alterations and subjected it to a thorough steaming and pressing, making the suit look as though it had been tailor-made. The new shirt was laundered and heavily starched. Lloyd Lockard, the proprietor of the only department store in Onansburg, generously contributed a second detachable collar and a narrow, diamond-pattern silk necktie.

Charles presented himself for inspection just after six p.m. on Friday evening, arriving home from work soon after four after being excused by John Richards before regular quitting time, as the Richards family had their own preparations to make for the evening. He'd excused himself from the supper table after dipping just a few spoonsful of rich tomato soup made from the summer bounty of tomatoes from the garden and cream skimmed from Pansy's milk.

After the supper dishes were cleared and washed, Charles had helped Rose fill the tin bathtub with hot water from the reservoir of the nearby cook stove and bathed carefully. Modestly, he looked around to determine Rose's whereabouts, then reached for the bath sheet Rose had laid out before absenting herself from the kitchen. Wrapped in the sheet, Charles stood in front of the small shaving mirror next to the back door, shaved for the second time that day, and combed his hair carefully.

He disappeared into his bedroom and next appeared wearing his new clothes. Rose, as accustomed to men's fashion as she was women's, helped him tie his new tie. "Over, around, up, and through. Four easy steps, Charles."

"Oh, Charles," she breathed. "You look just beautiful." Rose was relieved; this handsome young man was again the son she thought she had lost during the past months. He seemed pleased with himself, looking forward to his big evening. And who could tell? Maybe Lydia was sweet on him. Maybe they would start keeping company. Rose's hope lent her imagination a helping hand. She could see them engaged, then married, living on the Richards place, the Becker boy working for Charles. She hugged herself in excitement.

"Now, you'd best hurry and get ready. Where's Papa? Is he hitching the buggy? What are you going to wear? Let me see."

"Charles, you know your mother will be the prettiest girl at the exhibit! What're you worrying about her for?" C. D.'s booming voice preceded him from the kitchen, but when he entered the dining room, he stopped in astonishment at the sight of his son dressed in his first adult suit. Charles turned to face him, but a small frown creased C. D.'s forehead as he regarded a man who rivaled his own handsomeness. He delivered his assessment in carefully measured cadence.

"Well, now. You do look fine. You sure do look fine. That's a good-looking new suit. Yes, sir! A fine-looking suit."

He circled slowly as Charles stood motionless. He surveyed Charles's appearance carefully and flicked an imaginary piece of lint from his son's shoulder, gave the coat a little tug here and there. Tension hung between the two men, father and son; Charles stood rigid under C. D.'s scrutiny, at attention as a soldier undergoing inspection by a superior.

"Well, now. I'll just get my pocketbook, and we'll be ready. Charles? Will you ride with us?" Rose had earlier pre-empted C. D.'s usual request that Charles hitch the buggy with one of her own. "Darling, will you please get the horse and buggy ready while Charles gets dressed?"

"C. D., is the buggy ready?" C. D. answered in the affirmative, not too unhappily, and brought the skittery, ill-trained horse and the loose-wheeled buggy to the hitching rail in front.

The family exited from the dining room door. Rose, the last out with her small, hand-tooled leather bag hanging by its leather strap from her elbow, closed the door firmly then checked the closure on the kitchen door, just a few steps away. The two doors were twins, but not identical. Each featured a frosted glass pane centered on its upper half, but the dining room door had a pastoral scene etched into the glass. Charles guided Rose down the steps while C. D. climbed into the buggy and gathered the reins.

Charles had weighed the possible danger of riding with his parents in the rickety conveyance against the inconvenience of the two-mile walk in his new suit and freshly polished boots. The lesser of the evils won out. Rose, fashionably dressed in her black serge skirt and smart plaid jacket, held her purse out for Charles to hold, then let him help her into the buggy next to C. D. He handed her purse back and climbed in next to her.

Rose shifted her shoulders back and forth, rubbing them against each man, teasingly.

"Oh, this is so nice. The two best-looking men there, you'll be! I'm just so proud to be going with the both of you." Charles looked away in self-conscious pleasure.

C. D. was unusually silent, but then he spoke sharply. "You forgot the lantern. Get it."

"Don't you be cross now and spoil everything, Papa. You'll make Charles feel bad and him going to his first party here."

"Mama," groaned Charles. "It's not a party, it's the exhibit. It's Miss Lydia's, eh, the Highland School exhibit."

Charles retrieved the lantern, climbed back into the buggy, then pulled the horsehair lap robe from its rack and smoothed it over his new trousers and over Rose's skirt. The buggy with its uneasy occupants rattled off behind the devil horse in the direction of the school, following the distant lamp light of other buggies bound for the exhibit.

Upon their arrival, he and his parents admired the displays of art and examples of penmanship fastened to the walls and chalkboard and exclaimed their appreciation of same to the milling crowd of parents and children. They offered their respects to Lydia and her parents, and when Lydia clapped her hands for attention and asked everyone to take a seat for the program, the assembly complied quickly. The twenty or so students were directed to assemble backstage for their enactment of the entertainment.

When Charles along with Rose and C. D. first made their entrance into the school, a wave of attention rippled through the crowd. Not only were they strangers to many of those already assembled, but they were an extremely handsome trio. Lydia made the most of her opportunity, and it was apparent that she had the desired effect on Charles. He was smitten. No longer did he question himself as the object of her attention as he had when she flirted with him on the summer Saturday night.

The end of the festivities came all too soon to suit Charles. He had never had such a fine time; he reveled in the admiring glances of the women and girls, the unspoken, grudging acceptance by the men. At last, he felt noticed for his own attributes. He knew he looked fine.

No one spoke during the ride home. C. D. occasionally clucked to the horse but was otherwise silent; the evening had not been to his liking. He was generally the center of any untoward female attention even while he focused on their menfolk. Oh, no one could say that C. D., Charles Dawson Sr., had ever violated another man's home or leastwise had never entered without an invitation. He always felt welcomed.

Feeling diminished by the massive shoulders of the two men on either side of her, Rose sat at attention to counteract the discomfort of the jolting buggy ride and examined the events of the evening over and over in her mind. Despite her satisfaction over Charles's pleasure, she was uneasy, sensing that something yet undefined had somehow gone awry, and she was powerless to understand what it was. First the invitation, then Miss Lydia's behavior. Rose disliked feeling as though a plot was already in play with herself being the only actor who didn't know the lines.

The program had begun with John Richards welcoming the assembled parents and friends to the now crowded and overheated little schoolhouse and proudly introducing the "best little teacher Highlands Country School has ever had, my daughter, Miss Lydia Richards!" Lydia herself took the stage, a hastily gathered sheet strung on a clothesline at the front of the schoolroom, and never let it go. No one could fault her, at least publicly, for upstaging her students.

Thinking carefully, dissecting the evening bit by bit, recognition came slowly. Once the tableau began, Rose chanced to look toward where Lydia could be seen, ostensibly backstage but given the confines of the one-room country school, she was in view of those seated on the left side of the room as they faced the makeshift stage. Because Rose had been the first into the Dawson family seats, she had been the farthest to the left, and when she saw Lydia's gaze turn away from the stage for just the shortest moment, their eyes met. Rose responded with her generous smile but was met with the look of defiance and challenge from Lydia that every woman recognizes as a nonverbal call to arms.

The buggy creaked its way down the lane toward the dark house; the wheels bumped over the frozen marks of earlier passages. There was no gravel or rock spread over the top of the hard-packed dirt lane to ease the way. The fully risen moon passed from behind the clouds, casting enough light that C. D. could drive the buggy to where Rose could climb down onto the stump. Charles jumped out first and handed Rose first to the low stump and then down to the ground. C. D. dismounted and waited to hand the reins to Charles.

"Papa, I'm going to change from my new clothes before I put the horse away. Can I just tie him up?"

"Suit yourself," C. D. responded wearily, at which Charles and Rose both turned to him quizzically. Charles had fully expected that he would have commented on his request.

The three of them entered through the kitchen door, and Rose struck a match and lit the lamp that always held vigil just inside the back door on a wrought-iron bracket. To return to a dark house was preferable to the danger of leaving a kerosene lamp burning. C. D. draped his shirt, jacket, and trousers over a chair in the kitchen and kicked off his boots. Turning his back on Charles and Rose, who followed him to the door of his bedroom, he stripped off his union suit and without further ado climbed into bed. Rose's and Charles's gaze met and locked for an instant. Puzzled by C. D.'s uncustomary reticence, Rose spoke with concern. "C. D., are you all right? Do you feel okay?"

C. D. didn't answer. Charles stood in the doorway and regarded the still form. "Papa, you all right?"

C. D.'s voice came at last, faint and sleepy. "I'm fine. Go put the horse away."

Rose gestured, shooing Charles with both hands to do as he was told. Charles hurried to his own room, hurriedly changed from his new suit to work pants and shirt. In a few minutes, Charles emerged from his room, shrugged into his work coat, and took leave through the kitchen door.

Rose busied herself with measuring coffee and water into the granite-ware coffee pot for morning. Then she too stood in the doorway and regarded C. D.'s motionless form under the bed covers. There was usually not very much for which Rose could not provide a reasonable explanation, but this evening had been a mystery to her.

After quietly washing her face and brushing her teeth at the washstand in the corner of the kitchen, she crept into their bedroom, hung her clothes in the free-standing wardrobe as she shed them, and retrieved her nightgown from its hook. She decided to forego brushing her hair. Instead, she simply removed the pins and shook it loose, combing through it with her outstretched fingers. Slipping into bed beside C. D., she gave a shiver against the draft that wafted in after Charles entered the kitchen door from the outside, his work in the barn completed. Nestling under the pieced-woolen coverlet, she allowed herself a smile thinking of Charles's pleasure in the evening.

"Good night, son," she said softly when Charles went by the bedroom door on his way to his own room at the far end of the house. Charles didn't hear her benediction, or else, lost in his own thoughts, didn't respond. The old house groaned its night noises, the wind whistled through the empty upstairs rooms, now boarded against the elements, but her pleasure disappeared when her mind played the exhibit back for her.

She came quickly to address her gravest concern: the slight, flushed fullness of Lydia's unlined face and the thickening the clever little peplum at the waist of her green velvet dress helped disguise. Rose willed herself to escape, to sleep, postponing her questions for Charles. Had he and Lydia been seeing one another while he worked at the Richards' place? Rose was frightened for Charles. Had his inexperience gotten him and Lydia into trouble?

She shifted closer to C. D.'s bulk until she was warm again and closed her eyes, waiting for sleep to come, but they snapped open watchfully when she heard a hoot owl calling. The ghostly cry made her feel lonely and frightened, reminding her how vulnerable they were. Dependent on only the earnings she and Charles brought in, there seemed to be few choices for expanding their lives or their livelihood, but then she chided herself for her lack of faith and assured herself. She was resourceful, not afraid of hard work. They'd be all right. She shut her eyes once more and patiently offered up her prayers until sleep took her.

———————

C. D. and Charles were both up early the next morning, before the sunrise. C. D. poked the remaining coals in the stove into life, threw in the last of the kindling and a small measure of coal, but with the sun on the rise, he ordered Charles to fetch more wood. Without comment, even without his customary sullenness, Charles donned his work coat and hat and hastened out the door to the woodpile. The sound of the axe applied rhythmically to the wood stacked just off to the side of the broad front porch carried clearly through the clear, sharp air, and within half an hour, he carried in enough wood to last the day. Rose felt rather than heard the steady beat of the axe before she stirred. By the time she awakened, the morning had dawned cold and crisp, possessed with a snapping, electric energy. Charles's face, rosy from the sharp wind that caught him at the woodpile, was the first thing Rose laid eyes on when he poked his head in the door of her room. After the hours of nightmares featuring an enraged John Richards defending his daughter, it was a relief to see his face intact, that Rose's fears were temporarily soothed.

"Mama, come on. Get up. The chores are done. Let's eat! I have to get to work before eight o'clock." On Saturday, Charles could sleep an extra hour, but on any other day, except Sunday, the day off, work began at seven and was over when the sun set.

Charles turned and walked away, but not before Rose had an opportunity to notice his uncharacteristic exuberance. Rose sat up and swung her feet to the floor, modestly tugging her flower-sprigged flannel nightgown down over her knees. The set of his shoulders, the tilt of his head, both told her how he was feeling. She breathed a great, deep sigh. She hadn't realized how upset she had been until now, when her relief was so great that she thought it could be measured in buckets or even great huge bushel baskets. Everything looks better in the morning, she reminded herself. Rose practiced denial, the safe harbor for mothers, in its purest form.

Rose took time only to shove her feet into the fur-lined beaded moccasins she wore as house slippers and don a warm robe that had once been an old overcoat. Deftly, she wove her hair into a loose plait. Without making her bed, she plucked her apron from the hook in the pantry as she entered the kitchen. Embarrassed for having overslept, she made a busy clatter rattling the cast-iron skillet against the cook stove. C. D. had been up early and made coffee in the granite-ware pot, an unusual concession even to his own needs. Rose sliced and put thick slices of bacon to fry, forked it from the skillet, and added slices of leftover cornmeal mush to the sizzling fat. When the mush was fried crispy and brown, she served the plates to C. D. and Charles. But her heart sank as she filled her own plate and slid into her place at the short leg of the kitchen table. As she was seated, Charles began to complain even as he bent his head over his plate, chewing and swallowing.

"Mama, I'll never have mush on my table. And never sorghum! Only maple syrup!"

Rose and C. D. exchanged glances warily. This kind of outburst from Charles usually led only to a haughty reminder by C. D. that they were all lucky to have mush and so on, but suddenly Charles looked across the table to them. He swallowed the last bite of his breakfast even while Rose and C. D. had laid their forks down and studied their own plates in dismay.

"Wasn't bad for mush though, Mama. Excuse me, please."

He rose from the table, pulled his heavy-lined jacket and cap from the hook next to the door, and shrugged into the garments.

Patting the pockets for his work gloves, he opened the door. "I'll be going to work now."

But turning back, he closed the door, pulled off the denim work cap, retrieved the comb from the comb tray beneath the mirror, and carefully recombed and parted his already parted hair. Setting the cap precisely back in place, he hesitated. He opened the door and though the chill air made Rose flinch, she held her breath as Charles self-consciously searched for words.

"Mama, Papa, I am to ask Mr. Richards if it's all right for me to ask Miss Lydia, eh, Lydia, to keep company with me. You know. Me working for him and all." He exited quickly. As the door shut behind him, it sent a mighty blast of frigid air sweeping into the already drafty kitchen.

Charles immediately made good his intention to ask Lydia for her company. He knocked on the back door, as he always did to get his instructions for the day's work, and surprised John Richards with his request to call on Lydia. With no more than a slightly raised eyebrow, John Richards indicated, "Well, I guess there'd be no harm to it."

And to his own surprise, he then marched around the square-built house right up onto the Richards' front porch, rapped on the door, and when Mrs. Richards answered, he asked to speak to Lydia. Hugging herself for warmth, Lydia quickly stepped outside. She tossed her head and batted her eyes and when Charles issued a general invitation to "call on you, go somewhere, sometime," she countered with an invitation to a party at her best friend Joanna Allshouse's home on that very evening.

"There'll be just Joanna and Allen Tucker, they're almost engaged, y'know, her brother Grant and Rita Dentler, and you and me." She smiled winningly. Charles was so happy and so relieved that it had all been so easy that he didn't question such a tidy arrangement, that an evening had already been planned as if Lydia had known he'd be drawn to her.

On that first evening, he called for Lydia promptly at seven and, by prior arrangement made by Lydia, they rode to the party with Allen Tucker, who owned his own automobile. Charles was quiet and withdrawn, faced with the obvious superiority of someone both older (Allen was twenty-one) and with the wherewithal to own a car. But Lydia's lively chatter sought him out and carried him along in the conversation, and he was nearly at ease by the time they arrived at the Allshouses'.

"You two will probably have to walk home. I'll be staying a little longer, get me some smoochin' with my sweet Jo," Allen announced as they pulled into the drive. Lydia giggled when Allen waggled his eyebrows up and down along with a sinister smile. Charles leaned around Lydia to catch Allen's expression and then leaned back on the bench seat next to the door.

Laughing knowingly at Allen's chatter, Charles felt sophisticated and worldly, but he was more than surprised. Except for the evening at the first Old Settlers, he had entertained visions of Lydia and her friends as fairy princesses, unattainable, virginal. He was surprised by Allen's remarks, but he was determined to fit in with this older and more sophisticated group, and he'd show them he was as ready for a good time as they were.

Hopping down from the high running board, Charles helped Lydia down carefully, shivering in the chill outside air despite the warm Fair Isle sweater he wore under C. D.'s overcoat. Lydia tucked her arm in his, and they waited for Allen to join them. Stomping their feet in the chill of the recently arrived winter weather, the two of them hurried toward the house, but Allen's voice stopped them before they reached the porch.

"Want a little warm-up before we go in?"

Charles looked back to see that Allen had produced a small

flask from somewhere within the car. Allen took a quick pull and passed it to Lydia, who did the same. Charles could see her eyes dancing with mischief in the light of the bright moon as he took the flask from her outstretched arm. "Sure, why not?" Putting the flask to his lips, he took a cautious sip from the bottle with tight compressed lips.

"Naw, go on. Take a real snort," Allen urged.

And this time, Charles did. He opened his mouth for a sizeable swig but nearly choked as the fiery liquid scalded the back of his throat. His eyes watered furiously, but he retained control, quickly swallowing over and over while handing the bottle back casually.

"Good," he croaked. "Thanks."

"Come on, Lyddy-Girl. Let's go in. I hope Jo has something good for us to eat."

Allen, thankfully, didn't notice Charles's discomfort and swept Lydia along boisterously up the steps to the porch, where they pounded on the front door of the big square house. Charles surreptitiously wiped his watering eyes before Joanna threw the door open for them. With self-conscious laughter, introductions were made all around, even though Charles already knew their names, and they surely knew his.

"Hello, Joanna. Hello, Grant. It's nice of you to include me. Hi, Rita. No, I don't think we've met."

Mrs. Allshouse had allowed the door from the dining room to be left open so that the parlor would heat, and the rugs were rolled back to allow dancing. Joanna asked who would crank the Victrola, and Charles offered to take the first turn at the crank, relieved to have a job to do. He carefully wound the machine, taking care not to wind it too tight. Then, he observed while the others took turns as partners and decided he wouldn't have to take a back seat to their dancing. He and Rose and C. D., in happier days, had taken turns in just the same way. He had grown up dancing.

Lydia offered to sit out a turn, and the petite Rita asked Charles to dance. He thought he acquitted himself very well, jigging away to a lively tune, and as the Victrola slowed to a low growl, signaling its need to be rewound, he looked away from Rita to find Lydia appraising him with a new regard. Charles felt a surge of confidence and smiled at her, extending his hand. Lydia jumped up, rewound the record player, and they put their arms around one another.

Amazed to find her in his arms, Charles forgot his customary wary reserve and seized the opportunity to draw her closer. She had been a central character in his imagination for so long that she had loomed larger than life, and he was surprised to find her a woman of normal size, of a size to allow him to hold her in his arms. Charles felt energy from her body arc across the small distance between them. Across the room where the others were gathered around a tray of sandwiches and the no-longer-innocuous punch, Grant nudged Allen, then cleared his throat to attract Joanna and Rita's attention and nodded in the direction of the dancing couple. They knowingly smiled at one another.

The evening was a success on all counts. Charles felt he handled himself well. Grant and Allen stepped outside at regular intervals with the flask, and he and the young women periodically joined them. They all stifled laughter when Ted and Wretha Allshouse came from the dining room where they'd spent the evening playing cards and writing letters to bid them good night. They announced that they were retiring for the evening. Charles didn't recall meeting Mr. and Mrs. Allshouse at the exhibit, but he acknowledged them politely with a deferential nod of his head.

"My goodness," exclaimed Mrs. Allshouse. "You're all so flushed and rosy from dancing! Now don't get overheated and then go outside in this weather. You'll catch your death!"

The minute the door to the upstairs closed behind the older couple, the young people exploded into laughter. Grant mimed his mother mercilessly, dancing across the room, holding the skirt of his imaginary dress.

"You're all so flushed and rosy. Of course, it's just the dancing."

At ten o'clock, Lydia allowed that it was time she started for home, and Charles jumped up to indicate his willingness. When Allen groaned that he supposed he could take them home but that it would cut his evening short, Charles grinned wickedly at the reminder of Allen's intentions. "Yeah, I want you to take us home and spoil your plans," he said sarcastically. "Never mind. It's not that cold. Lydia and I'll just walk."

After taking several pulls from the flask, Charles felt that drinking with the others helped make him part of the group, not so much the outsider. To teasing and laughter about going straight back to the Richards' place, he and Lydia wrapped themselves in coats and scarves and pulled on their gloves. But as she pulled her red knitted hat down over her ears, a suddenly sobered Lydia caught Joanna with a glance from her dark eyes that Charles could only interpret as apprehension or uncertainty.

He was puzzled, yet this uncharacteristic display made him feel manly and powerful. Could she be uncertain about being alone with him? He preened himself, smoothing his coat over the heavy sweater, wished his new friends good night, and escorted Lydia out the door into the moonlight.

The room fell quiet with their departure. Stepping to the window and peering between the two panels of the curtains, Joanna kept them in her sight while they walked down the drive to the main road. She turned back to the others.

"What's she supposed to do?" She challenged the others defensively. "What else can she do?"

"Well," offered Grant, "there's Doc Ryan. And there's a new doc coming in so Doc can retire. A German fella—maybe he . . . or that Mrs. Burley down by Union . . . " his voice trailed off lamely.

There were no more suggestions.

Lydia and Charles picked their way carefully over the uneven rough ground that comes with a cold snap. The road was still frozen in the impression of the tracks left by the last vehicle or horse and wagon to pass over it before the temperature plummeted. Fifteen degrees Fahrenheit wouldn't be considered particularly cold for January, but for November, it qualified. Smacking his gloved hands together ostensibly for circulation but in fact to break the uneasy silence that had intervened in their evening, Charles stole a glance at Lydia's pensive expression.

"I sure had a good time, Lydia. I thank you for inviting me; your friends are real nice. They're, well, just swell."

With his satisfaction in himself and his conduct during the evening, he abandoned his usual grave countenance and manner. Customarily surly and withdrawn in a self-conscious attitude of superiority, he found himself experiencing new feelings of well-being. He smiled widely, showing his teeth, his mouth curled up at the corners.

Lydia smiled back at him and replied quietly, "We've all been good friends since we were little; we grew up together, went all through school together and everything." She made a sound in the back of her throat that passed for laughter and continued, "We used to fight a lot, you know, and have little quarrels. Just kid stuff." Charles peeked at her downcast face and noted her somber expression. "It'd be Joanna and me against Rita, or Grant and Allen mad at us girls. But now, we'd do about anything for each other."

Then at once, her attention focused again on Charles. She reached for his hand, ungainly in its heavy mitten, and teased, "What big hands you have, grandmother." Charles was puzzled for an instant but quickly recovered. He wanted to respond with some witty response, gay repartee, as a book he read once called it, but all he could think of was *What big breasts* you *have, grandmother.*

He quickly quashed the thought in his mind even though he had admired Lydia's breasts all evening. And the outline of her legs under her skirt.

Lamely, he shrugged and responded, "Well, they're the only ones I have."

They became more comfortable as they walked along the two-mile path to the Richards' place, and their conversation became easier incrementally with the warmth of their bodies from the exercise. Charles became overheated and even unbuttoned his overcoat. They were laughing and joking, replaying the best parts of the evening for one another when the distant lights of a car played on the landscape from behind them, warning of its presence before they heard the rhythmic chug of its motor.

Lydia jerked his arm with both hands just as the lights of the car were about to overtake them, drawing him into the small copse of trees that lined the road. She slid into his arms again with both arms around his waist, and he found himself clutching her shoulders with both hands. He moved to wrap his arms around her with more assurance when he realized that it was not by accident that they found themselves in an embrace. They stood motionless in the darkness while the car sped by, spitting fumes into its own trail. Charles's nostrils contracted involuntarily but flared again as he pressed his face against the side of Lydia's face and hair.

The warmth from her face radiated her essence into the cold air, and he felt himself stirring in response to her nearness. Experimentally, he nuzzled the top of her head with the side of his face, mentally registering each detail with surprise, the suppressed energy of the springy curls that escaped from beneath her hat, the curve of her brow, and her scent.

Lydia stepped back slightly, raised her arm, cupped the back of his neck with her hand, and pulled him toward her. Nearly frightened by her boldness, he caught a glimpse of her slightly parted lips just before she pressed their lush berry-softness against his own mouth. When the sweet kiss ended, Charles's eyes flew open in surprise to find her regarding him with a sardonic smile.

"Charles," she teased. "Have you ever kissed a girl before?"

Charles knew that had it not been dark, she would have seen the betraying color in his face. He had no experience with girls. He had not, as a child, had even the close friendships with other children, girls or boys, that might have, eventually, promoted such relationships with the opposite sex. He had never played parlor games simply because he had never been invited into someone's parlor for birthday parties or, for that matter, he had never been invited as a guest to the homes of schoolmates. In adolescence, he'd heard talk. Sometimes guilty, secretive talk and sometimes bragging, swaggering talk, not uncommon among the young men working in the fields. He was nearly always provoked to a response that made him turn away from the others, but apart from the shameful day he had walked in on C. D. and Rose in their mysterious but unmistakable act, he had no real knowledge of what happens between women and men.

Once more, Lydia reached for him and drew his mouth down to hers. This time, her kiss was different. Lydia's aggressive mouth crushed his. He moaned in spite of himself and marveled at her ability to give him pleasure. Every square inch of Charles's body craved release. Then, it was his turn.

He pulled Lydia close and kissed her roughly. Quickly, he stripped off his heavy mittens and clumsily unbuttoned her coat. He clutched her waist with outstretched hands then slid them down to her buttocks, pulling her close against his hardened body. After a few moments, Lydia pushed herself away and reached for his hands with her own. For an instant, Charles thought she would rebuff, rebuke him. But instead she moved his hands, still secreted under her coat, along her upper body to her breasts. She moved against the gentle pressure of his cupped hands and gazed up at him, her mouth slightly open, promising and inviting. She ran her tongue around the inside of her upper lip.

"Tomorrow," she whispered. "At the school. I'll tell my family I've work to do for next week. Meet me there after Sunday dinner. No one will be out and around then after church and dinner, and no one will be coming to the schoolhouse on Sunday."

Charles, emboldened by her invitation, caught her to him and kissed her clumsily once more.

"Lydia," he pleaded. "Let me . . . "

Quickly she stepped away from him and snatched up her hat from where it had fallen. "No, silly. It's too cold. And I should be home by now. Tomorrow. At the schoolhouse."

Charles watched as she pulled her hat back onto her head and, business-like, began to tuck her rambunctious curls in under its edges, then he bent painfully to pick up his mittens. She stepped close to him, grasped his lapels, and drew his face close to hers. "You do want me, don't you, Charles? You won't disappoint me, will you? Tomorrow?"

Before Charles could respond, she reached toward him (Charles thought she meant to kiss him once more) and bit his chin with her even white teeth. The bite was sharp enough that the surprise of it brought a rush of shock bordering on anger.

"Catch me if you can!" she called out, and before he could react, she was gone. Turning on her heel, she ran out from the grove of trees down the road toward her home, one hand clutching her hat to her head. He pounded after her with footfall echoed in his own ears. Catching up quickly, he loped easily alongside until they were both laughing and wheezing in the cold. Lydia was firm. Tomorrow, she promised him.

Charles and Lydia met at the schoolhouse that Sunday afternoon for their prearranged tryst, and Lydia led him skillfully. Charles was an apt pupil, and Lydia was, after all, a teacher. Her warm hand stilled his frantic thrusting and guided him into the dark velvet of her passageway. She tempered her amused tolerance for his inexperienced, clumsy lovemaking with her desperate need.

Lydia threw herself into the charade she and her friends had designed with such hope. And the plan might have succeeded.

———————

On an afternoon three weeks later, Charles blew into his cupped hands to warm both his mittened fingers and his face. His nose began to tingle, and his eyes watered from the contrasting warmth and the faint aroma of animals and their straw bedding that clung to his workman's gloves. The fresh snow made the going tough, and he began to wish he had used the road. Though the way by road was longer than the cross-country route from the Richards' farm to the school, the road would have seen traffic, so he could have walked in the frozen tracks of earlier traffic.

The early morning had brought a snowstorm that, coupled with the rising wind, threatened a blizzard. But the snow had tapered off and, though the wind still blew hard from the north, the storm had dissipated. Now the afternoon waned, and a fat cloud, trailing the earlier storm clouds, positioned itself like a dark feathered hat over the face of the descending sun, pink with embarrassment for the earlier display of nature's bad temper.

Anticipating a blizzard, Richards had earlier directed Charles to herd the cattle from open pasture into holding pens close to the barn. After distributing grain into the feed troughs and forking down extra hay, John suggested Charles could leave early. Charles was joyful, anticipating that Lydia might have sent the pupils home earlier than the usual dismissal at three-thirty.

Seeing opportunity for an unscheduled meeting at the schoolhouse, Charles left, first taking the short lane from the Richards farmhouse, but he quickly detoured to the cross-country route. If I follow the railroad tracks, he thought, I could leave from the tracks and cut off to the school at the Rasmussen place. But no, someone there might see him headed for the school. Lydia was careful that no one would know of their meetings at the school. It wasn't seemly, she told him, for the teacher to be carrying on there.

He snorted with satisfaction. And carry on they had in the three weeks since they began their well-designed courtship. Sometimes, they chased and played like gamboling puppies. They tested one another, their interest in the relationship. Sometimes Lydia played coy, affecting disinterest. And once, Charles told her with a perfectly straight face that he wouldn't be seeing her anymore, that he wanted to court someone else, little knowing the panic his play-acting set free for Lydia. But their games ended in the cloakroom on the hard, flat mattress of the cot that was the refuge for the occasional student who became ill at school.

The uncomfortable cot rocked and swayed with their combined weight and the increasingly hard use for which it was never designed. After its wooden leg finally broke, dumping them both on the floor in a heap, they took to making themselves a pallet with their heavy winter coats in the small narthex to the main schoolroom that also served as a cloakroom for the students. Sometimes after they were spent, they lay drowsily locked in embrace and made elaborate plans for their life together.

"Let's get married soon, Charles. Someday, we can farm my Papa's land. We'll build a little house for Mama and Papa right there on the place, and then we'll live in the big house with all our babies. Oh, Charles, think of it! Won't it be grand?"

Charles was secure and happy, warm and fulfilled in this new love. At last, someone had plans for him that were worthy of him, and someone worthy of him wanted to share a life. Lydia was everything he could have ever dreamed of. Secure in her position in the community as the eldest daughter of a respected and prominent church-going family, he would automatically ascend to become a man of some status, and respected. And he could give his mama the things that she deserved. Maybe they could build a little house for her as well. One with a front porch lined with rocking chairs and a swing. C. D. was never included in Charles's dream.

The enthusiasm of his reverie warmed him, discomfort was forgotten, and by the time he left the windy meadow and entered the stand of timber that surrounded the school, he only looked forward to his surprise visit. Concentrating on the uncertain footing in the grove, he tramped cautiously toward the clearing and the schoolhouse, advancing from the rear of the white frame building. A mounded pile of brush and firewood screened his approach to the windows of the building, and the strong wind muffled the sound of his heavy boots on the underbrush. Stepping carefully over underbrush and fallen trees, Charles emerged from a dense thicket and came face-to-face with El Diablo, tied behind the protective screen. Spooked by Charles's sudden appearance, El Diablo rolled his eyes, snorted, and pranced nervously when Charles edged nearer. The reins tethering the animal snapped taut as the horse tried to back away from him.

His mind rapidly considered the possibilities. Had the horse bolted and run? Strayed? Thrown his rider? Then, Charles noted that the reins were carefully tied to a stout branch under the overhang of a sheltering tree. The animal was not only out of the sight of anyone coming to the schoolhouse by the lane but also protected from the fierce, biting wind. It was no accident that he was here.

A frown creased two vertical furrows over Charles's nose. His lips made a hard line of his mouth, and a band of white appeared around his pinched nostrils. His pulse rhythmically hammered its tattoo on his brain.

His response was instinctive. The schoolyard was barren except for a forlorn swing tied to the long arm of the lone tree in the fenced-off plot. Two privies, one for the girls and one for the boys, squatted at the furthermost corner behind the building. There being no windows at the rear of the school from which he could be seen, Charles hesitated only long enough to check that there was no one present in the schoolyard, then he crept stealthily from behind the pile of brush. He hurried in a crouch to the nearest window. The sun had dropped farther into the western sky, and Charles knew that he would not be easily seen from the inside, where the kerosene lamps shone small beacons of yellow warmth. He dragged off his hat, cautiously rose to his full height, and peered inside. It took a few moments to search the darkening recesses of the big room before his eyes found what he had most feared.

Lydia and C. D. were together talking animatedly, heatedly, with Lydia gesturing, her hands stabbing the air. It was too apparent that they knew each other well. The sight of Lydia's face in profile told him she was angry and had been crying. He watched while C. D. tried to comfort her.

As if in a vacuum, unable to catch his breath, Charles sank into a squatting position, then slid into a slump against the support of the wooden building. He lay curled and near insensible in a fetal position until he was finally aroused by the guttural moan that he heard escaping from his own throat into the wind. He was surprised by the sound, but it continued unheard in the arctic cold that drove relentlessly through his body and pinioned him against the stark white building.

As awareness returned, his mind focused on the rent in the finger of his work glove from which his finger could be seen. It retrieved involuntarily from scrutiny like a grubworm retreats from the light when its rock is overturned. Like his most private parts shrank and retreated into the folds of his body when he was cold or frightened. The pink flesh gleamed obscenely from its hiding place. Vulnerable. Powerless. Mocking him. Shaming him.

Foolish. He knew he'd been foolish for believing he could be thought of as attractive or desirable. Mindless, lacking any awareness of what should have been questioned. Trusting, when it all seemed to fall into place too simply. Stupidly thinking he had gained a trajectory allowing himself self-governance; for thinking he could trust anything other than his own instincts. He became a misanthropist without knowing there was a word with which he could describe himself.

After a time, a reflex for survival more feral than human stirred Charles from his stupor before he could freeze and die from exposure. Gradually, as he began to move, full awareness returned. Tentative and stiff, he climbed to his feet, knowing as he did so that at least some of his toes were frostbitten or even frozen. As he flexed his cold-stiffened fingers, he knew he had lain on the ground for some while. He wondered at the loss of conscious thought that allowed this to happen.

Reassuming his same vantage point at the window, he brazenly made no attempt to hide himself as he surveyed the schoolroom. The broad, flat teacher's desk upon which he and Lydia had once pleasured themselves, the round iron stove in the corner under which a melted red crayon left a livid clot of wax, the stack of copybooks next to the desk awaiting grades; Charles examined the details carefully, each in its turn. The room was empty. Unwillingly, he turned his eyes to the open doorway of the cloakroom where he and Lydia had so many times sought refuge for their lovemaking.

Charles stood without moving, without taking his eyes from the door. Without questioning how long C. D. and Lydia had been in the cloakroom together. Without knowing how long he watched for them to reappear. It could have been minutes, but had it been hours, Charles would have stayed, a mute, frozen sentry at his self-appointed post.

When Lydia and C. D. re-entered the main room of the school, Charles knew with cold certainty that it was not the first time C. D. and Lydia had availed themselves of its privacy. He thought of his own performances on the pile of coats that had served as their bed. Objective and detached, he wondered if Lydia compared his prowess to that of his father.

Charles watched as C. D. sauntered from point to point in the room, picking up objects for examination, replacing them, jamming his hands into his pockets, removing them, and inspecting his fingernails carefully. Charles recognized the symptoms of C. D.'s boredom.

After ten or fifteen minutes, with staged reluctance, C. D. shrugged into his heavy coat, the one Charles had borrowed the first night when he and Lydia went to the Allshouse party.

Lydia began to weep, and Charles watched dispassionately as C. D. gathered her to him once more, tucking her against his chest, then unbuttoning his coat and drawing her inside its folds, sharing the comfort of his own body's warmth. Spreading his charm as he spread his sperm, without thought for the consequences. Charles thought of the first night he and Lydia had walked home when he, Charles, had held her close to him, inside the warmth of that same coat in the same way. Looking at her swollen face, blotched with tears, he wondered how he could ever have found her attractive.

C. D. finally took his leave with his broad, self-assured smile, a wink, and a chuck under the chin for Lydia. Not knowing which direction C. D. would turn when he left the front door of the school-house, Charles waited dry-eyed to confront his father. He waited for C. D. to discover that Charles had been witness to his debauchery. But C. D. turned to the side opposite from the window where Charles had watched and waited, leaving Charles unseen on his way to retrieve the horse. It was nearly full dark, but the moon hadn't risen, so he wasn't aware of the extra set of tracks in the snow leading from the thicket to where Charles stood. C. D. never suspected that he had been observed.

Charles watched his father disappear into the grove and waited until he had time to mount and ride away. He stood facing the brush pile, listening for the sounds of C. D.'s departure, the crunch of snow under the horse's feet. The wind began to drop even while he stood there, and Charles knew finally that C. D. was gone. Turning back to the window, Charles could see Lydia, sniveling, sometimes sobbing as she struck a match to light the lantern she carried to light her homeward journey. She banked the fire and gathered papers to grade and her lunch box. She donned her hat and coat, tied a woolen scarf around the collar of her coat, and exited through the door onto the wooden platform outside the door. She set her bundle of books and lunch box at the top of the three steps to the ground, holding her mittens in her left hand and the oversize key to the lock in her right. Charles watched, transfixed, but then moved purposefully to intercept Lydia.

Hurrying because it was so late, Lydia closed the door, turned the skeleton key, and when she heard the familiar cluck of the lock she turned to pick up her lantern, never expecting to see Charles. As she straightened with the lantern in her hand, he caught her with an open-handed blow that was deflected in part by the red hat and scarf he once thought so fetching. His hand, in its rough leather mitten, only scraped across her face, bloodying her nose, but the unexpected impact knocked her backward, causing her to stumble and fall against the door. The lantern rolled away, spilling oil and flame on the wooden stoop. Without hesitation, Charles directed a vicious kick to her side with the full force of his booted foot and felt the satisfying crunch as her ribs broke even through her winter coat. He turned and stalked away without further regard for Lydia or the flickering flame that danced down the steps of the school, following the trail of the lamp oil.

On the second consecutive morning that Charles did not report to the Richards' farm for work, Rose timidly ventured an inquiry as to his intentions. Charles only answered, "Mr. Richards doesn't need me anymore. Guess I'll have to look for something else."

Charles's closed countenance gave Rose no hints, and she was afraid to hear answers to the questions she so much wanted to ask. As she gathered her hat and coat for the ride into town to her own work, Charles appeared, wearing his second-best trousers and shirt under his overcoat, obviously planning to ride to town.

Before the end of that week in which Charles had inadvertently discovered his father's affair with Lydia Richards, Rose was to learn that Lydia would be married to the Becker boy. For a man like John Richards with no sons, Will Becker was heir apparent, and Lydia was twenty years old. It was time she married. Likewise, there was little surprise when their first son arrived two months short of his announced delivery date, five months short of his parents' first anniversary. After all, everyone knows first babies can come anytime; the rest take nine months.

And in the years to come, when Rose would see Lydia Becker with her oldest, she noted his resemblance to her own handsome son. His dark good looks. The same arch of the eyebrow over the deep-set blue eyes and high cheekbones in marked contrast to the lashless, rabbity blond, milky-eyed look of Lydia's other children. Fortunately, inquiring minds could catch a resemblance to Lydia's own dramatic coloring, and the startling Dawson blue eyes could be indexed to Will Becker, though his legacy was the more innocuous, benign blue.

The defiant challenge was gone from Lydia's expression. Her eyes searched Rose's face when they met, but Rose's learned and practiced response, her noncommittal smile, gave Lydia no quarter. Rose was kind, but she was no fool. Over the years, with the gradual erosion of her own defense mechanisms and her own reasoning, Rose would come to an understanding of what had transpired.

Charles found work in town. His sober appearance, serious manner, and obviously strong back made him the most eligible candidate for the position on the city work crew that was vacated when Snort Jackson dropped dead.

Charles found a job which, because of its security and lack of challenge, fit his needs perfectly.

And through the years during which he was promoted to foreman to supervisor to manager and eventually to chief city clerk, his life equation was never complete. X remained unresolved. He was a self-made man, a misanthropic philistine.

Nine

Trying to settle back into his routine at the store and in his office, Sonny started when the telephone jangled noisily just inches away. The somewhat discordant ring offended him and his ears. Sonny made it a practice not to buy products or services from businesses that used a ringing telephone in their radio or television advertising. There were enough annoying sounds in the world without adding to the din and clatter deliberately, particularly in the name of sales.

Sonny resisted the impulse to sweep the noisy instrument from his desk right into the wastebasket, but even as he reached for it, his second voice, the one on which he relied for best advice, advised him not to yield to his urge.

He picked up the receiver and answered evenly without betraying his impatience. "Franklin Hardware. This is Sonny Dawson."

He listened for a moment. "Yes. Kent. Thanks for returning my call."

His delivery was smooth. He took a deep breath before he continued. This was becoming hard work. This business of death.

What happens when a person with property, real estate, personal possessions dies and has no one? No one to clean up his affairs for

*him. What of a pet whose owner dies. and there's no one to take care
of the bereaved animal?*

At the last thought of a little pet, like the much-loved Spats, waiting for someone who would never return, his breath caught in a sob.
And his rational voice told him that he had to set aside such mawk-
ish sentiment to avoid falling into the trap of self-pity.

"Well, Kent, I need to get started on Polly's work. I guess *we* need
to get started on Polly's work." He punctuated his awkwardness
with a rough chuckle.

Both recognized that the request was actually a negotiation.
Though Kent and Sonny had been classmates from grade school
to high school graduation, they only now considered themselves
friends in business and community affairs, and Kent's help carried a
price tag. Such is the organization of professional work. The request
for services is characterized as help, politely phrased and negotiated
by the terms of the billing for services.

But Sonny had always known that a basic cultural difference
separated Sonny Dawson and Kent Field. Something far more fun-
damental than the fact that crustless sandwiches at Kent's house
were always sliced diagonally rather than straight across, and Kent's
father wore a suit at the dinner table with a monogrammed napkin
ceremoniously placed across his knees.

Eyes fixed on the instrument on the desk, Sonny was nodding in
voiceless agreement with the disembodied voice emanating from the
receiver. "Okay, Kent. One-thirty it is then. Yes, that will be fine.
Anything I should bring? All right, see you at one-thirty."

Even as he hung up the phone, Sonny felt the injustice his own
efficient self-sufficiency had forced on him. He'd read about grief
and its stages. Pastor Fred had offered a class on death and dying
for the adult Sunday school class that he and Polly attended. Then,
it had been an abstraction, something to consider for an hour or
two. Not this, not this grueling, interrupted process. Not this start
and stop, start and stop. Not this convention requiring a certain

performance from its subjects as now. His mind raced, recalling the stages of grief Pastor Fred described, remembering his angry tantrum with shame.

God knows I hope I am never that angry again.

Is it that time heals? In that case, one should just sit back and wait for comfort to arrive on schedule. Or alternatively, is it the process, the steps one paces off prescriptively, that is the key to recovery? Is there a script? A reflection of the self that measures progress along a continuum? If there is a script, what is ensured by adherence to the lines? Is there a process like a charm to be recited and then, magically, grief is concluded?

Sonny remembered a nursery rhyme from old times with Rose and his sisters. He was suddenly tired. Tired of the effort he was making. Tired of trying to understand his feelings. His shoulders drooped, and he slid the heel of his hand wearily across his forehead, then guiltily rubbed the slightly oily residue against his other hand. Never more the need to look around to see if Polly was watching. She would have sensed his mood, comforted him even as he would have tried to conceal his sadness. He longed for her. To feel the swell of her breasts brush against him as her arms gathered him close, to sense the fragrance of her skin and hair.

The malevolent heaviness descended upon him, relentless and invincible. He pulled a deep breath and held it, his chest growing miserable and tight with the effort, yet unable to release the pressure of the tension that held him.

Oh goddamn, goddamn. I'll never move again. I'll sit here paralyzed in this damn chair until I rot. I'll never get up again. They'll find me here tonight, tomorrow, next year. Locked up right here at this desk.

The weight held him, bearing on him until finally the breath was forced from him in short bursts. Coinciding with the last breath he expelled, his vocal cords sounded involuntarily with an utterance that was first more a grunt of effort, then it was a moan.

The desperate sense of anxiety that had always threatened him was absent. This was quite different. Now, there was no anxiety. The other shoe had dropped. The worst and unnamed fear was realized. He never thought he would be alone, that Polly would go first.

Again, unbidden memories forced their way into his consciousness.

"Sonny? Sonny? You in there?"

For the second time in as many days, someone was pounding on a door that should have ensured privacy. Yesterday, the men's room. Today, his own office. The voice claiming its trophy, knowing full well that he was in there, was not one he could ignore. He knew damn good and well that Wanda the Wicked would stand outside the door demanding entrance until he responded.

"Sonny, come on out. It's time to get down to the First National for the meeting."

Wanda was among the many who still referred to the South Side Café as the First National, which it had not been for thirty years.

Pound, pound, pound. The assault on the door continued. Sonny knew he couldn't delay much longer. Wanda Wainwright would not let anything so inconsequential as a heavy wooden door or any kind of sensitivity stand in her way. Sonny had known Wanda for a lifetime, since kindergarten with their teacher, the venerable Miss Marbel.

Sonny would long remember Miss Marbel's baleful glare when she spied Wanda, her attention drifting and blowing spit bubbles during reading group. Seated in a semi-circle on one of the miniature wooden chairs with Miss Marbel perched on her bony buttocks before them on a similar chair, the transgression was tantamount to heresy. Miss Marbel was a force to be reckoned with, even for Wanda, whom Miss Marbel had christened "Spitfire" in recognition of her spunky attitude.

To grade school, high school, the whole route. The munificent opulence of Kent Field's birthday parties from kindergarten through high school, the trepidation of seventh grade, which was the first year that students moved to the high school building for classes, and later in high school, late trips home on the pep team bus.

While the relationship between Sonny and Wanda had survived the years since school days, Polly and Wanda's relationship had been uneasy. Two women loving the same man was never the cause; rather it was that Polly knew their childhood held many hidden chapters.

"Sonny, come on. I'm not of a mind to be late. Let's get going. We're going to the committee meeting."

Wanda was officious, overbearing, loud, and obnoxious. She was also smart, one of the smartest people Sonny knew, and she had been his loyal friend for that many years. But sometimes, he wanted to wring her damned neck. Like now.

More than half annoyed, yet amused, Sonny pushed his desk chair back as he stood. Taking a deep breath, he crossed the room and reluctantly pulled the door open but deftly blocked Wanda's entrance. The room had too recently held fragile memories. He didn't want Wanda to see the wilted rose, the untidy stack of mail. The offending rose would have been swept into the wastebasket, the envelopes sliced open with surgical precision, the contents extracted and stacked for his eventual perusal, but not before Wanda's quick eye had taken in the contents to be stored for future reference. Sonny had always thought Wanda's mind was like a computer. Information long forgotten by anyone else was stored on her hard drive to be retrieved if one only knew which file to ask for. Like a computer, she was not discerning regarding the quality of the information she so readily stored.

"Why, she was bald. Bald as a billiard ball by the time she finally died."

"Cancer," she would say, her voice dropping as though she were saying an offensive word, but then, she continued. "Cancer, but it was probably the syph that really got her."

To a now-former friend: "Margaret, do you remember the time you took drunk and crawled to the car because you couldn't walk?"

"Wanda, you have lipstick on your teeth."

Without looking directly at her, Sonny knew that was a safe greeting. Wanda frequently had lipstick on her teeth, dark red Revlon lipstick, either Cherries in the Snow or Love That Red. Her incisor, the one that overlapped its canine partner, caught on the underside of her upper lip, and the result left her with a perennial jagged smile.

Wanda lorded her friendship with Sonny over his employees, but in return for her demanding friendship, Wanda bought everything she possibly could from Sonny's store, valiantly resisting the charms of the new Walmart store in nearby Centerton. Wanda always made sure Sonny knew how loyal she was to him and how important her purchasing power was at the store.

"Tell the girls we're off to the meeting. If they need you for something, the meeting's at the South Side."

This she directed imperiously, even as she had, with her arm linked firmly in his, drawn Sonny from his office out onto the sales floor of the store in full hearing range of Ruby and Thelma Jane. There were no secrets when Wanda gave full voice. Her voice might be considered melodic in that it rose and fell with the inflections of meaning, but her tone and accent ruined any possibility that it was pleasant.

Sonny, rolling his eyes at Ruby and Thelma Jane, gestured mutely, his extended forefinger pointing at the front door. Wanda, under full steam, mock-marched him out the door and into the street.

———

They emerged from the store into glittering white heat that had sliced the morning haze of humidity as neatly as a scalpel through soft recumbent flesh. When the sun dropped low in the late afternoon, the humidity would seep back, unwelcomed, and wrap Onansburg in its blanket of moisture. But now, the sun sucked at their pores, neatly extracting fluids before perspiration could form.

An abrasive light wind scratched against flesh that would too easily scorch in the baking sun.

The whistle sounded its regulatory call to cease work for the hallowed hour of the noon meal. Before the siren wound down and the occasional dog that still joined the descending chorus gave up his painful protest, a number of Onansburg citizens appeared on the street hurrying homeward or to the South Side Café. It was a point of honor with some that work didn't stop for lunch until the whistle gave its permission.

Upon entering the South Side, Wanda peered around from group to group, oblivious to Sonny's discomfort, waving at some, smiling toothily at others, all the while weaving through the occupied tables toward the closed door of the meeting room at the back of the café. The buzz of conversation, the clink of stainless steel cutlery against thick ironstone dishes dropped off suddenly and then resumed.

The three Shaw brothers were seated midway through the crowded dining room. When Darrell, Walter, and Tom caught sight of Sonny and Wanda, they pushed their half-eaten lunches away. Without words to one another, they pushed their chairs back, but the sudden chorus of the four legs of their three chairs scraping loudly in unison against the gritty linoleum flooring caused the other diners to turn toward them, forks suspended and eyebrows raised in question. Each of the brothers reached to his back pocket, extracted bills from his respective wallet, then laid the money on the table next to the dinner plate without waiting for his change.

They stood at the table as Sonny, slight in comparison to the weathered, raw-boned Shaw men, advanced past the brothers in the narrow corridor between tables, nodded to each in turn, and pronounced each name in grave, monosyllabic greeting. The two older brothers met Sonny's eyes but cut him dead with their glares. When he locked his gaze on Tom, the last to leave the table, Tom's face, with his clean-shaven fair skin already glossed to high color, went crimson. Tom, however, looked away, mutely acknowledging his discomfort.

Sonny watched the backs of the three brothers as they left the café, and without meeting the eyes of any of the other diners, he turned and followed to where Wanda was waiting for him at the door to the meeting room. Her round-eyed expression registered that she had witnessed the unspoken conflict.

"Ready?" she asked before she pushed the door open. He nodded silently.

Conversation flowed once again at the tables at his back.

Sonny remembered little else of the time at the South Side. The committee had convened at the back of the café and hadn't witnessed the mini-drama in the main dining room. But it was evident from the sudden drop in conversation when he and Wanda entered that his attendance at the meeting had been in question. And Wanda's triumphant "See, I told you he'd come" did little to make him feel less conspicuous. He ordered a glass of iced tea from the circulating waiter who happened to be the owner, Phil Larson, but declined to order lunch. The other committee members finished their lunch before taking up the business of the meeting.

The meeting passed uneventfully after polite but uncertain greetings were tendered. He tried to focus his attention on the business at hand and noted that mercifully, a printed agenda at each place didn't call for a report from him. He felt disoriented and dazed from the snub from Polly's brothers, and he was embarrassed that it had been in public. He shook his head sadly and caught Wanda looking at him quizzically.

At the conclusion of the meeting, before its members made ready to leave, Sonny asked for a moment to speak.

"Thank you, all of you, for stepping up for me during the last few days." His voice cracked, but he took a deep breath and continued. "You all know, my job is pretty much the same year after year with the setup of the benches in the Courthouse Park and the placement of the refreshment stands, so Dell and I and the rest of the city crew had gone over the arrangements last week. I'll be there tomorrow to see to the rest of the placements for the vendors and exhibits."

Then, with a start, he recalled that they had met last Friday afternoon and his report then had been much the same as that which he'd just given. Momentarily shaken, he continued uneasily, "Again, thanks to all of you." Several of those present gave half-hearted, close-mouthed smiles, as if concerned an open-mouthed smile might be deemed insensitive. Some nodded with compressed lips.

He sat down quickly, then realized the meeting was concluded. He stood again as the others studiously shuffled papers and took final swallows of their iced tea and coffee, avoiding direct eye contact. He glanced at his watch and hastily excused himself, in a quick aside to Wanda, without giving her more than an offhand "I've got an appointment, so I'll just get on my way. I'll see you and Robert soon."

As Sonny exited through the main dining room, he noted with relief that most of the diners who had witnessed the Shaws' snub were gone. Mary Lou Acheson gave him a half-wave as she sprayed and polished the counter but turned away too quickly and busied herself with replacing salt shakers and sugar shakers near the napkin dispensers.

Time to get on over to Kent's office. Damn, what is all this with the Shaws? I made peace with them years ago. Now what? A deal's a deal. No need for behavior like this!

As he'd recounted to Tom just yesterday, he had informally agreed with the Shaw family years before that he wouldn't try to lay claim to Polly's holdings in the family business. He and Polly had even joked about it, with him saying what's Polly's is Polly's and what's mine is Polly's, referring to their mutual ownership of their assets apart from the Shaw Family Farms stock that Polly owned. And likewise, Polly twitted him about it, teasing and laughing up at him. She had been so tiny even as compared to his moderate height.

"You're right, Sonny. What's mine is mine, and what's yours is mine!"

And now the stony silence with which he had been met bothered him more than he wanted to admit.

Shit! What a difference a few days make! Well, after I see Kent and he assures the Shaws that their precious land is safe, they'll come around. I told Tom that I'm not after their land! And the money. Who cares about the money, but goddamn, it's the principle. Polly was always so damned proud of her earnings from her family's business. But it'll be all right! It'll be all right!

Sonny tried to puzzle through what had happened even as he reassured himself. He regretted that half of the business community of Onansburg had witnessed the unspoken exchange. Despite the Shaw family's disappointment when Polly chose him as her life partner over Drennan, the relationship had always been amicable, and he and Polly had been close friends with Tom and Jenny as couples. Sunday lunch at one or the other of the brothers' farm homes had been as frequent as once every few weeks, and likewise, he and Polly had hosted a lunch or Sunday supper.

Sonny consciously repeated the incantation over and over to himself on his way to Kent's office.

It'll be all right! It'll be all right!

Once on the street again, Sonny scarcely noticed the dazzling heat. As was his practice, he followed the cement pathway in front of the stores over to Kent's office instead of cutting through the courtyard. He habitually avoided wrecking the shine on his penny loafers in the dusty grass.

Let's see. This is Thursday. They'll set up the wooden benches for the program around the bandstand early tomorrow.

It'll be all right. They'll see.

Sonny glanced at his watch. One-twenty-eight. Right on time. He pounded on, scarcely noticing the heat from the sidewalk searing his feet through the bottoms of his leather soles.

It'll be all right. It's okay. They'll see.

Sonny was so self-absorbed that he didn't hear the light tickety, tickety, tickety of the wheels of an expensive bicycle swooping up behind him despite the prohibition against riding on the sidewalks on the square. "Behind you, Sonny. On your left."

Sonny stopped, momentarily disoriented. A voice from nowhere. Then, the owner of the disembodied warning braked to a smart stop a yard in front of him at the entrance to Kent's office. It was Kent himself dismounting from the lightweight aluminum frame of the imported bike.

Kent had recently embraced cycling as a sport and was its newest disciple. In keeping with his methodical, pedantic approach to questions, issues, or his interests, Kent researched his subject well. Before ever climbing on the first bike he had set his seat to since his 1955 Schwinn (Kent, his brother, and his sister had each received Schwinn bicycles on their thirteenth birthdays), Kent studied reams of literature. He made numerous phone calls and trips to Des Moines to locate and purchase the equipment that his analysis had determined would best suit his needs. Today, his biking helmet perched on the top of his head like a fat, tan ham, its smooth molded buttocks enveloping the legendary Field brain. Sonny smiled automatically in greeting, his mouth pulling into a tight, flat line, threatening to crack and break his face. He stifled the urge to laugh out loud.

Kent was one of those persons who believed and made others believe he was intelligent because his parents had informed him of same at an early age. Sonny had personally believed that Kent was no smarter than himself or any one of a number of others with whom he had gone to school. It was just that Kent believed himself to be smarter, wiser, and endowed with special intuitive knowledge about all things. Kent created his own reality that, while not in dispute or question, was likewise never quite proven. It was widely assumed, as a matter of course, that Kent had graduated first in his class from law school at the University of Iowa, which in truth he did not. He never even suggested that he might have done so, but his family's self-importance carried a transcendent superiority.

Kent parked his bike precisely, removed the ham-helmet, tucked it military style into the cradle of his left arm, and smartly extended his right hand to Sonny. Everything about Kent postured as smart. His handshake, his starched white shirt under the tan poplin of the lightweight summer suit, the sharply creased trousers. Sonny conceded that few could survive the inferno of the day's heat and still look as cool and composed as Kent did.

Kent precisely pumped Sonny's arm twice in greeting and bent to the job of unlocking the door. Whenever Kent moved, he did so with a carefully studied, conservative use of energy, with little wasted motion.

"Come on in, Sonny, where it's cool."

Sonny and Polly had once speculated about the Fields' sex life. Sonny had argued that it was Monday, Wednesday, Friday at a predetermined time, while Polly was sure it was carefully scheduled but the act was timed also as to its duration. Precise and mechanical.

Waiting for Kent's key to find its connection in its mate, Sonny noted Kent's solemnity. No doubt his demeanor was the customary treatment for the recently bereaved, a relief from the spurious rasp of laughter with which Kent usually filled lapses in conversation. Sonny felt his sinuses wince from the air conditioning when he followed Kent through the heavy door. A nice door, but not so nice as the one Kent had tried to buy from Sonny.

Sonny smirked to himself, remembering Kent's not-too-long-ago remodeling and refurbishing of his office suite, after which it turned out looking exactly as it had after its last redo, which had occurred exactly thirty years before. All wooden appointments were refinished, the vintage wall coverings were replaced with the same basic burgundy and gold stripe, faintly reminiscent of old men's pajamas, each volume from the library was inspected for damage or dry rot and then either sent off to be rebound or carefully packed away until it was restored to its rightful place on the newly finished shelves. The heavy oak furniture was never in need of a complete refurbishing because of the meticulous care it was given on a day-to-day, week-to-week basis. It had long been Jessie's job to polish the venerable antique partner's desk with lemon and beeswax polish on Friday afternoons, as she had for Kent's father before him.

Jessie started working for Kent's father as a young woman, and she came to know more of the practice of law than any young person completing formal paralegal training would know for many years. At seventy-five years old now, she sensed that she was ending her usefulness to Kent. She observed Kent wanting to appear progressive and aggressive and above all, younger, with new strategies and ideas. His new interest in cycling was part of his newly emerging self-image, and she knew the picture of his father's elderly secretary still at her post as his legal assistant and guard to the inner sanctum of his office did not fit his evolving plan. She believed Kent paid deference to her importance to his father with her continued employment.

Sonny's eyes flashed with surprise that Jessie was not at her post. He couldn't remember a time he had come here that she had not greeted him courteously but officiously, her dignity ever reminding him of his good fortune in being allowed to spend his hard-earned money with the firm.

"Senior, please take line one. Junior, you have a call on line two. Senior, a call on one."

Sonny remembered Jessie's well-modulated tones announcing the summons to Field and Field. Senior and Junior. Neither would have dreamed of ignoring her. He could never imagine Kent working so many years with the venerable Jessie calling him "Junior" for years after there was no longer a reason to distinguish the two men.

"Kent, where's Jessie? I've never been in here that she hasn't been at her desk."

At her post like a German shepherd, was his unspoken thought. Inheritances indeed come in different forms.

"I told her to take the afternoon. Stay at home out of the heat. She still drives that old Buick, and I worry about her, Sonny. The engine throws off a ton of heat and then she locks it up and it's like a furnace when she gets into it, and frankly, after some former clients left this morning, she was rather shaken. They left, shall we say, rather abruptly. I told her she wouldn't need to come back in. She knew you were coming in and that I planned to take as much time with you as you need."

Kent waved Sonny on through the anterooms into his own office, where the antique partner's desk occupied the center of the room in the same spot it had held court for over one hundred years, since it was hauled by mule teams overland upon its arrival in St. Louis by steamer. Kent gestured to the partner's chair on the side opposite his own. This was a recently added innovation—to allow a client so close to his own personal space. And to be sure, it was a concession judiciously granted only to very important clients or friends. Sonny was both and couldn't have known that it was an honor that Kent afforded him, but he noted that on previous appointments, he'd been seated at a respectful distance, not at the desk.

Without Jessie, who as part of every client visit was to rap discreetly on the door and inquire if the gentlemen cared for coffee or tea, Kent turned immediately to business. He withdrew the file copy of Polly's will from within a locked drawer on the left-hand side of the desk, took it from its file folder, and laid it on top of the handsome, leather-bound blotter.

"Sonny, I'm sure you're familiar with the provisions of Polly's will. Do you have questions about the disposition of her estate?"

Sonny's eyes widened, and he exclaimed, "I've never seen her will! I've always had just a basic idea that her interests in our common property would be left to me, and her share of stock in Shaw Family Farms would go back to her family. I don't know how the two of you worked that out legally, but I've always agreed with the Shaws that I'd never have any ownership in their business."

Sonny saw a frown crease the wide space between Kent's eyebrows and noted that Kent's laugh, when it came to cover his surprise, was like the chatter of crisp fall leaves swirling against a lonely cement sidewalk, the harbinger of chill that reminded one of gloom and hardship of inclement weather ahead. With eyebrows raised in surprise, Kent queried, "Well then, Sonny, do you want to read this yourself or do you want me to read it to you now? We could postpone this to another day after you've had an opportunity to read through the will."

Sonny paused uncertainly, then responded, "I'd rather that you read it to me now, and I'll stop you when I have questions. Just cut out the pro forma stuff." He settled back, rested an elbow on the arm of the chair, and leaned his head against the comfortable angle formed by his forefinger and thumb.

Kent seemed uncharacteristically self-conscious, fidgeted in his chair, smoothed his trousers beneath him, and then patted the knife-edge crease into place across his thighs. Without opening his mouth, his rueful laugh expelled itself through his nose in short snorts. Sonny noted Kent wasn't smiling despite what seemed to be amusement on his part.

"You know, this isn't the way we ordinarily do this. Usually, there's no call for this formality of reading the will aloud. That's pretty much a fictional device for television or in books. Ordinarily I'd just do an overview of the assets, along with what was directed for disposition of the assets, and then we'd move on to the management of the will's provisions. We'd just follow what the will says with the requirements that go with it, filings and deeds to bequeathed property. But I guess if you've not read it . . . "

Kent looked to Sonny for agreement but quickly deduced from

Sonny's posture and quick hand gesture that he did in fact wish for
Kent to read the document and was waiting for him to begin.

"Last Will and Testament of Polly Shaw Dawson. I, Polly Shaw
Dawson, of Choctaw County, Iowa, publish and declare this to be
my Last Will and Testament . . . "

Sonny tuned out Kent's voice when he began to read the formal
introduction to Polly's will. He fixed his stare on the Oriental rug
and tried not to be annoyed with Kent looking up at him, coupled
with the nervous, involuntary sniff between paragraphs. He tried
to disassociate the will from Polly. Sonny surmised, having managed both his mother's and Grandma Rose's estates as executor,
that Polly's will would be consistent with his understanding of that
which had been agreed upon between them. There'd been no surprises from Grandma Rose's tidy bequests. But he shook his head,
remembering his mother's will.

There had been some $150,000 in cash and a savings account to
be distributed equally to her three children. While it was no fortune,
it was more than he'd expected. Sonny had thought it curious that
there had been no gift to the church that had seemingly occupied an
important place in the lives of their parents.

*Talk about surprises! How could anyone have known? The way
they lived, they could have been existing from paycheck to paycheck.*

"Sonny, should I go on? Is there something . . . ?"

Sonny started, then realized that Kent had seen his involuntary
headshake.

"No, sorry, Kent. My mind drifted."

Nodding his understanding, Kent continued.

" . . . hereby revoking all former Wills executed by me. I direct that
all my legally enforceable debts and funeral and testamentary expenses
be fully paid as soon after my death as can properly be done."

*Pay the bill for the funeral. Just go on and pay Steve this after-
noon. Don't wait for Steve to mail it. Get the damned bill and pay
it. Don't even look at it. I don't want to know what the charges are*

for. Hell, someone should pay survivors having to go through with the funeral. Just another piece of business.

Having made his plan without further debate, he felt recklessly giddy but then immediately guilty. Then he remembered his parents and their approach to money management and their no-debt philosophy. He tried to breathe deeper and from his diaphragm, recognizing his mounting anxiety.

Mother never had a dime to spend on her own, for herself or the three of us. Dad drove her to the grocery store on Saturday afternoon with the three of them, Cloris, Dolores, and himself, to watch how carefully shopping was conducted. Regardless of featured specials, Charles selected the higher-priced items, even the can of green beans or the much-hated spinach. He didn't want anyone to think he couldn't afford the better choice, by which he meant the more expensive, regularly priced goods.

Sonny had always known the cost of their home had been paid for with a check in its entirety when it was purchased. No mortgages for Charles Dawson. He only bought those things for which he could pay cash.

New was only when a predecessor was beyond use, such as a broom; a towel finding new service as cleaning rags. Sonny remembered, when he was quite small, wearing panties belonging first to Cloris and then Dolores. Outgrown, but not worn out. But that was another story, he mused.

He tried to cut off his thoughts of his family, but then he thought, *The apple doesn't fall far from the tree.* He realized his reluctance to wait for Steve's invoice was consistent with Dawson practice.

No one could have been nicer than Steve had been. He did everything he could to make it as easy as possible for me. Remember to thank him for that. Just say, thanks, Steve, I appreciate all you did. Just say that.

"However, it is not my desire that my executors accelerate and pay off the entire principal balance remaining on any mortgages, installment purchase contracts, promissory notes, or other evidences of my indebtedness unless there is some significant advantage in doing so. Said fiduciaries shall . . . "

Fiduciaries? Trustee. Yeah, a fiduciary is a trustee. Someone who is trusted. Like spouses trust one another. He thought of Tom and his accusation; an accusation based on a conjectured fear of a circumstance of which Sonny had no knowledge. And the three brothers and their insulting behavior, fueling the town's gossip.

Sonny's heart sank; his body sagged even within the confines of the upright, stiffly padded chair. He'd never thought of the possibility that Polly wouldn't follow her family pledge. He'd never thought of any parallels between Polly's family and his own family. Duplicity. Deceit. These were attributes of his own family, not the Shaw family.

And while his wish was to escape from what he was hearing, from Kent, he drifted too close to an abyss of memory he knew he should avoid. The recoil from the present sent him spinning toward the past. The stern character of Kent's office, its wood paneling, tomes of law, oeuvres of scholarly authors, and Kent's rigid demeanor took Sonny back to the austere church of his childhood.

He recalled his father's voice ringing out over the congregation, strident and self-assured.

"No ne shonny! Neoso cham dar wantu! Du do warnu plebto!

"No ne shonny! No ne shonny! No ne shonny!"

The voice, speaking in an unknown language but attributable to an understanding with a divinity, ripped through the tension in the church, but there was no sanctuary here for Cloris. When Charles Dawson had discovered the empty bed, open window, and absent daughter, he had sounded the alarm, and the rest of the Saturday night had been spent watching and waiting for Cloris's return.

And when she returned with the remnants of forbidden makeup smeared over her face and the strong smell of whiskey and cigarettes on her breath, she first faced parental action from Charles and Priscilla, which was backed up by vigilante action by the congregation of their church. After trying to beat the recalcitrant devil from her with a belt, Charles and Priscilla spent the remainder of the night praying over their daughter. At times, near stuporous from sleep deprivation, they barely moaned their prayers but then awoke to howl their furious supplication.

Cold and stiff with the blood congealing over the bruised flesh where the buckle end of his father's belt had broken the skin of her thighs and naked backside, Cloris had outlasted her parents' strength and rage. Admitting their own defeat at breaking her defiance, they hauled her into the Sunday service and delivered her to the congregation for judgment.

Sonny adroitly edged away from Dolores and away from his mother's grasping, pinching fingers that snaked along the back of the pew toward the vulnerable tendon atop his shoulder. He scooted his body down the pew from his mother's reach, leaning as far away from her as he could, only to have his escape cut off by his father's attention. Charles turned and glared at him. His stare crucified Sonny to the hard, wooden bench.

Sonny ducked his head, folded his hands, and assumed a safely pious posture. After a few moments when no further recriminations seemed imminent, he turned his head slightly from his prayerful position to steal a look at his parents.

His mother's hands were clasped tightly in front of her, the knuckles of her bony fingers white with the effort of clinging to control. Her dry lips clicked in silent prayer, her body rocked with silent passion, and Sonny hoped she wouldn't succumb to the power of the language that sometimes escaped from within her as it had from Charles. He hated when she spoke in strange tongues in a language that tore from her throat, in the voice of a total stranger. His surreptitious gaze shifted to his father, seated on the aisle with Cloris between the avenging parents.

The time had come in the service for public confession of sins, and Charles was sitting well forward on the hard bench, ready to spring to his feet to shout his supplications, to further exhort the congregation to help him, to guide him as he dealt with his wayward daughter, that she would confess, pray to be forgiven, and that absolution would be granted.

Charles stood up next to the pew occupied by his family, grasped Cloris by her upper arm, and hauled her down the center aisle of the church. Seizing her by her shoulders, he turned her to face the congregation and presented his damning case for judgment.

"This child's a sinner! Yes! I have prayed over this sinner! My own child! I am grieved by her. I am ashamed of her. She is willful. She is vain." His voice dropped, then rose on a crescendo of hysteria. "Her sluttish, whorish behavior. She has been with—listen to me—boys, even men from over all the county." His voice dropped then rose on a crescendo of hysteria. "Her name! My good name is a joke found on public restroom walls! She has the devil in her. The devil owns this child. She is one of his!"

Charles had done a more than adequate job of presenting Cloris's case to the congregation. But at five years old, Sonny found the proceedings a mystery. Without understanding her sin, Sonny only knew that Cloris had been bad before and would likely be bad again. The previous all-night session of physical punishment, prayer, and penance had left her weak and exhausted but still defiant. It would be merciful when the voice from heaven could finally be interpreted as pronouncing Cloris saved. Then Sonny knew, after the prayers were completed, they could go home for lunch, a cold lunch with preparation completed the previous day. Charles sat down next to his wife, leaving the seat between them for Cloris, but now, Cloris was left standing before the congregation to receive judgment.

Sonny observed surreptitiously the crosshatch of short, deep scratches on the soft flesh of Dolores's arm closest to him, then the tattooed black marks where a sharpened pencil point had penetrated the flesh between her knuckles. He studied the wounds critically, knowing their mother didn't allow Dolores or himself to use pens, pencils, even crayons, and certainly not scissors unsupervised. It was obvious to him that Dolores had disobeyed.

He studied the back of the wooden pew in front of him, the pronounced grain of the sturdy oak, and longed for one of the stubby pencils and a donation envelope from the metal repository affixed to the back of the pew. But children, even children so young as Sonny, were not allowed to distract themselves by drawing during services.

Lifting his eyes to the occupant of the pew ahead, he watched a boxelder bug make its way through the filigree of fine hairs that escaped the dowdy chignon fixed low on the neck of Sister Fox. The insect crawled back and forth, perhaps disoriented by its own out-of-season appearance, perhaps overwhelmed by the unwashed condition of the greasy locks fixed into a roll resembling oiled string. Vanity was not Sister Fox's sin, nor was cleanliness her virtue.

Sonny bowed his head again but strained to look up from beneath the ledges of his eyebrows at Cloris standing next to their father, dumbly awaiting the judgment of the congregation. Her eyes were dull and glazed, her face was pallid with an occasional blemish standing out against white skin. Her hair was neatly smoothed but with the length of the rich sable mane braided and wrapped in a coronet from ear to ear in a style dated and dowdy. Cloris was humiliated by the modest clothing her parents chose for her, and one of her frequent sins was sneaking from home and changing into friends' cast-offs or borrowed skirts and sweaters. Then, her hair released, and with the voluptuous length swinging without restraint, so it was with Cloris. She traveled Onansburg city streets and the town square with a so-called fast group of girls. The Norris sisters, on stealthy occasion, pushed their mother's Ford convertible from its roost in the detached garage. With Marian pushing and Martha driving, after a silent block or two, they started the engine, and the Ford was their ticket to popularity.

Most of Cloris's friends were already wearing their first nylon stockings and low club heels. The official debut for an Onansburg girl in her first hose hoisted into place by a garter belt and new pumps was Easter Sunday of eighth grade, but it had not been Cloris's lot to join her friends in the excitement of clothing heralding womanhood.

Cloris wore sturdy brown Oxfords and short white socks that tended to slip down on her heels. Her simple cotton dress of indiscriminate color fell shapeless from a yoke in a style that would have been suitable for a ten-year-old girl, but that seemed obscene trying to cover the full breasts of a soon-to-be sixteen-year-old. When its length already had been let down as far as it would go, Priscilla added an unseemly band of extra fabric left over from the original construction of the garment. Now, brightly new in contrast to the dress that was already faded from laundering, it seemed as foreign to the dress as did Cloris to the rest of her family. She longed to emulate her friends, but Charles and Priscilla set a different standard for Cloris, for their family.

"I want my family, my children, and my wife to be an example for everyone in the church to follow. No fol-de-rol or gee-gaws. We're plain, God-fearing, decent people, and I'm not going to hold with a bunch of fooling around with face paint and fancy, lacy dresses. And you will—make no mistake—you *will* behave."

When Cloris caught sight of Sonny peeping at her, her gaze widened, and she shot at him the look of pure, bold defiance which characterized her but which inflamed their father and grieved her mother. Then, she lowered the corner of one eye with just the slightest of winks in his direction. She dropped her eyes before anyone but Sonny caught her reassuring glance, and Sonny drew an involuntary gasp. He was so frightened, for Cloris and for himself.

He wanted Cloris to be good. Whatever good meant, he wanted Cloris to be that way so they could dispense with the sessions of fasting and prayer that didn't seem to make a difference anyway. Sometimes, he was angry with her. Angry that she brought her parents' wrath onto herself and then to all of them. At five years old, he couldn't understand what Cloris had done to make his parents behave as they were doing . . . shouting, slapping, whipping her.

He shifted his weight on his thighs, inching his body farther back onto the pew and leaning closer to Dolores. Head bowed, he studied his sturdy brown Oxfords, but when he slid a glance toward her, she put her hand over his and patted it with just the tips of her fingers, barely moving. It was hard not to look at the festering scars of the wounds on the back of her hands.

Attracted by the slight movements, Charles turned and reached across Dolores to grasp his shoulder in a pincer grip and hauled him bodily back to the front of the pew, from where his short legs could only dangle an uncomfortable distance from the floor. Charles grasped Sonny's hands and bent his fingers until they assumed a folded position of prayer. Sonny lowered his head and studied the place where Charles's fingernail had surely caused a permanent hole on the back of his hand.

The Council of Elders of the Church paraded from their pews, then caused Cloris to kneel before the altar, whereupon they pronounced judgment. It was merciful when the voice from heaven was finally interpreted as pronouncing Cloris saved.

"The Lord sends his love down to this Poor Sinner and to all of us. Hallelujah! She will be saved! We are witnesses to the Lord's salvation. Praise be to God. She will be saved from the eternal fires of hell. Praise be! Praise be! Praise be to God! He will lift her up!"

With the conclusion of exhortative prayers for her healing, Cloris was finally released to her family. Sonny held his breath until she stiffly entered the pew, brushing past her father. She started to slide past her mother, but Charles caught Priscilla's eye, and Cloris was directed to a place between them. Sonny could sense, even smell the emotion that radiated from her body.

The service concluded, and Charles, the avenging patriarch, ushered his family up the aisle. Charles and Priscilla faintly acknowledged the other members of the congregation as they passed by them. The congregants busied themselves in their places, allowing the Dawson family to precede them from the sanctuary. The distant nods and carefully averted eyes of the congregation were in tacit agreement with the informal sanction of the deviant Dawson family, even though it had been the Dawsons' choice to hold their own daughter out for formal castigation. The family was, by choice, shunned.

Sure, hold the poor kid up and pray over her so everyone else will think what good parents they were. Hedging their own chances to enter the Kingdom of Heaven. Damn you both. Poor Cloris. Jesus, the poor kid. As though from a distance, he could hear Kent's voice, but he couldn't make out the words. His right knee was trembling uncontrollably as was his right hand, as if palsied, when he realized that Kent had stopped, with brows raised in question. Sonny tried to clear the woolly fog of bewildered memory assaulting his consciousness and return his attention to Kent.

In response to Sonny's blank stare, Kent repeated himself. "Any questions yet, Sonny?"

"No. No questions." Sonny's answer was terse, yet his voice was unnaturally hoarse and strained as he fought to control the tremor that always coincided with the voice.

"Article lll . . . " Kent resumed. "I direct that all inheritance, estate, succession, or other similar taxes against my taxable estate or the properties . . . "

Properties. Property and position. Property and position. And the church. The sacrifices in the name of those three, think of it. Right up there with Father, Son, and Holy Ghost. Father and Mother spent every waking moment working or praying. And I thought they were working and praying for us. For us, our family.

Despite his distress, as Sonny's concentrated memories

unraveled into revelations, he began to understand Charles's and Priscilla's commitment to fallacious standards and disciplinary lifestyle. His sense was that their melded histories had accordingly colored their worldview.

———

More than likely in response to the profligate C. D., Charles had always worked hard. When he left the farm, he sensed that his ability to do hard physical work would earn him both his daily bread and respect from others, and his only definition of hard work was that of physical, not mental, toil. His limited definition set his course.

It was opportune that Charles presented himself to the foreman of the city crew, Big George Edwards, on the very day of a vacancy created when a less fortunate city employee dropped dead. Charles was a sober, suitable candidate for the job, and George knew that if someone was not hired quickly, he himself might have to turn a hand.

George's management style was authoritarian, dictatorial, and brooked no interference or suggestions from either insiders or outsiders. He was deferential to those elected officials by whom he was technically employed, but everyone knew that, in truth, Big George ran the city of Onansburg. Mayors might come and go, but George remained. And in truth he did it pretty well, even though the cause of his efficiency was really self-protection. George wanted no unexpected crisis to interrupt his even-paced life. Streets were maintained so there was no cause for complaint from the good citizens. The city's equipment was well maintained; breakdown was nearly out of the question. It seemed not even the occasional nail would dare puncture the tire of one of the city-owned trucks.

Charles admired George's mastery over his self-created domain. His control. The respect he commanded from the small staff. From his wife and daughter. The city works and the Edwards family's clocks were both set by Big George. The installation of a new city-owned and -maintained water system was delayed for Onansburg by at least five years because George Edwards was not in favor of it. Not only would that kind of progress bring more work for George, but the possibility also loomed that he might have to relinquish absolute control. Worse, he might have to incorporate "new" into his inflexible routine.

Charles found, without ever seeking, a role model to emulate. From the perspective of the topsy-turvy nomadic life he had led with Rose and C. D., George's rigidly patterned existence seemed admirable and attractive. It was a refuge into which he could slide safely, no questions asked.

Charles did work hard, and according to the prescription, kept his mouth shut, his nose clean, and life worked out just fine by his own definition. During the first years of his life in town, he led a quiet, solitary life, paced according to George-time. George owned Charles for the workday. At night, he retreated to a room at Mrs. Hedges's boarding house.

Those who bothered to notice were surprised, but it was most amazing to his mother when Charles eventually married Priscilla Edwards, George's only child. It would have been a subject of no interest to C. D., since homely women did not exist in his world. And no one could have called Pricilla anything but homely. Priscilla might have been excused from her countenance and stringy body if she had fostered a sparkling personality or some outstanding skill or undeniable charm. For the most part, all of Priscilla's personal attributes were overlooked, as was any recognition of her as an opposite-sex person from any male who happened to notice her.

Priscilla was the embodiment of a cliché, though most likely no one had given any thought to characterizing her at all. "Old maid" suggested that she once might have been a young maid, but Priscilla had most likely been born thin as a rail, flat as a board, and old. She was probably born at her full height of five feet, six inches with the mouse-brown hair, pale pinched mouth, and heavy-lidded eyes of nondescript color, all of which described her as an adult. She was Big George Edwards's only issue, the result of a hard-to-imagine coupling between a one-time less corpulent George and the tiny feisty woman that was Thelma Edwards, sometime before George attained full growth of his massive stomach and the legs of an elephant calf. (Local children gossiped that he was pregnant with a slow-growing fetus.) It was physically determined that the Edwards had to be content with one child.

Sonny didn't remember his Edwards grandparents. Big George was gone long before Sonny was born. Big George's funeral was one of Onansburg's largest and most memorable, since the rumor was circulated that George was to be buried in a piano case. By the time Sonny was born, Charles Dawson Jr. had long since inherited Big George's job, and the story of his burying passed into legend.

Sonny tried to retreat from the scourging memories of his own family's existence. In the quiet of the law office with only the rattle of Kent's reading, Sonny's trance led him to unwillingly recapture scenes that had appeared and reappeared over and over throughout his adult life.

Without understanding why, Sonny knew it was dangerous to see them, to examine them, to try to make sense of them. Charles and Priscilla were parents of discipline and responsibility, of harsh and strong moral teaching, of fear and anxiety. Charles had, early on in his relationship with Big George, attempted to curry favor by attending the same independent, fundamentalist church the Edwards attended. With his well-designed courtship of Priscilla, it was a given that he would become a member of that same church.

Sonny had always accepted the way things were. With his sisters, there was the unspoken, the *other* that separated them that he didn't understand, but he knew they were treated differently by their parents. But Cloris and Dolores acted as parents to him. They were his parents of love, affection, and laughter, of tenderness and gentleness. The three of them found refuge with Rose in her cottage whenever it was allowed. There, they played games, some of them rowdy, and read books and ate bread and jam between meals.

Be the best little boy you can be, Sonny. Be the best little boy.

He could still hear them crooning this to him when he was hurt or frightened. When he was very small, they held him on their laps.

Be the best little boy you can be, Sonny. Be the best little boy.

But the memories that troubled him most were nighttime memories, memories he could barely make out in his own mind. His memories were shrouded in the darkness of denial just as the darkness of night shrouded secrets concealed within the family home. Half-remembered, hazy, and uncertain in their detail. Darkness was his nemesis.

His mother, crying endlessly in the upstairs hall. Huddled, yet upright in her shapeless, colorless nightclothes, hugging her elbows close to her angular body, she rocked in rhythm to her own cries. The dim yellow light from the overhead fixture cast shadows on her cheeks, making her sallow features appear even more sunken with her death's-head skull. In his recollections, Sonny could always see her, never hear her, though he could see she was weeping. Her lips moved soundlessly but he knew it was not to him she had spoken. Was she praying? He regretted not knowing.

Sometimes, Sonny questioned the reliability of his memory, his own rational thinking. He realized later the light bulbs were always too small in their house since Charles thought larger bulbs cost significantly more to burn.

"Sonny? I need your attention. You need to listen to this next part carefully. "

Sonny jerked himself back to the present, to the soberly pleasant confines of Kent's office, away from the darkness that threatened him. Sonny was sure it was not important to hang on to Kent's every word, that reading the will wasn't necessary, even though Kent thought he was already familiar with it. He had no question that the conclusion he and Polly had discussed regarding her planning and individual estate would be set forth in the will, just as his directives had been set forth for his will. The fifty percent each owned of their mutual holdings would pass to the survivor, with the exception being Polly's stock in Shaw Family Farms, Inc.

Kent met Sonny with a polite but steady gaze. Sonny straightened his posture in the chair, leaned forward, took a deep breath, and rubbed his lips together to moisten them. Kent had cranked the thermostat controlling the relentless air conditioning down so far that Sonny's arms were cold; the air was dryer than it seemed could ever be expected in Iowa's late August. Or perhaps, he thought to himself, his memories were responsible for the chill he now felt.

Kent noted, then explained Sonny's discomfort. "The law library, Sonny. The books. The humidity is bad for them. We have extra humidity controls on our heating and cooling system. We did a lot of research to get just the right system to preserve these old volumes and the old records that are stored here. Did you know the Historical Society wants us to donate them to the Society's collection? Why, it'd be criminal after all these years. They can't hope to take half as good care of them as . . . " His voice trailed off when he realized that Sonny was not giving him the audience to which he was accustomed.

Sonny threw up his hands in a gesture of submission. They landed on the arms of the chair. He fell against the chairback and gave Kent a self-conscious smile.

"Sorry, Kent. I guess I just drifted off. Just got caught up in my own thoughts. Sorry. Don't go back. Don't read it again. I'll . . . I'll try to pay closer attention. Say, is this taking too much of your time? I can just read it on my own. Why don't I just take it with me. I basically know what's in it. I can just pick it up later at home and . . . "

Sliding forward on his chair, he grasped the edge of the desk in front of him with both hands as though to rise. Sonny heard his own apologetic stammering and was annoyed with himself.

Kent gestured across the desk with both hands, fingers splayed. Down. Sit down.

"All right, Sonny, now just take a minute. This all takes a little getting used to. We'll finish, then you can ask all the questions you like. I have as much time as you need this afternoon. We'll get everything, all the legal language, boiled down so that you understand it all and what's next to be done . . . Now, let's go back for a moment. We've been through everything through residence property and personal property. As you will recall, those were articles three and four. Any questions there?"

He continued. "Article Five. After complying with the foregoing provisions of my Will, all of the rest, residue, and remainder of my property, whether real, personal, or mixed, of every kind and description, of which I may die seized, may be entitled to, may be the owner of, or which I may have power to dispose of at my decease, wherever situated, I give, devise, and bequeath to Sonny C. Dawson."

Sonny heard the uncustomary "C" between his first and last name and remarked on it to himself. He and Cloris and Dolores all had just C for a middle initial but with no name indicated. He rarely, if ever, used the "C." He hoped it didn't stand in for Charles as his middle name or Charlene for his sisters. He always used just "Sonny Dawson" as his signature.

Then, he started. His mouth dropped when he began to recognize the meaning of what he'd just heard.

"Kent," he said in measured tones. "Please read that again. Please read . . . " he hesitated, groping through his memory of the last few minutes, "Article Five again."

Kent cleared his throat and swallowed. The dryness of his mouth caused his tongue to click as he read, like the rattle of dice thrown on a craps table.

"Article Five," he said. "After complying with the foregoing provisions of my Will, all of the rest, residue, and remainder of my property, whether real, personal, or mixed, of every kind and description, of which I may die seized, may be entitled to, may be the owner of, or which I may have power to dispose of at my decease, wherever situated, I give, devise, and bequeath to Sonny C. Dawson."

Kent read slowly and deliberately, punching out the last three words for emphasis. "Sonny . . . C . . . Dawson."

Sonny . . . C . . . Dawson. Sonny . . . C . . . Dawson. Kent's well-spaced words echoed over again in Sonny's mind. He could hear or think of nothing else. He was suddenly empty but for those words. His countenance was blank. His eyes were unseeing. He had no conscious thought of self or of being.

When the machinery started up again, when the well-oiled wheels of thought caught the charge and fired, it was with the explosive force of a gunshot. Sonny bounded to his feet, rocking the chair on its sturdy legs, and leaned across the desk, slapped the desk with the flats of his hands, making a thunderous crack on the smooth surface. Kent stared up into Sonny's face; his mouth dropped open in astonishment.

Sonny's face was flushed; his voice was strained and rose several decibels higher as he shouted at Kent. "She set me up, Kent! She set me up to get back at her family! God*damm*it, Kent! Did you *know?* Well, hell yes. You're the one that drew up the will. Of course, you knew! How could she have done this?"

Sonny continued, aware there was spittle forming at the corner of his lips. "Kent, all three of them, the Shaws, just cut me dead at the café. They looked at me like I was a piece of shit that they were ready to muck out of their high and mighty goddamn barn. Did you tell them about Polly's will? Before even *I* knew?"

Sonny leaned back from the desk, turning away from Kent. With widespread arms and outstretched hands, shaking in anger and frustration, he was again, suddenly, wordless. Whirling around, he pounded the top of the walnut desk with his now clenched fist.

Alarmed, Kent shot to his feet behind the desk.

"No, Sonny. Of course, I didn't tell them. And, I must say, I hardly expected this from you of all people. Collect yourself, man." Indignantly, Kent hitched his trousers at the knees and reseated himself. "I don't deserve this from you. Calm down. Get yourself together." He slowed the cadence of his speech, trying to restore order to the situation. "Without telling you exactly what business brought them in yesterday, I can tell you that in answer to their concerns and questions about Polly's will, I suggested they consult other counsel. That I represent you and Polly's estate. As simple as that, Sonny. They made their own inferences and obviously made a conclusion based on that conversation. They must have inferred that I have a potential conflict of interest and I couldn't advise them as to their interest in the disposition of Polly's estate."

Sonny, chastened, fell back into the chair, expelling a short, impatient breath. A few moments passed. Kent shifted uncomfortably in his chair, then stood and turned to face the credenza behind his desk. He retrieved a handsome, silver-rimmed walnut tray that held an ice bucket, a carafe of water, and several crystal glasses and placed it on the right side of his desk.

"I'm embarrassed, Kent." Sonny's voice was unemotional, flat.

"Some ice water, Sonny?"

Sonny took the tumbler of water from Kent's outstretched hand and noticed that in filling the glasses with ice and water, the ice, dropping into the glass from the ice tongs, had caused beaded droplets of water to form a pattern on the sleeve of the suntan suit. Sonny thought of the beaded buckskin jacket said to be Lakota Sioux that he and Polly had examined the last Sunday they'd been together in a dusty antique shop near Des Moines. It was hard to reconcile that idyllic day with the sudden sense of betrayal and anger he was feeling on this day.

Sonny took a sip of the water and leaned forward in his chair, his elbows resting on his knees, cradling the glass. Then, he stood and replaced the glass on the tray.

"Sonny, are you ready to go on? Shall we get on with this?" Without waiting for Sonny's response, Kent continued. "Sonny, we have been friends for a long time. Likewise, I've known the Shaw family for a long time. They have been clients of this firm longer than you have. In fact, my father drew up the articles of incorporation for their operation . . . let's see, that would have to have been in the fifties or early sixties after the old folks were gone. Father did their estate work and some strictly small stuff in the early seventies. They were Senior's clients.

"I find myself in a bit of a dilemma here. When Polly had me draw up her will with the provisions that you've heard today, I felt it my duty to point out to her what I understood from my previous conversations with you; the shares of Shaw Family Farms, Incorporated, stay in the family, to be eventually passed to their children. The brothers, and Dorothy as well, may have relied on marital trusts so that their surviving spouses have the income from the shares but never the actual ownership of the shares. The shares would be held in trust for the benefit of the named beneficiary. That's one of the ways it's done."

Sonny, anguished, pushed his hands against his thighs, arms bent at the elbows, shoulders raised. He shook his head, back and forth, sadly. Taking a deep breath, he looked pointedly at Kent. "Why would she have done this? Why couldn't you have warned me that this is what she was doing?"

"My conversations with Polly were privileged. Rest assured that I tried to represent your best interests as well as Polly's. I can tell you this, Sonny. Polly assured me that you would know how to handle this. She had absolute faith in you in that respect."

"Now, let's go ahead and get some of the nits and lice business matters cleaned up. The paperwork showing you as executor of her estate," he said. "You probably don't have a death certificate yet. That takes a while. A Quit Claim Deed for Polly's share of your home, and didn't you own your sister's home together? You'll have to tell me what you want to do about that. I'll go ahead and review the paperwork and filings on the store. We can meet in ten days or a couple of weeks, and get signatures on everything. You get some rest, take some time to think this through. You've had some surprises here. It's been a tough week."

Kent walked through the reception room with Sonny. The men shook hands at the door. Sonny began to reiterate his regret for his behavior, but Kent shook his head and put his hand up to wave it off.

"Forget it. I've already forgotten it, so you forget it as well."

The heavy door hurried Sonny out onto the wide steps. The firm closure pushed a noiseless whisper of conditioned air out in front of him in momentary denial of the torrid heat.

Ten

*S*uddenly, Sonny was self-conscious, as though anyone seeing him emerging from his attorney's office would know of his concerns, could see his dilemma. He was at a loss without his clear agenda, the self-prescribed regimen to take him through his day. His responsibilities, position, and autonomy had not changed. His very self had not changed except that Polly, who enabled every facet of his life, was gone. He was alone to carry on with the reality of the life they had created together.

Get on with it, Sonny. Just get on with it. Do what needs to be done.

Glancing at his watch, he quickly tried to think through a plan for the rest of the day. He had planned to call on Steve Fetters at the funeral home, pay the fees for his services, and finish any other paperwork there might be. Steve had mentioned the deed to the plot at the cemetery.

He thought with distaste of how he had gone through Polly's purse to retrieve the checkbook for their personal account. The checkbook cover was of a handsome tapestry fabric, and he felt like a thief removing it from the summer straw handbag.

Well, I sure as hell am not going to carry Polly's checkbook with

*me to pay Steve. I'll have to just take a couple of blank checks from
the pad and then fill in the register later.*

Though Sonny tried to distance himself from his newly realized
problem of having been named the heir to Polly's business holdings,
it was foremost in his mind. He pounded along the hot sidewalk,
feeling as though he walked with a stranger and knew he was dis-
placing his true issues with petty, irritating inconveniences.

When he reached the store, he gratefully welcomed the shade
afforded by the awning, but glancing at its dark green underside, he
didn't remember having cranked it out when he arrived earlier. As
he entered the store, it seemed dimly lit and cool after the scorch-
ing inferno of the out-of-doors. Alerted by the door chime, Ruby
hastened from the stockroom, but when she saw Sonny, she turned
and resumed dragging a carton of new leaf rakes for display. Sonny
could see a thin bead of perspiration on Ruby's upper lip.

"I'll bring those out for you, Ruby. I've told you not to fool with
these oversized boxes. Just wait, and I'll get to them."

He stopped and announced dramatically to the room at large,
but populated only by Ruby and Thelma Jane, and punctuated
each word with distinct and over-careful pronunciation. "We'll get
the fall displays done when we get the fall displays done. Just leave
them alone for now."

He stalked toward his office, hating the peevish sound of his
voice. Despite her happy-go-lucky personality and her frankness,
Ruby's feelings were sensitive and easily hurt. Sonny sensed that she
was doing everything she could to make things easier for him, and
he knew he'd been churlish. Thelma Jane averted her eyes when he
brushed by and directed her attention to the clear plastic boxes of
picture hangers together with their contents of tiny nails she was
counting out for display.

As Sonny continued his path toward his own office, Thelma
Jane's quiet voice followed him. At first, it was well modulated and
noncommittal.

"Julia Hayes, eh, Wildfang, was here again hoping to see you, Sonny. She came earlier when you were in your office, but we, I told her it wasn't a good time, you having just gotten in, first day back and all."

But she finished on a plaintive note, and Sonny heard the implied meaning of "and all." He resented the inference of Thelma Jane protecting him. He continued feeling put-upon and resentful of even good intentions.

What the hell could that Hayes-Wildfang woman want now! I can barely stand to be civil to the woman or her kid. Doesn't she have any sense? I can't take time for her now!

He gave short consideration to Julia and the last time he had seen her. She had called on him at the store to ask for space for the Historical Society's Old Settlers display in one of the store's front windows. That had been last May. The Legion sponsored a window, the Historical Society arranged one. The PEO sisters. Almost every civic and fraternal group. And he always gave space in one if not both of his display windows.

The dumb biddy. She should have known how active I've always been in the Old Settlers organization. Of course, I always let some group have my windows for a display.

Now, as he remembered, she had looked better that day than she had since Larry's injury. Not so desperately waiflike. And her appearance since Larry's injury had been one of the things that just griped the hell out of him. He regarded her victimization with both confusion and ambivalence. He allowed himself the dangerous thoughts. The kid was the victim. The mother, Julia, became a victim of the circumstances. Sonny couldn't think of what had happened to Larry without feelings of both anger for the abuser and the abused, yet he knew in his heart that blaming Larry was unjust.

And there were other feelings that he couldn't quite reach or touch. Sepia-toned memories. The naked light bulb hanging on a heavy cloth-covered electric cord with the switch attached to the socket, the dim light to be turned on or turned off only by Priscilla or Charles. Only adults could control important things that cost money. Sonny hated the darkness, when the bulb hung dead and useless on its thick, sinewy cord.

He so hated the sounds that were companions to the darkness, the sounds from Dolores's room when her bed knocked against the common wall in rhythm with her soft cries, presumably accompanied by her tears. He hated his own feelings of rage and helplessness that the memory triggered.

Sonny marched down the hall to his office, his thoughts ping-ponging with every step. Bounce. Bounce. Bounce.

"Ruby," he called loudly, as he swung into his office and first turned on the overhead light, "does Steve have a service this afternoon? Check on it for me, would you?" Sonny stopped to hear her response before he continued into the room.

In less than a heartbeat, Ruby replied. "Mrs. Everidge's service was at 11 this morning. Nothing at Steve's this afternoon."

Neatly spaced cards noting the time and place of services conducted at the funeral home were routinely distributed to businesses. Ruby relied on the information printed on the white index cards, which were displayed prominently beside the cash register in a slotted wooden cardholder that had been tailor-made for its purpose.

He turned on each lamp in turn, dispelling any remaining darkness missed by the ceiling fixture. His eyes fell on the note, a folded, single sheet of paper, his name carefully penned in prominent block letters that he'd earlier recognized as being from Larry. Impatiently, he unfolded it. He read the note quickly.

"Dear Sonny,

I know you've been very busy with all that happened. I hope you remember that I asked to come to work at 5 p.m. on Mondays and Wednesdays instead of right after school. Coach Jim who is the advisor for the Future Teachers of America at the high school asked me to tutor 5th and 6th graders after school on those days when school starts. I told him I'd need to ask you since I know you depend on me on those days.

From Larry"

On Monday, before Polly passed on Friday, Larry had politely asked to shorten his hours two days a week. Sonny hadn't answered immediately and then had forgotten about the request.

Dammit! I completely forgot about Larry's asking about his hours! Like I really depend on him. But suddenly, he was contrite, touched by Larry's assumption that his importance to the store was as great as the importance with which he held his job.

Sonny peeled two checks from the checkbook and turned off the light, but then he lurched back into his office, retrieved the checkbook, and noted the numbers of the two checks in the check register. He shut his office door firmly behind him, opened the door from the hallway, and leaned into the showroom long enough to say, "I'll be back pretty soon. Going on over to Fetters'."

With a glance at his watch, he noted that it was just after four pm, so he added a postscript to his message. "If I'm not back by five, go ahead and lock up. I'll bring the awning in later, no need to bother with it. And thanks, whoever put it out this morning." He paced down the hall to the back door, opened and closed it behind him, and exited reluctantly into the heat. He had shut it firmly but pushed against it to ensure it was locked.

Grasping the handle of the car door, he released it with an expletive under his breath, reflexively examined his hand, then gingerly jerked the door open. When the blast of hot air from the interior of the car first hit him, any hint of perspiration quickly evaporated and, for an instant, he felt the benefit of the comforting dryness. Just as quickly, small beads of sweat began to reappear on his forehead.

Sonny drove the short few blocks to Fetters Funeral Home, noting the absence of people on the streets. A few lengthening shadows suggested the afternoon was waning, and before long, the businesses and offices would empty their personnel into the late afternoon inferno. Sonny pulled his car onto the driveway leading to the double doors behind which the Fetters' hearse was garaged, adjusted the driver's side window and the passenger side window down halfway to allow circulation, even though Sonny didn't expect to stay long with his piece of business.

Slogging up the eight steps to the wide double doors of the old brick mansion, he stopped uncertainly at the entrance.

Should I knock or go on in? I didn't make an appointment, but it is a business.

Sonny turned the knob on the right of the two doors and stepped into the softly lit anteroom. He paused for a moment to let his eyes adjust to the soft lighting, then paced across the room to the closed door of the office he knew to be Steve's.

He stood before the heavy oak door, then rapped on it with his knuckles, saying, "Steve? It's Sonny Dawson. Do you have a few minutes? I came to settle up for Polly's services. Are you here? Is this time alright?"

Steve made it easy for Sonny. It was his business to do so. Death and survivors were both his to manage for the short two or three days of transition. He had worked in the business of disposing of remains in a manner that allowed past and future obligations to the deceased to be expiated. To manage the ceremonial aspects of ritualized liminality. To manage the observation of and compliance to bureaucratic rules for disposal. To manage dignity for some who had never defined it in their own lifetime. To serve as surrogate in accordance with the wishes of those who had. But the bottom line was service to the living. "The dead cared not" was a ubiquitous quote that served both parties in the transaction that ensued when funeral services were contracted.

He was seated behind his oak desk, new and functional, but styled to appear old in keeping with the appointments in the rest of the office. Coach lights retrieved from the original Fetters' horse-drawn hearse had been electrified and affixed to the wall behind the desk. Three wingback chairs upholstered in tastefully muted bargello fabric faced the desk, but a computer and printer on the side table at a right angle to the desk were an incongruous conces-sion to necessary business. Framed engravings of pastoral scenes lent a tranquil note to the room, and certificates of graduation from mortuary science training and certificates of state licenses for three generations of Fetters morticians bespoke the venerable nature of the business.

He motioned Sonny to one of the handsome chairs. "This is the final total, Sonny. I made sure everything is there." Steve glanced into his coffee cup, swirled its contents, and took an even drink. "You'd best take it home and go over it. Get back to me with any questions. Oh, and the deed to your plot is in the separate envelope."

Steve hadn't seemed surprised when Sonny knocked on the door of his office, despite Sonny not calling ahead. Early on in his career, Steve may have been surprised on occasion, but now, years later, Steve possessed a noncommittal countenance. Steve expected noth-ing. Steve expected everything.

Sonny mutely accepted the documents that were neatly done up in an important navy-blue folder.

How nice. Black would be too obvious. The navy is the right touch. Should I look them over while I'm here and write the check or should I take them home and go over everything? Check's in the mail, Steve, check's in the mail.

Sonny was uncertain, not sure that he had not been dismissed, but he was quite sure that he was not going to take the important folder home and pore over the itemized billing. For the second time in one day, he found himself on the opposite side of a desk, not liking the information with which he had been presented.

He opened the folder, noted the total, and flipped through the documents. His eyes sought and found almost immediately the list of services performed by Fetters Funeral Home. His eyes fell unwillingly but discriminately on the portion of the itemized statement titled "Additional Services," which he could see at a glance included fees for removal, embalming, cosmetic preparation. *Thank God,* he thought to himself, *it was not more descriptive,* but he could see that the list of services continued to a second page, discreet but definite. Sonny snapped the folder shut and withdrew the lower number of the two checks from his own slender wallet he had carried into Steve's office. He also withdrew a three-inch-by-five-inch lined note card on which he noted the check number and dollar figure.

Write the check and leave it with Steve. Go over the bill later when you can stand to deal with it. If there are any problems or questions, Steve will take care of them when I'm ready. Do it, Sonny, just do it. Just get on with it.

Steve gestured to the set of pens that were stationed on Sonny's side of the massive desk. Choosing the pen closest to himself, Sonny set the pen to the check and began carefully. "Pay to the order of . . . " Sonny began to write, "Steve Fetters," interrupting his progress on the second *t* of Fetters.

"Look what I've done." Sonny first pushed the check toward Steve, then snatched it back and ripped it quickly in two.

Steve began to speak as Sonny retrieved the check. "Forget it . . . you can make it out to . . . " his voice trailed off on the final "me" as Sonny tore the first check into pieces and retrieved the second check from his wallet.

Without taking his eyes from Sonny, he leaned across his own left arm, and with the index finger of his right hand, depressed the button on the intercom machine that was hardly noticeable where it was inset into the wall next to the desk.

"Tammy, Tammy! You there?"

An amplified voice answered, promptly preceded by the electronic pop of the "speak" button depressed from elsewhere in the vast, old mansion.

Tammy and Steve Fetters lived, as had the two generations preceding them, in the apartment on the second floor of the long-since-converted grand old home. Steve had been raised there, an only child of the second generation to occupy the mansion. The Fetters morticians had raised their families there, and friends and relatives alike quickly made their peace with the business that was never far away. Tammy and Steve had conceded to the demands of the profession in living on the premises, and their only concessions to the requirement were in terms of protecting their children from the constant intrusion of people into their space. While there was a private entrance that skirted the preparation room by not enough comfortable distance, most found the Fetters family at home by ringing the bell at the foot of the grand staircase located in the foyer of the funeral home. As toddlers, the Fetters children were protected from tumbling over the railing and to the first floor by the cargo net that was stretched, incongruously, from side to side of the rich walnut railing over the stairs.

"Tammy, would you please bring down a cup of my special coffee for Sonny and me. Here in my office? Bring one for yourself and join us."

Sonny shook his head, mouthing the words "No, no," but Steve waved him off, consulting his watch as he let go of the switch and leaned back in his chair. Sonny made out the second check, flipping open the folder to check once more for the total, then pushed it across the desk to Steve and gathered the papers to leave.

Steve fixed him with a discerning eye. "You know," he paused, "Let me say this because we're friends, have been for a long time. This isn't part of what I do for folks, but you came in here wound so tight your rubber band's about to break. Sit here for a few minutes. Tammy'll be right down."

For a name like Tammy, eternally ever-young, Tammy. But Sonny. Diminished, the diminutive of son. My son. His son. A son, not a boy. Not my boy, but my son. But Sonny, a flawed name. Neither my son nor my boy.

Steve's soothing voice brought Sonny back to attention. "Whatever it is, it'll wait. By this time of day, most things can wait. You know, you just can't get up the morning after, after you've lost the dearest one to you, and then go on with business as normal."

A quick knock on the door, and Tammy entered the room with a tray holding three handsome footed cups on individual coasters. Sliding the tray onto the corner of the desk, Tammy offered the nearest cup to Sonny with a smile that barely turned her mouth up at the corners. Tammy was a good-sized woman with broad hips and large breasts, but with an unlikely gamin countenance and attitude.

Puzzled, Sonny lowered his head to inspect his cup, but its icy exterior had betrayed its contents even before the aroma of the fine old Scotch announced itself. Sonny waited until Tammy seated herself with her own drink, then he leaned back in his chair and sighed. Steve regarded him soberly from across the desk. "It's after four o'clock. Just take a few minutes and enjoy your drink."

The sudden ache caught him off guard this time, but only for an instant. He recognized the onslaught of the surge of grief that threatened to send him reeling, unbalanced and nonfunctional, for what was left of the day. But, reaching into his arsenal of easy conversational topics, he asked polite questions about the Fetters children, their ages, their classes in school. Tammy took up the slack with observations about the weekend weather forecast, about the preparations for Old Settlers. They finished their drinks, but before Steve could offer another, Sonny looked at his watch, announced it was time to lock up at the store. He tendered his thanks to Tammy and took his leave.

He pulled the door carefully shut behind him, leaving Steve

and Tammy together on the other side in a whiskey-induced state of relaxation. Longing, then sadness rushed him physically with fatigue and uncertainty.

Get going, Sonny. Walk away. Make a plan. Dinner. It's almost dinnertime. This day has been too long already. It's after five o'clock. Ruby and Thelma Jane will have closed the store for the night.

As he walked to the car, he tried to deny his habit of anticipatory pleasure that the dinner hour fostered in him. He pushed himself away from his own image of Steve and Tammy in their companionable retreat to the second-floor apartment. He imagined them, hand in hand, ascending the staircase. Then Steve's arm circling Tammy's waist, his hand dropping to her ample behind. They laughed together, anticipating the end of the day, their dinner, their bedroom.

The aroma of cooking wafted along in Tammy's wake when she brought their drinks to them. Perhaps it clung to her hands, the attractive perfume of garlic and olive oil, green onions, and meaty red tomatoes. To Sonny, the fragrance would once have announced gazpacho. Or creamy pasta with melted Brie, basil, and tomatoes. He packaged his longing in a box, tied it up with heavy rope, and pushed it from his mind. He concentrated on his mental image of pushing the big box from the screen of his consciousness until it fell from the edge of the picture into oblivion.

The companionable drink with the Fetters had afforded a temporary respite from his pain. Scotch, a panacea. Another image immediately replaced the box. This time it was of himself, the actor in a black-and-white B-grade Western. He was writhing, twisting, and turning on a wooden table. Whiskey was forced down his throat as anesthetic against the knife that probed his body, searching, gouging, prying. If only a knife could cut out his grief. He pushed the image away. It had been so fleeting, not necessary to package it in a box.

The grass crunched, dry and brittle under his feet where he traversed the lawn. The stubble flattened under his weight and marked his path toward the car. He glanced around guiltily, realizing that he had blocked the driveway with his car. No one else could come or go, but he quickly forgave himself. Checking his watch again, he reassured himself.

I didn't mean to stay so long. And it was business.

The very fact that Steve had been inside doing business meant that the driveway that was used for the self-important hearse was not in use. But as he reached his car and opened the door, he started when the huge overhead door to the garage began to slide noiselessly up, retreating to its horizontal perch. Steve came around from the inside door to the front of the sleek blue-black carriage, parked always at the ready.

"Didn't mean to startle you, Sonny. Just got a call from Kent Field. It's poor old Jessie. Kent stopped off to make sure she was okay, guess she didn't work today. And . . . "

"This afternoon, Steve. Jessie didn't work this afternoon was all."

Sonny didn't understand why it was important to correct Steve's misunderstanding, but it seemed consistent with the character of the players, Kent and Jessie and their professional relationship, that it should be corrected and exactly stated.

"Anyway, Kent just found her, so I guess I'll be on my way. Later, Sonny."

"Yeah, later, Steve."

He climbed into the heat of the car. The air conditioning and its partner, the fan, were still turned to high just as they had been when Sonny arrived at Fetters, but despite his precautions, the interior of the car was stifling. When he caught the first hint of cool air coming from the air vent, he rolled the windows up from the halfway position, trying to merge the mechanical chilled air with the August heat trapped inside. He shifted the car into reverse, backed into the street, and allowed Steve to back out and head in the direction of the home from which Jessie would take her leave, feet first.

So, Jessie's gone. Poor little old stick of a lady. Wasn't much left of her but her loyalty to Kent. Really to Field, Senior. Poor old soul.

Sonny felt a sense of sadness out of proportion to his relationship to Jessie. Careful. Careful. His thoughts shifted to avert the rush of sadness, yet they continued in the same vein.

What about Steve? Does this ever get to Steve? Is it ever just another day's work?

Sonny slowly pulled away from the curb, watching in the rear-view mirror as the hearse rolled, majestic and slow, in the opposite direction. He drove along Wall Street, considering a token preparation of dinner from among the many plates of good food left by friends, but then he pushed the lonely image away. Giving himself a quick reprieve, he recalled that he needed to go by the store and bring the awning in for the night.

With renewed purpose, he headed back to the square and from the opposite side; he could see that the awning had been rolled up tight. He was thankful for his employees but was immediately faced once again with the prospect of finding dinner and eating it by himself.

Late summer Onansburg seemed deserted of energy, old and tired. Golden August to be followed by brassy September falling away to the copper hues of October. The town would assume its character from the land that held it capture. There were no children playing in the yards or riding bicycles, but robins and songbirds congregated to warn one another of the need to flee before the slow death of winter began. Sonny envied them their simple adherence to the instinct that drove them to arrive every spring as if it was their first and hurry about the business of building their nests, raising their young. Then, in the waning days of the cycle, they relied on one another to serve notice that it was time to make their migration to another land to survive.

Last week, Polly had pointed out to him how tired and worn the little robins looked. "Just look at them. They've worked so hard to find worms and feed their babies. Look how shabby they look now. They're exhausted from raising their families."

Like human families, Polly. They start out with shiny eyes and sleek, bright plumage, and by the time the job is done, they're a little tired, yes, and a little shabby. Unlike the bird-couples, however, they don't have to start the complete cycle over the next year. Cycles. Over and over. Round and round. God's creatures.

At the corner of Wall and Cedar, noting the hard glint of the west-setting sun, Sonny had turned north, homeward on Wall, when he saw the solid figure of his sister, Dolores, coming toward him. She had just passed from the sunlight into the shade offered by Mrs. Davenport's lilac bush, picking her way carefully on the uneven sidewalk. Years before planted too close to the sidewalk, or perhaps the sidewalk later encroached on the shrub's domain, the dense leaves were so dark, so covered with dust that in the shade they appeared near black. The gnarled limbs reached out to catch at passersby, plucking and picking at clothing or flesh, a reminder of the privileges of age.

The roots of the elderly shrub had long ago heaved the sidewalk out of place, and now Dolores stood just where countless collections of rainwater left a shallow pool of hard-packed mud. The black dirt would have seemed cool in contrast to the heat from the concrete. Townsfolk paid a summertime price for their precious streets and walks. The sun made them pay dearly in time spent waiting for the radiant heat to subside even while the countryside fanned itself gently in an evening breeze.

He was dismayed that her presence would likely delay his solitary dinner, yet he'd been perversely challenged by a need to push back against the challenge of the new life alone. Alone doesn't mean the same as lonely, he reasoned. He'd anticipated this time to begin sorting out the transition he faced. He was conflicted by his need to act as a caretaker to Dolores, while faced with reassembling a carefully constructed existence.

Sonny claimed a privilege of a small town, pulling into the left lane so that he could talk to Dolores without shouting across a lane of oncoming traffic of which there was none anyway. Cedar Street, Dolores's address, extended west from one corner of the square all the way to the outskirts of Onansburg, but was not heavily traveled. At Sonny's touch on the button, the window slid obediently into its hiding place in the door.

"Hey, Dolores. Where you going?"

Hearing first the sound of the engine and then Sonny's voice, her mouth was pursed into its shape of the perennial surprise, the "oh" of wonder. Her face manifested her damaged spirit; her eyes were vacant and dull as she trudged along, but then they brightened, and her brows raised expectantly, registering her pleasure at seeing her younger sibling. Dolores and Cloris had both inherited the facial structure of the Edwards family with rounder, softer features, unlike Sonny's longer jaw line and high cheekbones of the Dawsons.

Sonny leaned out his window and turned up a closed-mouthed smile at Dolores, the corners of his mouth barely elevated. With almost no inflection in his voice, Sonny greeted her.

"Where you going, sweetheart? You want a ride?" He relaxed his tight smile into a grin. He was surprised that he was happy to see her, but then immediately he recanted his pleasure and questioned himself sternly.

Are you only pleased to see her because you don't know what it is you are going home to do? Because Polly isn't at home waiting for you?

But with a jolt, he suddenly knew that while he had seen the same expression of despair on Dolores's face, over and over, this time he was seeing it from long-ago memory. Her eyes. He was lost, caught in them, drawn back to a forgotten puzzle. He lost control against the sudden force of cognition that foisted itself on him. His memory was spinning, reeling, disgorging information that he didn't want to know or acknowledge.

The rhythmic knocking came from Dolores's room. The steady bumping against his bedroom wall had wakened him yet again. He drifted, then awakened to the click of a door latch slipping into its notched opening with a solid confirmation that was suddenly much too loud in the void of a sleeping house. This time, he crept from his bed to follow the muffled, hushed sounds that before had indicated that others in the family were awake in activities that were guarded and secret from him. He winced at the cold of the wooden floor on the soles of his bare feet. He slipped into the dimly lit hall. His bony wrists and ankles protruded from the winter pajamas that were nearly too short for comfort. The seam of the pants rubbed uncomfortably on his crotch. The chill crept up his legs and arms and in and around the open neck of the mismatched flannel pajama shirt.

There was no one in the hall, but before he ventured further, his eyes fell on the door to his parents' bedroom. It was firmly closed. He stood stock still for a moment, debating whether to retreat to the safety of his own bed. Still, there was the sense of other life, a sense of movement that he could not see or touch. He could sense rather than hear the low, anxious voice of his mother that moaned and whined behind the closed door.

Now, suddenly, caught in flashes of frightening recall, Sonny cautioned himself against going any farther. He saw himself creeping into danger, even while safely seated in his own car. Even so, he coached himself.

No, no. Leave it alone. Go back, go back.

He tried to stop the scene of his own figure creeping along the dark hallway as if it were a figment of his imagination. But then he knew that it was memory and understanding, not imagination, that was playing in his consciousness.

He saw himself in a reenactment of the horrific memory. He remembered clearly the cold, dark hallway. In addition to the cold that gripped him, he sensed a chill of apprehension, and instinctively, he knew to be stealthily quiet. When he crept past his parents' bedroom and turned the corner from the hall to the bathroom, he could see light leaking out from underneath the door. It was not firmly closed, and someone was inside. Sonny listened for a moment. He could hear ragged, heavy breathing, a vocalization that was not articulated into words.

Sonny waited a few moments more, then pushed the door open. Dolores was standing with her back to him near the toilet. Her soft nightgown was bunched up where she clutched it under her arm and her bare backside was to him. She turned to him, dazed and not comprehending his presence, clutching the gown tighter to herself. He could see that she had been attempting to clean herself, ineffectively blotting herself with a square of toilet tissue. Sonny noted the thin square with unconscious approval since one at a time was all they were allowed. But then Sonny stared at the thin rivulet of blood that even as he watched traced its way down the inside of her thigh to the rag rug at her feet. More blood had soaked into the rug in uneven splotches. She covered her bald pubis with her hand but not before he had seen the bloody tear of her vagina. Her shoulders hunched over, protecting herself from his direct gaze even while she dabbed at a liver-like clot with the stiff tissue. She gasped involuntarily with pain. Raising her head from her task, her eyes found him, seeking, like a dumb animal pitifully awaiting its executioner, the last blow.

As he would have done with a bad dream, a nightmare, Sonny tried to shake himself loose from the memories. But the regression continued. He heard footsteps pounding rapidly up the wooden staircase and then into the hallway; the ribbed rubber treads affixed to each step did little to muffle the oncoming noise of human traffic. Cloris appeared at the top of the staircase wearing her coat and a triangular headscarf. He didn't question her appearance even as she was fully clothed in street wear as opposed to her nightclothes. His mother suddenly appeared with her chenille bathrobe clutched over her nightgown. With a cry, Cloris reached for him, shoving and pushing his mother away from him as they fought over him, tugging him first one way and then that.

He recalled that, curiously, neither went to Dolores, either to aid or to comfort her. Cloris snarled at their mother, her voice guttural, menacing.

"Don't touch him. Don't touch either of them!" she snarled, and pushed her aside roughly. Priscilla lurched and fell against the balustrade. She began to sob, a heaving crescendo of mewling cries escalating to outraged wails.

Dolores, sounding as if she were far away, began to moan a tuneless dirge of desperation. The same wordless horror would ever be present in her countenance. Cloris caught hold of the slight eight-year-old crouching at the opening to the bathroom door, his eyes wide in shock and splayed fingers over his gaping mouth. She lifted him easily as she had when he was a baby. Pressing his head into her shoulder, clasping him against her full bosom, she raced back to his bedroom, jerked back the covers of his bed, thrust him onto his bed, then drew the blankets up tight to his neck.

Fierce in her fury, she thrust her face close to his. Her pupils were dilated, her eyes protruded in their sockets. He was frightened of her and her anger. He didn't understand that he was not its focus.

"Forget you ever saw this, Sonny. Just be the best little boy you can be. Just be the best little boy you can be. Promise me. Cloris will take care of you. Just promise."

And for years, he forgot what he had seen and heard, just as Cloris told him to do. He had worked hard at being the best little boy he could be. But now, he knew from his instantaneous recollection that he was surely hearing the reverberations of a memory that had traveled silently through the years. He knew what his sisters had endured.

With the understanding of his childhood delivered by happenchance, Sonny found himself released from an unnamed burden. Without ever having full understanding of his hatred of his parents, Sonny had felt guilty and ashamed of his feelings toward them. The significance of his realization sent a thrill of exhilaration through him that was as quickly grounded in horror.

Dear God, my own sisters. Be the best little boy you can be, Sonny. Be the best little boy you can be.

They had taken care of him, protected him in the only way they could. Be the best little boy you can be. They instinctively knew to give him the only protection they could afford so that he was not in line for the same abuse they had endured. How could they have known what would turn his father away from him? And from the time he was old enough to follow their direction, he'd been the best little boy he could have been.

———

Sonny remained in the car, locked in the flash fire of memory while Dolores continued to regard Sonny quizzically. The dark cave formed by the lilac bush's hovering branches shielded her, but Dolores had made no concession to the heat, wearing a long-sleeved cotton dress that covered the self-inflicted scars on her forearms. Her round, fat face was flushed with the heat. With a start punctuated by a low guttural moan, he came back to the present.

"Dolores. Here. For godsake, get in the car. You'll have a stroke out here in this heat. Get in here where it's cool." Talking all the while, Sonny bolted from the car, and forgetting his distaste for marring his shoes, tramped through the dusty grass between the street and the sidewalk to escort Dolores to the car. He swung the big door open for her and tucked her inside, scooping the tail of her dress up and over her lap so it wouldn't be caught in the door. Before he firmly fixed the door shut, he lowered the window from the inside so he could remind her of the use of the seat belt that originated from behind the passenger's right shoulder. Obsessively, he focused on the detail at present even while pushing back against his odious memories.

"Here, let's make sure that you're fastened in good. Besides it's against the law for you to be without it. Let's be good and safe now. Where have you been? Were you at my house?"

"I . . . I left sandwiches for you," Dolores stammered slightly. "I, eh, I know you like them, and I thought you might not eat unless there was, eh, something you really liked. I put them in your refrigerator. Was that okay? The door wasn't locked. You don't mind, do you? Is it okay that I went in? I could have waited outside, but I didn't know when you'd be home."

"Well, sure it was okay. Your special sandwiches? Is that what you made for me? You know how I love your sandwiches. What kind this time? What did you make?" Sonny heard himself talking, near babbling, as though he would to one he considered simple or ill. Or to a small child. He continued a nonstop dialogue with himself since Dolores didn't speak but considered him thoughtfully. With a pleased but slightly embarrassed smile, she made no response.

With a brief signal of warning to himself, Sonny remembered the suggestion that she had made to him last night, which he had so neatly quashed. That she could live with him and keep his house suddenly didn't seem so offensive as it had the night before.

Timorously, she touched his arm. "Sonny, Sonny." The low pitch of her voice sought him and tugged at him, drawing him back from the dangerous place to which he had traveled. He knew suddenly that he must take care of his sisters.

Sonny had always had a sense of the strange contrast between the public and private life of the Dawson family, the chasm that separated the two. Like dirt that seems invisible, he had a sense of the evil that was unseen but treacherous.

The reverent adherence for participation in church, school, and community activities that was in marked contrast to the strict regimentation and frequent physical discipline of their homework and Bible study. And Charles's obsequious courtesies to the town's gentry, the mayor, the councilmen. And their wives and families. In contrast to his harsh treatment of his own wife and children.

Charles all but tugged on his forelock when some minor celebrity passed by him. To the wives, it was "How do you do today, Mrs. Kleckman, Mrs. Melson, Mrs. Jacobsen, Mrs. Lawyer Field? Mrs. Doctor Ryan's widow? How is this fine day treating you? Say hello, children!,'" in contrast to the rantings and ravings that the Dawsons heard about the imbeciles Kleckman, Melson, and Jacobsen around the supper table.

"Who does the council think they are? What do they know about the way we do business down at the city. They think it's just some easy job, think I don't know anything. They're so high and mighty. Just get down off your high horse, I'd like to say. See how business works here. Easy to give orders. It's another thing when you have to do the work yourself instead of just telling someone else to do it."

Self-righteous indignation felt good to Charles. The addiction of hatred and resentment was seductive to a man with a poor self-image, but no one would have known that Charles was so afflicted. Quiet, industrious, seemingly unassuming, Charles's progress through the ranks of the city works department to foreman, then on to assuming Big George's position, was inevitable and suitable.

Big George himself had laid the groundwork for his son-in-law to assume his position as foreman of the city works department when it was timely vacated. Charles's subsequent appointment to city clerk and manager was a surprise, however, since Mayor Kleckman had recommended Charles Dawson over the assistant city clerk, Rollie Stevenson. Rollie had always considered himself in line for the job when Jim McKelvy retired. There were a few days of discussion over the mystery of the selection process during morning coffee in Onansburg cafés, but there being no one with sufficient interest, apart from Rollie, in taking issue with a political appointee, interest in the topic soon died, leaving Charles Dawson Jr. at the height of his career and ambition, and Rollie Stevenson looking for a new job.

It could be said both for or against Charles that he saw his opportunity and did not hesitate to exploit it. But no one knew of the tenuous connection between Charles Dawson and the mayor, resulting in the appointment of a man to run the city's business possessing no more than an eighth-grade education, no bookkeeping experience, and no clear concept of the skills required by the job description. But Charles was not only cunning but smart. With study and by following meticulously calculated templates of bookkeeping set down by Jim McKelvy, he persevered and came to do a more than adequate job.

Charles's relationship with Mayor Kleckman was maintained at a respectful distance, with Charles deferring to his honor as appropriate. The mayor accorded Charles a certain wary respect based on having been inadvertently caught in a compromising situation, in all fairness, not of his own making. He recognized blackmail but felt powerless to thwart it, but Charles identified the situation only as that of opportunity.

Before ascending to the position to which he was appointed by the mayor, Charles's work was ostensibly of a physical nature. Oh, to be sure, he rarely handled a shovel or pickaxe, but he necessarily appeared on the job in work clothes and had to make the appearance that he could take on a tough job at any given moment. He might have been satisfied with the old George Edwards job, if it had not been for the necessity of wearing a working man's clothing.

Because of Charles's sober, hardworking nature, because of the respectability denoted by his serious approach to the business of maintaining his small rented property, because he was a family man, because of his strong back, and most of all because of a certain willingness to do certain dirty jobs, Doctor Deiter Dietrich employed him on an on-call basis.

Doctor Dietrich came to Onansburg to take over the practice vacated when old Doctor Ryan died. There being a dearth of physicians prepared to take up practice in rural Iowa in the mid-1950s, Doc Ryan stayed on to take care of the community's needs long after he should have taken care of his own.

Dietrich was a young man, fresh from medical school, and came ready to take on disease and pestilence but totally without knowledge of the social expectations of the position. The all-important legacy of the small-town practitioner was the aura of the anointed, the chosen one that was enjoyed by young physicians so courted and wooed by the communities that recruited them. He couldn't have known that the importance of the new doctor in town ranked right up there with the Second Coming. However, the transition to small-town practice from the ivory-towered atmosphere of the University of Chicago left the Dietrich idealism foundering.

He was a slight man. His elegantly slender physique, handsome, finely chiseled features, and slightly old-world manner of dress set him apart, as did his closely guarded secret. Dietrich brought a world-view to Onansburg that was greatly complicated by the baggage he carried, but his suitcase of secrets stayed firmly closed since it was unthinkable that a queer would have ascended to the doctor's throne. A queer for king! Indeed!

Keeping secrets, then, came naturally to the new doc. And neither history nor the *Choctaw County Recorder* would record the unspoken agreements to which those entrusted with the health and well-being of the citizens of a community were involved. Young Doctor Dietrich quickly found himself sorting through the carefully woven individual relationships that made up the fabric of the community, the carefully woven tapestry of financial and social relationships, the uneven patchwork of family lineages sometimes stitched with illicit alliances. Doctor D may have known more than most, but he guarded others' secrets as zealously as his own.

The law did not permit abortion in those years, and therefore many women did not consider it an option when faced with the prospect of yet another baby. The moral question upheld by the law meant that many would not seek the option, even when suspecting that it was an available alternative. Another child for many was inconvenient, ill-timed, an economic burden, but not life-threatening and not something over which one would go outside the law. Along with the need for therapeutic procedures to end troublesome pregnancies, it became quietly known that Dr. D performed abortions for unwed teenagers hauled before him when an expanding waistline, morning sickness, or the absence of the monthly cycle tipped off a watchful parent.

Deiter Dietrich was no fool. He charged a surfeit for the service, but not so much that a frightened family could not pay. The fee never appeared on a bill, and the cash payment never resided in his bank account. Payments, sometimes paid in installments, were in cash and delivered personally. The young women were both picked up and delivered to Doctor D's surgery in the wee hours of the night and then returned to their family within a relatively short while by Charles Dawson.

Charles was ideally suited to the work. It could be said that he and Doctor Dietrich understood one another, but more accurately, neither asked questions of the other. Each just did his own job with respect to the task at hand. Charles's work arrangement with Dr. D lasted until it was finally Mayor Kleckman's frightened daughter that Charles delivered to Doctor Dietrich's clinic in the dead of night.

Strong, reliable, close-mouthed. Ambitious and above all, devious, Charles realized the potential for reward immediately, and it wasn't long before he had the opportunity to remind his honor of a possible indebtedness that would be forever cancelled upon promotion to city clerk and manager. Charles got the job and kept his word.

As he was still a baby when the ill-conceived mismatch of opportunity occurred, Sonny couldn't have known of the illicit relationship between his father and Dr. Dietrich and Mayor Kleckman.

Eleven

---

riday's sun flamed into the sky bright and hot from first light. Even at six-thirty a.m., the fire vaporized the humidity that seeped into any cranny or crevice that was not protected by the astringency of air conditioning. The haze hung over the garden, and every plant sucked and gulped at the moist air.

Sonny pushed himself up through the discomforting layers of sleep that held him captive. He dreamed of balloons, floating pink and blue balloons. And miraculously, each one of them was Polly. He stretched and reached for them as they drifted near, a string dangling just close enough to tempt him to think he could grasp it. *Grab it! Grab it!* he urged himself. But each time, he was too late, moving in exaggerated slow motion, and each Polly balloon floated higher and farther away, leaving him first frustrated and then bereft.

He had awakened but dozed intermittently since shortly after five a.m. His pajamas were wet with perspiration. He ached, heavy and stiff, with a spirit so sore, so painful, that he broke into sobs immediately upon the disappointment of the return of full consciousness. He lay flat on his back on the smooth white cotton sheet. He dragged his fingertips along the sheet beneath him, sensing rather than feeling the slight resistance of its texture.

Sonny felt the light bounce with which Spats landed at the foot of the high old bed. Spats was called to duty to his human companions, and he knew it well. With no hesitation, with no question of his welcome, he curled his sleek body into the crook of Sonny's arm. Purring loudly, bringing the only comfort he knew how to give, he extended his neck and rested his whiskery chin on Sonny's shoulder. Sonny was immediately pleased and moved his arm to pull the supple body closer.

Careful, careful! He was pleased by the distraction Spats brought to him. In his dream, he'd lost his chance to have Polly with him again, and the memory of the dream was so painful, he knew he couldn't begin his day with it.

Disturbed by the motion, the cat raised his head and regarded Sonny with something less than his usual dispassionate gaze, and Sonny felt the kinship of the animal's loneliness. Spats returned his head to Sonny's shoulder. The broom-straw whiskers brushed Sonny's neck just so slightly, and the slanted eyes squinted open and then closed in feline appreciation. Sonny reached for Spats's front paw and felt for the black leather pads that were neatly separated by pristine white fur. Spats withdrew his paw from Sonny's examination and refolded it under the loaf of his body.

Are you happy, little guy? Are you? Or just relieved to have someone close?

Sonny lay morbidly still for longer than he cared to think, just to avoid disturbing the cat. One did not take such favors lightly. One could never be sure, given the nature of the beast, that he would ever be so chosen again.

He realized he'd slept in his underwear and was ashamed of his dishabille; Polly would have raised her eyebrows and smiled knowingly at his discomfort. Recounting his evening to himself, Sonny shook his head ruefully.

Shedding his underwear, he headed for the bathroom, but then the relief counseled by his overindulgence of alcohol last evening abandoned him. First Polly. Now the realization of the tragedy suffered by his sisters. He'd never been able to articulate his emotional detachment from his father. He could only feel an unexplained, prescient disgust toward him.

And his mother. A soul never illumined; a consciousness never awakened; a mind absent of perception and judgment. His father rewarded her willing servitude and passivity with approval.

Looking back at the empty bedroom, his despair overcame him. Polly would have been there, shaking her head at his messy trail across the room. He had always been considerate of her need for order.

He leaned against the doorjamb, and with loud sobs, he cupped his face in his hand and wept. Shoulders shaking, he howled his grief. Then he shrieked.

"Too much! Too much! My Polly! She enabled every facet of me. Now, who am I without her? She made me who I was. Am I the same man?"

He longed to hold her against his naked body, drawing from her scent, her warmth, her essence. He was bereft.

When he was finally without tears, having wrung what he thought was every emotion from every hollow of his mind, he was stilled by an overwhelming fatigue.

Drawing from his reserve of self-discipline, he willed himself to move ahead with the day at hand. *There's another entire day ahead, another without her. And it won't be over until it's over.*

He recalled his Grandma Rose admonishing him with "When you don't feel normal or like yourself, do normal things."

A stinging-hot shower did little to relieve his aching body but made the bathroom all but uninhabitable with steam.

He finished his morning routine quickly and then rubbed himself down with yet another fresh towel. Polly had kept a seemingly unending supply of fresh towels at the ready, neatly folded in thirds and stacked on the linen closet shelf. He looked guiltily at the towels from yesterday and the days before strewn around the bathroom.

He'd intended to choke the entire mound into the top of the washing machine, push a few buttons, and then later delegate the load to the power of the dryer, and it would be a job done.

But this may be the last of the clean underwear as well. It's not that I can't learn how to do laundry. There must be instructions somewhere. I can read, can't I?

He chose summer-tan slacks and a madras-plaid shirt, hating to add the additional layer over his tee shirt, but Sonny never wore knit shirts, only heavily starched one-hundred-percent cotton shirts, perfectly ironed by Charlene, the twice-a-week housekeeper.

He confirmed his own judgment of trading his penny loafers for Top-Siders when he thought of the possibility of numerous trips back and forth across the courthouse lawn, checking on the arrangements for the celebration. He inspected his suntans again and smoothed an imaginary crease as he headed for the door. The workday, the store, Old Settlers activities—his heart sank as he thought through the day that loomed over him. His fatigue crowded next to his aching heart.

At the top of the stairs, he stopped, puzzled. Going back into the bedroom, he frowned as he regarded the somnolent cat on the unmade bed. He hadn't made the bed yesterday either, yet he hadn't even noticed that when he climbed into it last night. He gave a little snort and chided himself. He had also been exhausted and had been feeling, more than a little, the effects of the frosty pitcher of some fruity, frothy drink that he found in the freezer, left from one of Polly's parties. He was pretty sure that he had been less than shit-faced, as some would describe it, but he knew he had been buzzed. It had seemed the perfect accompaniment to the tray of sandwiches that Dolores had deposited in the refrigerator. As he descended the stairs, Sonny started when he saw that all of the lights he'd so compulsively turned on the previous evening still burned brightly. Turning into the library, he saw the dried-out remains of the uneaten sandwiches and pitcher of now-melted cocktails.

He ordinarily preferred to eat earlier, but he had spent a few extra moments with Dolores, first chasing the bogeyman from her house, then admiring her flowers, inspecting an eaves trough that she imagined was loose without his customary impatience. He knew they would never talk about what had happened to her. He hoped her memories had been eradicated by the trauma she'd suffered, but then his heart plummeted when he understood that both sisters had likely experienced the same horror at the hands of their father. He knew he couldn't change what had happened just by having the recollection, the revelation.

He realized that he'd been deliberately postponing going home. It would fall to him to turn on the lights throughout the house that Polly had always switched on. She had always known of his aversion to dark shadows. There'd be no offer of a gin and tonic or aroma of a dinner ready to be served. Only Spats to share his aloneness.

He parked in the garage and pushed the closure button, lowering the garage door. He watched it descend and land with a resounding thunk. On the way to the back door of the house, he'd noted the plantings and flowers in his own yard looked thirsty, so he had given them a thorough watering with the hose. He knew that he was, all the while, making a tremendous effort to keep the incipient memory, the recent revelation, from his consciousness.

But after he brought in the mail, sorted through a now dwindling number of sympathy cards, and separated the bills from advertisements and appeals for contributions, he realized the sun had set more than an hour ago and it was nearly dark. He listened carefully to a couple of voicemail messages on the telephone confirming Old Settlers arrangements, then could no longer postpone being alone with his dinner.

The cool comfort of the library had embraced his somber mood. However, he turned on the lamps to relieve his abhorrence of the dark, sank into the embrace of the down-filled cushions of the loveseat, and watched a rerun of an inane sitcom that he had chosen not to watch the first time it aired. Without laughing yet trying to focus his attention on the program, he ate his sandwiches, drank the innocently seductive peach-flavored drink, and allowed himself to submit to its charms. He knew he was treading on dangerous ground. The intimate room, filled with framed photos, family keepsakes, and a collection of read and unread books both fiction and nonfiction, was the sanctuary where he and Polly had met, no matter what else the day had thrown at them, to unwind and play cribbage or gin rummy. Every single night, save a precious few when they were traveling or when one of them was ill.

He thought of his aloneness from a place deep within his core from which he could see himself looking out past his immediate concerns, to his future without Polly. He knew there would be loneliness coupled with his aloneness, but he knew they were not the same. As he felt the effect of the drink take hold, he welcomed the anesthetic relief, lifting him away from and outside of his own body. He drifted, almost pleasantly; in those moments, he could think of Polly and his aloneness without the surge of despair. He began to comprehend the enormity of the task before him in his grief process but knew there was a missing piece, something he was not understanding, and it eluded him. As he puzzled through his thoughts, he turned the television set off.

He had been fully prepared to let the swell of tears that he had consistently denied take hold. He gave himself permission to weep, to keen, to wail his grief, knowing that it was somehow overdue. Yet when he had consumed the food and sucked at the drink, the release was pushed further away. All that he hoped to experience was sublimated and distanced. Had he objectified the process with its deliberate choice? Had the food and drink intervened and given him comfort while what he sought was pain?

And the other. The new knowledge that had foisted itself upon him. He consciously segregated the chaos of the two dilemmas. There was Polly, and now then comes the other that he could never name or even articulate; but as he considered his newfound knowledge of his childhood, he recognized the piece that he'd been missing. It had been but a glimpse of a history of his family. How to fit that in with the grief over Polly. Too much. Too much.

The morning light illumined his recent understanding of the missing piece of his own history, only gained as an aftershock of having lost Polly. The darkness had brought him to a place of rebirth and awakening, even as he didn't comprehend the meaning it would have in the future. Even as he'd turned on lamps to dispel the fear that accompanied dark shadows, he'd turned to those same pockets of memory to recognize the evil that had changed the character of his life and that of his sisters.

As he hurried to the garage now, he noted the thermometer affixed in the doorway already registered seventy-eight degrees and wished he had chosen shorts instead of the tan trousers. He drove to the parking lot behind the store and pulled into his usual space in the back. It was early, seven-thirty a.m., and he recognized that Ruby and Thelma wouldn't be there yet. Once out of the car, he grabbed his metal tape measure and a can of spray paint from the trunk, then made sure he locked the doors of the car. Strangers in town for the celebration, he reminded himself. He hurried down the alley rather than cutting through the locked store, going through unlocking and relocking it, made a quick turn at the highway, then crossed Main Street to the Courthouse Park.

Once there, he checked the positions of the stands already partially constructed, the Cattlemen's barbecue booth and the Pork Producers' tent, then paced off the measurements for the remainder of the vendors who would bring their own tables. The bingo game run by the Lions Club and the dunk tank, along with the food stands, required work by members of the clubs and organization in advance of the opening night of Old Settlers.

First consulting his diagrams, then extending the tape measure on the grass, he marked dimensions for each vendor space with the spray paint. The spaces for the craft sale displays, for the Amish ice cream mega-churn, for the animal rescue group's petting zoo were allotted, numbered, and marked with spray paint.

Then he realized he'd forgotten he'd planned to be on the square last night when the carnival pulled in. Last year, the Ferris wheel had been set up by the carnival roadies at the corner of the square, which was also on the parade route. Sonny hadn't been about to take on the carnival workers at ten o'clock at night and try to make them move it, so the parade had detoured around it. The carnival was the same "Good Time Concessions" as last year, and a quick glance told him the parade route was, thankfully, clear. He'd listened to a voicemail last night from the city foreman, telling him the benches were in place in front of the stage.

Checking his watch, he knew that by now, eight o'clock, Ruby and Thelma Jane would have opened the store and would be getting ready for business. He reminded himself that the store would no doubt be busy with customers making last-minute preparations for floats for the parade; for food storage containers or new baking dishes in anticipation of arriving guests; for tape, poster board, and markers for the window displays. He anticipated being almost as busy as the liquor store and the Cozy.

I need to get in there, make sure the lights are on and people know we're open for business today. He crossed Main Street again, noting with approval that the lights were on inside the store and someone had thought to crank out the green awning under which spectators would gather during the next day's parade for respite from the sun.

Damn! I didn't clear out the windows for the Old Settlers display by the Class of 1969 and the Historical Society.

But with surprise, he saw the merchandise that had been in the window had been dismantled and cleared. Entering through the front door, he set the can of spray paint down on the checkout counter, then greeted Ruby and Thelma Jane.

"And I forgot to mention the display windows yesterday. The

Class of 1969—they're having their twenty-five-year reunion—and the Historical Society volunteers will probably be in soon to set up. Thanks again to whoever did that. Ruby? Or did you do it, Thelma Jane?"

Ruby put both hands on her hips and turned to face him.

"Larry did it last night before he left. I thought you were going to talk to him. Is today his last day, or is it tomorrow?"

"I didn't see him to mention it yesterday so we can just handle it tomorrow or even Monday. Let the kid have a good time at Old Settlers and . . . "

Ruby interrupted. "You can handle it, not 'we.' That's your deal, not mine." She finished counting opening change into the cash register and marched to the back room. Thelma Jane coughed discreetly to remind him of her presence.

"Well, I guess I know how she feels about that," he said to her. Thelma Jane didn't meet his eyes but scurried after Ruby to the rear of the store.

Now, he thought of Polly. He pictured reproach on her face, He hung his head as he might have as an ashamed child. *I know, I know, my sweet gentle girl. I was glib. I was crass, I was insensitive. Losing you has been hard for those two as well, and now this deal with Larry.*

Sonny put one hand on the checkout counter and leaned heavily on it. His eyes filled, and he felt the ache in his throat that presaged a breakdown into tears. He exited through the front door without a word to his employees but closed the door firmly enough for the sound to carry through the store to let them know he was gone. He heard the jingle of the store's entrance chimes even as he walked away.

He felt it necessary to make up for the days that he'd missed in doing his part for the Old Settlers committee. He knew Polly would have wanted him to carry on, to stay busy and not feel sad. As he encountered friends and acquaintances, he forestalled their polite commiserations of sympathy or the possibility of their concerned greetings of "How y'doin', Sonny?," giving each a smile, a comment, or just a nod in greeting as he hurried past.

Spotting the chairman of the omelet breakfast on Old Settlers morning, Harriet Percival, he asked if she had everything she needed and if she needed help setting up. Fixing him with a knowing eye, she responded, "Of course, we can always use more help. If you're free early in the morning, we'll be here by six-thirty, so we can start serving at eight."

Duke Hostetler, coach at the high school, cornered him with a complaint about the chairman of the kids' games and contests. "Sonny, what am I going to do about Donna? She thinks the start of the 10K race will get in the way of the kids' races. It's the same as it is every year, and she's been doing the kids' contests since God was a boy. We both do it the same every year, and it's never a problem."

And as he responded to the complaint from either Duke or Donna every year, depending on who came to him first, the response was the same: "I'll be seeing her, and we'll sort it out, like we always do."

The parade chairman, Roger, was marking out positions for each entry in the parade, based upon the category in which they'd entered. With his megaphone fully charged, at one o'clock sharp on Saturday, the Old Settlers parade would be underway. The Choctaw County Sheriff's patrol car, upon receiving the signal to start from Roger, would sound its siren and lead the parade on its ten-block route. Then each entry, in turn from the predetermined entry number, would be melded into the parade at Roger's direction.

"Hi, Roger. Need any help? Anything I can help you do here?"

"No, no. Everything's under control, at least until tomorrow. There's always some renegade entry that doesn't bother to sign up. Remember that goofy family that showed up in paper bag masks a couple years ago? The Unknown Family, they called themselves. Six or seven of 'em. They acted like they knew everyone in town, but no one knew who they were. They even called out to people by name.

We gave 'em a prize anyway. They came in fifth out of four entries for the best-decorated truck."

Sonny walked on. He knew the family. He stopped at the Cattlemen's stand and saw that they were already serving. He ordered a hamburger, realizing he hadn't eaten breakfast, before he checked back in at the store. He spent the rest of the day helping customers locate a particular screw, nail, or tool; bagged merchandise; and ran the cash register when Ruby and Thelma Jane took a lunch break. Larry had arrived earlier for his eleven-to-five shift, his summer hours. He busied himself with sweeping floors, dusting merchandise, intuitively staying out of Sonny's range of vision. Sonny heard pleasant chatter among the three employees when they encountered one another through the afternoon, but while he felt left out, conversely, he didn't want to join in their camaraderie.

Sonny's premonition had been correct; Business fell off toward the end of the day, so at four forty-five, Sonny directed the three employees to go on home, that he would close the store at five-thirty. Promptly at five-thirty, Sonny locked the front door and began to close out the cash register. He paced his way through the mundane tasks, switched off the showroom lights on his way to his office, and compulsively checked the back door, even then knowing it was locked. Half an hour later, emerging from his office with the bank bag locked in the safe, Sonny remembered that he hadn't rolled the awning in.

Dammit, as sure as I go out to bring the awning in, someone will see me and need something from the store or just want to have a word with me. But a thunderstorm or windstorm would take it down in a minute. I'd better bring it in.

He opened the door from the hallway into the showroom, but as he stepped through the door, he stopped abruptly. A figure at the door was silhouetted in the still-strong light from outside, cupping his hands around the sides of his face and peering into the store. Startled, Sonny stood still even though he was sure he couldn't be seen in the near-dark of the store and hidden as he was by the bulk of the merchandise gondolas.

It's Drennan McCormack! Well, too bad. He got here too late. I'm not about to go out and welcome him in.

But now, Drennan was knocking on the door, first with his knuckles, then louder with his fist against the solid mass of the wooden door. Sonny hesitated, but then Drennan dropped his arms, straightened to his full height, and walked in the direction of the Cozy. After a few seconds of thought, Sonny decisively hurried up the center aisle between the gondolas and through the showroom. He unlocked the door, jerked it open, and once on the street, he looked in the direction he'd seen Drennan take. First relieved, then chagrined, but seized with sudden purpose, he hoped Drennan was still in sight. He suddenly preferred to meet him face-to-face than be ambushed by him.

It's not as though I want to talk to him, but I'm starting to be curious. What could he want after all these years?

Sonny retrieved the awning crank from its hiding place at the junction of the awning and the front of the building, unfolded the handle, and twisted the crank, drawing the awning parallel to the building. With a last inspection of the awning, he replaced the crank, then turned to survey the town square. Looking both ways, and with rising anxiety, he surmised that Drennan had gone into the Cozy, yet he had no intention of seeking him out in a public gathering place. Having kept his emotions in check since his breakdown of the morning, his mind was clouded by his fatigue and anxiety at being stalked by Drennan.

Old Settlers started promptly at six p.m. with the opening of the carnival for business. The sun was just beginning its daily sinking spell, allowing welcome shade in front of the east-facing stores, and the shadows of the Courtyard Park trees began to lengthen.

A few early diners headed for the cool respite of the South Side Café—a prime rib special with salad and baked potato was the draw—but more celebrants took advantage of dinner in the Courthouse Park from the Cattlemen, the Pork Producers, and the carnival vendors now set up to do business. The cakewalk, sponsored by the junior class of Onansburg High, began more or less at six on the bandstand, with the high school band joined by a few band alumni taking the stage at seven o'clock.

Immediately following the band concert, the Harold Family Country Band would take the stage, then conclude the evening entertainment to an appreciative audience, some of whom sat on the temporary benches lined up in front of the stage. Others would take early possession of the wrought-iron park benches rendered with family names in memoriam, a modicum of comfort to well-padded and bony butts alike, donated by Onansburg families, both current and long gone.

Sonny had been invited to have a beer at six o'clock with the Old Settlers committee at the Legion Hall bar, but he'd begged off, as he'd planned to meet Dolores at six-thirty at the corner where the South Side and the First National Bank met daily for business— the financial district, so to speak. He'd suggested that Dolores walk uptown to meet him for the evening's entertainment, as he hadn't wanted to give up his parking space behind the store.

And Sonny was certain that he was not ready to be in the confines of his car alone with Dolores. There had been instances when Dolores's gentle heart intuited his underlying emotion, and he was reeling, not only with grief but also guilt born of his own oblivion to his sister's experience.

As it was not yet six-thirty, Sonny walked toward the corner to meet Dolores. Most of the early crowd was at the cakewalk, but Sonny stopped to look at a few of the display windows. He exchanged comments with a few others looking at the windows, greeted another merchant, Paul Levis, locking the door to the dry cleaners, which he owned and operated.

When Dolores saw Sonny walking toward her, she crooked her

arm at the elbow, and with her hand, motioned for him to hurry. She was frowning, yet he knew he wasn't late for their meeting. Her other arm held her much-used plaid blanket she'd brought along for cushioning the hard wooden bench seats. Upon seeing the blanket, Sonny knew it had been a hot walk for her even for the few blocks from her home.

"What's going on? What's the hurry?"

"It's that man, that man that was at Polly's funeral. He just walked past here, then he saw me and almost stopped. But then he walked that way," she said, gesturing toward the courtyard.

"I told you before, he's someone I knew a long time ago. He grew up here, and he's close to your age. You just don't remember him. Let's go across and find a place to sit. Here, let me carry your blanket for you. The band concert starts at seven." They jaywalked across the street, in front of the store to the park. Nodding to locals and even to those who seemed to recognize him, though he didn't necessarily remember their names, they found two places on one of the temporary benches. He unfolded Dolores's blanket across the spaces to make a cushion for the two of them on the bench. Before Sonny seated himself, he glanced around the crowd, seeking the face he'd seen in the doorway earlier at the store. But then he questioned himself.

So what would I do if I spotted Drennan? It's Drennan who wants to speak with me, but I'm tired of being shadowed by him; I'm tired of this cat-and-mouse game.

Precisely one hour later, the band concluded with a rendition of "Good Night, Ladies." The band members vacated the stage, packed up their instruments, and politely removed their chairs. The Harold Family Country Band, featuring lead guitar, fiddle, harmonica, percussion, and bass fiddle, took the stage and opened with the tune "Orange Blossom Special," featuring Alice Harold Madigan. But after half an hour, Sonny noted that Dolores was yawning, holding her fingers politely in front of her mouth. He thought she'd even nodded off, but as he observed the adult wreckage of the pretty little girl she'd been, he recanted earlier bursts of short temper and impatience.

"Sweetheart, are you ready to go home? Let's call it a night. I have to wake up early and get up here to be sure everything's in place for the day and then help with the omelet breakfast."

He stood up and noted with surprise that his knees were stiff from sitting, and his butt ached, despite the padding of Dolores's blanket. They joined the constantly milling crowd and followed the sidewalk path through the Courthouse Park to the street. When Dolores realized that Sonny was guiding her to the back of the store via the highway and the alley, she stopped.

"But why can't we go through the store? It's quicker, and besides, it's air-conditioned, and I'm hot."

"No, come on this way, but if you have to use the restroom, we'll stop in the store."

"Well, okay, I guess," she replied. "But I never miss a chance if a restroom is close, but I guess I can wait if . . . "

"Let's go around the back then. My car is parked back there."

They drove slowly away from the lights and flurry of the departing crowd, carefully avoiding those walking to their cars. Dolores seemed alert now, peering from the window to identify neighbors or anyone she knew. It was important to her to be seen riding with Sonny. She smiled and nodded complacently in satisfaction during the short ride to her home.

Sonny deposited Dolores in her living room, checked the back door and the windows for her, then stood on the porch until he heard her lock the front door. He swung back into his car, adjusted the fan, and headed for home. At the end of the block, he made a big U-turn, headed back to Dolores's cottage, and hurried to her front porch. The light was still burning, as it would until Dolores turned it off in the morning, so she opened the door quickly after peeking from behind the curtained window next to the door.

Her face was again fixed in the same expression of bewilderment that he had glimpsed the previous day when he encountered her walking toward his home. When she opened the door fully and unlocked the screened door, Sonny stepped through it and, despite her bulky frame, encircled her with his arms and hugged her tightly.

"What, Sonny? What did you forget?"

"Forgot to tell you good night and that I love you."

Dolores's face now registered wonderment, but she ducked her head and abashedly repeated his benediction. "I love you too, Sonny."

Twelve

---

*O*pening the door with the remote control, he idled the car into the garage but then closed the door without turning off the engine. He quickly turned the key to OFF, and the engine died. It would have been easy to leave the engine running and just drift away, but then he remembered Polly and her sweet guardianship of potential threats and harm to him— ever vigilant.

Sonny slipped through the service door that connected to the screened patio, then climbed the steps into the kitchen without turning on the yard light or kitchen lights. He first saw the white tip of the elegant tail before he saw its owner in the dark, but Spats immediately called attention to himself by scolding Sonny for being gone for so long. With a quick glance at the door to the basement, Sonny leaned over to meet and greet Spats. He took pleasure in stroking the satiny back that arched up to meet his hand.

Sonny visited the closest bathroom, the powder room, as Polly called it. He flushed the toilet, put the lid down carefully, as he'd been frequently reminded. A sob caught in his throat. He was forlorn.

She was here, she was just here, and now she's gone.

Shuffling aimlessly from the powder room, through the kitchen, into the dining room, he dismissed the stacks of mail and yet-to-be-written thank-you notes that lay untouched on the dining room table. In the living room, looking toward the street through the massive window with its drapes open, he admired the tidy lawn in light thrown off by the handsome Victorian lamp erected only last year to shine on the path leading up the front sidewalk. It was equipped with a sensor that automatically turned on the light at dusk, his own installation of which he was very pleased.

The brick sidewalk was a pain in the ass, as it came to be described by Sonny when he ran the snow blower or hand-shoveled new snow from it. Some of the bricks rescued from the old Choctaw County Courthouse were sold as souvenirs, but Sonny had come upon a cache of them after he purchased the store from the Franklin heirs. They were seemingly abandoned at the back of the store but carefully covered by a heavy oiled tarpaulin. *Curious,* he thought at the time. *Were they being preserved or hidden?* He worked diligently over several weeks to lay them in place, replacing the broken cement sidewalk.

The streetlight was the crowning touch to the entry to their Victorian home. They had come upon an ad in the *Des Moines Register* for streetlights that had once graced Grand Avenue in Des Moines but subsequently were relegated to an architectural salvage business. The sidewalk was positioned as a center walk to the front door, cutting diagonally from the corner of 5th and Wall Street straight to the steps to the porch that faced the corner. The brick walkway and the streetlight made a venerable pair, denoting age and character.

Polly had been so excited about the installation of the streetlight that she wanted to have a party: an erection party, she'd wanted to call it.

"Well sure, sweetheart! Let's have an erection party. We can serve hot dogs—wienies." He bent his head toward her, fixing her in his gaze, smirking as he did so.

"Sonny! Now you're making out something naughty about my party. Don't tease me so."

"Let's have a little party, yes. But let's call it something else, like a Let There Be Light Party."

Polly smiled knowingly then, and Sonny never knew for sure who was teasing whom.

Continuing through the living room now, Sonny glanced into what once would have been known as a parlor, and through the parlor windows, he could see someone—a man—on his front porch, his figure faintly illuminated by the streetlight. The figure was more than a shadow, standing with his back to the window. Then Sonny noticed the sleek, foreign automobile parked just beyond the streetlight, partially hidden in the shadows. Drennan McCormack!

Taking a deep breath, Sonny strode to the front door, jerked it open, and hailed Drennan.

"What the hell are you doing out here, Drennan? Lying in wait for me? You've been shadowing me since Polly's funeral. Yes, I got your note. No, I've not had time to call you up and get together for a good-old-boy chat about the woman we both loved. What the hell is going on in your mind?"

Drennan was smiling, a sheepish, self-conscious smile. But instead of retreating, he reached out to shake Sonny's hand. "It's good to finally see you, Sonny. Sorry I had to resort to sneaking up on you, but I wanted to get to you."

Sonny reluctantly extended his hand. After the two shook hands, Sonny stepped back. He raised his voice.

"Well, Drennan. You got to me alright. There've been a lot of folks around, quite a few came for Polly's service from out of town, but I really didn't expect you."

He was discomfited for a moment by Drennan's imposing height, his confidence, the fixed intensity of his eyes. He stepped back from the handshake and stopped speaking for a moment, not sure of the agenda for the meeting.

He continued, "We've never been friends. Anything I knew of

you, I knew from Polly." He dropped his head. His eyes filled, but Drennan looked away.

"Yeah, Sonny. I know. We didn't know one another. And it's because of Polly. I want to tell you what she meant to my life. I wish I could have told her in person, but now, I'm left to tell you. But it's important to me, and by God, I believe it's going to be important to you." The last he uttered as more prayer than threat.

"I don't know, I just don't know that I can stand here tonight and let you tell me about the time when you and Polly were together. I didn't know anything about that. Hell, I didn't even know you, but I remember seeing an article in the paper about local men serving in Vietnam, and you were one of them. Then someone just had to tell me that Polly had been your girl, and so Polly told me about you."

In angst, Sonny's voice rose again in strength and intensity. "There you were in that God-forsaken place, fighting a war no one wanted, and we were here, safe and sound, falling in love. You were over there killing villagers and babies, and we were here, comfortable, safe, and sound! We both, Polly and I, felt rotten about that."

Sonny knew he was taunting Drennan, and while he knew it was unfair, at that moment, he didn't care. In turn, Drennan raised his voice and pinned Sonny motionless with his vehemence. Both men were standing face-to-face, but both knew there would be no force beyond that of words. "Don't you ever say that! There was so much shit going on in that whole place, no one knew the truth of what was happening. Don't ever believe it, and don't you ever say it again. All of us that were there had to live with that, and too many good boys didn't ever come home. I always knew it would be better to be killed than to be taken prisoner! It was inhuman!"

He paused, then said, "I'm going to tell you what happened with Polly and me, and you're going to hear me out. I have a bottle in the car. Would you like some Scotch? Do you have some ice?

You're going to want something to take the edge off! And we might be here for a while."

"No. No more! You were *always* out there somewhere, from when we fell in love until she was gone. Gone from both of us now! She's gone, and she took you with her, your story, your memories together. I didn't ever want to hear them from her, and I sure as hell don't want to hear them from you. I'm the one that's left without her. You moved on, and she became another notch on your . . . " Sonny's voice cracked and became hoarse. He didn't want Drennan in his house. He couldn't bear having Drennan in the house he'd shared with Polly.

"Just you wait a minute! I thought I'd never get over what happened to Polly and me. I thought I'd never forgive her for what happened to us. But now, I can't imagine my life any other way than the way it's played out. And I can't imagine anything other than you and Polly together." Drennan paused thoughtfully, his anger suddenly gone. He took a deep breath and sighed deeply, but then he resumed his narration. "I'm so sad for all of us that she's gone. There was a time I thought the three of us might be friends, but I guess that was just a fantasy of mine, the three of us getting together when I came to town. I always loved her, you know, after I got over hating her for throwing me over for you."

Drennan smiled, but it was a sad, rueful smile. "Get the ice, Sonny. I'll get the bottle from the car. It's not late, and I want you to know and understand what happened to Polly and me. Not together, but what happened to us, the three of us—Polly, you, and me."

Drennan hesitated for a moment, then made his way to the car. Sonny watched him go. He'd not noticed previously that Drennan walked slowly, almost painfully. It made him seem a bit less powerful. He thought of going inside and just locking the door, but then, decisively, he turned and went through the dark rooms to the bar, formerly the butler's pantry, between the dining room and kitchen.

Flipping the switch on the small bar lamp, he filled an ice bucket

from the ice-maker beneath the bar, loaded a tray with two cylindri-
cal crystal glasses, the ice bucket, cocktail napkins, and at the last
moment, added his own bottle of Glenlivet to the tray. *I don't need
to depend on Drennan for a drink*, he thought childishly. He started
back to the porch but returned to the bar and retrieved the ice tongs.

Pacing back through the living room, Sonny paused when he
came to the door, but Drennan hastened to open the screened door,
and Sonny brought the loaded tray out to the porch. He motioned
Drennan to one of the wicker armchairs. Then, setting the tray on
the wicker table, he asked tersely, "What will it be, Drennan? I see
we both drink Glenlivet. How do you want yours?"

Sonny gave off signals that he was not regarding this meeting
as just a friendly get-together between acquaintances. He remained
standing in front of the chair he'd claimed for himself and watched
wordlessly when Drennan began to attend to the drinks.

Drennan poked the tongs into the ice bucket, coming out with
two cubes, then added two more to one of the glasses. Picking it up,
he studied it, then added another cube. "A big glass," he observed.
He gestured toward Sonny with the tongs. How many do you
want?" he asked politely.

Feeling as though Drennan had usurped him as host, Sonny all but
snatched the tongs from Drennan's hand. He said, simply, "I'll do my
own." He filled the remaining glass more than half full of cubes.

Drennan reached for his bottle of Scotch, added a generous portion to his glass. Extending the bottle to Sonny, he said, "I'll buy the
first round."

Sonny took the bottle, poured his own drink, and responded
with a slight smile, "And we'll see who lasts for the second round."

Drennan extended his arm, upraised with glass in hand. "To
Polly," he said with a catch in his voice.

Sonny felt the gut-wrench but choked out his own toast, "To
my Polly."

Both men leaned back against the ample cushions of the wicker armchairs, Drennan with his feet firmly planted on the floor, and Sonny with one foot cocked up on the opposite knee. Sonny took a deep drink from his glass and looked expectantly at Drennan. It was quiet for a few moments.

"Sonny, help me out here. I didn't know you in school. You were enough younger than me. It wasn't like we were a big school, but you were probably just one of the younger kids in the background. I was busy with football, then basketball and track. Did you go out for any sports?"

Sonny didn't know where Drennan was going with all this. He uncrossed his leg, pushed against the floor with both legs, straightened in his chair, and gave a negative headshake. He waited for Drennan to leave off his reminiscing and get to the point of the meeting he had initiated. "No, my family didn't do sports or any extracurricular activities." Sonny engaged in the conversation with a token contribution.

Taking Sonny's response as interest, Drennan leaned forward toward Sonny, resting his elbows on his knees, his drink cradled in both hands.

"Anyway, I worked a few hours a week at the gas station for some spending money. My brother, Mike, did too. Do you remember him?"

Sonny, becoming more impatient, mumbled a grudging assent. "Of course, I know Mike now, didn't really know him in school. He lives here in town—comes to the store for stuff once in a while." Sonny knew he sounded annoyed, but he was hard put to maintain interest in Drennan's queries about people he never knew when they were kids.

More intense now, Drennan moved the conversation on. "Didn't you have a sister? Seems like I remember a sister, yeah, and there was another sister, and you were the youngest. The older one was a year or so ahead of me, pretty girl too. Didn't she get married and leave town when she was still in school?"

Sonny's patience was finally exhausted. "Drennan, let's not waste time going down memory lane. You said you wanted to tell me about your time with Polly and what it's meant to you since you lost her."

Drennan leaned back, took a slow drink of his Scotch, paused a moment, then reflected.

"There were three, no four of us from here that went to Drake— two of the guys from our class and me and a girl, Donna. I had a track scholarship—used to be pretty fast, you know. Dad might not have let me go otherwise. We guys joined ROTC and played at being soldiers, marching and drilling, serving as color guards, but we knew the whole thing in Vietnam—"

Sonny waved his hand dismissively and interrupted Drennan's reminiscence. "Come on, Drennan—back to your life after Polly ended whatever you had together." He took a perverse pleasure in needling Drennan with the clarification that Polly had chosen him over Drennan.

Drennan continued as though he hadn't heard the interruption and resumed where he'd left off. "We partied hard, drank a lot . . . there was a place near campus called Peggy's that wasn't too fussy about our IDs. We had decent enough grades to stay in school—not what we could have had if we'd applied ourselves— but we got through the first couple of years. Polly and I were still together on weekends and with letters and phone calls, but it was really a pretty chaste relationship and . . . " He smiled and shrugged, his voice trailed off. For a moment, his expression softened.

"Drennan, dammit! I don't want to hear about you and Polly— what you did or didn't do together. I don't want to know!"

With a rueful smile and a nod, Drennan continued, as if he was delivering a soliloquy and hadn't heard Sonny.

"A Marine recruiter showed up during the spring of our second year; so Junior, Dean, and I, we decided we'd enlist in the Corps, serve our two years, then finish school on the GI Bill.

"We went to San Diego, got through basic training, but little did

I know, tough as basic was, that wasn't anything compared to the hell of Vietnam. No one would have guessed that a few months later, the other guys would be dead. At least, they weren't captured."

Sonny hadn't known anyone who'd died in combat. It was beyond the limits of his understanding. He'd known of students, roughly contemporaries, who'd died in auto accidents, but his recognition of them was of them as just being gone.

"I was usually sent out on a CH-46 with a squad doing whatever needed to be done." Sonny sat straighter in his chair and fixed his eyes on Drennan's face; he sensed the story Drennan was unfolding was outside of any experience belonging to himself or that he could imagine. He'd always wondered if he could stand up in combat with an enemy soldier.

"Sometimes, a Navy chaplain would go out with us. We gave him a tough time about being Navy, but he was a good guy. His name was Vince, but we called him Padre Vince or just Padre or even just Vince. I didn't know at the time, but because his nickname was Padre, I thought he was a Catholic priest. He didn't have to go out with us, but he did. The day I was wounded . . . "

Surprised, Sonny broke his silence. "Drennan, what the hell! I didn't know you'd been wounded! Did Polly know you were wounded?"

Drennan held his eyes evenly on Sonny, measuring the effect of his words. Slowly and emphatically, he replied, "Yes, Polly knew. My parents told her and let her know how to contact me once I was flown out of Da Nang. I'll tell you more, but then we'd better have another drink. You're buying this time."

Immediately, Sonny was nonplussed. Even in his surprise, he was embarrassed for Polly and himself. That she hadn't mentioned knowing of Drennan's injuries. For himself, that he'd never questioned her bygone alliance with Drennan.

Sonny was impatient to hear more of Drennan's story, even while wanting this evening to be over. More Scotch, he reasoned, might be a remedy for both. This time, he attended to the drinks, retrieving more ice, tipping his own bottle of Scotch in full measure of the glasses. *Polly knew! She knew Drennan had been wounded. She knew, but she'd never even mentioned Drennan, much less what happened to him.*

He sat down again across from Drennan, took a deep drink from his glass, the sliding ice cubes bumping his upper lip, splashing a bit of Scotch up under his nose.

"So, going in we were taking heavy fire from the word 'go.' We were all scared shitless but we knew there were wounded guys that needed to get out of there, so we just went on in. I could hear the copilot calling out coordinates to the guys on the ground that were trying to give us cover. He was a kid from Iowa—good pilot, I'd flown with him before—doing everything he could, but a big shell hit us, damaged the forward rotor."

Sonny sat up straighter, not having to feign his interest. "It burst into flames. The pilots were yelling, scrambling to keep us going, but the bird went over on its back, crashed and burned. I was lucky, I guess. I was thrown clear. I thought all the rest died then and there."

The personal devastation that Drennan had unfolded shook Sonny to his core. *This is an understanding beyond me.* "Have you told this story many times before?"

"No. I've never told it to anyone." Drennan took a long draw on his drink, then continued. "My injury was serious but not life-threatening. My hip was shattered when I was thrown clear.

"My folks got word that I was wounded, but I don't know what happened between them and Polly—maybe you two were already together before I was wounded. She took it hard when I left for Nam though."

Drennan leaned back in his chair. Sonny took a deep breath and let it out with a long sigh. Drennan had been a mystery to Sonny for as long as he'd known Polly. Drennan had existed on a level of thinking about which Sonny knew nothing. Drennan was a shadow, sometimes a cloud, when Sonny read of his academic achievements and opportunities. He looked questioningly to Drennan and nodded his assent to continue.

"I was in the hospital in San Diego for three months, first a series of surgeries to rebuild the hip. My folks came out to see me, but I wasn't very good company. With my mail all messed up, I didn't get Polly's letter, telling me about the two of you. She wrote to me again but assumed I'd received her first letter, so that second letter left me reeling. Everything I knew, I took from the second letter. She talked about the life the two of you were considering together and about Onansburg. She hoped I could forgive her and wished me a happy life. End of story."

Drennan resumed the telling of his biography, complete with an emotional edge sometimes bringing tears that never quite spilled over. "Pain was a constant; addiction was always a possibility. After a couple of months, fewer drugs, but then I looked around at the other men that were recovering in the hospital for truly life-changing injuries. Amputations, brain injuries, paralysis, burns, and always, addiction. Instead of realizing that I was relatively lucky and would eventually heal, I filled myself with the worst of everything I knew."

Drennan's words came haltingly. Minutes passed between his recollections; both men drank deeply from their glasses, but Sonny thought to do nothing but wait for Drennan to continue. Later, he might reflect on his lack of curiosity; but he knew himself well. To sit and absorb the story without question. Listen and learn. Then reflect and only then think of the questions he could have asked. *How would I have felt if Drennan had asked to visit with Polly and me? Would I have even considered meeting him with her present?*

"I turned myself over to hate, and I hated Polly and you the most. I held the two of you responsible for where I was and who and what I'd become. I filled myself with images of everything we all hate—I was cancerous, I was syphilitic, I was tubercular." He paused, searching for more vengeful words. "I was venomous, gangrenous, malevolent. I was cruel to myself and worse, to others. I wrote hate-filled letters to the two of you. I wrote to Polly and told her she was nothing but a prick-teaser; told her she was an alley cat in heat, so hot she couldn't wait for me. What I wrote to you was worse."

Sonny started, then fixed hard eyes on Drennan. "How could you, Drennan? How could you have done that to Polly? Writing to me, I understand that. But how could you have said those things to her?"

Drennan turned away from Sonny's stare, shaking his head, then dropping it to his chest. But then, he raised his head, grimaced as if in pain, and continued. Drennan answered in kind, stern and direct. "I didn't ever send them. They were filthy indictments of both of you." He continued slowly. "Even with all the poison that was filling me up and spilling onto others, I couldn't do that to her." Drennan stopped short, as if considering his next words more carefully. He inclined his head toward Sonny and looked deeply into Sonny's eyes.

Sonny wanted to look away. He had a prescient thought. *I don't want to hear what it is he will say next.*

"But for God's sake—look at yourself, Sonny. You're a man. You're a good man. You were Polly's choice of a good man." Drennan softened, but kept his gaze on Sonny. "I knew of you as a child, a little boy when you were growing up. But Sonny. I know, everyone in town knows you were born a female. The whole town thinks of you as a man, but biologically, you were born female."

Sonny was stricken. He gasped and stood up with his mouth agape but then clenched his jaw and spun around, his back to Drennan, to hide his face. He struggled for control, clasped his hands into fists to quiet his shaking.

Drennan said evenly, "Sonny, I want you to hear me out. How could I have not hated Polly for choosing you? How could I have not hated you for taking Polly from me?" Sonny heard Drennan's voice as if from a great distance; he recognized an unexpected gentleness in its deep timbre.

Drennan continued, "But now, I want to tell you where I've been for the last twenty-five years or so, since the seventies, and what's important is this—I want you to know you gave Polly the life she deserved, more than I ever could have given her. I regret so much I didn't get to tell her this."

Sonny couldn't speak, even though he wanted to respond.

Drennan's words continued to cut through the silence. "I promise you. We'll sort this out between us. I want us to be friends, the two men that loved her. And we'll both love her forever. You, for all the things she was to you, and me, for all the things I learned from loving her—all of the life she gave over to me when she chose you."

Still standing, Sonny cut him off, his voice hoarse with no inflection. "Give me a few minutes, Drennan." He made as if to get more ice, moving stiffly away, as though taut strings pulled between them. The strings were strung tight from one man to the other, and every movement hammered the tension.

Once inside, a chill seized him. The air-conditioned air hung without stirring but wrapped him in its cave-like essence. He didn't understand what Drennan was trying to tell him about a relationship between himself and Polly that had, in his own mind over the intervening years of separation, idealized a union that was nonexistent. An embryonic love that grew and matured into a relationship by proxy, not a marriage but one based on fantasy. Sonny returned to the porch without the ice.

Shaken to his very core, his heartbeat throbbing in his ears, Sonny tried to end the revelatory conversation. "Drennan, I'm not up for this. Let's call it a night." Sonny tried to gain control of the confrontation while understanding any rebuttal would be misunderstood.

"Come on, Sonny. Sit down. We may never be in a place for this conversation again. Sit down." Lamely, he added, "Please."

Drennan continued. His commanding presence allowed no interference in the message fueled by the need to convey his experience. "I was still a Marine, but then I was sent to the Naval Hospital in

Pensacola for more work on my hip, and Padre Vince was the first familiar face I saw when I got there.

"But Padre Vince saw me then for what I was; lost, just a body still filled with hate for life and what I thought it had done to me. He preached at the Chapel on base, and out of loyalty to a good guy, after a while there, I went on a Sunday for the service. The homily was based on Matthew 18:21–25. His sermon, the gospel from Matthew, was for me, I know it was directed to me through Padre Vince.

"Do not become the hate that you will come to loathe. It will eat you alive. Just as alcohol and drugs are addictive, so is hate. You cannot be forgiven unless you forgive. You don't have to forget, but you must forgive.

"From the time I heard him preach on that day in Pensacola, I had a sense that I could make it back, get a life, and expunge some of the hate and the shit that I laid on my family and my buddies. Being with him took me back to where the hell began and then let me come to life again.

"I forgave the guys that went to Canada to avoid the draft. If they didn't get to come back to America again, they were going to be as lost to their families as Junior and Dean were to theirs.

"I went back to college after being discharged. I transferred the Drake credits for my last two years at Duke University in Durham, then just forged right on through to the Duke Graduate School in sociology—the graduate program was a good one."

Sonny shifted in his chair and looked away.

"Once in graduate school, the short story is in trying to understand what happened when Polly chose you instead of me, I made an academic career."

Drennan's voice intensified as he warmed to his subject. "I needed to understand you and Polly and how you made your lives together, how the townspeople accepted you socially in business, community activities. What about your families? The Shaws?"

Upon hearing the Shaw name, Sonny slapped his hand flat on the painted, wooden top of the wicker table on which the tray of drinks was resting, and the sound cracked in the still night. The Scotch glasses, sweaty in the humidity, bounced on the silver tray. Drennan flinched involuntarily. Sonny dropped his voice, distinct and hostile.

"What I'm getting from you is that you've spent a lifetime rationalizing how Polly threw you over for me! Dammit! I'm not a lab rat! And Polly! You say you loved her then, and now some phony story about still loving her! You'd better leave." Sonny stood up and pushed Drennan's bottle away from himself.

Drennan persisted despite Sonny's dismissal. "Sonny, I don't want to leave you this way—This wasn't easy for you and Polly. It wasn't just the hometown sweethearts that became a couple. Crossdressing, assuming an identity not consistent with your biology, takes real work. You've always worked it. You've had a good life here; you're well-liked, respected, a businessman."

Sonny raised his head and fixed Drennan in a hard stare. "A man, you say. You call me a man? I don't know how you know what you think you know about us, but dammit, no one could have been a better man than I was for Polly." *I was the best man. I was the best man I could be.* The old mantra recurred. *Be the best little boy you can be, Sonny. Be the best little boy you can be.*

"I know that, Sonny. I know that. And why you are a man doesn't matter. It just doesn't matter. But I am interested in how you became a man. That's the part that has eluded me."

"Your family always lived here in town, didn't they?" Drennan began slowly when Sonny didn't respond. "I don't think I ever knew your parents. Your sisters were always a little . . . different. The older one. I didn't know her, but I knew Nate, the guy she dated and then married. They married young, didn't they? I remember Nate was one of the coolest ever, a James Dean lookalike, the Indian motorcycle, rolled-up sleeve with the cigarettes. Are they still together, Sonny?"

"I'll fill you in another time about Cloris." Sonny, with dismay, quickly realized he had assumed another meeting with Drennan.

I'll take care of you, Sonny. Promise me. Cloris will take care of you. Just promise.

"And yeah, I have another sister; she lives here in town, works at the school." Sonny wanted to head off Drennan's questioning about his family. There were too many hidden, dark secrets.

Forget you ever saw this, Sonny. Just be the best little boy you can be. Just be the best little boy you can be. Promise me. Cloris will take care of you. Just promise.

"Can we go inside, Sonny? The mosquitoes are starting to eat me alive."

Sonny hesitated, wanting Drennan to leave, but knew he couldn't walk away from this discussion. Drennan had long been a shadow, faintly haunting, faintly threatening. No one remembered or cared about Sonny's family, his upbringing.

But Polly! He had to defend her—shield her from his family's perversion and from Drennan's probing examination of her choice of himself.

Sonny slowly led the way into their home, from the front door through the foyer to their beautifully restored, exquisite home, to the living room. Sonny felt Polly's presence still. In relative dishabille from the aftermath of the funeral, Sonny thought Polly would not have wanted Drennan there. She would not have wanted his intrusion in their lives. He was someone from the outside looking in, a voyeur.

Sonny turned on the lamps, pulled the soft linen drapes closed. He pointed toward a chair, the Victorian rosewood chair covered in silk damask. He snorted to himself; the chair was one of a pair, one slightly larger and heavier than the other. A gentleman's chair and a lady's chair, as they were known. Drennan unknowingly had been directed to the lady's chair, leaving the gentleman's chair to himself.

Sonny perched himself toward the front of his selected chair. *He's only a little older than I am, but he looks a lot older.* Drennan's hair was thinning noticeably at the crown and had gone to salt and pepper at the temples. Vertical creases ran from his nose to below his mouth, like parentheses. A permanent vertical crease divided his forehead. Even so, Drennan had always been an attractive man. Sonny wondered if Polly would still find him so.

Reluctant to return to the earlier conversation, and going on the offensive, Sonny was on point to disallow Drennan's probing inquisition. "I thought I read once that you married. Are you still together?" Sonny said.

"That was over years and years ago, and no, we never got as far as the altar. Sue, Susan, was a daughter of the Old South. We were serious enough to be engaged, but I came to understand that I wasn't going to be more than an appendage to her life. She had scripted her future and needed a leading man." And Drennan recounted his realization that he was married to his research, and it left no time for a marriage. Uncharacteristically, Sonny wanted to taunt Drennan.

"So, being married to your research was like being married to—?" He left the rest of his thought unsaid.

"I know, around here and even on campus, I became known as the 'not the marryin' kind.' That euphemism is applied both to the role of playboy or gay man. Ever notice, Sonny, no one ever says that about a single woman who never marries?

"But that wouldn't have ever been a comment about you. You *were* the marryin' kind. This town takes good care of you, you and Polly. You were, by all outward appearances, a married couple. No one here would have pointed out to a stranger that you and Polly were not married because you are both female."

Sonny interrupted angrily. "You got it wrong, Drennan. I'm as much a man as you are. Polly thought so anyway." He couldn't resist the sarcasm this time.

Drennan seemed not to take notice of Sonny's comment or his

tone. "There's a sociological term for a community like Onansburg. This community is one that is characterized by common identity among its townsfolk. With relationships based on close ties. That's Onansburg, Sonny. Do you see where I'm going with this?"

"Hell yes, Drennan. I didn't just crawl out from under a rock. I know this community has been supportive of us."

Drennan raised his voice in protest. "But Sonny, you've lived here all your life! You were born here. Onansburg people have always accepted you, first as a little boy, then growing up into a man, when you are in truth trans-gender or cross-dresser. Those are just some of the names for who you are, what you are! But the fact remains, you're a man." Drennan's voice rose again with his emphasis on his explanation. Sonny was stunned at the mention of a label. He took a deep breath.

Dammit all! What's his next question going to be? I am who I am, who I've always been. Sonny's mind railed against what he heard come from Drennan. As if Drennan's knowledge and expertise entitled him to cross boundaries that no one had ever trespassed. Sonny thought of Drennan's crossing as a violation of privacy and decency. How dare he! That son of a bitch! He was exasperated; color flooded into his face.

"Drennan. I'm not about to let you turn this meeting into an exercise just to satisfy your curiosity even if you pretend it's for your research. And Polly—leave her out of this."

"Just sit down, Sonny. I know. I'm forcing this on you, and with losing Polly . . . " He paused. "There's no good time, but I'm trying to step this conversation up, so we both understand the same truth. I'm no therapist, but I want to understand how you became the man you are. I've told you how I became the man I am."

Sonny was suddenly drained of the adrenaline that had sponsored his attack of spoken and unspoken words. He was in turn weakened and confused, much as he'd been when he had first articulated Polly's death to her family. In retrospect, he would recognize that he was suffering another loss, this time a piece of himself that had been sacrosanct. Now, he was challenged by Drennan's assumptions and expectations of his response. His stomach roiled, and he was sickened by the exposure of his existence that Drennan was laying out.

When Drennan pushed on relentlessly regardless of Sonny's earlier protest, Sonny retreated into self-righteous indignation. *He wants me to just lay it all out for him. Between me and Polly, that is. He wants to tell me what he knows in hopes I'll fill in the gaps for him.*

Drennan continued, "What most people don't understand is that when a baby is born, be it a male or female, everyone is told its sex, male or female, and knows how to treat that baby boy or baby girl. Little clothes, gifts, toys. It's according to the baby's sex; it's how someone knows how to treat the baby, like a girl or a boy."

Sonny thought back to the infant-sized pseudo-football uniform he had delivered to the Thorensens' baby boy the day Polly died.

"These are social cues and may not mean anything. Those cues are how a person knows how to dress, walk, or talk. That's what I'm interested in knowing. I'm saying that masculine vs. feminine isn't dependent on what their biological sex is. It's all about what happens socially." Sonny turned his face away, as if he could shut out Drennan's voice.

"Usually there's a reason that someone acts different than the way their genitals suggest they should act. That's the 'why' question, but my interest is in how someone is assigned gender or chooses gender, either according to their biology or socialization."

Sonny hoped he had masked any involuntary response when Drennan mentioned the "why" question—why someone acts different than the behavior proscribed by their biological sex. He was not ready to acknowledge or understand what he had remembered about his family after so many years. He knew the "why."

Drennan continued, "As to 'how,' you were sustained in the gender identity that you chose as a little boy, then as a teen, then you as a grown man. It was how your family, the school, your friends treated you. You presented yourself as a boy, so you were treated as a boy.

"And then came Polly. Attracted to you as a man when you were young adults. And the community sustained and recognized you as a couple. You and Polly were, socially, a heterosexual couple.

"In short, life choices are made just as you made yours. And in the choice that you made, you created your own reality. And so, in the community and later, Polly was the mirror that reflected your masculinity."

Drennan stopped his explanation. He looked at Sonny keenly.

Sonny was leaning forward, his hands clasped between his knees, looking downward. He didn't want to look at Drennan; he was dismayed that what had always been natural and right about himself was so scrutinized. Or by others as well?

I've always been Sonny, the little brother.

"Sonny, can I ask you something? So far, I've told you what I know, and in some instances, what I think I know. Did you ever think of yourself as a girl or play like you were a girl when you were a little kid? I know that both biological males and females try on or play by taking the opposite gender role when they're kids."

Sonny looked up. His initial response was quick. "No, of course not. It wouldn't have been allowed."

Even given Drennan's skill at interviewing, asking questions to which he had already formulated an answer, an imaginary line had been crossed to a place in Sonny's mind that no one had ever gone. Sonny understood the conundrum Drennan had explained, and while he had acknowledged how he became masculine, he hadn't known why . . . until he experienced the regression in memory and its chilling revelation that day he saw Dolores on the street.

He knew that though he, Sonny, had been born female, a little girl they'd named Sonja, he was a little boy, the only son, Sonny. Dolores and Cloris, both used sexually by their father, had protected him the only way they could, knowing Charles would not abuse a little boy in the same way he had used them.

Now, he knew why his male identity had been chosen for him. And the "how" was the simple answer. He was a little boy, not a little girl. He grew into a man.

Be the best little boy you can be, Sonny. Promise me. Cloris will take care of you.

Sonny stood up abruptly. "Drennan," he said firmly. "Enough. This is enough for tonight. It's time for you to leave."

Drennan did as he was bidden. He stood retrieving his bottle of Scotch in his left hand, extending his right hand to Sonny. Sonny stood without offering his hand for several uncomfortable moments, but then he slowly extended it. Drennan grasped it and gave it a single firm shake.

"Let's be friends, Sonny. I need your friendship, no, I want your friendship, and perhaps you will want mine as well."

Sonny withdrew his hand and looked Drennan square in the face, meeting his eyes. *I am Sonny, the little brother, then the husband. Always have been and will be. Nothing's changed. Drennan isn't judging me. If I, born female, had been adopted as a baby boy, would that have changed my life?*

"Maybe, Drennan. It may be. Right now, I don't know."

Thirteen

Sonny slept the sleep of the dead, as he once would have described the kind of slumber he experienced after Drennan's leave-taking. The night before, he'd shuffled around, clearing the napkins, Scotch, and glasses, postponing the time to go upstairs to bed. Everything about the solitary rooms reminded him of his despair. Alone in the bathroom, he brushed his teeth relentlessly, then finally donning his pajamas, he hoisted himself into the lofty bed. Folding himself into the sheet and light blanket, he allowed the tears to come. He cried himself to sleep, quietly shedding tears for Polly, for himself, for his sisters, for Drennan. His tears were gentle, warm, and cathartic. Then he slid into restful slumber.

Sonny awakened early to the one hundred and eleventh birthday of Old Settlers, the Onansburg, Iowa, celebration and reunion. When he eased himself from the bed, sliding down along the mattress and box springs, he landed easily on his feet. Standing for a few seconds, he surveyed the handsome bedchamber; midnight-blue foulard wallpaper, burgundy, watered-silk drapes with swags and jabots, ornamented with heavy silk-tasseled trim.

The adjoining six-foot-by-six-foot square room holding Polly's collection of orchids and ferns appeared as a turret from the outside of the Victorian home. The features and appointments of the rooms were unchanged, taking no notice of Polly's absence. The air conditioning clicked on with its distinct mechanical buzz. The sentinel carriage-style clock stood watch.

Sonny knew he was the same man he'd been. Drennan's discourse had been his own exercise. He knew his story and his history were folded and enveloped into his recognition of how his life, his identity, his sexuality had been crafted. He was the same as he'd always been. His very being was locked into his soul.

But now there is no Polly, my love, my life. Nothing else has changed that can't be managed or accommodated. This mess with the Shaw family, I'll manage it somehow. They're missing her too. We're all shaken and lost without her. She was the darling of the family.

And Drennan. He thought he was laying a bombshell on me with his lofty explanation. No.

With a glance at the clock, Sonny crossed to the dresser and retrieved clean underwear and socks. He took off his pajamas and dumped them in the drawer where the underwear had been. With satisfaction, he saw that it was just five-forty.

Once in the bathroom, the pile of soggy towels from the day before was still piled on the floor. Borrowing a clean towel from the guest room supply in the highboy chest of drawers, he inhaled the subtle lavender fragrance from the sachets that she'd made years ago but refreshed every summer with freshly dried lavender blooms. He felt the beginning of the now familiar ache in the back of his throat; his eyes filled, but he blinked the tears away.

Hurrying now, Sonny slid into his favorite pair of khaki shorts that Polly had characterized as to be worn for snappy-casual occasions like golf or pool parties. With a crisp, coral short-sleeved Oxford Ralph Lauren shirt that had been Polly's favorite, plus socks and Top-Siders, he was ready for the day. He shoved his wallet into his pocket, then sliding his watch over his wrist, snapping the band closed, he checked the time. Six-fifteen.

"Perfect," he announced to Spats, who had appeared as Sonny finished dressing. "And where have you been, Mister? Did I get up too early for your royal highness? Well, it's Old Settlers, things to do, people to see."

With guarded surprise, he found himself looking forward to the day. Once in the kitchen, there was no Polly to hand him a to-go cup of coffee, as she would when he was rushing to an early appointment or meeting. While another pang of longing for her rushed over him, he took a deep breath, grabbed his car keys, and hurried down the steps and to the garage, through the enclosed porch, and with a quick swipe at the automatic opener button on the inside wall of the garage, the door ascended in its track. He opened the car door carefully, settled onto the leather seat, fastened the seat belt, and backed from the garage.

As he approached the town square, he began to see the busy work of the celebration. Triangular pennants marked the starting line for the races; the Amish family was unloading their ice cream churn; some vendors were already beginning to lay out their display of home-crafted goods; the trailer with the animals for the rescue group's petting zoo was pulling up to the stop sign just ahead of him at the corner of Main Street and Lone Tree Road.

Sonny parked behind the store, poked his key ring into his front pocket, but took the slightly circuitous route up the alley to the sidewalk along the highway, then crossed Main to the Courthouse Park. The breakfast committee was all but finished setting up. Harriet smiled when she saw him hurrying to the bandstand. "Sonny, I wasn't sure you'd make it in time. You've had a lot going on."

Sonny smiled but waved her off from further conversation. "Where do you want me? I can be here until seven forty-five. Need to get over to the store then."

"You're the official egg-cracker," she announced, extending a wet wipe, a butcher's apron, and vinyl gloves from the table behind her. "Just sit right here next to Helen. She'll be mixing and seasoning, so just crack eggs into this big bowl. Don't bother stirring them, just crack them and then put the shells in this waste can. Couldn't be easier."

Hell, I've never cracked an egg in my entire life. And I've sure as hell never worn an apron, but I guess it's time to try.

Sonny smiled, determined to be a good sport. Some seven or eight dozen eggs later, his gloved hands patched with dried egg white and egg yolk, he called it quits. "I'm out of here, Harriet. Time to open the store."

He returned the egg-cracking equipment, hopped down from the bandstand, and headed for the store. Going through the park again to the front of the store, he stopped to crank the awning out, then pushed the door key into the lock only to find it unlocked. Ruby stepped out from behind the cash register when Sonny entered but didn't raise her eyes to meet his. She spoke before he could greet her.

"I'm sorry that I was so cranky yesterday about Larry. It's your store to hire and fire who you want to work here. I was out of line, and I apologize."

Putting his hand on her shoulder, he reassured her. "We've all had a hard week, but we'll get through it. Let's just try to get through Old Settlers and have a nice day. We'll close the store just before the parade. I may be in and out a bit if I'm needed on the square, but I'll be here to close. Larry coming in today?"

"Yes, he's planning do his regular Saturday shift but only until we close, I guess. If you want him to come back in to sweep up after the parade, you know he'll be right here if you want him."

Sonny was unabashed by the import of Ruby's comment, but he was sensitive to what she was implying of Larry's loyalty and diligence. "We'll see, Ruby. We'll just see as the day goes on."

"Oh, Sonny. I near forgot. Wanda called and said some of your crowd are getting together in the Courthouse Park for lunch at twelve noon before the parade, something about a few from your class being in town and getting together, if you want to come."

"Thanks. Nice of Wanda to call. We'll see, but I'm guessing we'll still be open then. That reminds me though; I need to call Dolores to see if she needs a ride uptown for the parade."

After initiating the plans made to meet Dolores and Cloris after the parade, Sonny was excused from offering either of them a ride to town. Dolores had spoken with Cloris, who reported that Skip would drop them off on his way to the Legion Hall.

The morning was a busy one between customers making purchases and old friends stopping in to say hello to the three of them. It was awkward to hear the platitudes from those trying to express themselves to Sonny, but after only a few had come and gone, it was hard not to run and hide in his office. Sonny ran the cash register alternately with Ruby but took a few minutes to make a quick turn around the Courthouse Park around ten o'clock.

Hearing the racket of the gasoline engine cranking the ice cream churn, he made a note to himself to rethink its location for next year. Likewise, the petting zoo folks, while doing a nice little business with their animals, might be reminded about the logistical issues intrinsic to the pot-bellied pig.

Larry stayed busy marking inventory, dusting shelves and merchandise, making fresh pots of coffee for customers with the new Bunn fast-brew coffee maker that Sonny had added to the product line. He picked up trash from around the parking lot and changed liners on the waste cans strategically placed around the store.

Traffic into the store dwindled, and the spectators lined up on the sidewalk leading into the store began to block the entrance. Sonny glanced at his watch, surprised that it was already twelve-thirty. Members of the Onansburg High School Band, straggling along in twos and threes, were walking in the now-blocked-off street in front of the store toward the start of the parade route, carrying their horns, the sun glaring off the highly polished brass and silver finishes. Dressed for the hot-weather march, they were clad in black shorts and tailored white shirts.

Sonny turned to his crew that was winding up work in different sections of the store. "Hey, everyone—no one can get in the front door anyway, so let's call it a day." They looked at him expectantly, and he mimed locking the front door and flipped off the lights at the front of the store yet compulsively checked the spotlights on the display windows, which were never turned off. Each finished what they had been doing and headed for the back. Sonny called out to them. "If you want to leave your stuff in the back room, the doors will be locked and we can come back in before you go on home."

Ruby replied, "I'll just get my pocketbook now. I'll meet Harold out in front, watch the parade, maybe listen to the speakers, and then we'll probably just go on home."

Thelma Jane nodded her agreement and followed Ruby to the back room. After a few minutes, Sonny closed out the cash register and transferred the cash and checks to the bank bag, which he locked in the office safe. He finished turning off lights at the back of the room and joined Ruby and Thelma Jane as they were coming from the back room.

"Larry's still in the back working on assembling the new tool cabinet for display. We told him you were locking up, but he said he'd just finish the tool cabinet. Doesn't seem right. He needs to get out in the sun and watch the parade with the rest of us. It's Old Settlers."

"I'll meet you two and Harold out front if you're going to watch from there. We can stand under the awning. I'll just leave it out until after the sun goes down tonight, so people can stand in the shade."

Sonny knew he couldn't watch the parade by himself. There was a crowd out there, but he wanted company, someone with whom he could exchange comments; it had most always been he and Polly, usually Ruby and Harold and Thelma Jane watching from the same vantage point just outside the store under the awning.

When Ruby saw Harold strolling up the street from the Cozy, they exited to the street, and Sonny ushered them out the door and locked the door from the inside. A quick look at the clock told him that it had taken fifteen minutes for winding up the work, retrieval of hand-bags, last-minute restroom stops for a quick fluff of the hairdo and some lipstick. He hurried back to where Larry had been working on the tool cabinet, totally absorbed and hunkered over the assembly instructions. Sonny reiterated his invitation to watch the parade and finish the assembly job later.

"Well, alright, Sonny. I'll be out in just a few minutes."

The sheriff sounded the siren, announcing the start of the parade—several piercing whoops tapering to a series of bleats. The color guard advanced, following the patrol car. Three whistles from the band's drum majorette took control, and the drummers' cadence moved the band onto Main Street.

The floats followed the Old Settlers honorees, the parade mar-shal who would later be addressing the crowd, the Old Settler of the Year, also a designated speaker, and the Newcomer of the Year, all of whom were introduced by the perennial announcer, Phil Larson, owner of the South Side. Phil announced every parade entrant from the list provided by Roger, but went off extemporaneously with comments of his own about the origin and history of each. Every year, someone suggested that someone should take the microphone away from Phil, but the next year found him again inflicting his comments on the crowd.

The floats constructed by churches, clubs, and community orga-nizations passed by, some of which were elaborate and others not so, but each following the 1994 theme for Old Settlers, "Salute the Family." Some on floats threw candy, bubble gum, and unin-flated balloons to the children watching from the sidewalk that then scrambled to gather the booty. Members of Onansburg High gradu-ating classes celebrating reunions were seated miserably on bales of hay on flatbed trucks or wagons but gamely waving to friends and family. The reunions usually were organized at five-year intervals, which for some, allowed for a five-pound incremental weight gain at each reunion year.

The children's entries followed, tricycles and bicycles decorated with crepe paper streamers, paper flowers, and playing cards affixed to the spokes with clothespins that fluttered noisily with the turning of the wheels. The older kids, mostly boys on bikes, went for the Ninja warrior and camouflage look. The band played at least five or six times during their route, the Ferris wheel circled above, the merry-go-round added its pseudo-calliope music to the band's tune, and Phil Larson's commentary rang out over all. It was the Old Settlers parade in all its glory.

After the municipal armaments edged onto the parade route, commercial vehicles advertising for local businesses followed. The vacuum tanker truck dedicated to pumping out septic tanks and affectionately known as The Turd Hearse. The farm implement dealer with mammoth machines, tractors, harrows, disks.

Suddenly, Sonny realized Larry hadn't joined them. The parade was almost over. Annoyed, but not alarmed, Sonny unlocked the door and hurried to the back room, which he found empty yet fully lighted. The tool cabinet was still unfinished. Rushing back into the hallway to the rear entrance, Sonny jerked the door to the parking lot open and saw Larry slumped against the wall of the store.

As Sonny rushed toward him, he saw a figure disappear around the edge of the building, but Sonny made an instant decision not to give chase. Larry's eyes were closed, and a scratch above his left eye leaked a trickle of blood down the side of his face and onto his shirt. His glasses were on the ground next to him, the lenses broken, the frames bent. His eyes fluttered open and incongruously. He recognized Sonny with a slight smile. Then the smile widened to a grin, and he struggled to stand, but Sonny caught him, eased him back to the ground, and repeated his calm reassurances. Larry, still dazed upon seeing Sonny, gave him another incongruous grin. With his arms still around him, Sonny knelt next to him, noting Larry had other abrasions with a considerable bump on his forehead in addition to the scratch. Larry leaned his head against Sonny's shoulder.

Again, he smiled. Looking up at Sonny, he made a lame joke. "You should see the other guy, Sonny."

Sonny suddenly became aware of another voice, cursing, "Oh fuck, oh fuck," but then crying aloud, almost piteously, "Mamma, Mamma." Sonny scrambled to his feet, took a few steps from Larry, and discovered a man-sized figure face down on the ground behind his own Oldsmobile. He recognized him quickly from his longish hair and beard as one of the local toughs, not dangerous so much as an overbearing bully. But Sonny quickly realized Smokey Benson had this time gotten his just deserts.

Smoke, as he was called by his cohorts, was in a fetal position, clutching his crotch with an all-too-apparent injury, and Sonny, in a flash, recognized that the escapee he'd seen running away was most likely the so-called Dagger Sifert, Smoke's partner in soft crime, the possession of pot, speeding, and violation of Onansburg curfew.

Smoke began to retch, raised his head, and slobbered his lunch and perhaps a beer or two onto the ground beneath him. He rose to his knees, but in a flash of anger, Sonny directed a well-aimed shove to Smoke's backside with his foot, and Smoke fell face down in his own vomit.

"Just lay there in it, Smoke." Sonny's anger, fueled by adrenaline, didn't care in that instant that this was a kid, not more than eighteen years old.

The door of the store swung open, and Ruby and Thelma Jane emerged. Shocked by what they saw had unfolded in the parking lot, Ruby rushed forward, filched a packet of tissues from her purse, pushed Sonny gently aside to minister to Larry. Thelma Jane clutched her hands to her face, then hurried forward to help. His voice cracked, but he gave strong orders.

"Go find Julia. Tell her Larry's okay, but get her over here."

He turned to Larry. "What happened, Larry? I saw Dagger go around the corner just as I came out the door and then I saw you and then Smoke over there on the ground. Did those guys push you around? You're looking a little beat-up. We'll get your mom over here, then get Sheriff Ames."

Larry immediately shook his head.

"No, don't get the sheriff. It's all right, Sonny. Those two have been teasing me the past few weeks, but they didn't mean anything by it. Just having fun." Larry started to get up but then slumped back to the ground, but looking curiously smug, he haltingly told Sonny and Ruby what happened.

"I was getting ready to go out front to watch the parade, but I heard someone knocking on the back door. I looked out the window but didn't see anyone, so I thought maybe one of you had forgotten your key. I opened the door to look out, and Smoke and Dagger were waiting for me." He paused, took a breath, but continued. "They grabbed me, and at first, they were just pushing me around . . ." He hesitated, then said, "calling me a 'faggot and a rump-ranger,' but I stumbled and fell against the building. Really, Sonny, they didn't hurt me. I fell down, lost my glasses, and someone stepped on them. I got back on my feet, but I was weaving around and then they started toward me. I was scared, but I just pulled the oldest trick in the book. And they're not all that smart, you know. I pointed to the sky and yelled 'watch out,' then I landed a good one right between Smoke's legs, right in the gonads, the balls, you know." Dagger started running.

Sonny reflected briefly. *What kid but Larry would say "gonads"?* Then, as he realized how horrified, how frightened he'd been when he'd seen Larry, bleeding and scraped up, Julia rushed from the alley into the parking lot, followed closely by Thelma Jane and Sheriff Ames.

The sheriff took a look at the scene, turned to Julia. "It's pretty clear what's happened here. There will be some charges filed, but I'll have to question Larry and then take a garden hose to Smoke, clean him up before I want to question him."

Larry struggled to his feet, his broken glasses in one hand, and pressing a blood-soaked wad of tissue to the cut over his eye. "Sheriff, this was all an accident. Smoke and I were just here in the parking lot. I saw him from the window, just having a cigarette, so I came out to see him. I tripped over one of the cement bollards that mark the parking spaces, and fell against the building. I guess I don't know what happened to Smoke; maybe he drank too much and got sick."

Julia started forward, but Ruby put a precautionary hand on her arm. "Let Larry handle this." Julia saw that Larry had moved between Sheriff Ames and herself.

Ames gestured to Larry, and the two moved a few feet away from them. Sonny and the women turned discreetly away, and Sonny moved over to where Smoke had risen to a sitting position.

"Smoke, you feeling better? You going to be able to get up and get out of here? Larry's talking to the sheriff, but I think you and Dagger are going to catch a break on this one. But don't push your luck; just treat this guy as your new best friend." He grasped Smoke's shoulder, shaking it for emphasis, and continued, "No messing around with him, but I guess I don't need to tell you that. You should tell your mother not to expect you to give her any grandchildren."

He saw that Larry and the sheriff were winding up their conversation. Sonny gave Ruby a shake of his head, ran his hand along his jaw to the back of his neck, and said, "I think Old Settlers is over for me today. Julia, you and Larry need a ride home? Ruby, Thelma Jane, what about you?"

"If you'd drop Larry and me off at our place, I'd appreciate it. I walked up to where the float was in line for the parade, but we need a ride home now."

"Likewise for me. Harold went on home when I thought I might be needed here, said I'd find a phone somewhere and call him to pick me up. So, if you'd want to drop me off . . . "

With a wave, Thelma Jane excused herself, saying, "I'll just walk on home. I need a little exercise just now."

He kept up a one-sided conversation as they headed for the store's rear entrance. "The car's right here, but I'll start it up to cool it off. Let's go inside and wash up a little. We're a pretty motley-looking crew. Look at us; Larry's all dinged up, we're all hot and sweaty. Julia, you have everything you need for Larry before we head home? There's a first-aid kit in the bathroom, even has those butterfly bandages in it. Just take it on home with you. Larry, you feeling okay? Bet you're going to be stiff and sore tomorrow."

He dragged the keys from the pocket of his shorts, unlocked the door, then held it open as the three passed through. He went back to start the car, flipped the air conditioner to high, then joined the others inside the store. Ruby met him at the door when he opened it from the outside. With her eyebrows arched high, she gave him a satisfied nod of her head, along with a broad smile.

Julia and Larry chose the back seat together, and Sonny held the door for Ruby to climb into the passenger seat. He surreptitiously brushed some dirt and any tiny rocks from his knees, thinking it hadn't been a good day to wear shorts.

Sonny drove to the Hayeses' home. Leaning over the front seat toward them as they exited the right rear door of the car, he said, "Larry. If you want the day off on Monday, you take it off. You may still be feeling the effects of this then. Julia, take good care of him."

"Thanks, Sonny. I appreciate you being there for Larry, you know, before I got there. Thanks a lot."

Sonny waited until they disappeared into the front door of their house, then pulled away and headed for Ruby's home a few blocks away. Ruby smiled complacently, but neither tried for conversation during the short drive.

"See you on Monday, Sonny. Not sure I'll make it to church tomorrow, but I'll see you Monday for sure."

"Thanks, Ruby." Then he added, "You're a good soul."

Driving slowly away from the Sheltons', Sonny remembered the awning.

The damned thing is still out; guess it's easier now than later when the street dance is going on. And I'd better check on the girls. They might need a ride home. Damn, I'm tired. Must have had an adrenaline rush, and now I've crashed.

Despite his fatigue, Sonny turned back toward town and the store. He met a few folks who were walking slowly away from the celebration. Families, groups of children, a few of each winding their way home to rest before the evening's programs, and others that had likely concluded their Old Settlers observances. He glanced at his watch. A few minutes past three.

Another car pulled out from a parking place along the Courthouse Park, so Sonny slid the car into one of the few parallel-parking spots around the square. He sat in the car for a few moments, the motor and air conditioning still running.

He thought back to the scene behind the store. Smoke Benson crying for his mama, and Larry, apparently having acquitted himself well in a mismatched fight.

How will memory treat the incident? And how will Onansburg's memory treat Larry, the most unlikely winner of an unfair fight? He had either the most to gain or the least to lose. Sonny pondered the question for a few moments, then turned off the ignition.

Leaving the car, and crossing the street, he approached the store from an oblique angle, intending to roll in the awning, then go home. When the sun set in the west, the awning would offer no more shade to passersby; there was no need to leave it out as a courtesy. As he cranked the awning in and bestowed the crank to its hideaway, he spotted his sisters strolling along in front of the Cozy, then stopping to look at the window display at the *Choctaw County Republican*, the next-to-last display; only Sonny's store window remained for them to inspect.

"There you are," called out Cloris. "We wondered where you went. Did you see all that ruckus after the parade? The sheriff pulled up right in front of your store."

Sonny briefly recounted Larry's accident, wanting to relieve himself of the afternoon's drama. "So, are you ready to call it quits for the afternoon?"

"Just finishing the windows," she said, peering in, her hand shading her eyes. "We'll probably go on home. Dolores, are you ready to go home?"

"But I want to hear the evening program. We've been looking at the windows, but it's too early to get a seat for the entertainment. Well, I'm ready to go now, but I want . . . " Dolores vacillated.

Cloris stepped in with "Dolores, if you want to come back, I'll come with you. Sonny, are you coming back?"

Dolores and Sonny both looked at her uncertainly. "Don't you have plans tonight, Cloris? You and Skip usually have somewhere to go and people to see," he said, alluding to the Cozy, their customary hang-out and its denizens.

She shook her head "no" and stepped closer. "Not tonight. I'm not going out with Skip tonight; he's been at the Legion Hall bar all afternoon. I wasn't going to tell you two so soon, but I haven't had a drink since the night of Polly's funeral."

Sonny found himself at a loss for words. Another benchmark for the day of Polly's funeral. *The night of Polly's funeral.* Not wanting to trust his voice and on the verge of tears, Sonny stood motionless. A few moments passed, then he responded carefully. "Cloris, that's really fine. I'm happy for you, for your decision. Is there something Dolores and I can do to help?"

"I've thought about joining AA if I need some help. Dolores, for your information, AA is Alcoholics Anonymous."

Dolores responded indignantly, "I know what it is, Cloris. I don't need to go, but you sure do."

Sonny waved Dolores to silence, but put his hand in hers to soften his gesture of dismissal. He shifted the two of them closer to Cloris, then took her hand as well.

"I just decided to quit this week." Cloris cast her eyes downward. "I was embarrassed for all of us after that night of Polly's funeral. I was embarrassed that you and Dolores had to see Skip and me like that. And Claude, thinking you were drunk too, Sonny. I felt bad about that. It's hard work, but I think I'm ready. I don't want to be like that anymore."

Sonny smiled a benevolent smile, nodding his head when he met Cloris's eyes. "This is the Cloris I know. We're here for you. We've got your back."

After a few moments of companionable silence, Sonny spoke out. "Alright, girls. If you're coming up to hear the music, I'll come along. I can drive, we'll park behind the store."

"Let's just walk uptown. Someone will be in your parking place anyway, Sonny. So, let's just meet at the corner of Highway 2 and DeKalb Street at six-thirty. I'll walk by Dolores's, and we'll meet you. Then we can have a cold drink and . . . iced tea, Dolores. I'm talking about iced tea," she said in response to Dolores's look of surprise, "and get a seat in the park. The program starts at seven. Should be over by nine."

Sonny drove first to Dolores's, walked her to her small porch, peered in through her front door while she produced her key, looked around the small home quickly, pronounced it safe to enter, and exited himself. Once back in the car, he gave Cloris a quick look and a thumbs-up sign of approval.

"What?" she responded. "After all these years of bad decisions, I'm finally making a good one, but I'll need help, Sonny. I'll need a lot of help, and . . . " she paused. "This means it may be over for Easley and me. We'll just take it one day at a time with him, and see where it goes. My sobriety may be more than he can handle."

"You can count on me, Cloris. I've always counted on you, so now it's my turn."

Pulling into Cloris's drive, he leaned over, gave her a quick kiss on the cheek before she opened the door. She smiled, opened and closed the door, then walked around the car. Sonny rolled the window down from the controls at his left.

"See you about six-thirty then. And you'll go by for Dolores?"

"Yup," she said, and flashed him a thumbs-up sign. "Back atcha."

The park bench hosted them long enough to enjoy the community chorus highlighted by a professional baritone opera star, but at the conclusion of the program, the siblings agreed they were tired and stiff from sitting on the wooden platform and decided to take their leave. They exchanged their good nights with those seated nearby, some of whom they knew and some not.

The three of them picked their way along the sidewalk leading away from the town square. Leaving the revelry and street dance music behind after the musical entertainment concluded, they chose the route leading to Dolores's house on Cedar Street. They poked carefully along in the dark between the streetlights that hovered protectively over each corner. An occasional porch light invited an intrepid resident to run the gauntlet of nighttime insects or children's scattered toys. The old sidewalks were testaments to stubbed toes, trips and falls, but if not respected for their hazards, the concrete sections displaced by tree roots, broken and cracked by years of use, were taken for granted.

Sonny intertwined Dolores's left arm with his own right arm and clasped her hand with his. He placed his opposite hand protectively over their linked arms. Walking on the side nearest the street, Sonny solicitously exchanged positions when a right turn called for him to change sides at the corner.

Sonny mimicked the square dance caller and executed a few shuffling dance steps. Dolores smiled her secret smile at the attention from Sonny. Cloris, following behind, griped pleasantly at her brother's antics.

"What'll I do if you both fall down? Guess I'd just have to drag you home, one at a time. Dolores, I know you had your hair shampooed and set for Old Settlers. I'll try not to mess it up too much."

Dolores, defensively, put her hand to her hairdo, smoothing it as if to protect it from Cloris.

"Dolores, honey. I'm teasing you."

After checking Dolores into her home for the night, Sonny continued with Cloris. "Let's go on to my house. It's too far and too late to walk to your place now, so let's get my car." They walked in silence for the next half-block, then turned the corner toward Sonny's.

"What about Skip? I can't see how you can work on your own sobriety when you're married to an alcoholic. It's been your life as a couple. It's what you do together. The two of you make pretty decent money, I suppose, but you're not a good match if you're really going to make this work. Does he know all about this, about your decision?"

"Sonny, Skip and I were never married. There was never anyone that I could have married after Nate. Nate saved me, he loved me, and he saved me. He saved me from everything that happened to me here." She slowed her walk, and turned her head toward Sonny, but her eyes looked far away. "I refused to claim his body when it was shipped back from 'Nam. I wouldn't fill out the forms or give any direction about what to do with what they sent back. I let the Army take care of what was left! For me, he's still out there somewhere, and I came back here where I know he'll come looking for me."

Cloris was now matter-of-fact about her wasted years. "I drifted, and I drank a lot, and when I was so drunk and seeing double, I could imagine the guys I was with were Nate. And then afterward, Nate always came back to me. Looking for me." She grew quiet for a moment. "I was in the psych ward for a while at the base hospital. That's the time when you and Dolores didn't know where I was, Sonny. They tried to dry me out and help me get over Nate. That didn't happen, but I'm going to stay sober now. I don't care what happens to Easley. He's a good enough guy, but Nate will always be out there somewhere for me even if I can't ever touch him, feel him, hold him again. I feel like I finally know all of that now; I'm not nuts. Maybe I was for a long time, but not now. I'll always be married. To him, just him."

Cloris turned toward Sonny. "It's like you with Polly. She'll always be there for you. You made it good, Sonny! Polly took over where I left off with you. You needed a woman like Polly in your life. You were her man, and she was your woman. She gave you everything she had to give, and you did the same for her."

Soberly, he put his arm around her shoulder. "Cloris, Polly was my heart, my life. Just as Nate was for you. Nothing, no one will change that for either of us. They each made us whole. Our reality depended on them, still does. We both are who we are today because of them. You're fighting your way back to who you were when you were with Nate, loving and being loved. And me with Polly. She supported the man I became, and I'm a good man. We each saw who we are reflected in their eyes."

She responded in a measured, even tone. "Dolores, poor little girl, we'll both look after her; she can't make it without us, but you and I are here and now. This is home. We all get home, one place or another, where we know we belong. There were those years when they sent her away, and I'll always blame myself for leaving her, but I couldn't take her with me. Maybe I could have held her together if I'd been here, I don't know. But I had to leave, I had to save myself. Sonny, what happened to her? What happened to her at Clarinda?"

Without looking her way, Sonny responded quietly. "I have to think there was electroshock and God knows, given the times, maybe a lobotomy. There's no way of knowing for sure. She can't tell us, but she is how she is and does the best she can."

They turned the corner toward Fifth and Wall Street, and paced along quietly.

"Do you have your keys with you?"

"Of course, I have my keys. Men always have their keys with them," he replied with a smile.

"Just take me home then."

Sonny deposited Cloris in her driveway, leaned across the center console to give her a fleeting hug, then waited in the car until she opened her front door. She turned with a half-wave to let him know to leave.

Passing close to the town square on the way back to his own home, Sonny waved to a few stragglers walking to their cars; waved to the high school kids and their dates hurrying toward the edge of town to park and exchange sloppy kisses before reluctantly parting with promises to love one another forever.

Fourteen

Sonny continued his way home. As he pulled into his driveway, he looked across Polly's garden, the columbine and phlox pregnant with seeds stirring gently in the light breeze, but then he noted that Wanda and Robert's red Cadillac, complete with its white mud flaps decorated with studded reflective stars, was pulling into their garage next door. The garage swallowed their car; after a time, as Sonny continued to look on from his car, their garage lights were extinguished and the lights in their house were then extinguished one by one. Sonny ached with aloneness.

He opened his garage door with the remote and edged in carefully. For the first time since losing Polly, he turned and looked at her car quizzically.

Never thought about it in the last few days. It's a nice little car, but I don't need it. I'm not the convertible kind of guy, and it's not very practical in Iowa weather. Maybe I should sell it, but not today, not tomorrow. There'll be time to think about it. There's no hurry. I guess it would be nice to have the extra space when I pull in with my car.

Sonny exited his car carefully, but his musing was cut short. Tom Shaw pulled his car into the driveway just as Sonny pushed the remote button to close the door, leaving him against the garage door in the spotlight of Tom's headlights. Confused, Sonny stood motionless, but Tom climbed out of his car quickly and advanced toward Sonny purposefully. Sonny felt a fleeting moment of alarm. Tom was a big man, at least six feet tall, raw-boned and accustomed to hard work. Considering when last they'd met, Sonny could only wonder if he was to be challenged.

"I've been waiting for you. That was a hell of a thing that happened behind the store today; I heard that kid, the one that works for you, took a beating. I saw you from a distance and was hoping we'd get a chance to have a few words, but it wasn't going to happen after all that chaos. Is the kid all right?"

Drained of both mental and physical energy, Sonny could only wait for Tom to state his purpose. He turned his mouth down at the corners and gestured with his hands. "Come on, I'm waiting. Say whatever you're here to say."

"Can we go inside?" Tom asked. "I won't stay long, but . . . well, I need to talk to you about a few things."

"I don't think so. After you lost your temper here on the day of the funeral and after the cold shoulder you all gave me at the South Side, no. I don't think we have anything to talk about."

Sonny started up the sidewalk toward the door into the kitchen just as the sensor turned on the light over the four steps up to the kitchen door. For a moment, he was startled, thinking it was Polly who saw him approaching and turned the light on for him as she had before he installed the sensor.

Tom was right behind him as he mounted the first step. Sonny whirled around, drew himself up to his full height, and standing on the first step, he was near the same height as Tom. He fixed Tom with a hard stare.

"No! I said no, there's nothing more to say."

Tom, surprised, took a step back but replied evenly. "Yes, there is more to say, and you damned well better hear me out. It's to your benefit to listen to what I have to say."

Sonny recoiled. *This is the second night in a row that someone is telling me I need to hear what he's going to say.*

Sonny stomped up the remaining three steps, fished in the pocket of his shorts for the keys, then realized he'd left the door unlocked. Giving the door an unnecessarily hard shove, he saw that Spats, having come to greet him, was startled and skittered away. He reached for the switch, and the hanging lamp over the antique drop-leaf kitchen table brightened the window corner of the breakfast room. Another switch, and the pendant lights over the work island blinked on.

Sonny turned to face Tom, who'd stopped just inside the door.

"Sonny, can we sit down somewhere? Can we sit here at the kitchen table? You might want to get some paper and a pen, write a few things down."

After making Tom wait a moment, Sonny withdrew a pad of paper and a pen from the shallow drawer beneath the tabletop, pulled out the chair from beneath the drawer for himself, and gestured to Tom to take the chair opposite. With both men seated, Sonny waited for Tom to speak. He was dismayed by Tom's insistence. He was a force that Sonny didn't have the wherewithal to deny on this night.

"First, let me just say, I think we regret our actions at the café last Wednesday." In response to Sonny's questioning look, Tom stammered and Sonny broke in.

"Are you speaking of the collective 'we' meaning you, Darrell, and Walter, or do you really mean just you?"

"Just hear me out, will you? The three of us, plus Dorothy and Polly of course, us shareholders had been talking that we needed an agreement between us shareholders that we couldn't sell our shares to anyone else or use our individual shares as collateral for a mortgage or a loan, anything like that. And no one other than us Shaw blood relatives could own shares, like Carla, Molly, Jenny, or Ted couldn't own shares. So if one of us Shaws died, the widows or Ted couldn't own the shares. They'd just have the income from the shares, but the shares themselves would be in a trust for our kids, like my two kids, until Jenny died. This isn't just about you. We don't intend for anyone to own shares other than the Shaw family.

"Well, Polly pointed out that the two of you weren't legally married, and common-law marriage or whatever we wanted to call it would be a pretty murky set of circumstances. We knew there'd be some tough decisions. So, we all agreed we'd think about what to do; Ted, ever the attorney, y'know, said he'd do some research, no charge to the family, plus he isn't licensed to practice in Iowa. That's as far as we got, and then Polly . . . " Tom gulped and stopped speaking. He took a deep breath and continued. "So, we go in to see Kent Field to find out what to do since all we'd ever had was an understanding among us, nothing legal, but Sonny, you know how we are about the land."

"Yeah, Tom. I know how you all are about the land. And I've always told you that I don't want anything to do with Shaw Farms."

"But Sonny, Kent told us, in a nice professional way, to kiss off. He said he's your lawyer and Polly's, now her estate's lawyer." He paused and took another deep breath. "We don't know what the hell to do, but we pretty much inferred that Polly probably left her shares in Shaw Farms to you. We never got around to the shareholders' agreement or a plan for trusts or buy-sell agreements, so we feel like we're hanging out there in the wind, just seeing which way it's going to blow. So, Sonny, do you even know if Polly left her shares to you, or do you know if she did something else with them? We've gone through every possible scenario, but we don't have any idea what's going to happen if you own the shares. We feel like we've lost control of our business."

Sonny sat back in his chair, the spindly little chair that Polly had claimed was satisfactory for the breakfast table but hadn't ever been meant to be used for leisurely dining. He studied Tom's face, his discomfiture. Sonny shook his head slowly, and his anger and impatience began to surface. "Tom. Dammit! Just take a minute. Look at you. You're all worked up about something, but you don't even know what it is." Then he questioned himself.

Just a few days ago, I was worked up about the same circumstances, but now, it's just background to going forward. This is tough stuff. I need to draw a hard line here!

"Yes, Tom. Polly left her shares to me. It's not what I expected or wanted, and I felt she'd pitted me against your family. But when I've had a chance to think about it, and I have some ideas about what to do, I'll sort out the different options. I'll be fair, but whatever I do, I'll try to protect and preserve Polly's interests in Shaw Farms."

Sonny plunged on, suddenly clear of mind and resolute. "I am certain that Polly, in leaving me her shares, was trying to make sure we all would stay family. And just as I protected her financially with our assets in both our names, she was protecting me with what she had to give. She made sure I had her income to shore me up. Polly told Kent that I would know what to do with what she left me. We've been family for twenty-five years, but going forward, that's going to be up to you and your family. But Polly trusted all of us. I know she wanted us to remain family.

"Tomorrow is Sunday. There's not a thing to be done about this business on Sunday. Monday, we'll get after these questions, and we'll work things out. Polly planned it this way, and there's not a damn thing to be done about it now. Sorry that's a problem for you. Monday will be soon enough. This isn't a problem unless we call it a problem. Let's not let this happen. Between you and me, we can hold this thing together.

"Tomorrow, call Walter and Molly, Darrell and Carla. You and Jenny, all come over, and we'll have just a drink together. Just as family—we can talk about how to go forward. Rules of the game— no raised voices, no dirty looks. Just discussion, questions, and honest answers if we know. Like I've said, I didn't know of her will's provisions until last Thursday."

Tom looked away, without meeting eyes with Sonny. "Jenny and

I will come by, but I can't speak for the others. We're all hurting so about Polly, I just don't know if they'll . . . " Sonny interrupted. "Then you and Jenny come without them. You're not all joined at the hip, so just you and Jenny if the rest don't come. Like I said, we can hold it all together, make it happen. Just come on over. It has to be worked out, no choice."

Tom stood, pushed his chair back, and turned to leave. Then, with a rueful, downcast expression, he pulled a grimace that could have passed for a smile.

"See you Sunday."

Sonny watched through the open door until he heard Tom's engine start, then turned off the light over the walkway. Flipping the kitchen light switches to OFF, he shut the door quietly and engaged the dead lock.

Drained of all energy, Sonny leaned against the closed door, his hands and arms supporting his back. He let his head fall back and sighed deeply. *We'll make this work, sweetheart. You knew all of us so well. You knew we'll eventually all work to do the right thing. We might have to agree to disagree sometimes, but we'll make it work. I promise you, darling.*

Polly would have smiled, knowingly.

Acknowledgments

Special recognition goes to my friends who, over the years, patiently encouraged me and listened to my rambling about my work. Thank you from the bottom of my heart to all of you. I'll love you forever.

Thank you to the editors, Harrison Demchick and Jessica Choi, who helped me with this major life ambition.

About the Author

Peggy Lammers resides in Longboat Key, Florida, having left her much-loved Iowa in 2014. Active in her church and community activities on the Key and in Sarasota, she was born in Iowa to C. R. and Esther Pester ("Pester" is pronounced with a Long E). Her brother, Jack, and his extended family maintain close family ties, along with their ties to southern Iowa.

Peggy and her husband, David Lammers, were married for forty-five years before he passed away in 2005. David's family, a sister and a brother, remain close in heart and spirit.

Peggy and David's daughter, Lisabeth Lammers, has three outstanding children, as does their son, Jon Lammers, and his wife, Kathryn. So Peggy is blessed with six grandchildren.

A milestone in her life was graduation from Drake University at the age of forty-six. While working for the family business, she graduated magna cum laude with Phi Beta Kappa recognition. Another "hurdle" was learning to ride at age sixty, fulfilling a lifelong dream of owning horses and riding competitively, although not with the highest distinction.

Peggy believes that stories and characters are everywhere just for the telling. Many are ongoing; we know nothing of them, and they are forever lost. The others blend with a conjunction of fact and fiction. This novel evolved from 1959 and is set in 1994; the context was not defined until Peggy's better-late-than-never Bachelor of Arts degree in 1988.